SWORD OF FRANCE

A Novel

by

Hilary Condé-Mark

Indepenpress Publishing Ltd

Copyright © Hilary Condé-Mark 2009

All rights reserved

No part of this publication may be reproduced,
stored in a retrieval system, or transmitted
in any form or by any means, without
the prior permission in writing of the publisher,
nor be otherwise circulated in any form of binding or cover
other than that in which it is published and without a similar
condition including this condition being imposed on the
subsequent purchaser.

First published in Great Britain by
Indepenpress Publishing Ltd
25 Eastern PLace
Brighton
BN2 1GJ

ISBN 978-1-906710-83-5

Printed and bound in the UK

A catalogue record of this book is available from
the British Library

For Daddy who inspired me
and for my family who encouraged me.

If you can dream and not make dreams your master

Rudyard Kipling

History is an agreed upon fiction

Napoleon Bonaparte

Prologue

It has been said that genius is a form of madness.

If, for a moment, we accept that premise, then we must assume that all progress, all that we have become as human beings, indeed the very impulse of Evolution, has been driven by the uncontrolled caprice of the insane.

Such a thought could challenge the very limits of Reason itself!

Perhaps, then, it was such daunting reflections that summoned the fascination of the Ancients as they examined again in their literary forms the inexplicable phenomenon of the 'Hero'. Those rare individuals who strode across Time imposing upon their particular epoch a claim, and inextricably infused their presence within that era, thus forbidding the future to ignore them.

Such men, possessed of an extraordinary degree of strength and courage, came seldom, even in Ancient Times. Cult status elevation, subsequent to their death, usually immortalised them, resulting in a confused worship of something between a god and a man – "Greater, and yet lesser".

Yet undeniably such gifted individuals arrested the imagination of ordinary men through sheer mystique, removed by their physical feats of achievement, and by the superiority of their moral and intellectual qualities.

They were, however, essentially 'Human'. Unquestionably, therefore, they displayed singularly 'human' characteristics. These characteristics, however, lay dormant as the flowering of genius followed its path. But even as the surge of the Hero's destiny lifted his presence to stir the hearts and minds of the masses, sinister lay the threat of human weakness, ever ready to challenge the super human exterior, ever waiting to erode and destroy the growing mighty phenomenon.

The Pursuit of Honour was the noble principle that inspired the Hero. But such lofty ideals – preserve of the gods – met unavoidably with those corruptive elements of the Human condition. Incomprehension and jealousy led to betrayal from lesser individuals, inevitably manifesting an opposition resistant to the self-proclaimed singular catalytic proponent of Honour and Virtue through power. The weakness of the challenge induced an isolationist form of defence from the bemused hero, and the very thrust of his genius often inverted, becoming the means of its own extinction.

Thus the Ancients evolved the literary form of Tragedy.

But we do not here preface a story on Ancient times. Rather we look within the modern perspective to a recent time, there to examine a Tragedy, which is in many ways similar to those stories of distant classical periods.

Each individual holds their own view, positive or negative, of that enigmatic phenomenon who asserted his personality upon the face of Europe at the end of the eighteenth century. It cannot be denied, however, that the mighty presence of this small man changed the direction of political thought, inducing a great leap in progress, and thus presiding over the foundations of the systems by which we live today.

In the dark years that followed the fall of the Bastille in 1789, 'progress' was a word that might have been mocked by those who fled the horror that subsequently became manifest in the daily lives of the people of France.

'Revolution' – that bold, brutal and unimaginably bloody eruption of collective anger, expressed through a savage fury that defied reason, confirming the incoherent irrationality in violence that knew no restraints. As the bitter frustrations of long years of silently suffered degradation expelled their revenge, the country writhed under the lash of hatred. The momentum of that virulent mood, embracing in its entirety every aspect of the lives and thoughts of people everywhere, bit deeply into the fabric of Society with its acid demand: 'participation', insisting upon the total surrender of the population to its howling call 'to arms' in the struggle for Liberty.

But now, after almost ten years, France was tired. And in her weakened state the cry rose up begging, 'Leadership'. Wearied by anarchy, and disillusioned with the vanished promise of Mirabeau and Danton, the French fervently desired strength to lead them.

Order. How urgent was the need for order.

And somehow time demanded that some dignified solution, some practical articulation, some manifest embodiment of the noble spirit and principles of the Revolution demonstrate to the World that France had triumphed, despite the rivers of blood and tears. They yearned to shout their statutes with pride:

Liberté! Egalité! Fraternité!

They longed to confirm the legitimacy of 'The Rights of Man'.

And so they sought a 'Hero'. A man. A warrior. Someone who would lead them out of the darkness. Out of the shame of The Terror...

A man whose strength and courage would demand – no, command – respect for France. A man who, by being the embodiment of the Revolution, would finally legitimise the cause of their great struggle.

All eyes turned to Italy. There, in the military battlefields France's army had conquered.

BONAPARTE! How well he knew the desperate needs of the people. But the spirit of genius is guided by intuition, and he knew the time was not yet upon him. He left Paris for a foreign command in Egypt. The French found themselves governed instead by yet another incoherent body of inept politicians, The Directory, whose only virtue was that they were a little less bloodthirsty than their predecessors. We shall observe the course of events in our story.

We have mentioned that the downfall of a hero is brought about by the challenge of his innate human traits of character. But the weakness of those who surround him is manifest in jealousy, which ultimately induces them to treachery, and betrayal of their leader. What is it that provokes such vehement jealousy, which inevitably results in opposition, and eventual destruction?

It is interesting, therefore, to attempt to contrast the characteristics that distinguish genius from an undeniable brilliance that is still within the accepted norm of human standards.

Thus, mindful of this contrast, our story will unfold partly as seen through the eyes of the very man who betrayed our hero; the very man who was instrumental in both the ascent to, and the descent from, the summit of man's potential achievement — as reflected in the Tragedy of Europe's last conqueror. Only in such a form is it possible to see the true magnitude of such a mighty mind, as well as the full implication of the fragility of the human condition. Our fate is thrust upon the sway of conflicts and emotion of individual men. Men in whom we are inevitably forced to place our trust.

We cannot know the author of dreams, nor indeed its nature and purpose with regard to our particular path. All we do know is that we are inexplicably drawn along a course that, despite all reason, all logic, we know we must follow, regardless of consequence. The pursuit of Honour is an endeavour to contribute to the betterment of life for our fellow man. Thus, the fulfilment of our Destiny.

So thought the ancient Heroes of classical times.

So thought Napoleon Bonaparte…

Chapter I

I have always held a particular aversion to rats.

As a child I was exposed to their unpleasant company on occasion, since they were frequent visitors to the somewhat bleak quarters to which I was confined, my only other company being the rather slovenly presence of those appointed by my absent parents to care for and educate me. Such was the lot of the children of nobility in the days of the Ancien Régime!

All the same, I admit to a certain sympathy for the rats. After all, who could resist the temptation of easily salvaged pickings from the tables of such dirty and unkempt individuals. Perhaps the sense of revulsion I have continued to carry all my life for those rodents was easily compounded by a confusion between my contempt for both the animals themselves, and for those whose lazy habits induced the furtive scavenging of these skulking monsters.

I was hypnotised by the unblinking gaze of the hideous creature. The indelicate response of my heaving stomach was, however, happily restrained by my sense of astonishment. How very uncharacteristic of the species for the animal to depart from the protection of the shadows. Moreover, how extraordinary for it to appear to actually confront me, obstructing my progress down the narrow cobbled street.

It is strange how, in a sudden frozen moment, one's entire thought and feeling is invoked, and momentarily summarised. As my sensibilities recoiled from the penetration of that glassy stare, my mind appeared to focus upon a certain resolve: it had to stop.

This mess simply could no longer be tolerated. France had expunged her anger. And now she had celebrated her victory over The Terror. It was time for Order; otherwise she would slip into the arms of decadent despair. Revolution must cease.

A high-pitched giggle penetrated my thoughts. A light I had not been aware of was suddenly extinguished, somewhere in the dark recesses of a nearby wall.

The rat, no longer magnetised by the light, slowly backed into the shadow of the gutter, blending its joint-less hairy body with the complementary comfort in the filth of Paris refuse and mud. Once more my stomach surged in revulsion. I lifted some smelling salts to my nose, my head suddenly light as the full weight of the implications here, in these dreadful surroundings, hit me. Anarchy. We were virtually in a state of anarchy.

I pulled my coat more closely around my body, inevitably responding to the shiver that for a moment overcame my body. With a purposeful step I continued my journey. My mind was made up. I knew what the outcome of the forthcoming meeting must be. There must be no more procrastination. Besides, the news I had received that morning confirmed everything.

* * *

It had been an eventful ten years, to say the least. Nobody, throughout France, had escaped the effects of the mighty paroxysm of the Revolution. The entire concept of existing social patterns in French life had teen torn to shreds by its brutal methods.

Nonetheless, there had been much justification for the initial explosions of angry resentment, for no-one could deny that a gross disparity had existed between those whom chance had privileged, and those whose very existence seemed to have been forgotten by God himself.

As a representative of God in the form of a Bishop, I found myself irked by the church's hypocrisy in its attitude towards its flock. Political reform had been essential. Indeed, inevitable.

Violence, however, had not been in the spirit of the original revolution. Those heady days in 1789, when France's King had found himself monarch of a bankrupt country, and thus obliged to summon the States General – those had been days of excitement, of intellectual challenge, of positive change.

I, though both a Bishop and a nobleman, had willingly thrown in my lot with the Third Estate against the Nobility and the Clergy. Contrary to criticism against me, I made this transition entirely in logical sequence to my earlier recommendations to the Government.

Long had I been a liberal thinker, feeling a closer affinity to the Voltairian 'Age of Reason' than to the obsolete and impractical edicts of my mother church. Indeed, I had come to hold a very real contempt for the church, a subject upon which I was later to be challenged by my Imperial Master, whose practical expressions of devotion were no greater than my own.

But now, in 1789, I found myself with men who intrigued and excited me. Their political vision somehow accorded with my own beliefs. To me, it had long been obvious that the continuation of the policies of the Ancien Régime was impossible. The discontent on the faces of my Father's disreputable staff had informed me of that at an early age.

Thus, I had found myself a part of the new National Assembly. The Revolution had begun. We were to be the architects of a form of Democracy, under a constitutional Monarchy, somewhat similar to the English system of government. Mirabeau, dominating and pock-marked, enunciated with passion our noble cause, and rapid were those initial changes.

But there is something of a Pandora's box in the nature of passion. I myself am no advocate of excessive zeal. It is a certain route to disaster. The passion of Mirabeau and Danton, of the original leaders of The Revolution, was indeed inspiring and stimulating. But passion can unleash rage and resentment, more sinister in others who are often less intelligent and less distinguished than those using the means as an emotional incitement to Honour.

Within a short space of time the more extreme, more irrational elements of the Assembly were starting to take control, and even the powerful Mirabeau found himself helpless. The people were starving, and those hot furies at the assembly were intimating a real possibility of hope for them. The momentum of change was upon us. Unstoppable.

The untimely death of Mirabeau in 1791 was perhaps the herald that indicated we had reached a point of no return. As I listened to his dying breaths, I felt that I must carry the torch of this man, the 'Father of the Revolution'. And I must do it in the spirit in which it had been born. Yet even as I pronounced the funeral oration for my friend, I felt a strange presentiment. My eyes locked with those of Danton as the coffin was lowered into the ground. With us lay the last hope of tempering the revolutionary ardour that was increasing its vigour daily.

But the rabid Jacobins soon saw Danton's legal mind as being 'too moderate'. Aware of the looming crisis for the King, I now found it necessary to absent myself from what was to be, inevitably, the approaching degradation of my country. Danton aided me in the important matter of a passport and financial assistance, and it was upon my departure on the eve of impending disaster that we shook hands for the last time as we bid each other farewell at the Ministry of Justice. As at our friend's funeral, our eyes once more spoke that which knew no verbal expression. There was something very noble in this massive man's calm acceptance of his destiny. He knew his ugly fate.

News of the massacres reached me in England. I was in exile. The disgusting spectacle of savage behaviour induced such shame that I was able to bear the boredom and personal indignities of an embarrassing position with a degree of resignation.

I have always been appalled by the more bizarre traits of human behaviour. Displays of unfettered emotion expressed through such hideous means I found utterly repellent.

I recall the following years of exile with some pain. The murder of the King made it impossible for the British Government to accept me in their country. I thus found myself a 'double exile', on a ship bound for America. That people imagined I was in the pay of the French government as a spy was the most astonishing suggestion of all the absurd rumours that circulated at the time. I regarded the incoherent attempts at government by the committee of Public Safety to be a contemptible insult to Frenchmen. Moreover, their incitement of mass hysteria, expressed through the violence of frenzied bloodlust, was, in my opinion, inflicting harm upon the self-respect of Frenchmen. That damage would take a very long time to heal.

My stay in America was one of boredom and frustrated political impotence. I ensured, however, that my sanity prevailed by preventing the latter affliction from affecting me in other activities. The pursuit of women was always an attractive distraction for me!

My return to my beloved France was arranged through the good offices of Madame de Stael and her friends. Persuading the Convention that I was indeed a true Republican and not an émigré, my name was removed from the list of those whose lives were in danger if they returned to France. At last, I was free to go home.

France was now governed by a group of five men known as 'The Directors'. In the wake of the appalling convulsions inflicted upon the country by Robespierre and St Just, these men attempted to adopt a more humane approach to order. But whilst their intentions were good, they possessed an excessive propensity for exploiting the benefits of power – for instance, they had a penchant towards accepting bribes. Such weaknesses obscured their already limited political vision.

Seeing that they needed a man of experience, I contrived to meet the man who was, apparently, the real power within the Directory: Barras. However, the individual within that group who really interested me was an older acquaintance, Emmanuel Sieyés. He was a fellow churchman without vocation. Here was a man of interest, a man with whom I could work. Had he not, after all, been the man who had created the title of 'National Assembly' for the Third Estate back then at the birth of our Republic in 1789? Yes, this man interested me as an instrument towards my ends. Thus I began work with the Directors as Minister of Foreign Affairs.

* * *

'Good evening, citizen Talleyrand.'

The interruption of my reverie startled me. Quickly composing myself, I inclined my head in acknowledgement. Two young clerks from the Ministry…how irritating…and just as I was approaching my destination. Ruefully I eyed the squalid entrance to what I knew would be an even more sordid interior. I would have to proceed past and return unobserved. It was vital that no one should know of the forthcoming meeting.

I struck the cobbles smartly with my stick. An irksome business, walking. I disliked reminders of my disability, and walking induced tiredness in my lame leg. Oh for an end to this back street intrigue! I preferred the open surroundings of ballrooms and dinner parties. Such filthy locations, frankly, had always disgusted me.

Turning sharply into a narrow alleyway, I sank my head into the collar of my coat. But I knew it was impossible to retain anonymity from those who knew me, as it was impossible to disguise the dragging gait of my crippled leg. I would have to proceed to my destination via a diversion, remaining in that most unstable of conditions: hope. I did not relish the idea of prolonging my presence in the discomfort of this unsavoury area of Paris, simply to avoid chance encounters in the street. Such locations smacked of Fouché.

Fouché! I felt my face stretch in a grim smile. How I disliked that man. And yet it seemed that Fate was forever throwing us together. Indeed, he had been privy at one of the earlier meetings. I remembered it well because of Barras, whose blustering attendance we had invited to satisfy his suspicions, whilst not informing him of anything important. Indeed, that had been quite an amusing little entertainment due to the uncharacteristic passion of Sieyés. My face stretched once more.

'What we need is a *head* and a *sword*!' he had exclaimed with passion.

I had raised my eyebrows as I quietly observed the antics of the men in the room. Sieyés, smugly – and wrongly – certain of his own intellectual abilities to be the 'head'; Barras, graciously, ignorantly condescending in his belief that he was undoubtedly a combination of the two; Ducos, meekly subservient to Sieyés's every word; and Fouché, cold and dispassionate, his heavily lidded eyes icily claiming that he and his police network were indeed the controlling factor in France's destinies. I wondered if any of them had any idea at all about how the rest of the world outside France existed. I had wondered but briefly, assured of the answer.

I was now approaching a junction. Pausing, I peered into the gloom. The place appeared to be deserted, save for the sound of the scuffling of those dreadful creatures in a nearby gutter. I raised my sleeve to cover my nose as I proceeded through the alley that I knew would return me to my destination. The daunting odour of some nearby thick liquid substance of unknown origin hastened my step. I was becoming impatient.

The door, apparently opening of its own accord, greeted my knock instantly. Hesitatingly, I ventured into the dimly lit interior of this rather odd rendezvous. I looked down to see two large eyes staring at me, the child's dishevelled head leaning against the door handle that his small fist was still holding. I patted the boy on the head, thanking him for opening the door, and fleetingly wondering if I had contracted any disease from this filthy little street urchin, whose eyes held such innocence. Or apparent innocence. As my own eyes became accustomed to the darkness I noticed that the only light came from a large fire in the corner, to the right of the cavernous stone room. A very old woman appeared to be hunched over a stove, entirely absorbed by a pot, which bubbled with some evil-smelling boiling brew. An attempt at envisaging what the contents of that pot might be would have been too much for my already severely tested sensibilities. Starvation… The people were starving, pushed to the limits of their dignity, existing rather than living, reliant upon bones to live on. What a shocking state of affairs.

'Good evening, citizens,' I ventured. I met with no response. Either the woman was deaf or merely mesmerised by the horrors of the interior of her pot.

The little boy moved quickly to the foot of a narrow winding staircase. Pointing to the upper floor he beckoned me to follow him. The sound of two men's voices greeted my ears as I reached the summit of the long climb. My foot was now giving me considerable discomfort and I had no other thought in my mind than to rest it.

A shout from within acknowledged the child's knock, and the door was thrown open to reveal a room that was brightly lit, if a trifle spartan in its furnishings. There was one table in the centre of this small room, and three chairs. Nothing else, save one broken chair in the corner, and the candles lighting the place. A grimy piece of material that had once probably been rather an attractive curtain was dragged across the small window, too shrunken and tattered to cover it completely.

'Citizen Talleyrand.' Ducos sounded confident and strong, quite unlike his usual supplicating self. 'We have been concerned for your safety.'

Yes, I suppose I was rather late, and they knew me to be a man who observed scrupulously the manners of punctuality.

'Forgive me, gentlemen, I encountered an irritating delay.'

Sieyés was pushing back his chair, rising to his feet, impatiently gesticulating to the boy whose wide eyes had become wider as he appeared to stand immovably fascinated by the proceedings. As I caught the ex-Abbé's dismissive gesture to the small boy, I idly wondered who the child might be, why indeed this extraordinary place had been selected as a 'safe' location in which to meet. My fleeting thought vanished as, upon the sound of the door closing, the Abbé, now standing, for the first time turned his small colourless eyes upon me and, despite the effort that courtesy was to this man, nonetheless summoned the effort to smile.

'Good evening, citizen Talleyrand. I trust you are well.'

Observing my dragging limb, he indicated the chair that Ducos was obediently holding. With the assistance of the table and Ducos, I all but fell into the embrace of the hard and, no doubt under normal circumstances, uncomfortable chair. Extending the aching extremity, my body felt quite wracked by its recent physical exertion. Nonetheless, I was determined that I should not betray my physical discomforts to these two individuals. I had barely exhaled my sigh of relief when Sieyés began.

'Citizens, we must put our plans into operation without further delay. The Jacobin threat grows daily. We must seize our moment.' He paused, appearing to twitch a little. Flashing a look between the adoring Ducos and my own face, which I knew to be expressionless, he continued, '...we must seize our moment...'

There was something oddly comical about this small, cold, calculating yet ineffectual man, as he repeated his grandiose statement. I found it faintly ridiculous. Taking out my snuff-box, I sought to relieve my throbbing head in the midst of this bizarre experience. Pompously he continued, arms dramatically outstretched:

'The untimely death of General Joubert was an unfortunate blow to France. However, citizens, there are other candidates within the military...'

'What about Bernadotte?'

Ah, the glorious power of snuff! My delight in savouring the moment of inhalation happily saved my ears from some of the spluttering explosion that was the response to my question. Seemingly driven to distraction by the mere mention of the name, the agitated man proceeded to pace up and down the small room, his moving shadow enacting a frenetic dance with the already flickering candles, disturbed as they were by his flailing gesticulations. I felt my eyebrows rise a little. What extraordinary behaviour! I turned my head slowly to find the alarmed eyes of Ducos fixed upon me.

'He is a good and strong General, and has the support and confidence of the people...'

The spluttering erupted again, even more loudly and incoherently. The alarmed eyes, upon which my own gaze was still fixed, deepened in their horror. I suppressed a smile at the comic absurdity of this scenario.

The contents of my snuff-box once more came to my aid, but my deliberate actions were interrupted by the small man whose wig was now farcically askew, a sight that added to the unique comedy of it all. Sieyés continued to expound vehemently against Bernadotte, concluding, 'He looks like an eagle, but he is really a goose.'

He had thrown his arms in a wide gesture of exasperation upon the final word. Now, dropping them limply, he fell silent, and turned to the filthy window, moodily staring into the blackness beyond.

There was a long silence, and I felt the need upon me once more to sniff the remnants of snuff that lay within my lace handkerchief. I took the opportunity of stifling a yawn with that most exquisite specimen of lace. I was bored with my little game. I really must bring this sordid excursion to an end, and return to the civilized surroundings of my own home. Besides, I could not keep waiting the charming company that was to dine with me.

'Bonaparte…'

I was interrupted by a growl from the window. '…is in Egypt. There is no time to wait for him. No, Moreau is…'

'*Bonaparte…*'

I repeated the name, my voice lower even than normal. My firm emphasis silenced the menacing interjection from the window. The fidgeting presence of Ducos was adding to my irritation. Finally I was accorded my demanded attention.

'…has landed at Fréjus.'

There was a stunned silence. Both men appeared to be dumbfounded. It was curiously satisfying. I rewarded myself with further fortification from my snuff-box. How elegant an object it was, wholly incongruous with the surroundings. As I busied myself with the important business of sniffing, I was aware of fixed eyes staring at me in total disbelief. Bonaparte was not expected back from Egypt until the following spring at the earliest. I feigned a casual air as they stared.

'A-are you sure…?' The Abbe's tone had certainly changed. 'Wh-when…? How do you…?'

I clicked the beautiful enamel object shut. An exquisite work of art.

'Yesterday,' I returned crisply, slipping my snuff-box back into my pocket, and reaching for the silver nub of my walking stick. 'He is on his way back to Paris at this very moment.'

I straightened myself in my chair. Certainly it was not a chair designed for one such as I, who preferred the horizontal position to that upright inducement to discomfort. However, I was preparing to depart, wearied of this conversation.

'Gentlemen, Bonaparte has returned, and even as he approaches is being hailed as the victor of Vendemiaire, of Italy – and now of Egypt. The people have their confidence in him. He is the very man we need to put our plans into operation and set France on a new course to stability and prosperity. *He*, my dear Sieyés,' I spoke here in slow, deliberate tones, 'he is the *sword* you have talked about.'

I rose. And with my action, so did their heads lift, as though raised by invisible wires. From my superior height I looked down at them, abruptly concluding my laconic statement.

'Our plans are well laid, my friends. Now we have the man we need. There is no reason to delay longer. The moment is indeed upon us.'

Ducos now rose also. Sieyés, still apparently suffering from shock, straightened himself from his crumpled position.

'Bonaparte...' He said it with an air of disbelief, and a slight hint of apprehension. 'Bonaparte...' This last amounted to a muttered acceptance...

'Well, gentlemen, I must leave you. I have an engagement.'

Shaking hands with each of them, I moved towards the door. Turning, my hand on the door handle, I reminded them:

'Remember, good sirs, we must keep our counsel. The coming days will necessarily be active with situations which must be handled skilfully, and without error. It is vital that we maintain secrecy to the last. Our plans are well laid; nothing need go wrong as long as we employ caution. There is no turning back. We have our man.' I inclined my head in a gesture of farewell. 'We shall meet anon.' I concluded thankfully, anxious to be gone.

Ducos now sprang to assist me with the door.

'Au revoir, citizen.' Sieyés appeared to be preoccupied, his words almost inaudible.

'Au revoir, citizen.' The startled Ducos parroted the phrase, his words exhaled in nervous breathless spurts. I smiled at him. Poor man. He had a good mind, but what weakness of individual purpose.

I made my way down the narrow staircase and through the dark room below with a degree of haste, which approached the unseemly. At last, France's fortunes would change, and such back-street clandestine meetings would no longer be necessary. What a relief!

I gave the poor child a coin and, extricating myself from his demonstrations of gratitude, I left him again clutching the door, watching me fixedly as I hurried into the blackness.

And so it was done. I had asserted my view. All that remained now was to carry out the plan of action.

Ah, at last! I had, unusually quickly, left the hideous huddling streets of that gruesome part of Paris. I could hear the sound of the river, and the sight of the bridge loomed before me. My steps increased their haste, my limp scarcely hindering me. And as I crossed the bridge a surge of relief rose within me. My carriage. I could see it dimly outlined in the appointed position of rendez-vous at the other side.

I sank into the cushioned comfort of its interior. I was exhausted, but it had been a good evening's work. Closing my eyes, I heard the sound of the cobbles traversed by the wheels of my carriage. A wave of cold sweat overtook me momentarily. The harsh sound had fleetingly recalled the ghastly passage of the tumbrels. Never again must France return to such barbarism.

Bonaparte! I smiled to myself, recalling my thoughts when I had first met him following his return from Italy. The conqueror of Italy! How Paris had adored her hero. And he, how unusual was his appearance. Very small and thin, his pale face framed by long, dark, extremely untidy hair. Yet his frail looks belied the grim determination and natural authority of the soldier. Here was a man of immense intellect, and boundless energy.

But Napoleon Bonaparte was a man of many contradictions. On the one hand he appeared to be a young romantic who wanted nothing more than to have a quiet life, free to read the writings of Ossian and pursue the study of science. Upon his election to the Institute in Paris he had declared his life's ambition to be fulfilled. Indeed, his expedition to Egypt had included a team of scientists personally selected by him for the purpose of studying the hidden secrets of the Pharaohs.

Yet there was another side to this strange young man. The penetrating gaze of an unusual intelligence appeared, all the same, to mask something much bigger, much deeper. It was clear that his thoughts travelled at great speed, and the charming air of distraction that this gave him was sometimes marred by an occasional hint of impatience. But at this time, in youth, observation of that feature of personality required close scrutiny. His overriding characteristic was enthusiasm, and energy. An occasional hint of melancholy, too, served to further confuse. Even at the height of success and acclamation, when most youths would have relished the adulation, availing themselves of the benefits of such with alacrity, this young man seemed somehow removed from it all, somehow unimpressed. During a celebration in Paris to honour his Italian victories, he had observed to me: 'Triumph and disgrace are never very far apart. I have noticed on the world's great stage that the outcome of the greatest events always depends upon some trifle...'

I had smiled to myself. Love of glory makes a great hero, I thought. Contempt of it makes a great man. Perhaps in this pale, thin, almost frail young man lay the makings of the latter. And in the eyes of France he was already the former.

Love of glory, and the makings of a hero, however, could certainly be applied to Jean-Baptiste Bernadotte. I chuckled to myself, remembering Sieyés's reaction to my teasing. How odd that Sieyés should resent so rabidly this fellow Jacobin. But there, I suppose, lay the answer. Sieyés had more or less deserted his Jacobin cause, moderating his views quite drastically in the recent months. I shan't deny that I had had more than a small part in influencing such a change. Nonetheless, his dislike of Bernadotte seemed unnecessarily vigorous. Moreover, the distaste was reciprocated, particularly since Sieyés had forced the man to resign as Minister of War.

It had, as it happens, been a lamentable but necessary step. The fiery Gascon had been most successful and efficient during his tenure at the Ministry. Certainly he was a man to be much admired. The son of a lawyer, he had run away from home at an early age to join the army. Through the ranks he had worked his way up to General, and thence to Minister of War. Small wonder then that such a man should stand so firmly by the principles of the Republican constitution. Under the conditions of the Ancien Régime such a spectacular achievement would have been impossible for a poverty-stricken country boy. As a General he was popular with the army, commanding a degree of loyalty rivalled only by Bonaparte himself. Both Jacobin and Royalist factions had, in recent months, approached him in the hope that he might use his popularity with the army to effect a coup d'état on their behalf; that he might be their *sword*. But his regard and respect for the law and for the Revolution were his cause and inspiration, and thus he was resistant to anything that was unconstitutional. Indeed, I had thought of him myself as a suitable *sword*, but his stubborn attitudes had made me change my mind. Moreover, his declaration that he would shoot anyone who might try to challenge the order of Authority had made it necessary for us to remove such a power in view of our intentions. Thus Sieyés had forced him to resign his office.

There was an odd connection between these two very different but very talented generals. Bernadotte had married Bonaparte's former fiancée and first love, Désirée Clary. Though Bonaparte had married too – the widow Beauharnais, Josephine, former mistress of the director Barras – and though, in his poetic and dramatic way, he appeared besotted by love for the wife who had organised his position as commander-in-chief of the Italian Army, there still existed a very close tie between Napoleon and Désirée. Or 'Eugènie', as he called her... Moreover, Désirée's sister, Julie, had married Joseph Bonaparte, Napoleon's elder brother, so the family circle in the Bernadotte home at the Rue Cisalpine consisted entirely of Bonapartes. A particular friendship existed between Lucien, Napoleon's younger and most talented brother, and Bernadotte. The Corsican characteristic of family unity and closeness was strong in the Bonaparte family. Thus it was that Jean-Baptiste Bernadotte was seen by Napoleon Bonaparte as a part of his family.

Here, then, is perhaps the basic and essential key to the story that I shall now relate. This story of two men…

* * *

The carriage turned into the Rue Taitbout, where I resided. Idly I wondered where Bonaparte was in his passage from the south coast to Paris. I would know, no doubt, soon enough. 'The greatest events depend on a trifle…' Chance!

I smiled as the carriage slowed as we approached my house. It had indeed been chance that Joubert, the appointed *sword*, had been killed in battle in Italy. Certainly it was serendipitous for Bonaparte, whose only rival remained Bernadotte, a man who wanted none of it.

The carriage rolled to a halt, and a servant appeared to assist me descend from it.

Yes, these could be eventful days! The prospects were indeed exciting. Chuckling to myself, my thoughts turned to the forthcoming amusements of the evening.

Chapter II

'It's obvious they are not coming, Désirée. I think I'll return to my study. I have work to do.'

Jean-Baptiste Bernadotte's voice was brittle, masking a cold anger.

A piercing cry from a baby interrupted the indignant beginnings of a reply from its distraught mother. Gathering the baby to her, she rocked him gently, soothing words of comfort and reassurance issuing from her lips. Désirée Bernadotte flashed a look of irritation at the large form that stood silhouetted against the veranda door. His massive back to his wife, and to the pleasant oval room, Bernadotte stared morosely into the small and pretty garden beyond.

The baby's protestations silenced, Désirée began once more: 'Really, Jean-Baptiste, you are petulant these days. They're only twenty minutes late...' She paused, looking down at the tiny bundle in her arms, her eyes soft and loving, gazing into the unblinking stare of the three-month-old baby. 'Whatever is the matter with you, darling...?' Without attempting to hide her exasperation, she turned her head back to look at Bernadotte. 'You really mustn't take out your anger with that man Sieyés on me and Oscar.'

'Anger? Sieyés? What are you talking about?' His explosive response entirely contradicted his defensive reaction to her statement.

Désirée remained silent, her gaze, again soft, fixed once more on her gurgling son's face.

'*Well?*'

The bellowed word faded as he turned and saw the gentle presence of his wife and tiny son. His anger died as quickly as it had risen. Leaving the windows, he went to the pale pink sofa that held his precious family. Seating his large bulk awkwardly on the edge, he took his wife's free hand.

'Forgive me, my love…'

His lips caressed the small capable fingers. His eyes looked imploringly into hers, the many fine lines that framed them betraying a pain that was not apparent in his noble and proud bearing. The baby appeared to laugh, jerkily flailing his tiny arms and legs, an expression of determination on his little face, which had become suddenly puce with the effort of his heroic endeavour. The attention of both his parents was successfully arrested by the sheer wonder of such a feat. They were silent for a long moment.

'It doesn't matter,' murmured Désirée, her soft voice almost inaudible as they continued to gaze at their son. She hesitated before suddenly turning her wide eyes to look at Bernadotte again. 'B-but…you aren't…yourself just now, Jean-Baptiste.' She paused, uncertain of what she was trying to say, daunted by the looming dominating presence of her husband. 'I-I worry…' she finished lamely, choking slightly at her confused emotions.

He kissed her hand and rose, returning to the beckoning light of the glass doors. Resuming his moody stare into the autumn landscape, his attention fixed on a bird perched on the back of a garden seat, its head flicking from side to side as the bright eyes searched for food amid the carpet of autumn leaves.

'I know…' The words sounded harsh, thick with self-deprecation. 'I know, Désirée…I-I'm sorry.'

Bernadotte was not a man who found emotional situations easy to cope with. Discipline was ingrained into every facet of his character, and his behaviour seldom betrayed any inner turmoil that he, inevitably as a human being, might be wont to experience. His tough climb through the ranks of the army, a career embarked upon when he had yet been a boy, had hardened his attitude to the personal weaknesses of others, whom he felt should display similar degrees of self-discipline; and thus he imposed upon himself an even greater demand, omitting entirely the possibility of emotional dislocation. It was, no doubt, for these reasons that he had not married until the age of thirty-five. Now, in his marriage, little more than a year old, and a small baby son to seal the treasured union, he had found his Achilles' heel. How he loved his Désirée.

A mist seemed to cloud his eyes as he stared at the little bird. Désirée was so young, so sweet, so innocent. She trusted people, and seemed in that childish way to be able to love and understand everybody. She was everything that he was not. And she was so vulnerable. And he knew this hard and uncompromising world. He swallowed, his large handsome face slightly flushed in confusion. Didn't she know what was wrong with him? Didn't she understand that he had been forced to resign as Minister of War after nine weeks? Especially when he had raised the conscription by 140,000 men, and embarked upon so many other constructive plans. Couldn't she see what a humiliation it had been...? He blinked as the bird hopped on to a garden table, jabbing at the scattered leaves that lay upon it with its tiny beak. Humiliation. Yes, that was the word. Humiliating, not simply because he had been forced to resign – but because he knew the reason why. Yes, he knew. He felt it in his bones. He felt a surge of anger. It was never very far beneath the surface these days. Bonaparte...

'Jean-Baptiste...' The voice seemed to approach him through a fog. 'Jean-Baptiste?' Now she had approached him, gently taking his hand and pulling him. 'Darling, didn't you hear me? They're here.'

He wrenched himself out of his thoughts, drawing himself up to his full height, and straightening the stiff jacket of his uniform. Désirée's large eyes quickly searched his, an expression of concern darkening their amber colour. He smiled down at her, his heart twisting at the distress he knew he was causing her.

'Let us go and greet them, then.' His deep voice was warm and resonant. To protect her, that's all he wanted to do. Surely she knew that... He put his arm around her. 'Come.'

He guided her towards the door into the hall, from where the busy voices expressing greeting reached their ears. Quickly kissing the top of Désirée's head, he opened the door, a frown fleetingly passing across his forehead. Why had they come? What did they want? He felt he knew…

'Darling! You are looking well!'

Julie Bonaparte was very different from her sister. She had always reminded Bernadotte of a hen. Somehow she appeared to 'cluck' rather too much. However, her nervous behaviour masked nothing more than a constant fear of her responsibilities and obligations to the ambitious and very close family unit into which she had married. Undoubtedly she had always been troubled by a nervous disposition, lacking as she did both the intelligence and the natural reserve of her younger sister. But marriage to Joseph Bonaparte had served only to increase her feelings of inadequacy – sensitivities that were quite unfounded, for Julie Clary Bonaparte was a kind and unselfish young woman, who wanted nothing more than to please those whom she loved. Her relationship with Désirée was close, and Bernadotte had a deep affection for his sister-in-law, recognising as he did the agonies of her struggle with self-confidence.

Breaking away from Bernadotte, Désirée ran across the hall, embracing her sister with an uninhibited degree of demonstration, so characteristic of her animated nature.

'Julie!' she laughed, in an exultant girlish giggle.

As the girls hugged each other, the two men present stood – a considerable distance apart – observing the scene indulgently. Désirée's maid, her arms already filled with Julie's voluminous garment, was assisting Bernadotte's valet in relieving Joseph of his coat and cane. The circular hall was filled with the excitement of reunion. Beckoning to his servant, now also laden with clothing, Bernadotte quietly requested him to bring refreshment. Then, stiffly, he bowed to Julie who was now looking at him as Désirée embraced Joseph with a warm sisterly welcome.

'Julie.'

He smiled with formal friendliness and affection, extending his arm in the direction of the doors into the drawing room, inviting her to enter. Inclining her head with shy delight, Julie gracefully moved into the beautiful salon, her attention immediately arrested by the day-cot in the far corner of the room, near to the piano. Désirée, darting past Bernadotte, followed her sister as they both hurried to the lace-adorned object.

'Oscar!'

Julie almost screamed with delight at the sight of the tiny contents of the cot.

'Bonaparte.'

Bernadotte's tone had lost the warmth it had possessed in his greeting to Julie. Nonetheless, his bow was impeccably polite, its stiff formality cold but not unfriendly. His arm once more extended the invitation to proceed to the interior.

'Bernadotte! Good to see you, my friend. I haven't seen you since…'

Bernadotte stiffened. Joseph Bonaparte, who was not known for his forethought, nor indeed his tact, paused for a moment, realising he was on the point of touching a sensitive nerve.

'Ah…' Clasping and unclasping his hands, he continued his gushing, entirely changing the course of his conversation. '…I – quite expected to see my brother Lucien here. I know that you and he are often in each other's company…'

They passed into the drawing room, an uneasy silence between them following the somewhat stilted exchange of greetings. The tension was relieved by the excited exclamations of the two young women who were entirely absorbed by the gurgling entertainments of the baby's antics.

'Oh look how beautiful he is,' giggled Julie, her nervousness extinguished. 'I do think he has Jean-Baptist's nose.'

The sisters collapsed into further laughter. Bernadotte, who was renowned for the largeness of his nose – which, it was said, was after the noble style of the Great Condé – was somewhat bemused, not knowing if his son was receiving a compliment or not. Awkwardly he twitched a smile, and was relieved to hear his servant, Fernand, at his elbow, asking if the choice of wine and hot chocolate sufficed as suitable refreshment.

'Joseph, darling, come and hold him…' Julie was entirely concentrating on the baby, who obligingly smiled and demonstrated his physical prowess in the form of kicking and stretching. 'Won't Napoleone be pleased with his little godson when he sees him?'

Julie chattered on as Joseph gingerly tickled the child under the chin. 'What a strange name Napoleone chose for him: Oscar! But I like it…'

Bernadotte had stiffened as he bent over the tray of refreshments. Napoleon. Why did that name always induce this fierce racing of his blood, reminding him of the anger he tried so hard, and so successfully, thank goodness, to control? He busied himself with the refreshments.

'Chocolate for us,' called Désirée, her voice almost singing with the happiness of the closeness of her loved ones together.

Placing the two cups on a nearby table for the women, Bernadotte turned to Joseph. He had a strange feeling that Joseph's eyes were following him, firmly fixed, it seemed, on the back of his head.

Now as their eyes met he was convinced. He felt that Joseph had something on his mind, something to say to him. He smiled mechanically into the good looking but weak face, whose dark features so strongly resembled that other…

'Will you share your wife's preference for chocolate, or will you join me in a glass of wine?'

His politeness was cold, unnecessarily cold. He had nothing against this poor, rather simple creature, whose misfortune was to be the brother of one of unbridled ambition. He laughed bitterly to himself. He knew not why. Poor Joseph, he thought.

'That would be most welcome indeed.'

Joseph was, as ever, over-enthusiastic.

Deliberately, slowly, Bernadotte poured the two glasses of wine. He could feel Joseph fidgeting a little.

'Let us leave these two men to talk. We'll go and feed the poor starving birds, Julie. Oscar seems to have fallen asleep.'

Wrapping the sleeping child in thick blankets, Désirée passed the baby to her delighted sister. His wife's voice induced a dull thud in Bernadotte's breast. He would have to hear it out. Again.

The women passed through the veranda doors, still laughing. Bernadotte glanced ruefully after his departing wife. The room fell silent.

Joseph cleared his throat awkwardly a few times, his fidgets increasing, as he emptied his glass in three nervous gulps. Bernadotte, aware of Joseph's discomfort, continued to gaze upon the happy scene outside, remaining silent.

'Well, Bonaparte, what do you want?'

Bernadotte's voice, low and expressionless, seemed to heighten the very silence it had cut like a knife. Joseph, astonished by the directness of the question, hastily drained his already empty glass. Gulping slightly, and clearing his throat for the umpteenth time, he began to address Bernadotte's seated back from his standing position in front of the fireplace.

'The – ah – the Republic, Bernadotte,' he began. 'The Republic…' He paused, apparently making an enormous effort to overcome his nervousness, which was not helped by Bernadotte's silence. 'It's…'

Bernadotte slowly turned to face him, his whole body rotating on the scraping chair. Now he concentrated his full attention on Joseph, his dark eyes fixed disconcertingly on Joseph's shifting glances.

'It's in a bad state of affairs at the moment…' The words were tumbling out too quickly. 'The constitution is inadequate…the Republic needs strong men…like yourself…'

A hint of sweat glistened on Joseph's forehead as he went to continue.

'Stop patronising me, Bonaparte.'

Bernadotte's abrupt interjection seemed to momentarily stun Joseph. Catching his breath, he tried to regain his composure.

'I-I assure you, Bernadotte, I would never insult such a great General as yourself by…'

Bernadotte was staring at the wine in his glass, his face cold and expressionless. Joseph, appearing to suddenly forget his nervousness, assumed a more assertive tone. Leaning towards

Bernadotte he began, 'Let's be frank, Bernadotte...'

'Yes, let's be frank.'

The General's interruption was not abrupt this time, but slow, cold – his eyes lifting from his glass to look straight and hard into his brother-in-law's blinking eyes.

Joseph was taken aback. This was proving even more difficult that he had imagined. He swallowed, his head swimming. Why did this man have to be so inordinately proud?

'Yes...' He paused. 'Ah – the position in the Republic is diabolical – there is no coherence in the government, the Directory is corrupt and...'

He broke off, pausing in his passionate, rehearsed speech as he saw Bernadotte raise his eyebrows. He could feel a pulse beating in his temple. Why could this man not respond as he wanted him to? It could all be so easy. On a fervent note he finished, imploringly looking at Bernadotte's arrogant face:

'It can only be saved by leadership, strong leadership.' Again he paused, choosing his words. Then, with utter resolution, he flatly concluded, 'Only two men can save it. One is in Egypt – and the other is here in this room.'

Bernadotte stared at him in the long silence that followed. His careful discipline maintained a rigid mask on his emotions. So, they had finally revealed their intention, these Bonapartes.

'The campaign in Egypt has floundered in disaster. Your brother, my dear Joseph...'

Bernadotte's crisp reply was interrupted by a suddenly angry Joseph. 'My brother's talents are being wasted!' Vigorously he defended his brilliant brother, whose fortunes so deeply affected his own. Attempting to control himself, he lowered his voice and earnestly leaned towards Bernadotte. 'Look at his record in Italy! He has shown himself to be not only a great General, but also a master at the art of diplomacy and government.' He paused. 'Very little can develop now in the Oriental expedition...'

Bernadotte smiled to himself, an expression of sarcasm preceding his words: 'The Oriental expedition – what a mad escapade that was!'

23

Flushing, Joseph continued: 'One would be inclined to believe that my brother's abilities could be better employed...' He stopped. Eyeing the motionless Bernadotte, he once more cleared his throat. 'What would your position be, Bernadotte, if Napoleon were to return from Egypt?'

So, it was out at last. Napoleon Bonaparte was going to return from Egypt before his tenure of office there expired. And yes, everything was now very clear. Very clear indeed. Bernadotte felt an icy wave of cold revulsion momentarily seize his body; that familiar surge of anger once more rising within him. He remembered a conversation with Sieyés, Joseph and Lucien, which had taken place only a few weeks ago. Sieyés, that colourless and cowardly individual, whom he so disliked, had asked him what he had thought of the idea of Napoleon being recalled from Egypt, implying that Barras was more than favourable to the possibility. It was clear that these three were intent upon changing the constitution. Bernadotte, who had himself been approached on a number of occasions by both Bourbons and Jacobins with the proposal that he effect a coup d'état, was vigorously resistant to the idea. Loyalty to the existing government had always been Bernadotte's determined practice, even in the days of the Ancien Régime. Now, as Minister of War – appointed by the Directory – his loyalty was to the constitution. The constitution they represented. It was clear why the recall of Bonaparte from Egypt would be required... Moreover, he had made it clear that if Bonaparte returned without being instructed officially by the Minister of War, he would be shot, according to the military rules regarding such an act of disobedience. Sieyés, who had never liked the Gascon General anyway, had sourly turned to the others saying, 'We are no longer of any account. Nobody heeds us. It is the Minister of War who constitutes this government.'

Thereafter Sieyés had set about preparing actively for his dismissal from the Ministry.

What exactly was going on at the moment? Bernadotte wondered. Why was Joseph once more trying to draft him onto their side? Were they frightened that he might attempt to use his own considerable influence with the army? But surely his record had shown that he was consistent in his adherence to the constitution. The situation had changed, he could tell that by Joseph's behaviour. Something had actually happened, he felt sure.

He took a deep breath and, rising from his seated position, walked to the French windows behind the piano, which faced a quiet leafy corner of the garden, away from the area where the two wives, now seated on the garden chairs, still chattered and laughed, surrounded by birds. Standing quite still, his back once more to Joseph, he finally replied. Quietly.

'He would not be able to return to France unless he had been recalled by the Minister of War. You know this, Joseph, we have discussed the matter before.'

Joseph, who was still standing in his position by the fireplace, took out a handkerchief, mopping his brow, which was now displaying beads of perspiration. He was becoming a little desperate. This large man, so imposing in his stiff uniform, was not making it easy for him.

'But what if there should be a *need*...?'

Bernadotte turned his head abruptly as Joseph flung this last word at him. His eyes blazing, he looked hard into Joseph's imploring gaze.

'What *"need"*?' He bit the words out in cold anger, finally unable to contain the emotion any longer.

Joseph, utterly confused, hesitatingly began to splutter an explanation. 'There – there are a number of...of...plots ...against the Republic being...'

'I am not without knowledge of the political position, Bonaparte.'

Bernadotte was now facing Joseph, his arrogant interjection snapped with the force of one who knows he is winning. Joseph took in an uneven breath, valiantly protesting.

'But if the government is threatened with conspiracies, would it not be advisable to have a strong man...?' He stumbled '...strong men...to deal with...'

'To deal with the "conspiracies"?' Bernadotte laughed a harsh,

25

mocking laugh as he cut in. Moving towards Joseph now, he thrust his advantage, his eyes, hard and uncompromising, holding Joseph's once again. 'Bonaparte, the Police Force is the properly constituted and authorised body to deal with plots against the government. Leave it to them. The army has its own function to fulfil for France.'

Joseph, glancing out of the windows at his wife and sister-in-law, doggedly refused to concede.

'But...are they capable, Bernadotte? It might be that they are unable to contain the conspirators who will stop at...'

'Who is going to stop them? The conspirators themselves?' Bernadotte's impatient sarcasm silenced Joseph's efforts at persuasion. Their eyes met again, holding their stare for a long moment, each taking full measure of the other. Bernadotte finally moved, gripping the back of a nearby chair, breaking the icy impasse.

'Why don't you be honest, Bonaparte?' He paused as Joseph adopted an expression of defiance. 'Your brother is aware of the mounting political tensions here in Paris. He is aware of the possibility that a motion could be launched in the Assembly to attempt an overthrow of the government, and – if some would have their way – impose a form of dictatorship in its place. God knows, man, I have myself been approached, on four separate occasions, to play the part of the strong man.'

Bernadotte was exasperated. Joseph, beginning to protest, was not allowed his voice as Bernadotte continued threateningly.

'Why do you not admit it, Bonaparte? Your brother wishes to be recalled in order to put in an appearance on that day – and apply for the vacant position.' Bernadotte's contemptuous sarcasm was succeeded by a heavy silence, penetrated suddenly by a shriek from outside. Désirée and Julie had risen. It seemed they were moving to return inside.

'Talleyrand...he...he seems to favour constitutional reform...' Joseph's last desperate attempt seemed suddenly to lack conviction, as he knew he was beaten.

'I am aware of Talleyrand's thoughts.'

Bernadotte was tired of this conversation. He was tired of Joseph, tired of the Bonapartes and their ambitious little schemes. Lucien was the only one amongst them with whom he felt any affinity. As he looked at Joseph, who appeared to suddenly wilt, he once again felt pity for him; and for Julie. He would always be at the beck and call of his imperious brother.

'Bonaparte..' Bernadotte's voice was biting, though he tried to assume a tone of kindness as he addressed Joseph in a final declaration. 'I have sworn an oath to the Republic. I shall be loyal to the constitution, whatever happens. If it falls to my responsibility I shall have shot anyone who threatens that which I am bound to protect. All this you have heard me say before. My position is unchanged, despite my removal from the Ministry of War.' These last words he seemed to chew with bitter sarcasm. He paused, looking at the defeated Joseph. 'Do I make myself clear, Bonaparte?'

His final thrust was countered by the bursting sound of the garden doors opening, admitting the breathless presence of the two invigorated sisters and the baby.

Bernadotte and Joseph remained for a moment locked in silent duel. Suddenly, Bernadotte, stiffly bowing to the company, excused himself.

'Forgive me, I have business to attend to.'

The young women, astonished, were momentarily silenced. Désirée started to follow him, but was restrained by Julie, who had just seen the expression on Joseph's face. Helplessly the three stared at the disappearing back of Jean-Baptiste Bernadotte as he opened the double doors towards him with a little too much of a theatrical flourish.

* * *

'I-I must ring for Marie.' Désirée was confused and embarrassed, moving towards the bell-pull beside the fireplace. 'I-it's time for Oscar's feed.' She tugged at the bell savagely.

'Do-do sit down,' she pleaded with her sister and brother-in-law, passing her hand nervously across her forehead. 'It will soon be time for luncheon...Joseph, your glass is empty...'

Marie entered and took the baby. Désirée poured three glasses of wine, her pretty face slightly flushed.

'Oh, Désirée darling, I almost forgot that you probably hadn't heard...'

Julie, an expression of loving concern on her face as she looked at Désirée, was trying to lighten the atmosphere following the abrupt departure of Jean-Baptiste.

'Napoleone is back! He landed at Fréjus yesterday. He should be in Paris at any moment...'

Chapter III

Désirée was in Oscar's room. Gently she was rocking the sleepy baby's cot, softly singing in a pure and sweet voice. Singing had always been a love of hers. Indeed, Napoleone had encouraged her to practise this art when they had been betrothed. He had always loved her voice, and though he couldn't sing a note himself, he loved music. She smiled to herself as she remembered: 'Music is the soul of Love...' Enthusiasm, that was one of the great qualities about Napoleone. It was probably that very quality, she thought, that endeared him to everyone; after all, most people seemed to fall under the spell of his charm. But it had always been the same: anything he found interesting or challenging he responded to with an extraordinarily vigorous excitement. For some reason that feeling seemed always to affect everyone around him too. He drew everyone with whom he had contact into the tide of his own enthusiasm, sometimes even against their will. There was something irresistible about Napoleone's will... Her smile deepened. Perhaps it was because she knew him so well. And yet for all his strength of character and power over others, there was something strangely vulnerable about him. She had always felt that he was a bit like a little boy. He had such a huge imagination, and somehow he managed to live within it. Momentarily a frown passed over her face.

Her gaze returned to the inside of the cot. Little Oscar was asleep now. How innocent he was. Suddenly an unexpected fear seemed to grip her. What would happen to him? What was his *destiny*? She had always believed in destiny. How many times had she and Napoleone discussed that subject in those distant days long ago in Marseilles. He had believed in destiny too. 'I have a great destiny to fulfil,' he had informed her. She remembered that she had concealed a giggle, for it had seemed a slightly incongruous statement coming from the skinny, untidy, penniless, unemployed General. She smiled again at the memory of it, her eyes soft.

How different he was from Jean-Baptiste. Jean-Baptiste. Her smile vanished, a troubled expression taking its place across her pretty dark features. What was wrong with him at the moment? She loved him so much. But in recent weeks she simply had not been able to communicate with him. He had always been reserved, but these days he hardly spoke. Indeed, he never seemed to emerge at all from his study, his concentration buried in those large books all the time. It had been ever since he left the Ministry of War. But why? After all, he had always said he didn't want the job, that he would prefer another military command. Well, now he was in a position to be given another command. Why then was he so moody? Really, men were a very strange breed! Perhaps none of them ever grow up, she thought flippantly.

At that moment she thought she heard the sound of a carriage on the pebbles of the driveway. She was not sure though, for now the noise appeared to cease. Quietly she tiptoed to the window. Oscar's room overlooked the semicircular approach to the front of the house. It was raining lightly. But at the end of the drive, amongst the trees, she could dimly make out the outline of a small black carriage. As she looked she saw a small figure suddenly emerge from the carriage, stopping to speak to the coachman. Désirée's heart leapt in a sudden surge of excitement. How well she knew that small figure! Hastily she checked the cot again, gently placing a kiss on the baby's little forehead. Silently she hurried from the room, her hands expertly adjusting the pins in her hair.

'Eugènie!'

His voice was unexpectedly deep, the heavy accent giving it a strange musicality, its resonance somehow enlarging the presence of its small owner. He wasn't very much taller than her, yet as she fell into those familiar arms she was, as always, struck by the sheer power and force of character that seemed to emanate from his small frame.

'Napoleone,' she breathed, 'I-I thought it was you...'

A wave of memories seemed to engulf her as she buried her head in his shoulder, temporarily overcome by the depth of feeling that still existed between them. Images abounded. Warm summer nights, gazing at the Mediterranean sky. 'Our souls are suspended in the Universe,' he had said, deeply entranced by the stars. 'Vastness and immensity can make you forget a great many defects in life.' It was as though they had travelled a magic journey together. He, transported by nature and the works of tragic literature, had related his dreams; his hopes, his fears. 'I love the whisper of the wind and the waves of the sea...they harmonise with my nature.' How well she had understood that statement. Beneath that practical exterior; beneath the constant assertions that 'two and two makes four', Désirée had known there existed a wild imagination, and an intellect far beyond her capacity for comprehension. Sometimes she had wondered if she too was the creation of his imagination, so immersed in his unique personality had she become. But Fate had not meant their innocent love to last. In separation they had grown their different identities, and in the place of that youthful flight of passion had grown a deep and mature friendship based on the firm foundation of their young love.

'You have come to see your godson...' Her amber eyes glistened as he held her away from him, tenderly taking in every feature of that dearly loved face.

'Not just my godson, Eugènie...' His blue-grey gaze was soft in his tanned face, his dark hair, as always, long and untidy.

They looked into each other's eyes silently for a long moment in the darkness of the damp autumn night. The light from inside stole out to catch his handsome features in its aura.

'Believe in me always, Eugènie,' he had said to her long ago. A small spasm seemed to momentarily twist something inside her. How alone he was. That cruel isolation he had always lived in seemed to have grown.

31

'Come.' Gently she took the familiar arm. 'Come inside, Napoleone. We're getting wet.'

'How is Oscar?'

The deep musical voice spoke the words as ever quickly, intense with interest and enthusiastic enquiry. Whatever his focus of interest, it always seemed to be the most important thing in the world at that particular moment.

'Well, Napoleone! He is very well. In a moment you shall see him.'

Désirée was helping him to remove his grey coat, handing his military bicorn hat to her maid, who had been summoned by the unexpected sound of voices in the hall.

'Good evening, Marie.'

He was friendly and warm as he greeted this woman of long acquaintance, genuinely pleased to see her once more. Désirée smiled at her blushing servant of whom she was so fond, handing her the heavy coat.

'G-good evening, mon General…'

Marie was unsure how she should behave toward this young man who, when betrothed to her mistress, had been so poor and inconsequential, and now was the famous Conqueror of Italy, and yet who, despite his fame, still treated everyone with the same simple courtesy and genuine interest. How charming he was.

'And Bernadotte?' Freed from the heavy clothes, he clasped his hands behind his back in his characteristic way as he glanced around the circular hall. 'How is that brave General?'

As Marie turned away, laden with the heavy coat, the radiant Désirée lightly touched his arm, beckoning gently, her large eyes alight with mischievous amusement.

'He is well too, Napoleone.' She paused, pointing down a corridor off to the left of the hall. Light streamed from underneath a closed door. 'He is in there. Go in and see him, it will give him a happy surprise. He's been a little miserable ever since he left the Ministry of War.'

Her smile vanished as she remembered an earlier conversation between her and Jean-Baptiste. Her brow creased faintly as the memory momentarily troubled her eyes. Napoleon, immediately sensing the moment of unease, gently touched her cheek. She acknowledged his tenderness with a rueful smile, then, pushing him gently in the direction of Bernadotte's study, she murmured softly:

'You go in and see him, Napoleone. I shall go and find someone to bring some wine – and see if little Oscar is awake.' Lightly kissing him again on the cheek, she uttered spontaneously, almost without knowing it: 'I-I'm so happy to see you again, Napoleone.'

Turning quickly, she hurried from the hall towards the kitchen, leaving Napoleon standing in the hall.

* * *

Napoleon paused for a moment before going to Bernadotte's study. He glanced about the hall once more, his eyes coming to rest on a large portrait of Désirée hanging on the right hand side of the double doors, which he knew to be the entrance of the drawing room.

First love! Strange how that first flush of youth seemed forever to remain. There was something so free about that first closeness to another person. Somehow it was never as demanding as any other relationship. Youth was so much better able to share, because communication seemed to be more abstract, perhaps more spiritual, experiencing that great sense of wonder and excitement at the invitation of life's immense potentials. Youth knew no obstacles, only dreams, and certainty that the attainment of those dreams was possible. How sad that life shattered those dreams so early. He smiled at the portrait. She was the symbol of his youth, of his uncorrupted innocence, before he had learned that the paths to one's goals were blocked by deceit and guile, borne by men whose purpose in life aspired to nothing more than the pursuits of self-interest.

His lips curled in contempt as he thought of them. Bankers; ambitious politicians who accepted bribes with both hands. How low was the sense of values held by some people. And those people, it seemed, were always in a position of power. What about the People? The People of France? Those who gave their sons so readily to fight for the honour of the principles of the Revolution; those who had sacrificed and starved in a country drained of financial resources, to prove that 'The Rights of Man and the Citizen' had given them dignity and freedom. But they couldn't maintain that dignity whilst they continued to starve. They must be rewarded for their fortitude; they must see a benefit from their newly found equality. People could not sacrifice forever.

His eyes returned once more to the portrait of his Eugènie. He had learned that he must fight, not simply in the battlefield, to achieve the dreams they had discussed so long ago in the Mediterranean breezes of Marseilles. He knew the course would not be easy. Yet within that gentle heart, he thought, gazing at Désirée's lovely face framed by her dark ringlets, there remained the abiding trust and understanding of the one who knew his unavoidable destiny. It gave him a strange sensation, a comfort from that unending churning and frustration from which he seemed to suffer. This gentle creature understood him as no other; even his beloved Josephine.

He cast a last glance at the face. Then, turning briskly, he moved quickly in the direction of Jean-Baptiste Bernadotte's study.

* * *

Napoleon hesitated as he lifted his hand to knock. Bernadotte! What a strange fellow his Eugènie had married. He hoped Bernadotte made her happy, that was very important to him. All the same, he was an odd fellow, quite different from Napoleon's other peers. Bernadotte was a loner. Well, he could respect that, after all, so was he. At least the man was honest. A rare quality, that. One that he admired greatly.

His smart knock exacted an immediate crisp invitation to enter. 'I'm almost…'

Bernadotte's preoccupied address to the intruder ceased as he felt the powerful presence of an unusual visitor. Slowly he raised his head from the writing in which he had been busily engaged. The hand holding his pen sank to the desk as, across his small and comfortable study, cluttered with books, scattered papers and maps, his eyes met those of Napoleon Bonaparte. An expression of disbelief crossed his dark brown eyes, as, against his will, he continued to stare into those blue-grey magnets in the fine-featured Corsican face. He flushed, suddenly aware of the heat coming from the dancing flames in the fireplace.

'My dear Bernadotte! How are you, old friend?' Napoleon's voice was warm and effervescent, almost affectionate. 'Eugènie told me I would find you in here.'

Bernadotte twitched at the familiar use of his wife's pet name from her childhood. He felt the beginnings of that strange surge of anger within him. But as Napoleon, closing the door behind him, advanced into the room, the feeling died as he saw the sincerity of Bonaparte's pleasure at their reunion. With a sudden wave of shame confusing him, Bernadotte rose, towering over the small man who, nonetheless, appeared to occupy the room in its entirety, his quick movements and intense enthusiasm entirely dismissing any hint of hesitancy or reserve of welcome on the part of his fellow General.

'Good to see you...'

Napoleon gripped Bernadotte's hand in a vigorous and firm handshake. Bernadotte, recovered from his astonishment, now smiled, a thin, uneasy smile that somehow touched his eyes only fleetingly.

'Bonaparte.' He nodded as they shook hands. 'Be seated.'

Bernadotte indicated a large comfortable leather chair that faced a similar one, both placed close to the blazing fire. The leaping flames cast enormous moving shadows across the room, dancing with those of the many candles that contributed to the warm reddish glow lighting the small study. Napoleon laughed with childlike exultancy, clasping his hands together, vibrant with his intense enthusiasm and high spirits.

'Be seated? My dear Bernadotte, here we are at the most critical juncture of our country's history, and you say "Be seated"! How droll you are, sir.'

Napoleon laughed again with boyish absence of inhibition, taking up a standing position, his feet apart and his hands warming at the fire behind his back. His natural authority asserted its presence even here, in the company of this most formidable of rivals. Bernadotte stared at him, unamused. Quietly he moved to his own chair and slowly seated himself, crossing his long legs, deliberately contrasting his slowness of movement with Napoleon's quick, excited gesticulations.

Napoleon, sensing a slightly hostile response to his statement, suddenly became serious. Looking intensely into Bernadotte's eyes, he continued: 'Bernadotte, the country is in a position of great peril.'

Bernadotte, unable to contain himself, interrupted icily: 'The position is not at all critical, Bonaparte. You are misinformed.'

Napoleon started at the bitter repudiation of his statement. For a moment he studied the large, handsome Gascon who was staring morosely into the fire. The flickering shadows of the room seemed to accentuate the dark features of his massive head. This enigmatic individual must be handled with care.

'Isn't it?'

Napoleon's voice was low, quietly deliberate, his eyes wide open, the hint of a pleasant smile on his face. Bernadotte twitched, irritated by the smiling friendliness of this man he did not wish to see. He raised his head to look at Napoleon's face.

'Why have you come back, Bonaparte? France's frontiers are secure. We have a hundred and fifty thousand men in the field to defend her.'

He paused, about to continue, but Napoleon, again quietly, interrupted. 'Yet I have been told since my return that the Government is no longer in control of the situation. The threat comes not from without, my friend, but from within.'

'There is no threat.' Bernadotte was cold, his tone almost mocking in its dismissal of Napoleon's statement. 'That is a figment in the imagination of your somewhat volatile and excitable relations.'

He paused. 'It's that hot Corsican blood.'

Napoleon was silent, continuing his perusal of the dispassionate face, its gaze apparently mesmerised by the orange flames whose crackling and hissing seemed almost deafening. Napoleon's low voice broke the silence.

'I am told, old friend, that you would have had me court-marshalled or shot upon my return, had you still been Minister of War.'

Bernadotte's gaze remained fixed, his emotion betrayed only by the momentary tightening of a jaw muscle. He paused a moment before replying with heavy sarcasm, 'How fortunate, then, that I was so suddenly relieved of my position.'

Now his head lifted as his eyes met Napoleon's in a hard and meaningful stare. Napoleon remained unmoved, a good-natured smile still playing about his lips.

Suddenly exasperated, Bernadotte went on: 'Bonaparte, you know the regulations as well as I.' He paused, the bitter sarcasm resuming as he continued. 'Indeed, you should know them better, since you were fortunate enough to go to the Military Academy and began your active service as an officer, whereas I served in the ranks...'

Abruptly he stopped, swallowing as he returned his attention to the flames, which had died down a little. Leaning forward, he picked up a log from the stack beside the fireplace. How stupid, he thought as he dropped the piece of wood onto the hissing blaze; how stupid to get carried away by the personal differences between us. Why was it that everything about this man seemed to rankle him? Everything seemed to just fall into the man's lap. He had never had to really struggle. Well, not in the way that Bernadotte had done anyway. At least Bonaparte had not had to wait eleven years to get a commission. A muscle again moved in Jean-Baptiste's face as he remembered his own slow climb through the ranks. How could a soldier who had been to the Brienne Military Academy know what it was like to run away from home at seventeen years old; to join the army as a recruit; to sleep in filthy barracks, two in a bed, carrying out the most menial and unpleasant jobs that had little to do with soldiering? Life had been easy for Bonaparte, no wonder he could indulge his intellectual fantasies.

Bernadotte's turbulent thoughts were suddenly interrupted by Napoleon's voice, strong and authoritative.

'Bernadotte, we must stand together. In the present desperate position of the Republic, I can...'

Bernadotte's mind seemed to explode. His thoughts, so confused and bitter, now lost their coherence. The successfully suppressed anger he had contained now escaped its restraints.

'*What "desperate" position?*' he erupted in a venomous shout. Then, controlling himself, he continued: 'The Russians have been defeated in Switzerland and retreated into Bohemia. The line of defence between the Alps and the Appenines is maintained and we are in possession of Geneva. Holland is saved; the English Army has been forced to capitulate at Helda...'

His arms flailed in wild gesticulation as his anxiety mounted, the words biting in anger. Suddenly he rose, striding into the middle of the room and turning to look at Napoleon as he finished with a final bitter thrust: 'I do not despair of the Republic, Bonaparte. I am convinced that she will resist her enemies, both foreign...and domestic.'

The eyes of the two men locked for a moment in the silence that followed Bernadotte's outburst. Suddenly Bernadotte seemed to sag, tired from the passion of his now expired anger. Napoleon had remained calm throughout, not moving from his position in front of the fireplace, his hands still clasped behind his back. Indeed, his face had maintained a look of amused admiration at Bernadotte's passionate defence of the Republic, and he did not appear to feel hurt or offended by any apparent personal hostility from the taller though slightly less commanding man.

Silence again fell between them. Suddenly Bernadotte threw up his hands and shrugged his shoulders, his head shaking in a bemused fashion.

'I'm sorry you feel this way, Bernadotte.'

Napoleon's voice held a quite genuine note of disappointment. He knew that Bernadotte was refusing to support him, and that saddened him for both personal and professional reasons. Bernadotte was one of the strongest and most influential Generals in the French Army. Napoleon would prefer to have such a person on his side rather than allow the possibility of him becoming an opposition. All the same, he could not help but admire the soldier's loyalty to his cause. Certainly he was a man of honour, this Bernadotte.

The soft expression of admiration on Napoleon's motionless face seemed to neutralise the bitter enmity Bernadotte had felt moments earlier. He moved slowly to stand beside his fellow General, next to the flames that leapt once more with vigour. Sighing, he suddenly put his hand heavily on the smaller man's shoulder. Looking into his face he earnestly began. 'I fought under your command in Italy, my friend. I know your genius, and I realise that France has no greater commander than you...' He paused, hardly believing that he was speaking such words to this man who induced such extremes of emotion in him. '...But these political machinations are not worthy of a General of the Republican Army.'

Again he paused, imploringly searching the fine features of the good-looking Corsican. His hand increased its pressure on Napoleon's shoulder. Into his eyes came a meaningful expression, implying that he knew of that secret about which they had not actually spoken. 'Don't do it, Bonaparte. Don't do it.'

Napoleon's face was serious now as he felt the strong grip on his shoulder of this strange man. His eyes were riveted by the dark gaze that spoke to him with such imploring urgency. He felt a twinge of sadness. If only he could make him understand. But he knew it now to be hopeless. He could only hope that time would demonstrate that which it was impossible to explain to this man.

A light knock at the door ended their silent exchange. Désirée, her arms carrying the small white bundle that was Oscar, came into the room, followed by Marie carrying a tray of wine and glasses.

'Here he is, Napoleone.' Désirée was radiant as she proudly

held her son towards Napoleon. 'Look, Oscar, little man, it's your godfather.'

Lovingly she spoke to the child as Napoleon, without inhibition, lifted the baby from his mother's arms, his face displaying the affection he felt for all children, and now particularly for his small godson.

Bernadotte looked on, his feelings again confused. Bonaparte was a man of surprises. He had not expected this man, who was undoubtedly some sort of military genius, to be so at ease with children, especially babies. Yet here he was, genuinely delighted to be playing with the gurgling child. Bernadotte looked at Désirée, who was pouring the wine, a look of rapturous contentment on her face. A lump came into his throat as he felt the pain of his love for her. Why was he so stiff and undemonstrative? Even with his own baby, he could not play in the way Bonaparte appeared able. He watched Désirée as she took a glass of wine to Napoleon who, now seated, held the baby comfortably in the crook of his left arm, cheerfully making strange sounds into its happily bemused face.

'Thank you, Eugènie.'

Bernadotte felt an angry twist of jealousy as Napoleon took the glass from Désirée. He felt a strange sensation of being left out. Did Désirée still love this man? The question he had been avoiding ever since he had met Bonaparte had finally surfaced. He felt as though he had been hit by a thunderbolt. But now Désirée was standing in front of him, extending a glass of wine to him, her soft eyes looking into his with love and happiness. She touched his hand with a light, fleeting caress. The silent message communicated itself. His rising doubts extinguished. No, his Désirée loved him, he knew. What then of her affection for this love of her youth? Bernadotte felt suddenly tired. He could not think about it any longer. Bonaparte. Would he always be inextricably linked with this man he could not comprehend?

'You must stay for dinner, Napoleone.'

Désirée's happy voice confirmed his answer for him.

Chapter IV

It was the morning of the ninth of November. At last!

There seems little point in continuing to refer to the Republican calendar, for it was soon to be dispensed with. 'Eighteen Brumaire' would mean little to the French who chose to forget the rather more eccentric reminders of The Terror.

Easily forgettable too was the cold grey mist of that November morning. However, weather conditions mattered not. The moment of change was finally upon us. It remained only that those of us involved would carry out our individual participation without any unnecessary blunders. However, our plans had been carefully laid and left little room for error. Thus, as my servant woke me from a peaceful night's sleep, I was calm, and delighted at the prospect of the forthcoming forty-eight hours. Indeed, I shall confess to a degree of near excitement as I rose at that disagreeable hour of the morning, to which I am happily unaccustomed. The world is not at its best in the murky mists of a November dawn. However, great events in the history of the world are few, and such require the breaking of habit, and often the endurement of discomfort. As I stretched and yawned, moving the bedclothes aside, loath to leave the comfort of their warmth, I heard voices coming from the direction of the hall.

'Monsieur Roederer has arrived, sir.' My servant, holding my dressing gown in readiness for me, needed no enquiry. 'He has brought his son. Also, Monsieur Montond awaits you.'

Finally I stood, wincing slightly at my lame foot's morning reminder of its awkward presence. 'Thank you, François. I shall see them presently. Assist me with my toilette.'

Without further delay, I busied myself with my ablutions. As François expertly shaved my face, I recalled with amusement the events of the past few days.

Napoleon Bonaparte had secured the support of everyone that mattered. Everyone, that is, except Bernadotte. Various members of the Bonaparte family, including his close friend Lucien, had also tried to persuade this stubborn man, but none had succeeded. However, the support of the army seemed assured as Murat, Berthier, Lannes and Leclerc were all sworn to support Bonaparte. I had myself ensured that any other potential opposition had been appropriately dealt with. It remained only to furnish Barras with a lucrative compensation, which would assure his physical departure from Paris before the coming events. Paul Barras was a man with a penchant for comforts of an exceedingly expensive nature, and thus I had no doubts as to his willingness to overcome any hesitation he might entertain to the proposal that he must absent himself from Paris.

Undoubtedly it had been a source of much regret for Napoleon that he had not been able to acquire the support of Bernadotte, a man whom he clearly admired and to whom, moreover, he felt personally bound. I, however, considered such an absence to be of little consequence. Indeed, I was in an exceedingly good humour this autumn morning.

'Invite the gentlemen to attend me in my dressing room,' I bid François as he handed me a warm towel to hold to my cleanly shaven face. The man departed momentarily to direct an attendant servant outside my room to deliver my invitation. I looked in the mirror as I pulled my silk dressing gown closed over my clean shirt and breeches. I didn't really feel forty-five years old. Strange, I felt as though life was really only just beginning.

'Good morning, Excellency.'

My visitors were brisk and alert, chorusing their morning greeting as I entered my dressing room. Certainly there was an atmosphere of rapt anticipation and controlled excitement here in my house on this cold and foggy morning. I seated myself on the chair in front of the mirror whilst François completed the preparation of the wig he was to place on my head.

'Seat yourselves, gentlemen.'

My friends looked a little surprised at the hint of joviality in my voice. Indeed, I was a little surprised myself. I have never been known for any display of passion, considering it imperative that one maintains a constant sense of decorum. Today, however, was a moment of exception. Long had I worked towards this day. *Order!* At last we would have Order in France.

'We must employ our time in completing the resignation of Monsieur Barras,' I said as François painstakingly fitted my wig, tucking under it any escaping evidence of my own greying hair. 'Montrond, my good man, have you a copy of the one we have already drafted?'

François was puffing powder lavishly over the now comfortably fitting wig. I closed my eyes to avoid the invasion of the white particles of dust.

'Indeed, Monsieur Talleyrand.'

Montrond was, as usual, lively and positive. A pleasant fellow, this Montrond. I was fond of him. He was known as 'Le beau Montrond', such was this handsome young man's reputation with the ladies. We had worked together for some considerable time, and he was most particularly useful to me in my English negotiations, for he was extremely popular with those often humourless members of the English court.

I asked Roederer if he would make a completed fine copy from that draft which Montrond now handed him upon my instruction. I have never seen the merit in unnecessary employment of my energy, and Roederer appeared to require a task to occupy this idle moment. Roederer therefore completed the brief statement, dictating it to the tidy hand of his son. His son had already been of invaluable assistance to us in his capacity as a printer's apprentice, wherefrom he had printed notices of the forthcoming events for the benefit of the people of Paris. Even at this moment these notices were being plastered to walls all over the city.

'Excellent.'

I was pleased with the smooth and efficient responses of our small company. François was handing me a mirror that I might examine my profile in the other, longer mirror.

'We shall polish him off – before breakfast, sir!'

Montrond had a dry mode of expression. I laughed, amused at the prospect of our unheralded visit to Barras.

'An appropriate phrase, my dear Montrond...You have a way with words.' I paused a moment. 'Barras, however, is the least of our worries. He will soon be safely ensconced in the country, minding his own business, and his own insignificant little affairs.' I rose from my chair, the appearance of my wig now to my satisfaction. 'The least of our worries...' I was half musing to myself. 'He is under control, like the Ancients...'

I confirmed in my mind the preparations, and I nodded to myself as I removed my dressing gown. François was holding out my coat to receive my arms. Dipping my back slightly as he slid the velvet garment up to rest upon my shoulders, I continued: 'It's the Council of Five Hundred with whom we must concern ourselves.' Pulling my lace cuffs from entrapment under the coat sleeve I continued. 'There appears to be considerable opposition amongst that unruly congregation.'

I was aware of my note of irritation, and saw its message register on the pleasant features of the good Montrond. Loathe to cast a dampening effect upon the optimistic gathering, I hastened to relieve the tension I had unnecessarily induced. 'How do I look?'

Taking my cane from François, I perused myself in the full-length mirror, turning to view my back and sides. The familiar and charming smile returned to Montrond's face.

'Marvellous, Excellency...Exquisite.'

I was satisfied with their appreciation of my carefully tended appearance. 'My snuff?' I held out my hand to receive the small box and lace handkerchief that François was now extending. 'Let us hope Lucien Bonaparte can play his part satisfactorily. He is the key, you know.' I addressed them with the crystallised thought that had been playing on my mind. 'We must not lose control of those emotional simpletons in the Five Hundred. They have frustrated the course of sanity in France for far too long.' I laughed, invigorated by my good humour. 'Understand, old chap?' I clapped Montond on the back as I moved to proceed downstairs.

'Indeed, Excellency.'

The Roederers fell in behind us as we descended the carved staircase into the hall.

'Admiral Bruix has just arrived, Excellency.' A servant informed me as we reached the hall that my choice of individual to serve Barras with his document of resignation had arrived.

'Ah – good, good.' Yes, all was going smoothly. 'Now, is the carriage ready? Let us depart, gentlemen, and exercise the careful operation of our plans.'

François now enveloped me in a warm cloak, whilst other members of my household assisted my compatriots to their winter protections. I took in a deep breath as the glass doors were opened for us to descend the steps to my waiting carriage.

'Let us proceed, gentlemen.'

I led the way into the cold, damp autumn air. Our task had begun.

* * *

Residents of the Rue Chantereine were wakened early that cold November morning by the persistent sounds of busy comings and goings at the small house wherein resided the Conqueror of Italy. Clanking spurs and snorting horses complemented the creaking sounds of arriving military carriages bearing Generals regally garbed in their imposing uniforms of blue and gold. Silently, obediently, confusedly waited the soldiers from the entourage of the greatest military luminaries in France, glancing nervously at one another as they held the restless animals during their long vigil amongst the fallen leaves of autumn in the quiet street, shrouded by the chill of the morning mist.

Inside, small groups of men, their numbers swelling as the

morning grew older, conversed quietly. The pretty hall and corridors were filled to capacity already with senior officers, who had been invited to attend Napoleon Bonaparte at seven o'clock. As their numbers increased, so gradually filled the garden and steps with the small tentative groups.

Napoleon, meanwhile, was in his study, attended by a growing number of Generals. The hum of excitement was restrained as Napoleon exchanged quiet and brief words with each of the individuals in turn. Taut and alert, Napoleon appeared composed and assertive, displaying his considerable authority simply and efficiently, without over insistence.

He was in conversation with Berthier, his Chief of Staff, when his attention was arrested by a new arrival at the entrance to the room. Napoleon's conversation died on his lips, the colour of his eyes appeared to change to a steel grey as their pupils dilated in sudden, uncharacteristic anger.

The tall figure of Jean-Baptiste Bernadotte moved commandingly into the room. Blithely he acknowledged his fellow Generals whose mouths appeared to fall open at the sight of their colleague. He was dressed entirely in civilian attire, contrasting quite incongruously with the formal military presence of blue, gold braid, swords and revolutionary sashes.

The room fell silent, all eyes on the tall, arrogant figure.

'How is this? You are not in uniform?' Napoleon's angered voice bit into the uneasy silence. Bernadotte met his steely stare insolently.

'I never am on a morning when I am not on duty.' Bernadotte's reply was laconic, affecting a casual tone.

'You will be on duty presently.' Napoleon snapped his retort, maintaining a cold control over his anger.

'I have not heard word of it. I should have received my orders sooner.' Bernadotte shrugged with an apparent lack of interest. He appeared to be enjoying the discomfort he knew himself to be creating amongst the assembled company.

'A word with you, sir.'

Napoleon's command was abrupt, almost savage. He turned

and walked quickly into an adjoining room. Bernadotte slowly followed, smiling at his astonished peers, moving with a sauntering air of disdain.

The door to the room was closed smartly, leaving the Generals to break out in fervent speculation.

Napoleon's head seemed to be bursting with the effort of trying to control his temper. Damn him! he thought. Why did he have to do it this way? Why had he just not turned up? How would this affect the others?

He was seething now, barely able to contain himself as he watched the tall figure stroll arrogantly into the small room.

'What do you mean by this, Bernadotte?' Napoleon's tone was menacing as the sound of the closing door drowned the low voice to Bernadotte's ear.

'I beg your pardon?' Bernadotte was arrogantly polite.

Napoleon was silent, collecting himself, determined that he would not unleash his anger. 'You received my request to attend me. Thank you for coming.' Napoleon's crisp words sounded strangled as he maintained his control. Bernadotte remained silent, his face betraying no emotion as he stared defiantly at the smaller man.

'A plot has been discovered, the safety of the Council is at risk...' Napoleon continued, his tone brisk and commanding, hands clasped behind his back as he faced squarely the tall hostility of his fellow General. '...We must stand by in readiness.'

A loud guffaw silenced Napoleon's words. Bernadotte threw his head back as the harsh mocking laughter filled the room. Napoleon's face flushed, he could feel the hot anger rising. He knew it would overtake him.

At that moment a knock was heard at the door. Napoleon, glaring at Bernadotte, shouted the invitation to enter. His secretary, Bourrienne, appeared.

'General, this note has just been delivered for you. Its bearer said it was urgent, he is waiting...'

Napoleon snatched the piece of paper, reading it quickly. His face betrayed no indication of the document's contents. His temper now restrained, he looked at Bernadotte with cool composure.

'If you do not wish to join us, then I suggest you withdraw, sir.'

With these icy words he abruptly left the room, his arrival amongst the assembly of Generals silencing the buzzing conversations. A small civilian made his way through the large Generals to Napoleon, beckoned by Bourienne. He exchanged a few low words with Napoleon, who then turned to the company.

'Citizen Generals, it seems that the Republic is endangered. Citizen Cornet brings us a message from Citizen Sieyes. The Council of Ancients has held an emergency session concerning the discovery of a Jacobin plot to overthrow the Republic. It has been voted that the session be adjourned to the Palace of St Cloud, and the Council has appointed me commander of the Paris district to ensure the safety of both the Council of Ancients and that of the Five Hundred.' He paused, looking at each of his military peers in turn. Slowly he concluded, with low authority: 'Gentlemen, you know your duties. Attend to them.'

There was a moment of still silence. Then, as Napoleon, his movements as ever quick and decisive, began issuing orders to Bourienne, the rest of the Generals seemed to erupt into action. The mood of dispersal rippled through the dozens of soldiers gathered both inside and out. In a flurry of excitement, carriages began to roll away; horses, whinnying and stamping, were spurred into instant swift canters. The events of the coup d'état had begun.

Napoleon, busying himself to leave with all haste after first informing his wife Josephine of his appointment, forgot all about Bernadotte.

Bernadotte, meanwhile, slipped quietly away. Returning to his home in the Rue Cisalpine, he burst into Oscar's bedroom where Désirée and Marie were feeding the child. His suave composure gone, Bernadotte was now approaching panic.

'Désirée, my love! Prepare yourself to leave Paris.' His shouted words were almost incoherent. Désirée was startled at the breathless sight of her husband who, moreover, she had seldom seen attired in civilian clothing. Her protestations were interrupted by his rough insistence. 'Do as I say. *Immediately.*'

Without further protest, Désirée, a little frightened, followed his orders. Bernadotte, shutting himself in his study, sank into a chair, burying his head in his hands. What have I done? he wondered. What have I done...

* * *

Barras presented little trouble, as I had anticipated. Having been led to believe that he was a part of the conspiracy, indeed feeling himself to be the very inspiration of change, he now found himself confused and more than a little surprised to find events in motion that were beyond his comprehension. He had learned to his chagrin that Sieyés and Ducos had disappeared. Paris was crawling with soldiers, and his other two somewhat weak-minded colleagues, Gohier and Moulin, were loudly bleating for assistance from him. Barras, dazed at the continual stream of reports, remained in the bath, hoping that General Bonaparte would arrive at the Luxembourg Palace to see him. Instead he learned that Napoleon had been sworn in, at ten o'clock, by the Ancients as Commander of the Paris district.

Thus, by the time my small company arrived at the Luxembourg to join him for breakfast, Barras knew he had been fooled. Remembering the fate of past Revolutionary leaders, he also knew, as he saw the white document of resignation complementing his coffee, that it was time to cease his faint-hearted and impotent gestures of resistance. Well-practised in accepting bribes, he acceded with indecent haste to our insistence, and gladly accepted an armed escort to ensure his safe arrival at his country house.

He left – after breakfast.

* * *

The events of the ninth were going well. Sieyés ensured through his majority in the special meeting of the Council that due to the 'dangerous plot' by the Jacobins, it was necessary in the interests of safety to adjourn to St Cloud on the next day, protected by General Bonaparte. Happily, sixty members, with somewhat zealous moral scruples, had failed to receive their summons to the meeting due to a small manoeuvre on my part. I do not believe in inviting the possibility of opposition if it is possible to avoid it.

Later in the day the Assembly met to receive the decision of Council to recess. Lucien Bonaparte, in the serendipitous position of President, thus hastily declared the meeting adjourned, before giving them time to consider.

Yes, events were running smoothly, and according to plan. I returned home following our little business transaction in the Luxembourg. There I was kept informed of the rest of the day's events. I had left Napoleon in conversation with Sieyés in the Tuileries. Already I could see a potential rift between these two uneasy collaborators. Sieyés, pompously certain of his intellectual superiority, did not appear to recognise the extraordinary abilities of the small General whom he erroneously thought he was 'using'. That he would be felled by his own sword was a fate I knew would ultimately assail Sieyés. The thought amused me.

Fatigued and rather bored by Sieyés's self-important posturing, I had departed, the events of the morrow more prevalent on my mind than the turgid philosophising of the ex-Abbé. The procedures of the next day, I knew, would be a little more complicated to execute than the relatively simple actions of the ninth.

I had arranged for a house to be put at my disposal in the vicinity of St Cloud. There I could find myself better placed to control the situation whilst retaining a degree of comfort. I find these emotional gatherings somewhat noisy and tiresome, too exhausting altogether to get directly involved in. Moreover, I have always felt it necessarily politic to absent myself from the actual scenes of illegal activities.

Thus, on the morning of the tenth of November, accompanied by the Roederers and des Renaud, I travelled to St Cloud. At our nearby position Montrond would keep us informed of the sequence of events.

* * *

Napoleon was staring at the place where the guillotine had stood. Momentarily he felt sickened as he imagined what an observer of all that had taken place in this square this past decade might have witnessed. His gaze remained fixed, his thoughts recalling horror, but he could feel his body being jerked up and down to the sound of the fast moving carriage wheels on the cobbles. As though from a distance he could hear a conversation. In his peripheral vision he could see them. Joseph and Sieyés were only a few inches away in the dark confines of the small carriage. Poor Joseph. It was his turn to be bored with the endless prattling of that man Sieyés. A bitter taste seemed to suddenly come into his mouth. He had to admit, he really did not like this ex-churchman. There was something so pretentious about him. He thinks he's using me, Napoleon wryly amused himself. He would soon know better. Napoleon felt a wave of disgust at the very idea that anyone should imagine that they could 'use' him. He, the Conqueror of Italy! All the same, he would remain silent, put up with this cold, cowardly individual until things were sorted out. All that was important was France.

He cast a last look at the empty square as they left it. It must never happen again. Never. France must never again be so degraded. He would ensure that. He would ensure that France and Frenchmen would be the most respected race on the earth. He would bury their shame that it might never again be remembered. He knew this was his mission, his *destiny*. He believed totally and utterly in his 'star'. He knew he was different from others. That was why people like Sieyés disgusted him. They were too limited and narrow in their vision to be able to understand that.

Fate. Suddenly that word seemed to present itself in his mind with an ominous discord. Fate was quite different from destiny, though most people seemed to confuse it. Fate was somehow an element in the human condition that was beyond the control of the individual. Yet it was that very element that ultimately determined success or failure. Fate was somehow the necessity through which human beings had to perform their deeds, yet destiny was that which must be performed in order to fulfil the task of life. Destiny was sublime, magnificent in its spiritual illumination. Yet fate was somehow corruptible, like men; like politics; inflicting guilt without criminal cooperation. Fate played to make you a victim. Napoleon shuddered, a strange and hitherto never experienced sense of foreboding suddenly overcoming him. He felt a little dizzy. Someone was speaking to him.

'Well, the Ancients are under control, Napoleon.' Joseph was attempting to lighten the atmosphere in the carriage, seeing his brother's serious expression as he stared out of the window.

Napoleon turned from his reverie, taking in his two fellow travellers seated opposite. He felt removed from them, entirely alien. I feel like a fragment of rock thrown into space, he thought. How often did he think that...?

Slightly dazed, he looked at his brother. 'Sorry?' he enquired, having not heard his brother's statement clearly.

Joseph leaned forward, raising his voice slightly above the sound of the racing carriage wheels. 'I said the Ancients, at least, are under control, Napoleon.'

He smiled fondly into his brother's serious face. Napoleon, pulling himself from his thoughts, reciprocated the smile, his grey eyes soft, though carrying a hint of melancholy. Quietly and slowly he spoke. 'I have made the calculations, Joseph. Fate will do the rest.'

Joseph sat back in his seat. How odd Napoleon was. This was a moment when he would have thought he would be elated. Instead, he seemed to have slipped into that strange mood of his. Oh well, he had a lot on his mind; he'd snap out of it soon enough.

'I wonder if Bernadotte...'

Napoleon was surprised to hear his own voice, indeed surprised to hear his words. He broke off. The rhythm of the galloping hooves of the horses seemed to beat into his mind. Bernadotte. He felt a twist of pain at the thought of yesterday's episode at the Rue Chantereine. He hoped he would not repeat such a display of poor behaviour; it made it all so difficult. He didn't want to fight with Bernadotte – didn't the man see that? He had wanted him to stand with him in this great cause. Couldn't he see the magnitude of what they were about to do for France? Yet he couldn't find it in his heart to be really angry with the man. After all, he was related to him. And he was married to Eugènie, damn it. Why did the fellow have to be so inordinately proud?

'The army will stand by its agreement with the Five Hundred if there's any trouble.' Joseph was trying once more to be businesslike. Napoleon's grey gaze rested unseeingly on Joseph's kind face.

Sieyés, looking from one to the other, addressed himself to Bourrienne, Napoleon's secretary who had been silently engrossed in some papers throughout the entire journey in his seat beside Napoleon.

'How long is to St Cloud?' His colourless eyes were without expression.

Bourrienne opened his mouth to reply, but was interrupted by a shout from the coachman outside, answering the question for him.

'St Cloud, mon Général.'

Napoleon remained unmoved for a moment. Then, as the carriage slowed, he appeared to spring a transformation. Tightening his sash, and fingering his sword, he cast a quick glance at the three other occupants of the carriage. His eyes were suddenly alert and determined, his natural expression of authority entirely supplanting the preoccupied detachment he had displayed during the journey.

'Gentlemen, our time has come.'

He moved quickly, impatient to begin, as the door of the carriage was thrown open, the vehicle had not even come to a halt. Suddenly he had vanished, and was seen striding quickly and purposefully towards the Palace, immediately surrounded by a group of questioning soldiers, even before Joseph, Sieyés and Bourrienne had begun to move.

* * *

An atmosphere of fevered speculation enveloped the Palace of St Cloud that morning. Small groups of people were seen conversing intently, and arrivals at the Palace noticed that there was a heavy military presence mingling with the growing number of Council members collecting in the formal gardens.

As Napoleon made his swift exit from the still moving carriage, Lucien, who had been waiting impatiently for the arrival of his brother, approached him instantly. Lucien's agitated figure was followed closely by the tall and dashingly flamboyant presence of Murat, characteristically theatrical in appearance, but uncharacteristically serious and tentative. The two fell into step with the rapid strides of their small leader as he approached the entrance to the Palace with an expression of grim determination on his face. The scattered group of people seemed to turn as one to look at the body of soldiers who were disappearing into the Palace with such haste.

'What's going on?'

Napoleon kept his eyes fixed ahead as he crisply asked his brother for an explanation regarding the groups of people outside, apparently not engaged in session.

'The sitting is unable to begin...' Lucien paused, a fleeting expression of anguish passing over his face, his hands moving nervously. 'The workmen have not finished installing the benches, hangings, and all the rest of it – the place isn't ready.' He finished on a note of exasperation, throwing his hands up in a gesture of helplessness.

They were inside the Palace now; the sound of footsteps and clanking steel from Napoleon and his retinue echoed around the columned emptiness of the vast hall. Napoleon halted, an expression of horror on his face as he looked in disbelief at Lucien. Before he could say anything Lucien took the arm of his thunderstruck brother. Hurriedly he pushed him in the direction of an imposing staircase, glancing up at the galleried floor above.

'Come. We'll find a room for you. Have some wine. It'll calm your nerves.'

Lucien was in control now, glancing anxiously around at a few clusters of members who conversed quietly in the shadow of the great hall, whilst casting sidelong glances at the small group of soldiers with whom their President was speaking.

* * *

'What sort of a mood are the troops in, Murat?'

Napoleon had overcome his shocked reaction to the slight setback that had greeted his arrival. He was standing in front of a fire, in a small room on the first floor of the Palace. The tall Murat positioned himself by the window, quietly observing the scene in the gardens below. Sieyés, meanwhile, had taken a seat also close to the fire. Crouched in the chair, he appeared huddled and tentative, his pale face staring intently into the flames behind Napoleon's parted legs. Murat, his eyes still perusing the scene below, replied quietly and simply:

'We shall see.'

Momentarily a hush fell upon the room. The sound of splashing liquid interrupted as, in the corner, Lucien was pouring wine, nervously missing the glasses as he began. Murat, suddenly moving from the window, wordlessly left the room, indicating only with a jerk of his head to Napoleon that he was going to review the situation. Napoleon nodded, accepting a glass from Lucien, who was also extending one to the oblivious Sieyés.

'I had better go and see if they have begun to assemble yet.' Lucien's voice was firm as he looked at his brother with unspoken understanding, placing Sieyés's glass on a small table nearby.

Taking a sip from his own glass, Napoleon calmly and quietly urged his brother, 'Try and gauge their mood, Luciano.' It was Lucien's pet name from their childhood. Then, with a dramatic gesture of his arm, he continued, 'This all depends on mood…the army…the Council…mood!'

Sieyés's' expressionless eyes moved to Napoleon's face as he spoke, and Napoleon, unable to resist the potential for comedy in the situation opened his eyes wide and, looking mischievously at Sieyés repeated, '*Mood* – eh, Sieyés?!'

Sieyés, confounded by this peculiar man who indeed was a man of many 'moods', looked at Napoleon, slightly bemused. Twitching his thin lips, he attempted a nervous smile, then hastily returned his gaze to the fire. He kept seeing the flash of that falling blade: Madame la Guillotine... Suddenly he was nervous. What if he, who had survived The Terror, had made a wrong judgement? He picked up his glass and gulped the liquid without tasting it. He could hear his *sword* laughing. The sound struck a strange presentiment in him. His attention returned to the face of the handsome soldier who was addressing him once more.

'Don't worry, Sieyés...it will be alright. Lucien is President. Murat has the troops standing by. What can go wrong?'

Napoleon's words seemed a little less confident as he finished. Each man put his glass to his lips as the heavy silence fell upon the room once more. They both returned to the contemplation of their own thoughts as they resigned themselves to a long wait.

* * *

The sound of 'La Marseillaise' opened the session of the Council. The Ancients had heard of the resignation of four Directors, and moved that the Assembly of Five Hundred should propose a list of suitable Directors from which they could decide upon successors. Following their decision, the sitting was suspended. Napoleon was flabbergasted. He had imagined that the Ancients would move to create a committee to form a new legislation.

The adjourning Ancients were astonished to see the small figure of General Bonaparte, accompanied by Berthier and Bourrienne, suddenly appear in their midst. A breathless silence fell as he began to speak, the sheer audacity of the action compelling them to listen.

'Representatives of the people! Do not underestimate the gravity of the situation. Let me speak to you candidly, as a soldier...' Napoleon addressed them with the vigour and command of a General inciting his troops to battle. 'Let no one search the past for examples that might slow down our advance! Nothing in all history resembles the last years of the eighteenth century; nothing in the last years of the eighteenth century resembles the present moment...'

The Councillors began to look at each other, uneasy with this lofty, military style address.

'At all costs we must save the principles for which France has sacrificed too much: Liberty and Equality...'

A hum went round the chamber. '*Save?*'

Was this young man implying that there was a conspiracy? Who then were the conspirators? What was this young upstart talking about? Was this the man they had asked to 'protect' them? Had they made a mistake?

'What about the constitution?' shouted one of the Ancients.

Napoleon's voice rose with even greater passion. 'Precisely! Conspiracies were being planned in its name, because of its *inadequacies*...'

A swell of anger rose from the venerable gathering. They simply would not tolerate such impudence. Napoleon began to hesitate, sensing his audience to be hostile. Valiantly he tried to explain himself, but they became increasingly vigorous in their antipathy towards him.

'We must take the appropriate steps to form a committee to deal with the dangers...'

His last attempt was silenced by shouts telling him to remove himself. He felt a pressure under his left arm.

'We must leave, mon Géneral.' Bourrienne was speaking urgently into his ear, sensing what might happen if the Council got out of control.

Abruptly, Napoleon ceased his attempts to address the Council. Glaring at them, he turned and walked out of the chamber, closely escorted by Bourrienne and Berthier.

His head held high, and walking with singular purpose, he decided to proceed to the Orangerie where the Assembly of Five Hundred were in session. He would address them instead.

* * *

The Orangerie of the Palace of St Cloud was a forbidding place. Its huge bare windows looking vacantly out on the grey November skies seemed to cast a grim light on the vast, unadorned interior. Now, filled as it was with the noisy Assembly of the Five Hundred, whose collective mood was growing more ugly by the minute, the Orangerie was indeed a daunting prospect.

As Napoleon and his two faithful companions approached the hall, the roar of apparent pandemonium greeted them. People were still pouring into the assembly, each man so preoccupied with the heated debate that even those who passed the small soldier in the corridor did not notice who he was.

Inside, Lucien was standing on the platform, regally dressed in his official toque and toga, attempting to perform his duty as President. His efforts were in vain, as the sound of his voice was drowned out by the angry voices of incensed members. The Speaker, banging his gavel insistently, was being entirely ignored by the shouting, gesticulating crowd. A small group of members, entirely carried away, began trying to ascend the platform. This was too much. They were driven back by the Assembly Guards, and the Speaker stood up assertively, savagely crashing the gavel, forcing the attention of those unruly members. Suddenly the noise appeared to subside as the members realised they were behaving without any semblance of dignity.

A voice from the crowd appeared to cut across the subsiding hum. 'Is it true? Are these rumours true?'

Lucien searched the crowd to find the owner of the angry shout, which had forgotten all formal etiquette.

'Is it true that the traitor is here?'

A second voice, shouting even more loudly, came from the same direction. Lucien's racing thoughts charged his searching eyes. It was organised, this havoc. He knew it; he felt it.

'The Ancients have endorsed him...'

'No, no, he's just been thrown out of the Council.'

Lucien had located the small group. Yes, he knew them: a Jacobin faction. In vain he tried to interject, but was drowned out by the first waving group, who were successfully inciting the anger in the rest of the Assembly.

'He won't get far here…'

Threateningly the shouts continued, now exciting reciprocal yells from the other side of the hall.

'Talleyrand controls the Ancients…this smacks of his work.'

'Yes, but Bonaparte won't get anywhere with us.'

The temperature in the hall was rising once more as the shouting began to break out savagely throughout the hall. The Speaker again attempted his angry motions to silence them. Lucien looked at him, shrugging his shoulders helplessly, an expression of grim rage on his face.

Napoleon had arrived at the doors. The menacing sound of the hubbub shocked him. Joseph, who had been standing at the entrance waiting, looked at him in helpless desperation. 'Lucien can't get a word in…'

His voice was despairing, exasperated. Napoleon, his hands clasped behind his back, began to pace up and down, his eyes fixed on the floor, his chin buried, apparently deeply in thought. Berthier and Bourrienne exchanged an apprehensive look with Joseph.

'Joseph, see if you can assist Lucien. He…'

Napoleon's words ceased as the hammering sound of the gavel appeared to achieve its effect. The angry shouting died down, and order appeared to be restored again. The small group at the door craned their necks to see what was going on. Murat had now joined them.

Lucien stood up once more. Calmly he lifted a long document, which he ceremoniously unfolded. 'Gentlemen! I have the honour to inform the Assembly that the following resignations from the Directory of the Republic have been received: Sieyés, Ducos, Gohier, Moulins…' Gasps came from the thunderstruck members as the names were read out. '…Barras…'

As Lucien read the last name, bitter fury erupted again, this time bringing the proceedings to the verge of a riot.

In the corridor outside the hall a small group of soldiers had begun to congregate, hearing the furore coming from within.

'What's happening along there?' a confused looking young soldier asked a fellow as they curiously looked along the dim passage towards the entrance to the Orangerie.

'It sounds as though they're out of control. There'll be a massacre in a minute...'

The small group were distinctly uneasy.

'What's Bonaparte doing?' asked one, who had caught sight of the small commanding figure of their General amid the group at the doors.

'God knows. It's his fault anyway. You can't interfere with the constitution. After all, that's what we fought for in 1789. The Rights of Man..'

The young men were shaking their heads, confused and saddened at the hysterical shouting of the Assembly. They were joined by another small group of young soldiers, similarly speculating.

'Where's Bernadotte?' one young soldier asked abruptly. 'He's the only one who can handle this...'

'Yes, he cares about the Republic – at least, he respects the constitution.'

The rejoinder was instant from another member of the group.

'But Bonaparte is our commander-in-chief, we must be loyal to him. Look what he's done for France in Italy!'

The soldiers continued their debate without rancour, looking over their shoulders at the growing group by the door, now joined by Sieyés, and by Montrond, who had come with a message from Talleyrand for Napoleon.

Without warning, Napoleon roughly pushed aside the soldiers standing to attention on guard at the door of the Assembly. Striding into the hall, he advanced towards the platform, ascending it quickly.

'Gentlemen! We are on the verge of civil war! France is threatened. Leadership is required to safeguard the Ideals of the Revolution. We must...'

Napoleon's shouts were halting and unsure. As he looked at the contorted faces, reddened with an anger that appeared to be directed solely at him, he felt suddenly light-headed and dizzy. The sound of their hostility seemed to blend into a deafening cacophony; the flailing arms and fists, the blazing eyes, floated before him in a nightmare of slow motion. It couldn't be real. Surely this could not really be happening? What had gone wrong? Didn't these people understand that he had come to save them? That he was there in their interests? Look what their incompetence had done with France? They were at war on all fronts, their economy was non-existent, and their rule of law was obsolete. Surely these useless individuals had some concept of what it was their positions were supposed to require? And, therefore, if their true interest were France, they would know that he, Napoleon Bonaparte, was in a position to save them.

The faces seemed to drift before him in the ghastly din. He felt numb, that familiar sense of alienation separating him from the reality.

Someone had scratched his face. He could feel the hot passage of the blood as it oozed slowly down his head. People were pushing him. A hand was crushing his arm with unrelenting savagery. The red faces were close to his own. He could smell their stinking breath as they spat their words at him. Animals. They weren't men, they were animals. They knew nothing of Honour; of the Glory of France…He felt a wave of sick disgust rising from his stomach. Someone was pulling the collar of his coat. He felt a strangled, nauseated, revulsion for this ignorant mob.

'I refuse to be the man of any Party!'

He knew that he had shouted those words. They could kill him, but they would not demean him. Deep inside, as he felt the dizziness increase, a cold anger began to rise; a contempt for these rabid animals who were pushing him and pulling him, dragging him from the platform. His words had seemed to inject an even greater rage into their mood. High-pitched screams erupted:

'How dare you?'
'Who does he think he is?'
'Down with the tyrant!'
'Dictator!'

He could hear the violent invective reaching him through his daze, and was aware of the increasing savagery of their physical abuse. Now he could see Lucien fighting his way towards him. And Joseph. Their expressions were frozen in horror.

'*Outlaw him! Hors la loi!*'

And now a cold sweat broke out all over his body. Those were the words that had sent Louis XVI to the Guillotine. The penalty for outlawry was death. Momentarily everything appeared to become silent. Some tall soldiers were hauling him out of the hall. Lucien was close beside him.

'*Hors la loi…!*'

The animals were receding from him, the whites of their eyes and teeth flashing. Again he felt that sensation of sick contempt.

'Outlaw him!'

His eyes closed for a moment. It hadn't worked. He would have to resort to the measures that he had hoped would not be necessary. It was not possible to make those assassins understand. They were more barbarous than anything found on a battlefield.

* * *

'If they seek to outlaw you, then they are outlawed themselves.'

Napoleon opened his eyes to see Sieyés's pale face looking intently into his. The colourless expression was calm and controlled. He was leaning his head back against the wall behind the seat where he had been placed, having been dragged from the hall into the corridor. Still slightly dazed, he could hear the sound of the riot from inside. He stared silently, unseeingly, into the face of the ex-Abbé. Taking out his handkerchief, he pressed it against his bleeding face. Staring into nothingness, he collected his thoughts.

Suddenly he appeared to tense his body. Rising quickly, he strode to the doors of the hall once more.

Inside, Lucien was again attempting to pacify the crowd. Glancing at the door, he saw his brother. Unnoticed, he scribbled a note, and passed it to a soldier. 'For the General,' he murmured.

'*You have ten minutes to act.*' Lucien's scribble was almost illegible.

Napoleon looked up from reading the piece of paper. His brother was now dramatically addressing the members who, suddenly alarmed at his words, were listening.

'Since I can no longer perform my duty as President for you, I shall lay aside the insignia...'

Slowly, deliberately, with theatrical exaggeration, Lucien began to divest himself of his robes of office. The members appeared to be taken aback by his actions. Had they gone too far? What was the President doing?

Napoleon, meanwhile, had summoned the senior officers from the division of the soldiers present. Soldiers had built up along the corridor, horrified at the news that members of the Assembly had assaulted their Commander.

'Soldiers! I have led you to victory.' Napoleon's voice echoed its authority to the grouping soldiers far back at the Palace entrance. 'France is in need of you! Can she count on you? We must save the Republic!'

There was a momentary pause as the soldiers looked at one another, still slightly confused and uncertain. Suddenly the voice of an old soldier shouted: 'Vive Bonaparte!'

Another shout, further back: 'Vive la République!'

A chorus began: 'Vive Bonaparte! Vive la République!'

Echoes of the soldiers' growing cheers filled the corridors, hall and entrance, spreading to the attentive groups outside.

Napoleon, glancing quickly at Lucien as he continued his gallant performance, turned sternly to Murat. 'General, the President is imperilled. He is in danger of suffering an attack to his person. It is the duty of the army to save him from physical violence...'

His meaningful stare into Murat's eyes now moved to the soldiers behind him. Raising his voice, he again asserted: 'The President of the elected representative body of the People of France is in mortal danger... Defend him!'

There was a pause, then: 'Aux armes! Aux armes!'

Napoleon's deep authoritative tones hypnotised the soldiers.

Abruptly Murat shouted his orders to prepare for attack in

immediate response to his Commander's rallying command. He beckoned for his horse to be brought inside. The drums were signalled to begin, and an order was issued to fix bayonets for foot soldiers, whilst Murat mounted his horse, as did his personal guard.

Lucien allowed himself a sigh of relief as he saw Murat's dramatic entry to the hall. The clattering of horses' hooves on wooden floors, accompanied by the clanking of steel armour from the mounted soldiers, was a terrifying and unprecedented sight. The Members of the Assembly, who had been confused and spellbound by Lucien's theatrical display, appeared to be taken unawares. Gasps exhaled from their horrified faces as they realised what exactly was happening. They seemed to shrink as one body, while more and more soldiers poured into the hall, surrounding the platform with rank upon rank of armed protection. The earlier rage of the members seemed suddenly to turn into a quaking fear, as they knew they were beaten. Quickly, silently, in the face of the threatening soldiers, they dispersed, melting away through windows and doors, skulking into the protection of the gardens now darkened by night.

Napoleon stood in the entrance hall of St Cloud. He was alone, as soldiers held their positions both inside the assembly hall and outside the palace. His face was expressionless, his grey eyes betraying no emotion. It was done. He felt nothing now.

'Sir, the task is accomplished.' Murat was pleased with himself, bowing to Napoleon with characteristic panache.

Napoleon looked at him in silence. His gaze wandered into the middle distance. 'I have refused to be the man of any party.'

He repeated the words he had used earlier in the screaming teeth of the riot. Now they echoed softly, barely audible even to Murat. The flamboyantly handsome General coughed, a little uneasy at his master's serious face.

Without warning Napoleon flashed his irresistible smile at him. Clapping him on the back, he transformed into the dynamic General he knew so well. 'Good work, Murat! Good work! Come, let us find Lucien, Sieyés, Joseph and the others…'

Napoleon's deep voice was warm and elated. Striding with a

sudden lightness of step and accompanied by Murat, he moved towards the doors of the Orangerie.

* * *

I was informed of the successful outcome of the day's events just as we were about to dine that evening.

Emotional events are usually forgotten quickly when a successful conclusion is reached. Thus, I did not doubt that the somewhat chaotic occurrences of this day would soon be consigned to oblivion. Following the violent scenes a calm had settled upon the Palace of St Cloud. A small body of members had re-assembled, and had docilely declared the Directory to be at an end. Napoleon Bonaparte, Sieyés and Ducos were sworn in as a temporary measure to protect the Republic.

A coup d'état is a tiresome necessity which one would wish to avoid. But the peace and stability of France was at stake. Whatever the means, the end was imperative. All the same, the precarious events now concluded, I was relieved to be able to enjoy my dinner in the firm knowledge that our mission had been accomplished.

France had reached a new threshold.

Chapter V

The Bourbon Lily! I was amused to see its tattered remains on the dirty carpet underfoot. That such a furnishing, displaying such an emotive emblem, should still be clinging to the floor of a Tuileries corridor after ten years was indeed some sort of feat. All the same, I wasn't quite sure for whom. Whether for the unfortunate Bourbons; or as testimony to some sort of restraint in the ardour of the Revolutionaries; or perhaps for the simple art of good weaving prevailing upon the sanity of practicality. At any rate, it proved one thing: that quality lasted, in carpet weaving at least!

I glanced about me as I progressed slowly along the long corridor. Other remnants of a bygone age, broken or covered, were evidenced intermittently. What a mess! But then, how else? After all, the place had been somewhat hastily occupied.

I smiled, recalling the past few months since the coup d'état Brumaire. How things had changed. How indeed...

* * *

I liked Napoleon.

In those early days I was drawn to him by that irresistible attraction that defies definition: the spell of great genius. His enthusiasm and eagerness to learn were almost childlike in their charm. Moreover, his anxious desire to acquire knowledge about every facet of government, and anything else he felt he needed to know, meant that he was never ashamed, or too proud, to be taught.

Indeed he sought advice, listening intently, absorbing with a voracity that only increased his yearning to take in more. His energy was inexhaustible; his delight and excitement with his work so intense and vigorous that everyone with whom he engaged became infected with his high-spirited enthusiasm. He was possessed of a brilliant, clear vision for the reconstruction of France and the stabilisation of Europe, and such was the animated power of his 'dreams' that we were all drawn into the euphoric momentum of working within the requirements to realise that great vision. How happy he was then...

Indeed, how happy we all were. I myself, though naturally of an idle disposition, and not given to excessive demonstrations of passion, even I found myself infatuated both by the charm of the young man himself, and by the brilliance and imagination of his vision, which he so passionately expounded upon at every available opportunity. His zealous nature amused me, though I was forever warning him against excessive display of such extreme emotions. But yes, those were happy days...

Events had occurred rapidly following the coup d'état. Napoleon had quickly found himself at odds with Sieyés and Ducos. Firmly he held to his belief that, through plebiscites, the 'Will of the People' should be expressed 'through the ruling executive'. Sieyés, however, was in favour of a removed executive body, who would not be subject to the caprice of the people. Thus, disagreement ensued about the structure of the proposed executive. Finally, following advice from the councils, Napoleon's will prevailed.

There would be three consuls. The First Consul would assume the supreme position of authority; the second and third would remain performing purely consultative functions. They would be elected for ten years, at the end of which time they would be eligible for re-election. Thus Napoleon became provisional First Consul. Cambaceros, a most able lawyer and drafter of legislation, became Second Consul. As Third Consul, Napoleon selected Lebrun, a brilliant economist who had served in the Ancien Régime. Now, with a firm structure of government, they could draft a new constitution.

The result of their concentrated efforts was published at the end of December, barely six weeks after the coup d'état. The people were presented with a document to vote upon which introduced a system that seemed to be heralding an approaching democracy. At last – a new, coherent, direction. France was delighted, and the constitution and the Consulate were endorsed by the elated people, and voted into power overwhelmingly.

Ergo! Napoleon became First Consul, and in February moved from the temporary abode of the Luxembourg Palace into the Tuileries. The Revolution had ended.

* * *

I had passed out of the depressing corridor, and was now making my way through a large room, which seemed to vibrate, despite its dilapidated condition, with the impulse of energy emitted by its young occupants. A bevy of secretaries were hard at work. Some scurried between desks, intently conferring with colleagues; others hunched over their writing, wholly absorbed in tasks that excluded all external interruption; all were surrounded by mountains of papers. As I walked through their busy atmosphere, acknowledging their respectful greetings, it passed through my mind that here, in this small body of dedicated young people, was expressed the spirit of that which Napoleon Bonaparte had brought to France. Youthful unbounded activity pulsated here. Optimism, dedication, and a fearless desire to tackle the daunting legacy of chaos left by the Revolution and, through hard work, create an order that would bring France peace.

'I have only one passion, one mistress, and that is France…' he had once said to me in that dramatic way, so characteristic of him. And though the theatrical phrasing amused me, I knew there to be a truth in his statement. This young man was totally and wholly dedicated to the land of his adoption. His talents were, it was becoming increasingly apparent, even greater than I had realised in those days when we had sought a *sword* for France.

I felt pleased with the outcome of events in general. Thus it was with warm thoughts that I remember entering his study on that spring morning of 1800.

* * *

'The First Consul is in the bath, Monsieur de Talleyrand.' The ever-faithful Bourrienne rose from a table placed close to Napoleon's littered desk. 'He asks if you would care to attend him in there, sir,' continued the secretary, moving in the direction of a door that led into a small dressing room.

I followed him, smiling to myself. Certainly the young genius had his eccentricities! Long hours did he spend in the bath, claiming that an hour immersed in the warm, soapy suds was equivalent to four hours of sleep in its contribution to general relaxation and strength. Thus comfortably ensconced, he liked to hold discussions concerning the more philosophical aspects of his 'dreams', and these were pleasant and stimulating gatherings, when the young man was often at his most creative and imaginative.

As we approached the room of his toilette through the small dressing room, I could hear voices. I could also breathe the escaping steam, which was finding its passage into far distances from its source. Napoleon liked his baths hot. Very hot! As I reached the door I could hardly see through the thick vapour. I could hear the end of a sentence spoken by Tronchet, the venerable lawyer for whom Napoleon held so much respect. Evidently he was also in attendance that morning.

'...and so it seems, sir, that there is actually no such thing as "French Law". We have only many regional – and sometimes very obscure – codes, and there are hundreds of autonomous courts. Also...'

A sudden splash came from the most concentrated area of steam, interrupting Tronchet's quiet statement, and closing the surprised opening mouth of Bourrienne, who was about to announce me.

Through the swirling mists broke the glistening face of the First Consul. Wet hair – shorter these days – plastered against his reddened features, his eyes were gleaming with excited animation, his white teeth flashing in that magnificent smile that seemed to light up his whole being when he so projected it.

'My dear Tronchet, we are embarked upon the most formidable task ever given to a Frenchman...Mon Dieu...!'

This childlike image of intoxicated idealism was one that was to remain in my memory always, even when time would sour the magic of his immense vision, and bury the flame of his unrestrained enthusiasm and energy.

'...We are a nation with three hundred books of laws, yet we have no *law*...?' He spoke in wonder, softly, half to himself, his gaze carrying from Tronchet into the unseeing middle distance.

'Monsieur de Talleyrand, sir.' Bourrienne had recovered himself from the sudden action of his unpredictable master.

'Ah, Talleyrand! Good morning.' Napoleon's greeting was hearty and jubilant as he lifted a long brush to tend to the less accessible regions of his back. 'Sit down! Sit down!'

Napoleon ignored the more formal observations of etiquette required of his position when he was in the bathroom. Here grew the intellectual articulations of his dreams. We were all equal contributors here.

'More hot water, Constant.'

He addressed the hitherto unnoticed presence of his valet who was silently busying himself, no doubt with some visual difficulty, with a task in the misty recesses to the rear of the room. As the valet quietly attended to the wish of his adored master, boosting still more the thick shroud of steam that enveloped us, Napoleon continued, vigorously moving the brush in its awkward position.

'Tronchet here and I have just been discussing the Laws of France...' He laughed exultantly, the deep musical tones reminding me of Plato's reference to the 'halloo of the hunters' as they tracked down an intellectual truth. '...or the lack of them!'

He was sponging himself, returning to his reclining position, only his head above the deep water. He paused for a moment, becoming serious and still, his brow creased in a sudden frown. 'A Frenchman is a Citizen, first and foremost. Soldiers come second.'

His voice, now quiet and deliberate, reflected the complete transformation of his mood from youthful vigour to weighty thoughtfulness. These were the dynamics that typified this young man. Without warning he could change his mood entirely. His now serious eyes moved in the still face, its chin sinking into the water. Soberly he looked at Tronchet, then at me, his grey-eyed intelligence penetrating my own returning gaze.

'I must give them a fair and just society...' He paused, continuing with a hint of growing passion. 'We must create a coherent and just civil code. Then a criminal code.'

His gaze had again shifted from my face into that sightless gaze into the middle distance. The awesome vision he was now apparently challenging seemed to touch his voice, rippling beneath his words through a brittle catch in his throat. 'I shall re-build France that it may combine the best of the Old Laws – with the Rights of Man.'

His voice was now rising in excitement as he returned his darting eyes to Tronchet and myself. 'We shall have one great code of Law for all Frenchmen... As we have strangled the corrupt practices of usurious bankers and financiers that they may not drain our citizens of the little they have, we shall now provide those citizens with their natural Right of recourse to Law – a just and fair law, common to *all Frenchmen*.'

He paused, overcome by his own passion. I could not help but hide a smile at the incongruity of such a speech, more fitting for the newly formed Council of State, coming from such a strange setting. And yet, it was so typical of the man, whose very existence was driven by his cause. Regardless of circumstance he was continually preoccupied with France. Nothing else mattered, at any time.

Suddenly he lurched forward once again, his penetrating gaze fixed on Tronchet. 'I give you six months to give me a civil code, Tronchet.' He was intent, crisp, authoritative. 'I want equality before the law; all feudal rights and duties must cease. We must have freedom of conscience; freedom to choose one's work – most especially we must attend to the protection of the Family unit. We must make the Family *strong*. That is the very *basis* of a healthy society. We must ensure inviolability of property…'

He broke off suddenly, intently leaning towards the lawyer, his face soaked with beads of sweat from the heat of the bath. 'Tronchet, you already have my thoughts on these matters. These principles must be codified, do you understand? Six months…a draft…'

'Sir, the Minister for the Interior.' Bourrienne's voice cut across the passionate exposition.

'What…?' Napoleon's voice trailed, preoccupied with his vision of a civil code. Turning his attention to the door, he wrenched himself from the passionate discourse. Unperturbed, the bespectacled Tronchet too turned to the entrance, as did I.

'Luciano!' Napoleon had returned to this boyish heartiness. His bare arm extended, beckoning the figure of Lucien, which had just appeared from behind Bourrienne. 'Come in! Come in, my dear brother. What a gathering we have here this morning!'

Napoleon indicated to Constant that he was going to get out, and the good valet obligingly approached him with a large enveloping towel, which he wrapped around his master as he rose from the deep, spilling, water.

Lucien advanced into the room politely, inclining his head at Tronchet and myself, casting a brief look in the direction of his brother. His glance at the latter betrayed a somewhat surly undercurrent. I had heard that there had been disagreements between these two in the months since Brumaire. Lucien had envisaged, at that time, more of an equal partnership with his brother. But time had proved that the extraordinary qualities and charismatic character possessed by Napoleon were beyond equality with anyone else, even one as acutely intelligent as Lucien.

Napoleon, however, appeared not to notice any hints of reservation. Fixing a towel around his waist as Constant vigorously rubbed his back with another, he enthusiastically addressed Lucien, casting a mischievous glance in my direction, which rather confounded me as it seemed to conceal a hidden amusement in the vibrant young man.

His eyes wide with twinkling anticipation, he enquired of Lucien, 'Well?'

Then suddenly, inexplicably, he turned to me. 'We shall see, my dear friend, if you are right…or I am!'

Turning then to Tronchet, he politely included him in what he clearly regarded as our private joke, and as though by way of explanation he stated simply: 'There are two forces in the world: the Sword and the Spirit. By Spirit I mean civil and religious instruction. In the long run the Sword will always be defeated by the Spirit.'

Now I understood! Shaking my head slightly I marvelled at his subtleties. This young rascal was undeniably unique.

Lucien had seated himself, silent throughout Napoleon's humorous theatrics.

'Well, brother?' Napoleon demanded. 'Don't keep me in suspense. What is the outcome of your survey? What do the people in the county districts want?'

Lucien paused. 'They wish the return of the Faith, Napoleone. As we thought…'

The loud guffaws of Napoleon's laughter rang through my numbed mind. I was flabbergasted. Speechlessly I stared at the convulsed First Consul.

We had, of course, discussed the possibilities of a re-establishment of Religion, the Revolution having dispensed with it. However, I mistakenly imagined that I had successfully dissuaded Napoleon from such thoughts. My own personal feelings about Religion need little explanation.

I cleared my throat, stunned that he had taken such an initiative without my knowledge. 'You are making a grave mistake, sir, if you are seriously contemplating the re-introduction of Religion.'

Napoleon was pulling his dressing gown across his chest. Abruptly his laughter ceased. Sternly he looked at me. 'The Law needs the church as her ally.' His voice was firm, indicating that his mind was made up. Tying the belt of his gown he turned to

Tronchet who had risen, gathering his papers together in preparation to leave. 'Tronchet, speak to Portalis. We must begin to draft our documents.'

Smiling at the departing figure of the older man, his eyes returned to me as Constant put his shaving equipment into his hands. Opening his eyes wide, a gleaming look of amusement in his eyes, he whispered teasingly: 'My dear Talleyrand, I see in Religion not the mystery of the Incarnation, but the mystery of social order!'

He grinned, turning to the mirror to attend to his shaving. Vigorously slapping soap over his face he continued, now serious and firm: 'How can there be any order in a State without Religion? Society cannot exist without inequality of fortune, and inequality of fortune cannot exist without Religion.'

He paused, looking pensive for a moment, ceasing his actions. His voice lowered as he slowly murmured, half to himself, 'Religion associates with Heaven an idea of equality which prevents the rich from being massacred by the poor.' Lifting his razor he leaned towards the mirror being held by Constant. 'Religion is the vaccine of the imagination, my dear Talleyrand. It preserves us from all dangerous and absurd doctrines. It is enough for a Christian Brother to tell a man of the lower class, "This life is but a transition". It gives them hope, Talleyrand. *Hope*. Then they can bear their miserable existences...'

His voice trailed thoughtfully. The scraping of his razor was the only sound in the room. I was still bereft of words, turning over the implications of his intentions in my mind. Suddenly he turned, his face half shaven, and, gesticulating with the long blade, looked at Lucien and myself in turn.

'My policy is to govern men as the majority wish. That, I believe, is the only way to re-organise sovereignty of the people. It was by turning Muslim that I gained a hold in Egypt; by turning ultramontane that I won over the people in Italy. If I were governing Jews I should re-build Solomon's Temple...'

He shrugged, grinning as he returned to his shaving. Casting a sidelong glance at me he spoke through the contorted accommodation of his mouth to the shaving action. 'Besides, I have myself never doubted God. For if my reason did not suffice to understand him, yet my inner feelings accepted him. My nerves are in sympathy with that feeling.'

I felt my eyebrows raise in surprise. I had not expected such a statement from this man. Once more I had been taken aback by the traditional conformity of his thoughts.

Napoleon was pressing the warm towel, handed to him by Constant, to his cheeks. Quickly he patted his face. Then, passing the towel back to Constant, he strode towards the door. 'Come, gentlemen. Let us go to my study.'

Taking my arm affectionately, he smiled into my face, tweaking my ear painfully with his other hand. It was a habit he had of displaying his feelings of endearment, usually creating much discomfort for the recipient since he appeared to be unaware of his considerable strength. I was not usually honoured thus, reserving as he did such demonstrative actions for younger objects of his affection. However, his good humour today appeared to ignore his usual restraints.

'Come now, my dear friend, not so glum! You'll get used to it! After all, you are a bishop!'

He twinkled as he guided me towards his study, now warmed by the freshly attended blazing fire. Becoming suddenly serious he quizzically looked at me, tilting his head slightly to one side.

'You know, old friend, it might be a good idea to examine again your own feelings about Religion.' As I began to protest, he lifted his hand as he shook his head, smiling. '…Yes, yes, yes! I am fully aware of your antipathy towards the church, Talleyrand. I understand your views, and can even agree with some of your criticisms about the practical aspects that have been so abused in the past…' He paused before continuing. '…But Faith! The nature of Faith! There is an interesting polemic to conjecture.'

His grey eyes looked deeply into mine, challenging me, as he continued: 'It is, after all, an extraordinary thing to ask someone to believe in God. The sheer absurdity of an abstract invisible deity is unbelievable, to say the least!' Again he paused. 'And yet, despite the strictest application by Reason – inexplicably we somehow come, mysteriously, to find ourselves evolving that unimaginable: Faith! Moreover, the very futility of Reason in the face of such an abstract idea renders the challenge of that very "Reason" to become the underwriter of Faith itself! The Act of Faith, therefore, occurs as the action of the overcoming of doubt!'

He threw his arms wide. Shrugging, he grinned at me. We had reached the fireplace. Napoleon reached his arm out to rest it on the mantelpiece. I was transfixed by him. Amazed as ever by the broad scope of his thinking.

'You are saying, then, that the transformation of the negative issue into a positive form comes through the intellectual process of Reason? That is, we "reason" doubt away...?' I confess that my tone held a hint of cynicism, and yet I knew there to be a certain logic in all this.

'Precisely, my dear friend. Precisely.' His eyes were dancing with excitement. He was speaking quickly and intently. 'Now, let us therefore examine the phenomenon of courage. Not necessarily physical courage, but moral courage. Courage in itself represents some strange form of faith. And the inevitable and natural fear inherent in us in some way corresponds to the doubt we have spoken of. Now, the oriental warriors believed...'

'Sir!' Napoleon's bubbling enthusiasm was interrupted suddenly by a soldier who had, unannounced, entered the room unexpectedly.

'What is it?' Napoleon snapped at the soldier, angered at being interrupted.

'Sir...' The soldier bowed. 'Sir, the Austrians have delivered a surprise attack in Italy.'

The First Consul froze, stunned into silence, staring at the soldier who was awkwardly shifting under his penetrating stare. I was more than a little shocked myself, though my intelligence had informed me of the continuing possibilities of such.

There was a long, charged silence. Finally Napoleon, collecting himself, muttered to the soldier, 'Moreau...?'

'General Moreau and the army of the Rhine have been alerted, sir.'

Napoleon nodded, waving his dismissal to the soldier as he accepted the document proffered to him. His shoulders seemed to droop, suddenly tired. He glanced at the document, then, putting it down on his desk, he walked to the window.

Silently, he stared down at the courtyard below. Motionless, he appeared to be in a state of shock. The long silence was broken by his low murmur as he seemed to sigh to himself: 'The purpose of the Republic making war is to win Peace… Peace… I must have Peace to re-build France…'

His voice trailed. I felt a twist of pain for him. He really was a man of peace, it seemed at that moment. Now he knew he must go to war, when what he wanted was to address his energies to the reconstruction of France.

But aggressions from abroad were not all that our young First Consul had to disturb the planning of his dreams for France…

Chapter VI

'Bonaparte?'

Napoleon was roused from his doze by the mellow tones of his wife's voice. Opening his eyes drowsily, he looked up into her wide, dark, enquiring gaze. Gently placing her hand on his, she knelt beside the large comfortable chair that held her tired husband. Only the crackling of the fire momentarily filled the room with sound, as the First Consul and his wife looked at each other in silence. Moving his hand to enclose hers, his face melted into a warm and loving gaze, sleep receding as he responded to her question.

'Josephine…?'

His face had filled out a little during his year as First Consul. The dark hair, though still quite long, was nonetheless cut more tidily.

Now, as he smiled into the face he so dearly loved, he was a deeply contented and satisfied man. This last year had certainly been a challenge. The Republican opposition had, in fact, posed a serious threat and had been gaining an alarming momentum. But Marengo had put an end to all that. The people had been ecstatic at his success over the Austrians.

'My love, are you not coming? Have you forgotten?'

He was jolted by her quiet voice. Josephine squeezed his hand, smiling at his bemused expression.

'The opera, darling. You said you would come. It's "The Creation" by the German composer Handel, remember? It's never been heard before here in Paris. Everyone is so excited about it.' Her voice was pleading slightly. 'Hortense and I have so much looked forward to it, and Caroline is here to come with us too…' She paused, tilting her head appealingly to one side. 'Please…?'

Napoleon could never resist her smile. How utterly feminine she was! He did not really want to attend the opera that evening. He was tired, and besides, he had intended looking over the draft for the forthcoming treaty with the Austrians.

'I'll stay here with you, my darling, if you are tired. The others can go on without us.'

Josephine was unable to conceal the disappointment in her voice. With his other hand Napoleon suddenly pinched her cheek affectionately, moving in his chair in preparation to rise. Kissing her quickly on the forehead he said, 'Order the carriages to be brought round. We'll go.'

He cast her an amused sidelong glance. Women! She had known all along that he would not disappoint her. He chuckled to himself, shaking his head a little as she, beaming at him with a long look through her dark eyelashes, quickly rose and hurried out of the room, calling back to him from the door, 'You had better hurry, my love, we'll be late. Joseph and Julie will be meeting us there, also Désirée and Bernadotte…' The voice trailed away as Josephine disappeared.

Napoleon rose from the comfort of his chair, walking to the fireplace to warm his hands. It was chilly tonight. But then of course it was the twenty-fourth of December. Christmas Eve! How happy he would be when he had ensured the official return of the Religious calendar. Some of the idiosyncrasies of the Revolution irked him, and not least was the 'calendar'. Noble ideas and lofty ideals were one thing, but a disregard for tradition was quite another. Most sentiments, Christmas for instance, were traditions. We experience them because they have preceded us, and because the pattern of history and civilisation was guided by such recurring occasions. Besides, it was a unifying factor in society, and indeed between nations. Virtually not a single human activity, he thought, is determined by the simple impulse of man's will. From early childhood we live under the sway of laws and habits, adhering to the rituals and cultural customs handed down by our ancestors. How important it was to recognise the spiritual values of such great traditions.

His lip curled slightly as he thought of the revolutionary rabble, tearing at the heart of their cultural heritage without anything of consequence to put in its place. Well, he would ensure that the new order would embrace all that the Ancien Regime had stood for, but with accessibility to the moral and material enrichment for ordinary people, not simply the privileged few...

'Papa...' Hortense's shy interruption lifted his intense preoccupations, pulling his eyes away from the dancing flames in the fireplace. 'Mama asks if you are ready...?'

'Yes, yes my dear. Indeed.' Pulling her ear, he grinned at her, quickly disappearing into an interior room. '...I'll be with you in just a moment.'

Completing his quick personal preparations, Napoleon looked at himself in the mirror, drying his hands on the towel hanging nearby. He was changing... Well, so was life!

He had consolidated his power after the Italian campaign. Now he was at peace with Austria and Russia. That mad Russian Tsar was certainly an odd fellow. Still, Napoleon did not complain about the infatuated communications from Paul I, Tsar of all Russia. He cared little for the rumours about the cruelties supposedly practised by the Russian ruler. After all, he was the son of Catherine the Great, that 'student of Rousseau'! He smiled wryly to himself. How decadent were some of these European royal families. Fleetingly he thought of the Bourbons... Decadence was a tumour in society that must be got rid of.

But he wouldn't think about such unpalatable thoughts this evening. It was Christmas Eve, and he was spending it with his family, assured of his success. He was at peace with all save England, and even there negotiations had already been initiated. The reconstruction of his beloved France had begun.

His pale face stared back at him from the mirror. Yes, he could certainly celebrate this Christmas. In the next room he could hear the voices of the three ladies, chattering and laughing. He smiled to himself. His family meant so much to him. What a pity that Luciano...

His brow creased with the fleeting troubled thought of his difficult brother. But he must not entertain such worries tonight. He shrugged unconsciously as he reached the door.

'Good evening, ladies.' His deep musical tones immediately silenced the feminine conversation, his charming resonance entirely arresting the attention of all three. 'How beautiful you look, my dear.' He took Josephine's hand, pressing it to his lips in admiration of her tasteful white dress, offsetting her strange dark beauty so perfectly. 'Indeed, how charming you all look...'

He bowed to each of the others, affectionately extending his arms. As he passed his gaze over his sister, his eyes lingered a moment on her stomach. 'And how is Murat's heir, sister? Well, I trust? Another great General for France?'

He laughed uproariously, unaware that his remark was a little tasteless. Caroline blushed, spontaneously putting her hand to the swelling beneath her dress.

'Napoleone...don't be so crude.' But his sister was amused.

They all laughed. It was understood that Napoleon was quite ignorant of the nuances of fashionable behaviour. He said whatever he felt like saying, oblivious of whether or not it was considered polite. Nonetheless, he was fussy about clothing and a sense of decorum and propriety in ladies, and carefully scrutinised everything his wife and family wore in public. At the outset of the Consulate the scanty attire favoured by the fashionable ladies of the day such as Madame de Tallien and that friend of Talleyrand's, Madame de Rémusat, had horrified him. He had ordered Josephine to address herself to changing the fashions of the Consular court, thus setting an example throughout France. Josephine had naturally complied and the fashion now was of elegant simplicity.

Approvingly he nodded. Then, briskly offering his arms to Josephine and Caroline, and glancing paternally at Josephine's daughter Hortense, he issued: 'Let us depart, ladies.'

With his customary speed, Napoleon guided his three companions down the wide staircase towards the palace entrance. They were attended by Josephine's maid as they passed bowing footmen in the course of their rapid progress. As they reached the doors, however, the flaming torches of the entrance throwing their moving light over the stationary waiting carriages, Josephine suddenly shivered, despite her covering cloak.

'Marie,' she turned to her maid, 'please could you fetch me my shawl…you know the one I mean?'

Marie curtsied, nodding to the kind tones of Josephine's voice. 'Of course, Madame.'

Josephine squeezed Napoleon's arm, looking up into his eyes. 'Bonaparte, my love, you go on, please. Marie will only be a moment and we will follow on behind you. The others waiting at the Opera will be disappointed if we are all delayed. Besides, you may wish to speak to Bernadotte if he has managed to return in time…? Anyway, we'll probably catch you up…'

Soothingly, with practised experience, she coaxed him into going alone.

'Very well then, but do not delay, Madame.' Napoleon was brisk and formal as, first kissing his wife's hand, he strode out to the waiting carriage.

Hunching down into the cushioned interior of the dark carriage, Napoleon felt unexpectedly uneasy. How irritating it was when things didn't go absolutely as planned. He often felt that it was an intimation that something catastrophic was going to happen. But he knew it was silly to think such things. Anyway, Josephine was right. He would like to have a word with Bernadotte if he had returned from La Vendée. He shook his head to himself. It was a troubled region, La Vendée, a regular hotbed of intrigue. He must keep a careful eye on it. Indeed, that was where the supposed Royalist conspiracies were hatched, inspired by the fanatical loyalty to the Bourbons of Georges Cadoudal – 'Georges', as he was more popularly known. He had become quite a folk hero, this 'Georges' – for the Royalist cause.

Bonaparte hunched more deeply into his coat. His eyes closed, half dozing, as he listened to the rhythm of the hooves of his horses, and the clatter of the accompanying guard of grenadiers.

Still, he couldn't have a better man to cope with Royalists than Bernadotte. His face stretched in a wry smile. Bernadotte! He hated the Royalists even more than he hated the First Consul!

Napoleon laughed to himself. No, he should not make jokes about Bernadotte, even to himself. After all, the man was part of his family circle. Moreover, he was proving his loyalty, in spite of his rather faltering start. But then, he could respect the man's original repugnance for the overthrow of the Directorate. At least it displayed a healthy regard for the law and the constitution. He liked that in a man. It showed loyalty and integrity. Now Bernadotte's loyalty was to him, and to the Consulate. Exploiting his sense of honour must absorb his Jacobin tendencies. Yes, he admired the man, no doubt about it. In spite of his little foibles, and misguided Jacobin ideals. Goodness knows what he and Luciano talked about. They seemed to be very close indeed. Why was it that he, Napoleon, just could not communicate with that particular brother of his these days?

He shook his head in the darkness of the carriage. Raising his eyes, he looked out of the window, that small twist of pain he always felt when thinking about Lucien touching him again.

Moodily he stared out into the night. He could feel his body moving with the motion of the carriage, the clatter of the hooves on the cobbles pounding a rhythm in his tired mind. It was raining slightly, and he could see shapes moving about in the street they were passing through.

Suddenly a strange feeling of foreboding seemed to grip him. It was inexplicable somehow; he couldn't quite put his finger on it. But he was certain that something was wrong. Dreadfully, horribly wrong. It was like having an abrupt premonition that one was on the very brink of disaster. Where were they? The Rue Saint-Nicaise...

He sat up suddenly, his body taut and tense. In the darkness the sound of the galloping hooves seemed to hammer relentlessly inside his brain.

Looking through the small back window, he could see Josephine's carriage behind, following. Yes, they were catching up as she had promised, though they were still well behind. Now he craned his neck to try to see up to the front of his own carriage, through the side windows. They were travelling at quite a speed. Too fast in such a narrow street. The strange feeling was turning into a quite unreasonable fear, almost a panic. He felt suddenly trapped in this small rattling box.

There seemed to be an object, a large object, apparently pulled across the road in front of them. It was difficult to see clearly through the side window... But surely it must be in the way? And yet they weren't slowing down. Why? Was the driver drunk? It was Christmas Eve...

But then maybe there was a way through the obstruction that he couldn't see. After all, the Grenadier guard must be passing it by now... But the street was so narrow and that obstructing object, which he could now see was a cart, was so large. It was getting closer. And closer. The Grenadiers must have passed it... And now he could see two more of those furtive figures, moving somehow very suspiciously.

Running away...?

He pressed his face to the window. He knew, suddenly, with absolute certainty, something was very wrong. But *why weren't they slowing down*? His head was bursting. The clattering hooves seemed to be deafening. It couldn't...oh no...

The pitch of the sound became intolerable. He seemed to explode from inside. But the bright orange of the explosion told him it was outside. He felt he could hear himself scream – or was it someone else...? The horses were shrieking...in shrill terror... they...

But now it didn't really matter. That unbearable thrust of climactic sound had ceased. He seemed now to be floating. The small black box of his carriage interior was hurtling through some silent netherworld. And he, no longer in his seat, was helplessly clinging to what appeared to be the roof, pinned by a force beyond either his coherent comprehension, or control.

Perhaps...perhaps he was dead...

And then it became black nothingness.

* * *

'Bonaparte...!'

The piercing scream seemed to jolt his aching body. Moving his arm slightly, he heard the sound of crumbling wreckage as his carriage door and roof, whose unintended coupling had been supporting him, collapsed. He was thrown into a supine position. Blankly he stared at the sky. It had stopped raining. He could even see a star...

Why was he lying here? Where was he? Why did every part of his body hurt so much, and why was he so lethargic that he was incapable of movement? He didn't even seem to be able to blink.

'Bonaparte...Darling...Where are you...?'

The scream was hysterical. It seemed to approach him from a long way away, through some dazed veil. He seemed to know that voice. He felt the wreckage move again. The sound gave him a surprise. It had all been so still. So eerie...

And now a sickening sense of horror washed over him. A horse's hoof plunged through the moving debris, flailing near to his face. A terrible moan came from the mound of fragmented wood, as again the hoof kicked feebly into the thick, smoke-filled air. Now he could smell that acrid smoke, and the blood of animals...and humans...

He felt sick. Still he was dizzy, yet the numb daze was receding. Now he understood. He began to remember. One by one the realities of the carnage now dispelled the terrible momentary silence that follows horror.

Screams of pain and delayed shock came from scattered human beings. Hysterical whinnying and stamping from frightened horses, whilst their less fortunate counterparts, ravaged by the blast, rolled in shrieking agony amidst broken wood and dead human bodies.

As the reality hit him, Napoleon shook himself. Painfully he sat up, pulling himself unsteadily to a standing position with the aid of the tangled harness still attached to his crushed carriage. He looked around, aghast at the slaughter he now witnessed. Many times had he seen such sights on a battlefield, but somehow the indescribable horror of such carnage in a Paris street was a less bearable assault to his sensibilities. In war one lived with the expectation of death. But the unannounced cowardice of such an attempt at what he now knew to be murder – his murder – was without justification of any sort, and bore no relation to honour.

Sickened with a convulsion of disgust, he turned as a nearby animal, lying in screaming agony, arrested his attention. At that moment a distraught officer rushed up to him.

'Sir...sir...thank god...'

'Your gun, sir!' Napoleon snapped at the distraught soldier, who was staring at the writhing animal.

'A-a-are you alright, sir? We couldn't find...'

'Your gun, man!'

Napoleon could not wrest his eyes from the sight of the struggling horse whose head, bathed in the froth of its saliva mingled with blood, was jerking hopelessly beneath the weight of the unrecognisable carriage. His hand waited while the confused soldier passed him his gun, transfixed by the suffering animal.

The sound of the gunshot seemed to momentarily silence the rising hysteria of the scene. Napoleon stared numbly at the inert body of the dead horse. His eyes carried over the ugly scene to rest on the sprawled body of his carriage driver. Thoughtfully, dully, he stared at the dead man. It would have happened anyway, even if he had taken it a little more slowly.

'*Darling*..!'

The hysterical crying of Josephine interrupted his thoughts. As he looked around for her approaching presence, he could see more and more people running to the scene to tend to the wounded and the dead.

His eye was caught by the pulverised body of a little girl, her bloody hand still clutching the reins of her dead horse. Suddenly the smell and sight of the horror overcame him. He felt anger such as he had never experienced before. He shook with the sheer force of the emotion. Who had done this? Who?

'My darling...!' Josephine threw herself into his arms, her tears spilling uncontrollably, trembling with fear and relief as she gazed up into the blackened face of her dishevelled husband.

'I'm alright, Josephine. I'm alright.' His voice was calm and quiet. As he held her quivering body, he looked around at the scene, his rage somehow controlled by the sensation of disbelief. Moving a little, his arm around Josephine, he put a soothing hand on the neck of a nearby quaking horse. Absent-mindedly he calmed the terrified animal, his shaking wife buried in the embrace of his other arm.

As he stared into the middle distance the scene suddenly seemed to detach itself from his mind. He was aware that now that he had been located, panicked members of his family and household were approaching, crowding around him, concerned and shocked, but relieved to find him alive.

Who? Who? The question hammered in his mind, oblivious to the panicked chattering around him. The Bourbons? Royalist fanatics? Jacobins? No, this wasn't their style. Suddenly he heard a voice from the chattering speculation around him.

'General Bernadotte, perhaps?'

Turning ferociously on the speaker of Bernadotte's name, Napoleon snapped, 'No, it was not General Bernadotte.'

The group were silenced, staring in a shocked hush at the rigid, stone-faced First Consul.

'Of course it would not be Bernadotte,' he repeated, a little more kindly now. 'It would be Royalists, or Jacobins...' His voice trailed. 'Yes, Jacobins...' he repeated, nodding. Surely it couldn't be Royalists? No, not Royalists.

Glancing at the horse, he once more patted the now calm animal. Moving heavily, he began to walk away, assisted by Josephine and a soldier.

Suddenly he stopped, hearing a whispered speculation as to who would have succeeded him had he been killed. Addressing the unseen voice in the crowd, he refuted the suggested name he had heard: Moreau.

'No, it would have been General Bernadotte...' He paused at the stunned response from the crowd. He smiled bitterly, the pain of the last hour's events suddenly ageing his handsome face. '...Like Anthony, he would have presented to the excited people the blood-stained robe of Caesar.'

A ripple of horror seemed to convulse the crowd. Silently they watched as their First Consul was escorted slowly, with his terrified family, into a newly arrived carriage. As the vehicle turned to roll slowly back to the Tuileries, away from the smoky scene of bleeding flesh and death, the terrified bystanders looked at each other in confused silence.

Someone had tried to kill their First Consul...

In the silence of the carriage, Napoleon stared numbly ahead. Josephine, Caroline and Hortense were trying to control their frightened tears. Suddenly his choked voice penetrated the silence. 'This is how vulnerable I am...'

A heavy silence fell once more amongst the occupants of the dark interior. Each once listened numbly to the slow rhythm of the horses' hooves on the cobbles, too dazed to think.

Moving his bruised body painfully, Napoleon stared out of the window at the frightened speculators who had suddenly swarmed on to the Paris streets as news of the assassination attempt on the First Consul spread rapidly through the city.

He had almost been killed! The unbelievable reality of his escape from death was hammering in his mind, unrelenting in its insistence upon his racing thoughts. His head ached painfully. Vulnerable... Yes, he was so vulnerable...

He closed his eyes. Something would have to be done. He could hear now people shouting occasionally at the carriage as it passed them.

Vive Bonaparte!'...

They were relieved that their First Consul was alive. Yes...but something would have to be done to stop him from being so vulnerable. His features tightened into a grim mask. He would ensure that this would never happen again. Never…

He had to make himself invulnerable to such crazed attacks. And he would. For France.

Chapter VII

I had always been amazed by Napoleon's ambivalent attitude to the Bourbons. His dogged refusal, at first, to believe that Royalists had made the attempt on his life was, to say the least, puzzling.

Clearly he held a deep contempt for the Jacobins, considering them to be intellectually inept in voicing what he considered to be naive and impossible ideas. He had a deeply practical side to his nature, and despised the unrealistic demands of lofty idealism that disregarded the human needs of ordinary people. He was only too aware of human nature, and recognised the divisions and weaknesses therein. Perhaps it was thus natural for him to immediately blame the Jacobins.

I, however, believe that there was a deeper reason for his refusal to blame the Royalists. Napoleon had always held a sneaking regard for the monarchical system of government. Perhaps it was his own patrician nature, his father having been a nobleman. Whatever his reasons, and despite his deep commitment to the Republican cause, Napoleon nonetheless seemed to crave some form of recognition from the deposed Bourbons, and simply would not accept that they considered him to be an audacious military adventurer.

He had considered that the British had incited the risings in the Vendée region, the geographical proximity of England indicating the ease with which this could be done. Through relaxing the restrictions for the émigré aristocrats, Napoleon had actively begun to encourage the return of the exiled members of the Nobility. Indeed, he had made it abundantly clear to them that they were welcome, and tried to ease their difficulties in returning as best he could. Thus he continued to believe that the Jacobins had tried to murder him, and it was with deep shock that he examined the irrefutable evidence produced by Fouché that proved that the plot had indeed been Royalist, carried out under the leadership of the redoubtable 'Georges'.

Such indeed was his chagrin that he even grew suspicious of Fouché himself, believing him to have been the guiding force behind the attempt, through his devious dealings with the Jacobins.

Deep down, however, he knew. I too knew that without doubt it was a Royalist endeavour to rid France of 'the Corsican', and I was, myself, secretly alarmed. The incident proved for me an indication that had long created a growing unease within me – namely, that the Bourbons hated Bonaparte, and would never gracefully accept the preferred will of the people of France. They would not rest until they had killed the man they considered to be a usurper.

I had encouraged Napoleon's monarchical tendencies, for I believed it important to restore the Old Nobility. Furthermore, I did not believe in having festering potential for opposition abroad. I had not, however, reckoned upon the Bourbon cause commanding a significant threat. Now, it seemed, Napoleon and I may have been wrong, and something would have to be done to end their activities. My entire adult life had been dedicated to striving for peace and prosperity in France, and a balance of power between the nations of Europe. Now the former of these aspirations was taking a positive form, and Napoleon Bonaparte was the architect of an inspirational programme for a strong and vigorous society. I did not feel I could see it all destroyed by a petulant pretender.

Thus were my thoughts on a warm day in mid-July. I was being driven in my open carriage through the streets of Paris towards the Champs de Mars. The people of the city were thronging, moving in merry groups, towards the dense crowds that already lined the streets, long before the Victory parade for the Battle of Marengo had even begun.

I did not like parades actually, but I had promised Napoleon that I would put in an appearance because of the importance of the occasion for the people of France. Thus I found myself doffing my hat to the acknowledging shouts of Parisian revellers. How I disliked such displays of raw emotion.

The Peace signed with the Austrians following their defeat at Marengo had happily been a most successful diplomatic achievement for France. I was naturally pleased when the negotiations for the Treaty of Lunéville had been concluded in February, as I was responsible for drafting the terms.

The left bank of the Rhine, and territories beyond, became our eastern frontier. We retained possession of Piedmont – and Belgium and Luxembourg were acknowledged to be part of France. The Cisalpine Republic and Liguria remained under our protection, and the King of Naples found himself obliged to maintain a French military presence.

The people of France were ecstatic, as indeed the carnival atmosphere of Paris on this summer's day reflected. French dominion had been expanded farther than ever before, and we had defeated and made peace with all our enemies – save England.

England… I was concentrating all my energies on the English negotiations at present, though much of my attention had also been required by Napoleon's determined efforts to agree a treaty with the Vatican. The 'Concordat', as it was known, had just been signed, and I was bound to admit that Napoleon had been correct in his estimation of its import for the People of France. That it contributed to the spiritual need of equality was an assertion I could no longer deny. Napoleon and I had often discussed the semantic properties of the Revolutionary slogan: 'Liberty – Equality – Fraternity'.

'Liberty,' he had said, 'is a need felt by a small class of people whom nature has endowed with nobler minds than the mass of men. Consequently, it may be repressed with impunity.' Remembering the rabble of the Five Hundred at Brumaire, I had hidden a smile! 'Liberty means a good civil code. The only thing modern nations care for is property. Equality, on the other hand, pleases the masses, yet there can never be equality of fortunes in society.

Thus, when a man is dying of hunger by the side of one who gourmandises, it is impossible for him to agree to the difference unless there be some Authority to say to him: "God wills it so". There must be poor and rich in this world, but afterwards and during eternity, the division will be made otherwise. You see, my dear Talleyrand? That is spiritual equality.'

Certainly the response of the French people had proved that his perception of how they felt was indeed correct. They had thrown open the doors to their churches with a joy that must have warmed the very heart of the Almighty himself. As for me, I was amused to find that I was impressed, even though I had been proven wrong.

But England... Here was not such an easy matter.

Negotiations were underway, indeed the preliminaries would be signed this coming autumn. I smiled as I thought of le beau Montrond, playing his part most excellently in the diplomatic requirements of the English court. Nonetheless, I was uneasy. William Pitt had resigned in March, and whilst Addington was easier to deal with, a peace made with Pitt would have been worth more in the long run. Moreover, in the same month of March the 'mad Tsar', Paul, had been assassinated, and his succeeding son, Alexander, was a zealous anglophile, determined upon reforming Russian relations with England.

A strange sense of foreboding overtook me. However, one must take things as they come, and it was more important to think of the immediate future and its effect on the growing confidence of the French nation. With the accommodation of Addington, a Treaty would soon be signed. We would be at peace with England. For the moment, at least.

We had arrived at the focal point of the day's festivities. I was feeling a little hot in the midday sun, and felt that I would willingly be almost anywhere but out here amongst the extraordinary spectacle of celebrating crowds. It was of course gratifying that theirs was a happy mood, indeed that one had contributed to their celebration. But the crude form of their behaviour I found to be a little rigorous upon my sensibilities.

Slowly we drove into the enclosed area for the dignitaries attending the ceremony. The platform was already almost filled with seated officials. Indeed, as I followed their fixed attention I could see down the length of the Champs de Mars where the first soldiers in the parade were already approaching, passing the cheering crowds vigorously marching to the sound of their military music, their leaders carrying the torn and tattered colours of the defeated armies, as well as the meticulous standards of their own.

I declined the proffered assistance of my coachman to dismount and ascend the platform. I felt I could quite adequately see the events from the comfortable seating in my carriage. Getting about was a painful enough task, without having to waste extra energy in descending steps, only to ascend yet more; then to find oneself seated on a hard and uncomfortable chair, surrounded by boring officials passing polite but inconsequential remarks. I knew it would be some time before the revue area would be filled by the various regiments, and therefore before Napoleon himself appeared to address them. I would pass the time as best I could observing the proceedings from a shaded spot behind the immediate fenced-off crowds.

Indicating a small closed carriage, which, I had noticed, was positioned in an excellent place, I told my coachman to manoeuvre our own conveyance into a similar mode. Leaning back, I looked around at the crowds, satisfied that I had found a suitable viewing spot beneath some large trees, thus shielded at least from the ever-rising heat of the sun.

The rippling cheers of the crowd filled my ears as the coachman most expertly manipulated the cumbersome contraption. Finally we were most perfectly placed, immediately next to the small black carriage. Pleased and relieved, I fortified myself for the tedious wait with the pleasant assistance of the contents of my snuff-box. I was really rather enjoying it all now; at least the crowds were at a respectable distance away from me.

The soldiers filed on, disciplined and smart. What a contrast to the motley mob that had been the French Revolutionary Army! Napoleon had certainly freshened up the military. Indeed, his regard and care for the well-being of his soldiers was yet another admirable trait in the man's character. And his consideration for his men was rewarded by a fanatical loyalty, which seemed to increase each day.

'A man does not have himself killed, my dear Talleyrand, for a few halfpence a day, or a paltry distinction,' he had informed me with characteristic intensity one day as we had watched the changing of his guard from his study window. 'You must speak to the soul in order to electrify the man.'

Electrify the men was certainly what Napoleon Bonaparte was able to do, and the scene before my eyes was a testimony to that fact, and to the Honour of the French Army.

The Veterans of Marengo had begun to file into the arena now – those who had been wounded on the Italian plains. A hush fell upon the crowd. This dignified little band of men commanded a guilty lull in the high spirits of the mesmerised crowd.

The reality of sacrifice was borne bravely by those now eyeless; legless; armless; or maimed by their wounds in other equally horrifying ways. Some were still bandaged, the red stains of congealed blood discolouring the dirty material. Many had arms in slings, others hobbled on crutches, or aided by walking sticks. All held the expression of pride and dignity as they made their slow progress along the dusty Champs de Mars on that hot July afternoon, proudly displaying their wounds.

'Vive la France!'

Like the crowd, I felt a little sick at the vivid reminder of the actualities of war. Peace made cruel demands of men. I looked away, and for the first time my eyes fell upon the figures of my fellow spectators in the carriage next to me. The darkness of the interior cast a heavy shadow upon the man and the woman. Nonetheless, there was something familiar about them. I was sure I knew them… The man – he was in uniform…

* * *

Jean-Baptiste Bernadotte was said to look like the portraits of the Great Condé. Undoubtedly he had a nobleness of appearance, as he had of manners, which pertained favourably to such a comparison.

He was rigid, staring without expression at the moving column of blue and white. His wife Désirée, by contrast, was in a mood of elation, clearly enjoying the spectacle of the victorious army of France. Sitting on the edge of her seat, she craned her neck to catch sight of everything she could, determined to miss nothing of this exciting celebration.

Uncharacteristically, Jean-Baptiste suddenly took his wife's hand, his eyes remaining firmly fixed on the pervading soldiers, his face impassive. The sight of the Marengo Veterans abruptly changed the excited mood of Désirée. Her free hand flying to her mouth, an appalled gasp escaped as she witnessed the horror of war.

'Oh! Jean-Baptiste...' The strangled words escaped in a hoarse whisper, as suddenly she realised that such were the sights daily witnessed by her husband. Looking up at his aquiline profile, she saw him register only the tightening of a muscle in his jaw, his eyes and face still remaining expressionless. He squeezed her hand as she lifted his to her cheek. How was it one could be so ignorant of war, even when part of a soldier's family? The overwhelming realisation that her husband might, at any moment, meet a fate such as these crippled veterans, or death itself...

Tears fell as the chilling thought swept over her. She pressed her damp cheek upon his large hand.

A mighty surge in the crowds dispelled the growing morbidity of her thoughts. Craning to see the focus of the deafening cheers her features broke out into her childlike smile once more, a little rueful at first.

'It must be Napoleone, darling...' Softly she spoke. Stretching her neck, her eyes searching through the heads of the crowds, she appeared to be oblivious of her husband's taut and rigid stillness, his silent stare fixed and unblinking.

Suddenly catching sight of Napoleon riding on a large white horse, flanked by his Guard, Désirée completely forgot her earlier misgivings. 'There he is, Jean-Baptiste! Oh, doesn't he look well...!' She giggled affectionately. '...I do think his new haircut looks a little strange under his hat though!' Still craning her neck, she continued: '...You know, he has named his horse Marengo, darling...he...'

Abruptly she ceased her chattering as, for the first time, she became aware of Jean-Baptiste's stiff impassivity, his eyes now fixed on the figure of the First Consul.

'Jean-Baptiste...?'

Her concerned enquiry, as she looked up earnestly into the expressionless eyes, was interrupted by a deafening cheer from the nearby crowds.

Turning her attention back to the passing parade, her face melted once more at the sight of Napoleon. How had life changed since long ago in Marseilles...

But now she could feel a dark presence coming from Jean-Baptiste. Why was he so silent and stern? This was a great moment for France. As she watched Napoleon ascend the platform, and heard the crowds hush to hear his words, her brain hammered with an odd confusion. What was wrong with Jean-Baptiste? Why couldn't he be happy like everybody else? The only time he seemed to be happy was when he was with Madame de Stael, Benjamin Constant, and those other 'intellectual' friends of his. She didn't really know them, anyway, after all they didn't include *her* in their 'soirées'. She felt a bitter twinge of resentment. Perhaps they thought her too stupid to understand their conversations! It didn't matter anyway. If Jean-Baptiste wanted to keep his friends separate from her that was all right – after all, she was part of the Bonaparte circle, and was happy to be there. They were much more fun than those dreadful 'know-it-alls' who were just jealous of Napoleone.

And what about that Madame de Recamier...? She was actually *critical* of Napoleone. She cast a sudden glance up at her husband's face. No, it couldn't be... Yet... Could there be something between Jean-Baptiste and...?

* * *

'Frenchmen! We have peace in northern Italy…'

Napoleon had begun his speech. The crowd were hypnotised by him as he dramatically delivered the glorious message of victory to their ears, long starved of any news of success.

'The day of Marengo will remain famous throughout History…'

She could hear only snatches of the powerful speech, the large figure beside her having become almost waxen, almost appearing to have ceased breathing.

'…The Emperor and I have agreed terms. Thousands of Frenchmen and Austrians are no more due to the hostilities induced by the cunning English…'

His voice rose in vehemence upon the last two words, and shouts of 'Peacemaker', 'Vive Bonaparte!' rang from the crowd whose collective tension was mounting with the thrilling words of their First Consul.

Désirée tried to concentrate, but the brooding presence of her large husband seemed to bear down on her, prohibiting her absorption.

'…the prospect of such horrors is of great distress to me – a lasting and fruitful Peace is the objective of your First Consul…'

Napoleon stretched to his full height, his head proud. The cheers from the crowd grew ecstatic, delirious with joy at the great inspiration of Peace that was their leader.

'Peacemaker! Peacemaker!' Wildly, the chanting grew: 'VIVE BONAPARTE! VIVE LA FRANCE!'

Somewhere some singing burst out, and like wildfire the mood ripped through the crowd.

'Allons enfants de la patrie…'

'La Marseillaise' rang out, louder and louder, as every Frenchman in the dense crowds fixed their adoring gaze on the small figure of Napoleon Bonaparte.

Désirée felt her hand being gripped. He was hurting her, crushing it with his massive strength. Startled, she swung her attention from the happy scene outside to his slightly flushed face still staring intently at the figure on the platform.

His low voice penetrated the silence for the first time, whilst his eyes remained intent upon the First Consul. 'I have a strange presentiment…'

His low statement was almost inaudible to Désirée. She was certain he wasn't addressing her, for he seemed abstracted, as though involuntarily voicing a hitherto unspoken thought.

'Our beloved France has passed its finest hour…' His voice trailed, dreamlike.

Désirée swallowed, uncertain of what she should do. Patting his hand soothingly, she cast a quick look back at the platform, aware that her husband's intent gaze remained fixed. Peripherally she noticed the carriage next to them. A man was looking at her.

'Why, it's Monsieur de Talleyrand!' she exclaimed, without thinking. She smiled at him, inclining her head as he doffed his hat to her politely. Bernadotte appeared not to hear her, absorbed in his own sombre thoughts.

Noticing that Talleyrand's coachman was making preparations to leave, Désirée turned abruptly to her husband, determined to end this discomfort that had resulted from a moment she had looked forward to. She wanted to get out of this claustrophobic carriage, she wanted to see her sister, her family, the Bonapartes, she wanted to get away from this strange person who was her husband, but a husband she suddenly felt she did not know, in spite of how much she loved him.

'Monsieur de Talleyrand is leaving,' she suddenly blurted. 'He is probably going to the reception too. Perhaps we also should depart before the crowds disperse…?' Looking uneasily up at her husband's strong face she finished quickly, '…besides, we're supposed to arrive before the First Consul.'

Without any sign of emotion Bernadotte lifted his baton, banging a signal to the coachman on the roof. Once more he squeezed her hand as they pulled away.

Désirée gazed unseeingly out of the window, her eyes swimming with unshed tears. Suddenly she reached up and kissed him on the cheek. How strange, his cheek seemed to be clammy and dampened, as though by perspiration. Her head ached. There was a part of Jean-Baptiste she did not understand. She wondered if she ever would. Did he even understand himself? she wondered...

* * *

But if Bernadotte had his own lament about the vanishing dreams of the Republic, the people of France did not share it. The victory of Marengo in June 1800 had further strengthened the reputation Napoleon held, and firmly consolidated his power. I did not know it then but he was now approaching the zenith of his creative and mental activity. I was, however, aware that an important choice was soon to be faced, both for the much-loved First Consul, and for the people themselves.

Yet, although I knew what it was that he ought to do in the interests of France, as I looked at the small figure on the platform, motionless as he drank in the adulation of the crowd, I was suddenly uncertain that he would seize the correct course.

He had several options. I, personally, favoured a federal system – which leaves each ruler, after his own defeat, still master in his own territory, but on conditions favourable to the victor. But did Bonaparte intend to unite and to incorporate? Or would he enter upon a course to which there was no end...?

We shall soon see which choice Napoleon Bonaparte was to take....

Chapter VIII

Paris was an exciting city in the late spring of 1802. A contrast indeed to the disgusting squalor of three years previous. The improvements brought about by the Consular administration had transformed not only the appearance of the city, but also the behaviour of the ordinary citizens. They carried about them an air of pride and self-confidence these days. Somehow the twinkling warmth of the newly installed Paris street lighting system seemed to reflect the new mood of optimism that Napoleon Bonaparte had brought to France.

We were at peace with England. At last. On the twenty-seventh of March a treaty had been signed with the English at Amiens. France now found herself, once more, in possession of most of her colonial territories, and in general the treaty was more favourable to France than it was to England. This fact disconcerted me. I had hoped for a stronger accord..

However, France was celebrating once again, and I did not wish to cloud the revelries with pessimistic speculations upon future possibilities. Nonetheless, I was sensible to the peculiar characteristics of the British people, whom I much admired, and I was aware that their sense of pride would find the terms of the Treaty too conciliatory to a long-time enemy.

But now, as my coach turned in towards the blazing gaiety of the Tuileries entrance on this spring night, the sight of hiving activity as coaches deposited beautiful ladies in full evening dress and their distinguished looking escorts at the ballroom doors, through which the sound of music faintly filtered, quickly dispelled my apprehensive thoughts.

I always adore a celebration ball. The air seems to seethe with subtle intrigue mingled with the overtly banal vanity of the participants in this fascinating world of politics. It is all very amusing!

As my coach drew to a halt the door was thrown open. Exiting coaches is always an awkward business for me, but I found myself ably assisted by numerous liveried palace servants.

It crossed my mind, as I descended the steps of the coach, how increasingly monarchical the Consular Court had become. The Council of State had recently ratified a motion to extend the tenure of First Consul for a further five years to Napoleon, who had now ceased to use his father's name of Bonaparte, and was to be known only as 'Napoleon', save by his lovely wife Josephine, who always addressed him as Bonaparte. However, the gratitude of the French nation had expressed itself in a move to make Napoleon First Consul for Life, and that very day a current report for the office of the Minister for the Interior had indicated that the response to the plebiscite being carried out was proving overwhelmingly in favour of such an accolade.

Fleetingly I wondered how that former Minister of the Interior, Lucien, would have reacted to such a departure from the dreams of Brumaire. But this most intelligent of Napoleon's brothers would not be here in the Tuileries to inform me, for he had quarrelled violently with his brother and had resigned his position in the government.

I straightened up, aware of the stolen glances of admiration from my fellow attendants to the ball. Drawing myself up to my full height, I moved my stick to aid me in my procedure towards the entrance. Slowly I moved behind the ushering servants towards the interior, politely acknowledging the kind attentions, and inwardly delighting in my tailor's artistry. The affectation of vanity is a useful mask when there is business to be done. And in such gatherings, especially this night, I had much business to attend to.

* * *

'Have you heard that the Tsar has been murdered…?'

I smiled to myself as the soaring pitch of society's faceless dictator floated across the loud hum of this gathering of the Consular Court. Rumour and gossip: the meat and drink of politics. Often rich pickings for the skilled diplomat!

'…But my dear, I do believe from a most *reliable* source that the instigator of the assassination was none other than his son, Alexander…'

'…They never got on, you know, and now he's the new Tsar!…I believe he's a most handsome and dashing young man. But they say he likes the English…'

The conversation passed out of earshot as I moved through the parting crowd in my progress across the vast room to a dais at the far end.

I have never ceased to marvel, despite my long years of political involvement, at the sheer frivolity with which the fashionable leaders of society casually discuss the most weighty of international political developments. Moreover, that so much political intrigue amongst statesmen and diplomats should take place in the salons of these social butterflies had always induced a sense of bemused wonder in me. The important role played by women in politics is one that I had fortunately never made the mistake of underestimating, and indeed, I found it both amusing and profitable to use the pleasant facilities of such an extraordinary quirk of human behaviour to my best advantage.

Napoleon despised the power of the Ladies' Salons, and I had often tried to encourage him to see the potential value of such a system – for 'system' it is. But such was the temperament of the young First Consul that to my cool observation that 'women *are* politics', he retorted a rude rejection, and an assertion that he would most certainly never be dictated to by what he considered to be the inferior intellect of women. For even though Napoleon was fond of the fair sex, he disdained that they might have any claim to offer society more than was their wont, namely to produce children and ensure the smooth and happy running of the home for their male superiors. That such was his firm belief – though without intent to offend, for as I have said, he was fond of women – incurred much resentment, and indeed wrath, from intellectual women such as Madame de Stael. This intelligent and gifted daughter of the banker Necker, whose activities Napoleon also despised, had originally been one of Napoleon Bonaparte's strongest supporters. However, several unfortunate encounters, during which Napoleon's views on women had been articulated in his characteristically undiplomatic language, had expressed its response in the truly feminine trait of 'a woman scorned', resulting in her becoming the focal point of an anti-Bonapartist group. It did not take much imagination to speculate on the views that abounded in her Salon!

'…but they say that the English are not satisfied with the terms…imagine!'

Another floating conversation interrupted my thoughts. I felt my eyebrows involuntarily crease for a moment. So, such rumours were already circulating amongst the gossip-mongers of society. It struck a note of concern, for such chatter was an important guide to the sentiments expressed between the members of the English and French Court who constantly moved back and forth across the Channel. That such a remark might be a reflection of a growing unease confirming my fears was, I knew, more than a mere possibility.

'Monsieur de Talleyrand?'

The charming greeting of a most exquisite young creature, whose name I could not quite remember, again interrupted my thoughts.

'Good evening, Madame…' I kissed her hand, vainly searching my memory for her name.

Fortunately I was saved as she continued, batting both her eyelashes and her fan, seemingly in rhythm, 'How elegant you look, Monsieur de Talleyrand. As always eclipsing every other man in the room. Will you not divulge to me the name of your extraordinary tailor, sir? All Paris speculates, you know…'

Bowing once more I passed some polite comment, and turned

to the approaching figure of Joseph. The feigned coyness of some members of the opposite sex often becomes a trifle tedious. I congratulated myself, as indeed I did daily, that whilst I had never had to moderate my indulgence in the delights of women, I nonetheless had managed to have the good fortune not to have to marry one of them. Whilst I adored the company of women, and was eternally fascinated by them, I could not imagine a worse fate than seeing the same one daily. The church had done little for me, but at least it had saved me that dreaded fate!

'Good evening, sir. Welcome! Welcome!'

Joseph's beaming face was before me, unctuously inclining itself as he greeted me with a predictable degree of over-enthusiasm. That the young genius could have such relative simpletons – albeit charming simpletons – as part of his family was a continuous source of astonishment to me. Lucien alone posited any form of challenge, though even he did not approach the supreme talent concentrated in the small form of Napoleon.

Joseph, in his stupidity, had assumed a somewhat pompous posture since his brother had become First Consul. One year his brother's senior in age, Joseph seemed to have inflated ideas of his own station, probably due to the fact that his brother apparently entrusted to him so much responsibility. The truth of the matter was that Joseph, though competent, was merely Napoleon's puppet, and was little informed of any matters of real import. However, such reality escaped him, and he remained mistakenly and blissfully in the belief that he was the second most important person in the French Government; and indeed that when his brother assumed the title of First Consul for Life he, Joseph, would be his heir.

'A great moment for France...'

Joseph was guiding me towards the family gathering of Bonapartes on the dais. His rather pretentious graciousness of tone was complemented by his almost comic responses to the sycophantic acknowledgements from various members of the small groups we passed. I felt a sort of irritated pity for Joseph, knowing that he could not see through the superficial facades of these transparently 'charming' individuals. How different he was from his brother...

'It is indeed a great moment for France, Monsieur Bonaparte.' I too was acknowledging the respectful greetings of those we passed. Without illusions. 'However...' I continued '...we must ensure that we temper our emotions and contain our delight in recognition of realities...' I broke off briefly to kiss the hand of a particularly handsome lady friend of mine. 'England is a great Power, and a proud nation. The due respect for her, and the preservation of her constitution, is of paramount importance to the stability of Europe.' I paused again, bowing to an old acquaintance, before continuing: '...Victory is one thing – humiliation quite another.'

We had reached the three shallow steps that rose to the slightly raised dais. I turned to look into Joseph's startled eyes. 'We must take care not to deprive her of her dignity, Monsieur Bonaparte. The result of such an act of folly would have dire consequences for France.'

Joseph appeared to be lost for words. Flushing slightly, he cleared his throat, clearly nonplussed by my statement. I smiled at him, a little saddened that he should find my remarks so extraordinary. Whilst France was naturally my central concern, it was nonetheless my added determination that my life would be dedicated to the cause of creating a coherent and harmonious balance in Europe amongst her great, and very different, nations.

'I-I don't think...'

'Monsieur de Talleyrand, good evening.'

Joseph's stuttering reply was interrupted, to his great relief, by the shy greeting of his wife, Julie. I turned immediately, taking her hand. She was a delicate little person, Julie, and one felt a certain concern for her nervous disposition being placed at the mercy of the competitive and ambitious Bonapartes.

'Why, how charming you look, Madame Bonaparte.'

She blushed demurely at my sincerely felt compliment. Dropping her eyes shyly, she curtsied to cover her embarrassment.

'Tell me, does your sister do this assembly the honour of her presence?'

Looking at me, her eyes wide and innocent, she smiled. 'Oh yes, sir. She's just over here...' She indicated a small group of people crowded around a seated figure, near to a column. 'And Madame Letitia is here...'

'Ah! I must pay my respects to her.'

I offered the diffident Julie my arm that we might approach her mother-in-law together. Joseph, meanwhile, had become engaged in condescending conversation with some enthusiastic admirer of his brother.

I glanced quickly across the vast hall as we walked towards Napoleon's mother. It was quite a magnificent sight. The oval room was filled with people, simply and tastefully attired in the formal dress fashionable at this time. Small groups of people were vivaciously conversing, some in the centre, some retiringly grouped in the columned recesses in the periphery of the beautiful ballroom, obscured by plants and the movement of busy servants. The breathtaking beauty of hundreds of candelabra crowned the whole, their myriad candles flickering a magical light upon the excited gathering.

I confess to feeling, at that moment, a sensation of satisfaction that this occasion was to celebrate a life-long ambition of mine, now finally achieved. Peace with England!

* * *

Madame Letitia Bonaparte was little older than myself, but though the struggles of her difficult life had served to increase the indomitable strength and courage that this dignified Corsican woman was renowned for, time had worn her once considerable beauty, and now the mother of the thirty-three year old First Consul looked more than her fifty-two years. The true meaning of the word 'matriarch' was embodied in this sternly practical woman. Widowed at thirty-five, she had brought up her eight children alone, being forced to move from her beloved native Corsica in 1793, due to the unpopular political activities of her sons. She had never felt at home in France, and the spectacular achievements of her children, and most particularly of her second son, appeared to have had little effect upon her. Indeed, I sometimes wondered when I looked at her faded dark beauty, if she really understood the full implications of the extraordinary genius of her son.

That she ruled her family with a rod of iron was without doubt. Her children, their continued well-being, and their relationships with each other, was her sole preoccupation. A deeply religious woman, she had tried to instil into each of her strongly individualistic children the moral values of the Catholic tradition. The fact that she had failed with most of them was odd since her influence over them was so great. Yet I felt that in Napoleon, the most unlikely of them all, these values had taken a deep rooting. Indeed, I felt sure that his determination to restore the position of the church in France had been heavily influenced by his mother.

Her current preoccupation was the rift between her two favourite sons, Napoleon and Lucien. The latter was still employed by the state as Ambassador to Spain, but the rancour between the brothers was not dulled by distance, and neither one was making any effort to heal their broken relationship. A rumour, currently circulating, that Lucien and his close friend Bernadotte were intriguing against Napoleon had shocked her, even though it was found to be groundless. Worse was the fact that she was fond of Jean-Baptiste Bernadotte, and was often in his company due to the regular family gatherings. She had a particular affection for Bernadotte's wife Désirée, who had so nearly been her own daughter-in-law, and whom indeed she treated as some sort of daughter.

Even now as Julie and I approached the formidable figure of the First Consul's mother, it was to Désirée that she was giving her attention. She was surrounded attentively by the rest of her unpredictable children as they awaited the entrance of the First Consul – the most difficult of them all.

On his arm would be the woman he had married, and with whom he was happy. But her mother-in-law disliked Josephine, with an intensity that was difficult to understand in view of the Creole's kind nature. But Madame Letitia would never accept that her son had married a woman who had apparently, in the past, displayed loose morals, and moreover was his senior and unable to give him children. His mother's attitude to Josephine saddened Napoleon, who was always trying to bring them together, without success. Personally I held the view that Madame Letitia, accustomed to the complete devotion of all her children, had been horrified by the passion that Napoleon had displayed for his unusual wife when first they had been married. That another woman could command so entirely the singular affections of her son came as an unpleasant shock.

'Good evening, Madame Letitia, this is indeed a pleasure.'

I bowed respectfully over the hand irreparably roughened and reddened by years of hard physical labour. The dark intelligent gaze, so like her famous son's, flicked over me, unsmiling. The niceties of court etiquette were of no interest to this woman, who did not attempt to disguise the fact that she would willingly absent herself from such pretentious gatherings. Nodding a little impatiently, she quickly withdrew her hand. With grudging politeness she gesticulated towards the humming ballroom, and in the thickly accented language she so disliked, commented dryly, 'Quite an assembly, is it not, Monsieur Talleyrand?'

'Indeed,' I replied, following her indication and passing a glance over the happy scene, flickering with the movement of dancing lights and dancing fans. 'An excellent example of the power of women over men!'

At last I had managed to find a little humoured response from those usually expressionless eyes.

'Is the Minister for Foreign Affairs alone tonight?' a voice suddenly boomed. 'Where is the ever-present snake, Fouché? Examining somebody's personal belongings in their absence, no doubt.'

There was something about Joachim Murat that I disliked. My feeling was, I think, one shared by his mother-in-law, Madame Letitia. Now, as I heard his loud voice, already amplified by alcohol, I stiffened, maintaining however a polite and casual address as I bowed an indifferent greeting. Perhaps it was his ostentation I disliked, for he showed a distinct lack of taste. All the same, I knew him to be a brave soldier, and one who inspired much devotion from his men. His remarks, however, had annoyed me, though I knew them to be relatively harmless from this intellectually rather stupid man.

Choosing my words carefully, I paused as I studied the good-looking if rather ruddy face before me. Slowly I replied, looking fixedly into his eyes: 'Strong Government, Murat, requires different talents...' I leaned towards him, determined to drive home my point. 'Though it is, no doubt, probably of little interest to a man of action such as yourself, it is important to some that there are differences in varying approaches to politics. To me, the settlement of dynastic, constitutional or diplomatic problems is often served well in environments such as this – or in the atmosphere of a dinner party. To Fouché...?' I paused, wondering why I should in any way uphold Fouché's methods. '...Fouché has a preference for alleys and street corners...' I sniffed involuntarily at the luxurious folds of my lace handkerchief as I thought of it. '...But the games of Politics require different characteristics from those so admirably displayed by the army, Murat. Without such ill-matched bedfellows there would be few occasions for celebrations such as we have the honour of enjoying tonight. The road to Peace is comprised of a mixed composition of varying talents. The subtlety of that balance is of paramount importance, Murat.'

He blushed slightly under my direct gaze. I was aware that the coolness of my tone had been somewhat severe, and I had emphasized the word 'subtlety'. But the blustering ignorance of soldiers often irritated me. How fortunate that the First Consul did not possess such regrettable characteristics. But then, he would never have become First Consul had he done so.

Another soldier who happily did not demonstrate this was Bernadotte, whose wife Désirée was now rising from her attentive position beside Madame Letitia. She had been a smiling spectator to my greeting to the Bonaparte matriarch, as well as the uncalled for interruption from her sister's brother-in-law. However, now, sensing an awkward impasse in the conversation, she had decided to intervene.

'Monsieur Talleyrand.' Warmly, charmingly, she held her hand out to me, smiling her infectious smile as I placed her hand to my lips. 'How happy I am to see you, sir. You must come and speak to Jean-Baptiste. You haven't seen him since he returned from La Vendée.'

Utterly captivated by her fresh sweetness, I was delighted when she slipped her arm through mine to guide me the short distance to where Bernadotte was talking to Murat's ambitious wife, Napoleon's sister Caroline. After the customary exchange of greetings, Désirée returned to the side of Madame Letitia, taking with her the matriarch's youngest daughter. Bernadotte and I were alone. I was pleased, for I had a little matter to clear up with him.

Bernadotte was a man of few words. This I found to be an admirable characteristic, being myself of a somewhat reserved nature. His reticence, however, was often misunderstood. But I had always been drawn to this interesting man who was something of an enigma.

I invited him to share some of my snuff, and we observed the mounting excitement as the expected arrival of the First Consul drew closer. The comfortable silence between us seemed to heighten the fevered chattering of the expectant crowd.

Relishing the effects of the excellent tobacco, I began casually, still glancing about the hall. 'Fouché, it appears, has been busying himself with yet another of his plots.' I paused, turning to look into the handsome face. 'This time he seems to have found one in the soldiery – in the army of the west.'

Bernadotte's face remained expressionless, his polite impassiveness betraying no emotion whatsoever. That he himself had just been compelled to relinquish the command of that Army, due to the peace with England, was a fact of which he knew I was mindful. With equally casual tones he replied, a trifle sardonically: 'So I have heard. I believe that my friend Moreau and I are both implicated.' Seeing the humour in my eyes he smiled, and we both laughed briefly.

'This definitely appears to be Fouché's responsibility, I suppose.'

I inclined my head to a passing lady. Twitching what appeared to be an approaching acknowledgement to the same female of our mutual acquaintance, Bernadotte returned: 'Oh I don't know, Talleyrand. I wouldn't have thought that the Minister of Police was in a position to interfere with military matters.'

Knowing that our discourse could continue for some time in this amusing but slow form, I turned to face him, directing my gaze straight into his eyes. There was an urgent reason for my conversation with this man.

'A good time of the year, don't you think, my dear Bernadotte, to take the waters at Plombières?'

He was aware that I was delivering him an important message, and returned my look with serious intensity. Our meaningful, silent exchange was interrupted as the incidental music that had been playing unobtrusively in the background broke off, and the orchestra started to play the stirring opening bars of 'La Marseillaise'.

Through the enormous doors at the opposite end of the ballroom emerged the small figures of Napoleon and Josephine. The crowd, having divided to fall back for the passage of the First Consul, were now silent, transfixed by the couple: he in a plain, unadorned formal General's uniform; she dressed with exquisite taste as always in white, her brow adorned with a diamond diadem.

As the anthem of the Revolution ended, Napoleon and his wife moved to cross the floor. Joseph, with characteristic fuss, hurried to meet them, accompanying them back to the dais. Josephine was her usual gracious self, charmingly smiling and passing occasional remarks as she moved gracefully through the crowd. Napoleon, his presence emanating a powerful silencing effect on people, nodded briskly here and there, intent upon crossing the short space as quickly as possible. Once or twice he stopped to talk to someone, and once his boyish laugh rang out, arousing confused ripples of polite, responsive laughter.

But Napoleon had little liking for such rituals. Joseph, meanwhile, was rather pompously imitating his brother's nods and bows, and I smiled, amused by the comical aspect of his behaviour.

Quickly they passed through the crowd, and ascending the slightly raised platform Napoleon immediately greeted his mother with his usual demonstrative affection.

The light music resumed and the crowd broke out in muted, controlled chatter. One need hardly guess as to the undoubted subject of their conversations!

Bernadotte and I had been joined briefly by one of his fellow unemployed Generals, but, seeing that we were engaged in serious conversation, the man had moved on. However, we had barely had time to resume that exchange when we were interrupted.

'France does you honour tonight, Talleyrand.'

The well-known voice came from behind us, compelling us to turn, his presence nullifying our superior height.

'Peace with the English is important for France, and the Treaty of Amiens is due to your efforts.' His deep voice was kind, and I knew his sentiments to be sincere. Napoleon, at this time, was never afraid to give credit where it was due.

Inclining my head to him, I expressed my gratitude. 'I am honoured to be able to contribute to the prosperity of our Great France, sir. My efforts at diplomacy are, as you know, like my life, dedicated at all times to the pursuit of Peace.'

Napoleon laughed boisterously, clapping me suddenly on the back. With boyish humour he twinkled: 'Don't tell me, my dear friend, that the pursuit of Peace has a greater hold on your loyalties than...' He jerked his head towards some nearby ladies '...the pursuit of the fair sex?' He laughed uproariously. Napoleon always found his own jokes the most amusing.

Josephine had joined us, the cold rebuttal in Madame Letitia's greeting driving her from the Bonaparte gathering. Glancing at the people still standing in their groups, Napoleon looked affectionately at his wife.

'They are waiting for us to begin the dancing...' he said. Then, turning to me, he went on, 'Talleyrand, perhaps you will spare me the ordeal of my duty?' Smiling at Josephine, he continued: 'I am not as adept at such social niceties as this French aristocrat.'

As he laughed again, I felt a little perturbed. He seemed to be making more than frequent sour comments about the French aristocracy these days, too often alluding to the Ancien Régime in sarcastic quips. Knowing him as I did, I felt it probably intimated some as yet uncrystallised thought. However, I knew him to be honouring me and as I gave my arm to guide Josephine to the floor, I put it to the back of my mind. I knew he had something to say to Bernadotte.

* * *

'Have you convinced the peasants of La Vendée of our great Republican cause yet?'

Napoleon's eyes were following the graceful movements of his wife's dancing figure. The tall Gascon beside him stiffened, momentarily disconcerted, though his mask-like lack of expression betrayed no emotion. Now he was compelled to return the First Consul's gaze. The kind enquiry in the Corsican's grey eyes dispelled the uneasiness he was feeling.

'There are signs of improvement, but the close proximity of England seems to invite the rather too frequent visits of royalist agents.'

They were silent, both observing the growing number of dancers. Napoleon, casting a sidelong glance at his tall companion, continued in an amused tone, his face smiling genially. 'It seems, does it not, that La Vendée is a regular hotbed for all kinds of plots, my dear Bernadotte?'

Bernadotte was impassive. Quietly he returned, 'I know little of any other than Royalist plots, sir.' He paused. Then, turning to Napoleon, his voice became brittle. 'My command in La Vendée is long finished, as you well know, sir. I await a new command.'

Napoleon continued to watch the dancers. He appeared to be unmoved. Bernadotte, who was testing his control, was beginning to fidget. A tension was building up between them; neither man seemed to be saying that which he felt.

'Your wife looks charming this evening, Bernadotte.'

Napoleon's bright remark seemed to trigger an explosion in

the big General. Exerting as much control as he was able, his face reddened with frustration at the mild geniality of his companion. Rounding on the First Consul, he burst out: 'Sir, I await two things: the release of my friend Moreau who has been arrested on an unjust charge; and…and…a new command.'

'It occurs to me that your wife is looking a little pale,' Napoleon continued calmly, apparently oblivious to Bernadotte's angry outburst. 'Perhaps a short stay in Plombières might return the roses to her cheeks?' Now he turned, looking meaningfully through his smile into the dark face of the Gascon. Bernadotte, suddenly understanding, lowered his head, his anger, indeed his very energy, entirely spent. He felt Napoleon's hand on his shoulder. Quietly, the First Consul continued: 'Following your visit to Plombières, I hope that France may benefit from your talents when you assume the administration of Hanover.'

Bernadotte jerked his head up. Startled, he looked into the grey eyes, warm and kind. He felt his face grow hot as he blushed in shame and confusion. Why did he always misjudge this man?

Now the grey eyes grew stern, even as the low voice became meaningful. *'Plombières…'*

As the meaning of the message transmitted itself, the long silence between the two men was broken by the return of the dancers.

Chapter IX

'Monsieur Fouché has also arrived, sir.' Constant's voice was gentle, aware that he was intruding into the deep preoccupations of his adored master.

Napoleon unconsciously granted an acknowledgement, his pensive gaze fixed on the winding paths and light green hedges that gave the garden of Malmaison its simple symmetry. He could hear the birds chirping with abandoned gaiety at the freshness of the early spring morning, the pale blue skies brushed with the merest wisp of white, promising a day of sunshine and warmth. How beautiful it was here! He always felt a deep sense of peace in this place.

He smiled as his gaze fell upon the neat rows of budding rose bushes. His Josephine's passion. How she adored her roses! It was a perfect reflection, somehow, of her utter femininity. A slight frown now clouded his brow as he recalled the conversation he had just had with her before he had left her room to take his toilette here in his dressing room. She seemed to require an excessive degree of reassurance these days. Continually she referred to the circumstances of their marriage, and his assumption of the Command of Italy at that time due to the influence of her former lover Barras. She appeared to harbour some gnawing doubt that perhaps he had married her to further his career. How ludicrous! He, who had displayed such ardent passions towards his bride; such emotions, which she had laughed at then. Indeed, she had even humiliated him by turning her attentions to a worthless hussar in his absence. But since his return they had been happy, and though his passion had moderated – after all, passion must always be governed by reason – still they were content in their marriage. Perhaps her worry was because they didn't seem to be able to have any children? Once more his brow creased. Yes, that was a problem, especially now that he was First Consul for Life. He needed an heir. It was something he had to think about.

Automatically his thoughts turned to his family. A sinking feeling accompanied the flood of complex emotions that the thought induced. Involuntarily he sighed, passing his hand unconsciously across his forehead as he looked at the innocent flicking movements of a bird in a nearby tree. His family! Oh why did they trouble him so? Didn't they understand that by their association with him they were inevitably a *political* family? He was the leader of the greatest nation in the world; they couldn't behave like undisciplined children. They must do their duty. Duty was everything. How could they forget that? Goodness knew he reminded them often enough. Couldn't they see that he was doing his best to ensure their positions and security? But in return they must adhere to his wishes as far as their personal behaviour was concerned.

Lucien! He was the worst of them. Napoleon could feel his heart beating a little faster. The very thought of Lucien always did this to him these days. Alright, he had forgiven him that dreadful error in marrying an innkeeper's daughter. After all, it had been a long time ago, and the unfortunate girl had since died. But it was inexcusable that he should openly defy the wishes of his brother in the matter of his second marriage.

Napoleon's head suddenly ached as he remembered how shocked he had been when he had heard that Lucien had married that dreadful widow Jouberthon. What a disaster, especially when he had laid plans to make a brilliant political marriage for him. Napoleon's hand again involuntarily went to his forehead. He had decided he really couldn't see Lucien again, and had sent him to Rome where he could live with that vulgar woman away from his sight. Inside he felt a bitter sting of anger. How *could* Lucien have been so irresponsible?

Suddenly tired, his thoughts ran quickly over the rest of his brothers and sisters. He loved them: they were his family. And he would always look after them. But sometimes he wondered if he really liked them very much. Except Pauline. He smiled at the pleasant thought of his most beautiful, if slightly flippant, sister. She at least amused him!

He knew that Joseph hoped to be his heir. Joseph... He did his best. Yes, he was competent. But he could never head the administration of France; head the greatest nation in the world. No, he would have to adopt an heir. A soldier.

Murat knew that. He could see that ambition rising in his flamboyant brother-in-law. But Murat's vanity somehow impeded his intellect, and though he was a good soldier, he could never understand the complexities of government.

Napoleon's stare was unseeing, as his thoughts seemed to mist, swirling around the central name that he knew, in his heart, would be the best heir he could provide for France, if he had no blood relative.

He smiled wryly to himself. Life had its ironies. Yet personal doubts and wounds must be disregarded when the Future of the nation was in the balance. He had heard that some called him 'the last of the Romans'. He smiled again, slightly bitterly. All the same, it was true. There was only one man who could continue the work he had started, were something to happen to him.

Bernadotte.

Abruptly, Napoleon turned from the window. Calling to Constant to bring him his jacket, he brushed his hair briskly. Well, nothing was going to happen to him. He was going to be here for a very long time. He had much to do. He had begun the re-building of France. And he had a few ideas for Europe, though they weren't yet ripe... But there was enough similarity among the nations of Europe. European society needed regeneration, but there must be a superior power to dominate all the other powers, with enough authority to force them to live in harmony with one another. And France was the best placed for that purpose.

Yes, he had lots of dreams. No need for an heir at the moment.

He smiled wryly to himself. Bernadotte! Putting his arms into the jacket Constant now held for him, Napoleon shook his head a little. He had better get down to his study and clear up this little problem about 'the last Roman'! He felt an amused exasperation. Really, Bernadotte would have to choose his friends a little better. He really must stop associating with these petty intriguers. Moreau! Stupid, hen-pecked individual. Bernadotte was above such people. All the same, he would land himself in serious trouble one of these days if he continued to implicate himself in dubious activities by association with other people of doubtful repute. It was fortunate that his integrity and sense of honour transcended the petty temptations of vanity. But then, that was what he admired about Bernadotte, and why he knew he could trust him whatever the personal discrepancies that sometimes existed between them. Besides, the man was married to Désirée.

As he turned to leave, Napoleon was aware of a slight movement from the bedroom door. He looked up from his thoughts to see the still white presence of Josephine, silently looking at him.

'Why darling, you are up already?' Napoleon's gentle voice gave no hint of their earlier difficult conversation. Striding the short distance between them, he took the small, lace-covered form in his arms. Pressing his lips into her dark curls he softly told her: 'I must go down. They are waiting for me.'

He could feel her body almost indiscernibly quivering as he held her. He gathered her closer, kissing her tenderly. He loved her so deeply; surely she knew that – even though he knew he was not always very demonstrative nowadays. But he was so busy, and…

'I-I'm sorry.' Her voice was thick and husky, choked with the emotion of both the worries she could not rid herself of, and the regret of voicing them to him whom she now so passionately loved, and whom she knew must not be worried by her silly insecurities.

His grip on her tightened, almost hurting her. Kissing her on the forehead, he looked into her eyes, lovingly and kindly. 'Don't be silly,' he whispered tenderly.

Why did he always feel awkward with women? Even his beloved Josephine. He really didn't understand them at all. They became so emotional about the most trivial things! Perhaps, though, that was their charm. At any rate they should be indulged.

Gently holding her away from him, he guided her towards a chair. 'Talleyrand will lunch with us today, darling. You must prepare yourself. But I must see Fouché first – he is waiting.' He paused as she sank gracefully on to the chair, looking up at him, her eyes glinting with unshed tears. Suddenly, breaking into a boyish grin, he tweaked her ear playfully. 'It's a beautiful day!'

His high-spirited remark was complemented with a wide movement of his arm. Briskly he straightened himself, and his jacket. Placing a quick kiss once more on her head he turned, and without further ado walked quickly from the room.

Josephine, motionless in the luxurious folds of her negligée, stared after him. As his footsteps disappeared she turned her head slowly, looking out into the tranquil beauty of her beloved garden. She felt a lump grow in her throat, and knew that the tears were now rolling slowly down her cheeks. Yes, she knew he loved her. But why did she have this terrible presentiment? Why was she so sure that ultimately he would leave her?

* * *

'I apologise for my delay, gentlemen.'

Napoleon's presence erupted suddenly into the striped 'tented' surroundings of his study.

I started, my stick irritatingly refusing to meet the floor without sliding uncontrollably as I tried to struggle hastily to my feet. The hand of the First Consul happily restrained the useless endeavour as I felt its pressure on my shoulder from behind. The good-natured voice commanded kindly, 'Don't bother, old friend. Rest that foot of yours.'

Walking quickly to his desk, Napoleon's tone changed in his next terse demand. 'Well, Fouché? What do you want?'

Briskly he was busying himself with his papers, ignoring the insinuating figure of the Minister of Police who was standing near the window through which he had been looking when our master had appeared.

As I settled myself back into my preferred horizontal position on the chair, I couldn't help once more thinking of my aversion to rodents. There was something distinctly rat-like about Fouché. Frankly, at times the similarities induced a hint of nausea in my stomach. Now, as he appeared to ooze his way towards the preoccupied First Consul, I could feel that inclination.

'Sir, the documents.'

Fouché's simpering overture was cut short by Napoleon's barked interruption. 'So! This is your "evidence" of the plot in the army, Fouché?'

Napoleon was looking coldly at the sheaf of papers that Fouché was extending towards him, an expression of distaste hovering at his mouth. Suddenly he leaned forward, savagely snatching the documents from the surprised Minister of Police. Flicking contemptuously through a few of the sheets, Napoleon laughed harshly, disgust registered on his face. Throwing them down on his desk in repugnance, he crossed his arms; his steely gaze bored into Fouché's heavily hooded, colourless eyes. He was silent for a moment, his fixed gaze making the usually composed, sly Minister distinctly uncomfortable.

As the silence continued, Fouché began to twitch slightly under the unrelenting stare of the angered First Consul.

'Is Moreau under arrest?' Napoleon's crisp question bit into the silence.

Stammering slightly, Fouché began a reply. 'Y-yes sir, but Bernadotte is...'

'*Is not here!*' Fouché blinked at the wild anger of Napoleon's shouted interruption. Controlling his outburst, Napoleon lowered his tone. With a bitter tone of irony he continued, 'You are misinformed, Fouché. Clearly you do not have the facts. How could general Bernadotte be involved? He and his wife are at present taking the waters at Plombières.'

'I…but sir, I assure…'

Fouché's protestations were silenced.

'The case is closed!' Napoleon snapped the command coldly.

Fouché doggedly refused to give in. 'Sir…'

'I *said*, man – the case is *closed.*'

Napoleon's voice was rising once more, as he made an impatient gesture with his arm. Turning away from us, he looked down at his desk. As though involuntarily, he snarled bitterly, 'I'm so sick of these "plots"…something will have…'

He ceased suddenly, appearing to take a hold on himself. Walking to the window, he stood, staring morosely into the gardens beyond, his hands behind his motionless back, which faced us.

'Leave us, Fouché.' The arrogant command erupted unexpectedly.

Fouché looked at me. Once more he began his protestations.

'That is all, Fouché. I repeat, leave us.' The cold order had a monarchical ring to it.

Fouché, knowing himself to be beaten, bowed stiffly to the small back, then he left the room. The First Consul remained, hands still clasped behind his back, staring through the long window. After hearing the sound of the door close, Napoleon remained silently in his position a few moments longer.

Turning suddenly without warning, he beamed at me. That charming smile that few could resist. How odd was this strange man, that he could entirely transform his mood within a few moments. Jerking his head at the door, he rolled his eyes.

'That man, Talleyrand – he becomes increasingly tiresome.'

I smiled as the First Consul echoed a recurrent thought of my own.

'Indeed,' I replied quietly. 'His lack of sensitivity can sometimes appear to be something of a bore, or perhaps…' I was a little uneasy '…perhaps something potentially more dangerous.'

The First Consul was looking thoughtfully into the middle distance, past my face. Like me he was conjecturing upon the possibilities of Fouché's own participation in conspiracies against the Government, and Napoleon himself.

'Possibly,' I ventured, 'a period of relief from his position of Minister of Police might temper his excesses?'

My cool statement withdrew Napoleon from his preoccupations. His broad smile spread over his still handsome face. Amused, he twinkled his reply. 'Possibly! Possibly, my dear Talleyrand!'

His eyes met mine in a meaningful exchange. With a youthful laugh he suddenly strode towards a cabinet in the corner of the room. 'How remiss of me, old friend! A glass of wine...?'

With his quick movements he began pouring two glasses of wine. Now had arrived the moment I had not been looking forward to. There was little point in delaying, however, so as he busied himself I began bluntly: 'Sir, Addington has resigned...'

I had expected a shocked or stunned response. Surprise, at the very least. Napoleon, however, was more engrossed in examining the colour of the wine, lifting it to the light before handing me my glass.

As he lifted his glass to his lips he finally responded, shrugging his shoulders. 'A short tenure of office. But what has that got to do with France? One Englishman is much like another. "Prime Ministers" are all alike...'

Again he shrugged, losing interest at once.

I sipped my wine, collecting my thoughts in the wake of my surprise at his lack of comprehension at the implications of this news. Seeing my unease, he leaned forward, patting me on the shoulder in boyish affection.

'My dear old friend, you understand these English.' He chuckled suddenly. 'Bah – the English constitution is merely a charter of privileges! They are behind the times, eh Talleyrand?' His flippant attitude worried me, but I was disarmed by his boyish trust as he went on, 'I know you will find an understanding with his successor.'

Without warning he suddenly jumped to his feet. 'Come, my dear Talleyrand, let us take a walk in my wife's garden. The sight of her rose bushes will dispel any gloomy thoughts you may have on this beautiful day.'

Helping me to my feet, he guided me through the glass door into the garden. Once more his almost childlike enthusiasm had restrained me from speaking my true feelings. The natural exuberance of his youth and genius were so fresh and spellbinding, and I could not bring myself to introduce prophecies of doom.

But I had every reason to entertain such thoughts. Napoleon's contempt for Englishmen blinded him to their individual characteristics. Whilst the Treaty of Amiens had been acclaimed as a great success for France, I had always carried uneasy feelings about it. The ease with which it had been concluded had bothered me. My long experience with these proud people, the English, had taught me that they were not easily understood. Had the Treaty been agreed with Pitt or Fox I would have been happier. It would then have been an agreement, which, though possibly less favourable to us, would nonetheless have lasted, for it would have been truly 'English'. Addington was a weak man, uncharacteristic of the English leaders. The terms of Amiens had never been accepted by the ordinary English people. Now, in the event of his resignation, and in the light of Napoleon's recent high-handed behaviour towards limiting outlets for British trade in Europe, I knew the peace with Britain would end.

Napoleon, however, appeared to be oblivious to such possibilities. He was naturally savouring the fruits of his popularity. In two short years he had built France from a humiliated, internally strife-ridden land, into a supreme power, respected abroad and prosperous at home. He had much to be proud of.

But my natural caution warned me to temper his zeal. History had shown that such enthusiasms could quickly turn – to something much more sinister.

* * *

I was smiling to myself. The sight of Josephine's garden was indeed exquisite. But in truth this intense young man walking beside me, with unaccustomed slowness in consideration of my disability, did not notice the delicate fragrance of the air, far too deeply engrossed was he in the ebullient enunciations of his 'dreams'. The creative energy of his intellectual vision seemed to race. Sometimes, indeed, it seemed to be in advance of the man himself, and some of the things he was wont to say in those moments often alarmed me. Now was one of those moments.

I had been congratulating him on the Senate's decision to make him First Consul once more. His reaction was a strange one, displaying that characteristic I had observed in the past. It was as though the honour hardly touched him. He, Napoleon, was of course gratified, but without undue excitement or surprise. It was as though he knew it to be inevitable – his due – and had therefore expected it from the outset. Yet the more honours he received, the more detached he became from those who gave him those honours. Unconsciously he became more and more wrapped in his own great vision. I knew that he liked to talk with me because he felt I could understand what he was trying to do. Increasingly he seemed to feel that others did not understand him.

Thus, as we conversed, his old enthusiasm returned. 'Yes, yes, Talleyrand. In France there is but a single party and a single will.'

I experienced a slightly startled reaction to his grand tones, almost liquid in ecstatic response to the clarity of his internal vision. Looking intently ahead, without seeing the neat rows of his wife's beautiful roses, I was sure, he continued in his almost delirious excitement, relating to me his dreams for France which he felt was the greatest nation on earth.

'I want the title of French Citizen to become the finest and most desirable on earth, Talleyrand. I want every Frenchman travelling anywhere in Europe to be able to believe himself at home...'
He turned to me abruptly, ceasing his broad gesticulations as he stopped. His grey eyes, wide and earnest, looked deeply into mine. 'We must re-build, and re-build *solidly*, my dear Talleyrand. I have opened up a vast road. He who marches straight ahead shall be safe. But he who strays to the right or left shall be punished... France will grow even greater – nothing must stop her progress...'

We had started walking once more, and I was relieved, for the intensity of his words was disconcerting. Now he seemed to be becoming entirely carried away by the creative vision of his imagination. He was talking on, quickly, intensely, concentrating on an unseen sight ahead.

'The grand order that rules the entire world must also regulate each of its parts. At the centre of a society, like the sun, is the government. The various institutions must revolve around it without ever straying from their orbits. Thus the government must regulate the mechanism of each institution in such a manner that all concur in preserving general harmony. In the system of the Universe, nothing is left to chance, and in the social system nothing must be left to individual caprice.'

We had stopped again, having reached a small garden seat. Again the grey eyes were looking deeply into mine, their earnest sincerity lit by the gleam of light that I knew was a reflection of the genius of the man. The presence of the small First Consul loomed over me; he seemed larger than life, consumed by some supernatural force. I felt a little dizzy, and my foot ached.

'We can do much together, Talleyrand. You must help me. France…' His voice trailed. I felt he was oblivious to everything, even to me. I coughed uncomfortably.

'Indeed, sir. Indeed.' I paused. 'Permit me, sir, my foot…' I was indicating the seat longingly, my one thought to sit down.

'My dear friend! How inconsiderate of me. Forgive me.'

Like a small boy he seemed to jump to help me. I knew his apologies were genuine. Napoleon was a kind and thoughtful young man. Indeed, he had the most generous and forgiving nature I had ever encountered. His regret was deeply felt if he knew he had been in any way careless of consideration.

As I settled myself on the seat, relieved to feel the pain of exercise ebb from my troubled limb, I looked up at the young man who was looking around at the spring landscape with pleasured approval registered on his handsome face.

'I must ensure that you do not become carried away with those great dreams of yours, young sir.' I was adopting the paternal tone that I knew the young genius liked, and which he appeared to respect. 'Sometimes I wish you were a little lazier. A little less zeal, my young friend.'

He laughed exultantly, and my stern expression as I tried to temper his enthusiasm was, once again, melted by his disarming boyishness. As we laughed together, he suddenly put his head to one side, his eyes mischievously twinkling in his beaming face.

'And I have a little advice for you, my old friend.' His voice had adopted a tone of firm affection.

'Indeed?' My enquiry held the mutual fondness, though I knew that the forthcoming statement would, nonetheless, contain a proposed intention from the First Consul, which could not be disputed.

Seating himself beside me, Napoleon looked a little uncomfortable for a moment, hesitating slightly. Then, clearing his throat, he began. 'A .. delicate matter, sir.'

As I looked expectantly at him he appeared, uncharacteristically, to be searching for words. Looking kindly into my eyes, a faint twinkle playing about those blue grey magnets, he continued, 'It's about your impending marriage.'

For a moment I thought I had misheard. Leaning forward I enquired, 'Forgive me, sir?'

'Your – ah – marriage, Talleyrand. Marriage!' The expression of astonishment on my face seemed to be embarrassing the First Consul.

Reaching for my snuff-box, I endeavoured to maintain my customary composure. 'I assure you, my dear friend, I have no intention of…'

His grey eyes were boring into me, kindly but insistent. His interruption was firm and quiet. Kind. 'But you must, sir. I cannot have my Minister for Foreign Affairs living openly with his mistress.'

I was silent for a moment, searching my confused thoughts. This was indeed an unexpected command from the young First Consul. Yet when I thought about it, I realised that it had been inevitable.

Napoleon had a deep respect for convention, and a profound sense of morality. Moreover, he was determined that his court should be respected both at home and abroad, and had been insistent that many of the more frivolous pastimes and fashions of those associated with him should be regularised.

I understood his viewpoint, of course, but the horrification I found in contemplating the idea of marriage was almost overpowering. I hastily comforted myself with liberal quantities of snuff.

Indeed, it had been well known that I had been living with a certain Madame Grand for some time. A creature of spectacular beauty, she was nonetheless a trifle silly, and the thought of making her my wife would never have even entered my head. Frankly, she rather bored me, though I had a fondness for her.

The grey eyes were still looking at me. Though I knew it would be useless, I nonetheless raised the vain protest. 'Sir, I have taken vows...'

The smiling eyes deepened their expression as his face broke into that charming grin. 'I shall resolve that little matter of your former association with the church. It is a minor concession to request of the Pope at this moment...'

His soothing tones expressed a note of sympathy. Napoleon was aware of my antipathy towards the prospect of such a step. Brightly he continued, quietly persuading me to accept the demand. 'Anyway, my dear Talleyrand, bachelorhood is no longer fashionable in modern France!' He was skilfully addressing my own regard for the traditions of society. 'You will enjoy marriage, it is an honourable estate...' He gesticulated, his arm indicating his house and gardens. 'It is the estate that my constitution values above all.'

His voice had lowered to a serious tone as he spoke those last words. I knew I was beaten as I looked into those earnest grey eyes. For the sake of peace I would marry the woman. In truth it mattered little to me, since I had no regard whatsoever for the religious implications, and I knew my lifestyle would be little curtailed. If it were so important to him then I would not resist.

Indeed, I appreciated the argument he was now putting before me.

'They must have *example* from us, Talleyrand. They cannot be expected to accept one code of behaviour from us when we expect them to adhere to the moral standards required by the constitution. It is simply not fair. That is why I am so delighted with the Vatican agreement, my dear friend.'

I could see that he was deeply sincere. Looking around him, he went on, 'Last Sunday I was here, walking in the solitude and silence of Nature. Suddenly the sound of the church bells of Rueil struck my ears. I felt moved, so strong is the power of childhood habits and upbringing. Then I told myself, "What an impression this must make on simple and credulous people!" What can your philosophers and ideologists answer to that, Talleyrand? The people need religion…'

His eyes had been soft, doubtless recalling his Corsican childhood. Now he looked at me with a more steely expression. 'And that is why we must set an example of dignity for them, Talleyrand. We must respect the religious principles too.'

* * *

'Good to see you, Montrond.' The still jovial Napoleon dispelled Montrond's nervousness as I took the extended envelope from his hand. 'Still charming those English ladies?' Napoleon's good humour was now directed at Montrond as I opened the document.

I glanced quickly at the contents of the single sheet of paper, my heart sinking as I realised the implicit message, and the deeper ramifications. Reading it through once more, I folded it neatly, returning it to its envelope. My fears had been confirmed.

Napoleon, acutely sensitive to my sudden silence, turned to me, enquiring casually, 'Anything of interest, sir?'

I remained silent a moment or two longer, searching vainly for a way in which to soften the blow I knew I had to deliver. There was no way in which I could cushion it. Handing him the document, I bluntly announce, 'Sir, the Bourbon Pretender has refused your terms. He will not relinquish the Bourbon claim to the throne of France.'

I had anticipated anger. Rage. And indeed that was to come. But the initial response from Napoleon was somehow even more poignant. A shade of dark scarlet rose from his neck, engulfing his face in a deep blush of apparent mortification. He appeared stunned, wounded as though he had been struck.

For a few moments he remained quite still, apparently numbed. Slowly he opened the document and read it through, placing it deliberately on the seat beside him when he had finished.

'How dare they...' The husky whisper seemed to exhale through almost unmoving lips, rising from his throat. Staring straight ahead he fell into silence once more.

Then: '*How dare they?*'

His anger had unleashed itself as the momentum of his rage propelled him on to his feet in unison with his yell. His eyes blazing in uncontrollable anger, he looked at Montrond and me, throwing his arms wide.

'I won't have these imbeciles insult me... I won't have it... Don't they understand the wishes of the *people?*...The *people*...They *have no claim.. no claim...*' He was almost incoherent, blinded by rage, wildly gesticulating. 'Don't they understand?...I *am* France!'

He had drawn himself up to his full height, a sudden arrogance rising through his anger. Narrowing his eyes in a menacing expression I had never seen before, he lowered his voice to a threatening snarl. He appeared oblivious to the presence of Montrond and myself. 'I'll show them... I'll show them...'

He had transformed into a character I had never seen before. Utterly humiliated, he repeated: '*I am* France...they will have to learn that.' His voice trembled slightly with bitterness as he stared unseeingly into nothingness.

And so, his reaction had been more extreme than I had even imagined – or feared. At that moment I believe that the course of History was changed. At that moment the charming, loveable genius seemed to die.

In its place was born a genius who instead was to be scarred forever by the wound of humiliation, a wound that had killed the naive trust with which he had been blessed. Never would he recover from the insult of being considered a *parvenu* by the Bourbons.

He had made a most generous offer to the Bourbons, had been prepared to restore substantially their proprietary claims in France. But in return he had asked the unforgivable from those who claimed 'divine right'. Never would the Bourbons renounce their rights to the throne of France; never would they accept a Corsican General as the ruler of 'their' land.

At that moment was born a man of bitterness. That characteristic was to manifest itself in varying forms of destructive acts of aggression. Not least of those was the one that now planted its seeds in his mind...

Chapter X

Spring had made an early arrival to Germany in that year of 1804. In their fragile delicacy, the first buds of the year were already beginning to thrust their life through the threshold of winter's restraints. And blending with the light greens of infant leaves, the willows hung their slender yellow arms gracefully, gently brushing the gurgling waters of the small river here at Ettenheim, near to the town of Baden. It was a peaceful scene, an idyllic setting for a romance. And love, indeed, was in the air!

Louis Antoine Henri de Bourbon Condé, the Duc d'Enghien, had been happy in this beautiful place. Walking by the sparkling river here on this fresh spring day, he breathed in deeply, gently stroking the head of his adored and faithful dog that was, as ever, by his side. He was in love, deeply in love. He smiled to himself at the sensation that the thought of this emotion induced in him.

Charlotte! A sigh of ecstasy escaped him as he thought of the exquisite beauty, sensitivity and unsurpassed gentleness of Cardinal de Rohan's niece, whose hand he was shortly to take in marriage. He glanced at the large house in the distance behind him. Yes, it had been a happy time here in this comfortable place, but he had only been here because of Charlotte. Soon they would be married, and then he must address himself to his family duty.

Ceasing his strolling, he stood staring thoughtfully into the smooth flow of the river. He could see the rippling reflection of himself and his dog in the clean clarity of the silver water. He was a true Condé, the pride and hope, he knew, of his grandfather, now exiled in England; and of his father, now attempting to rally the Royalist Army that had lost its coherent strategy. The princes of Condé had long been associated with the very spirit of military honour in France. Indeed, it was said that Bonaparte had a bust of the Great Condé, that extraordinary General, in a gallery at the Tuileries along with other heroes he admired: Alexander, Caesar, Hannibal, Cicero, Demosthenes, and others. So it was that the young Duke too had inherited that mantle of chivalry, and he knew it to be his duty, his destiny, to fight for the Bourbon cause, to restore his family's rights and dignity. Indeed, he had already been contemplating the possibility of an invasion of the Alsace region, but there was as yet no actual plan. Liaisons between the separated factions of emigrés took time.

Meanwhile, he was basking in the contentment of love, though he had been disturbed at the news he had learned a few days since of the uncovering of a plot in Paris, resulting in the imprisonment of Georges Cadoudal and General Pichegru. The garbled reports he had heard indicated that they had intended to abduct the First Consul, but that Cadoudal had mentioned after his arrest that Bonaparte would not have been attacked until 'the arrival of the Bourbon Prince'. Naturally his friends and household were concerned and alarmed, fearing that the identity of 'the Bourbon Prince' referred to was being misconstrued – thus implicating him. But he had laughed at such a suggestion. Quite simply it was not true, and was a frankly far-fetched possibility, for his reasons for being here at Ettenheim were well known.

He felt the head of his dog suddenly turn under the absent-minded fondling of his hand. The stiffened attention of the animal was succeeded by a delighted wagging of his tail at the arrival of a familiar figure. The Duke turned, smiling his beautiful smile at the approach of his elderly valet, a man he had known all his life, and in whom he placed his entire trust and confidence. A fleeting look of surprise passed over his aristocratic features at the sight of this much-loved man, whose expression now wore an uncharacteristic gravity.

'Pierre?' The youthful voice, set against the tall, fair beauty of the Duke, made him seem younger than his thirty-one years.

'Sir, my lady has arrived...'

The elderly man had clearly not made his way to the river without purpose. He could, after all, have sent a younger member of the household to announce the arrival of Princess Charlotte de Rohan-Rochefort.

The Duke's handsome face creased into a deep smile, his blue eyes shining. 'Perhaps you would ask her to join me...?' His reply ended in enquiry; he was well aware that his faithful servant had a more pressing purpose for his long walk.

As he cleared his throat nervously, the old man's face seemed to fall into uncontrollable agitation and an expression of alarm crossed his features.

'Sir, there are Bonapartist agents in Baden. They have been here these past twenty-four hours.' He paused, his worried eyes searching the Duke's bemused face. Opening his mouth to reply, the young man was pre-empted by the agitated continuation of the paternal urgings from his valet. 'Sir, you must leave Baden. Your life is in danger...'

Pierre paused briefly, pleadingly looking into the innocent blue eyes of vigorous youth. 'There are rumours that a meeting was held between Talleyrand and Bonaparte following the arrest of Cadoudal and Pichegru...' The man's agitation was growing. 'Sir, your name is being implicated in the Cadoudal plot to overthrow Bonaparte, and the proposal of the Talleyrand-Bonaparte meeting has been put to the Council of State.'

The young Duke's expression of bemused incomprehension had given way to the uncomfortable amusement of disbelief. 'Oh come, Pierre, you cannot be serious!' He laughed uneasily. '*You* know – *they* must know – I had absolutely no inkling of that plot! I knew nothing about it whatsoever. How can I be "implicated" in something about which I am ignorant?' He laughed, gently patting the old man on the back, trying to comfort the rising panic of his faithful retainer.

'Sir...' The old man's agitation was now mingled with frustration at the calm response from his master. 'Sir – you must listen. You are in great danger... That meeting of the Council was on the tenth of March. It is now the thirteenth. The presence of Bonapartist agents in Baden is not innocent. They have made enquiries…'

The emotion was becoming too much for the old man. Gripping his master's arm, he looked with pleading affection into the blue eyes. 'Sir, you *must* leave. You *must*.'

The Duke was silent, looking with serious concern at the old man's anguished face. He could feel the warm lick of the dog's nuzzling comfort as it sensed the disquiet between the two men. Looking kindly at the anxious face of the man he knew so well, the Duke spoke quietly. 'Send someone to find out more information, Pierre. If the situation becomes dangerous, yes, I shall leave.' He smiled reassuringly. 'Now, ask my lady to join me, will you…?'

Bowing, the old man withdrew, suddenly bent as though by an invisible burden, his brow creased in a worried frown. As he walked back quickly towards the big house, he knew that time was short. But there might still be a chance if they could convince the Duke…

Turning his face once more to the river, the young Duke passed his hand nervously before his eyes. Suddenly he felt a little sick, gripped by some strange presentiment. It was madness! The whole idea was utter madness. He had not even been aware that there had ever been such a plot. Of course he was a Bourbon; of course he was committed to the Bourbon restoration. But this particular conspiracy had been nothing to do with him. Surely Bonaparte couldn't implicate one who was known to be innocent? Surely he wouldn't stoop to such insane treachery…?

The Duke moved to a nearby seat, taking a small book out of his pocket. He must rid himself of this dreadful sense of foreboding. Bonaparte was a soldier. For that reason he would inevitably abide by the codes of Honour.

'Lesser than Macbeth, and greater…Not so happy, yet much happier…Thou shalt get kings, though thou be none…So all hail Macbeth and Banquo!'

The page before him seemed almost to vibrate at the sheer

intensity of the words of the great English bard, staring relentlessly up at him from the small page.

All at once the full weight of the implication of his position as a Bourbon seemed to engulf him. For the first time, it seemed, he was aware of the very real danger he was in constantly, due to his relationship of first cousin to the Capetian Pretender – indeed, due to his being a potential pretender himself to the throne of France. He felt stunned, as though he had stumbled upon a truth. He realised that though he had always known the superficial realities of his position, he had nonetheless never fully understood the awesome actualities of it. A surge of panic began to rise, as a lump seemed to form in his throat. He stared mesmerised at Shakespeare's words.

'*The fate of Kings…*'

The involuntary exhalation of breath seemed to whisper the words to the soft spring breeze without touching the lips of the young man's beautiful face. The motionless Duke was oblivious to the world in his frozen state of shock, even to his own melancholy phrase.

'Louis?'

The gentle voice of Charlotte de Rohan-Rochefort failed to penetrate the still trance of the young Duke.

'Louis…? My love, how serious you look today…'

Gently, she took his hand, sinking like liquid onto the seat beside him, her large blue eyes wide and concerned as they gazed lovingly into his transfixed stare. With a start he appeared to jump slightly, abruptly wrenching himself from the paralysing terror of his preoccupations. The beauty of her soft face, animated by her loving smile, served to dissolve entirely the growing horror of his indefinable premonitions.

Rising immediately, he kissed her hand tenderly. His face returned to its happy expression of love as he looked deeply into her eyes. Taking the still open book from his hand, Charlotte's gentle voice laughingly enquired, 'What manner of story is this that it should so induce such a melancholy expression from my love…?' She giggled softly as she looked at the page, knowing well the work before her. 'Ah, the English master…but, my lord, this is not a day for the depressing tragedies of strife between princes…'

Throwing the small book down on to the seat, she rose, taking both of her fiancé's hands in hers. 'It's spring, my love! Look how beautiful it is today! We must think of the future…not fill our heads with melancholy images of Celtic history…'

She had linked her arm through his, picking up a stick to throw for the large dog, whose delight at seeing his future mistress was inducing a frenetic wagging movement of his entire body.

'Come, let us walk a little, my lord. We'll dispel Shakespeare's gloom…'

Hugging his arm, she gently pulled him to walk with her as the dog ran after the stick she had thrown. Enclosing her delicate hand in his, he looked down at her, overcome by the rush of emotion he felt as he gazed at the object of his most passionate and ardent love. Ruefully he smiled at her, patting her hand gently. 'You are right, my darling…' He paused, checking an unnecessary explanation of his thoughtfulness. Then, glancing at the small book, he murmured, 'History seems choked with gory incidents such as we see in this tragedy, "Macbeth".' He hesitated, momentarily thoughtful once more. 'Innocence or guilt appears to be an irrelevant element in the destinies of Royalty…' His voice trailed as he gazed into the middle distance.

Suddenly the panting form of his dog presenting the retrieved stick almost knocked him over. Looking into the worried face of his fiancée, he suddenly broke into a youthful laugh. 'Lucky it was me – you wouldn't have stood a chance! He's bigger than you!'

Relieved, she joined him in laughter, while the breathless animal looked on, wagging his powerful tail. Holding the stick, the Duke drew his arm back slowly – then expelled some of his pent-up emotion by hurling the stick some considerable distance for the excited dog to charge after once again. Laughingly, he turned to Charlotte, his face suddenly becoming serious as he said softly, 'Forgive me, my darling.'

Her eyes watered slightly as he drew her into his arms. How deeply she loved him. She couldn't bear to see him saddened by anything, this noble and dignified fiancé of hers. Yet as their faces moved closer, her lips yielding to the tender touch of his, she felt that she had seen some strangely haunted look at the back of his eyes, some hint of fear.

But now, as he gathered her more closely into his arms, and she responded to the growing passion of their kiss, her tentative worries were drowned as the tide of her love overtook her. It was silly to cloud their happiness with senseless speculations. Nothing could ever spoil their love.

* * *

The sound of galloping hooves was unrelenting. It seemed somehow to be growing gradually louder, its menacing rhythm now accompanied by the clink of spurs and the creak of saddle leather.

The Duc d'Enghien tossed and turned in his bed. He was not quite sure if he was awake or asleep. He felt hot, terribly hot. His blonde locks were damp, as indeed were, it seemed, his nightclothes. Opening his eyes, he could vaguely make out the familiar shapes of his own room, and as he felt his hand pass over his aching head, he could hear the concerned whine of his dog from his place at the side of his master's bed. Stretching his hand to pat reassurance to the much-loved animal, the young Duke closed his eyes once more, falling again into that heavy doze that seemed to take him only to the bare threshold of sleep, forbidding the luxury of restful oblivion.

The unremitting hammering of hooves beat louder and louder, seeming to come from inside him. He could feel a sweat breaking out on his body. He felt as though he was in some dark nether world, without visual definition. The swirling darkness was penetrated only by the unbroken rhythm of that threatening sound that seemed to grip his mind in a relentless torment, refusing him either sleep or wakefulness.

Now, images began to rise intermittently before his eyes, surging up out of the rushing mists of darkness, disembodied and distorted, briefly materialising, only to vanish suddenly, swallowed by the folds of the insatiable blackness, whose deepening shades pulsated to the unending rhythm of the swelling sound.

The Duke writhed on his bed, entrapped by the suffocating embrace of his growing nightmare. Louder and louder beat the sound in his head. Now he could see the flaring nostrils of a galloping horse, the whites of its eyes flashing in the eerie blackness, some sinister silver light glinting off the flash of the bit in the animal's open, frothing mouth. And as the wild image of the horse disappeared, ranks of the same flailing vision surged up from behind, rising and falling in a tight body that moved to the rhythm of that dread sound.

And now, as he tried to wrench himself unsuccessfully from the cold grip of the paroxysm of horror, the Duke could see two eyes emerge from the mists. Like gimlets they burned into him from beneath the military hat. The fixed expression of purpose penetrated without falter, as the image rose and fell too with the ghastly rhythm. Again the single image vanished, to be superseded by the slowly materialising vision of ranks of the same, their hats at different heights, nonetheless moving up and down in a unified movement, as an advancing body bearing down on him.

The agonised form of the sleeping Duke twisted and turned frenetically now. His dog, alarmed at his master's seizure, lifted his front paws to the side of the bed, leaning his head over his beloved master to administer a pacifying lick. But the Duke was still held by his tortured dream.

That unrelenting sound of the hooves had risen to a deafening pitch. His head felt as though it was about to burst. And now he could see the hooves cleaving their frantic passage through the silvery dust of eerie country lanes lit only by the glistening whiteness of the full moon in the clear March night. Louder and louder. Nearer and nearer. The images seemed to flow and ebb before his eyes like an ephemeral tide of horror.

Now suddenly the sound changed. The rhythm remained the same, but the hooves were striking a different surface, no longer the worn hardness of a country lane, but the clatter of hoof beats upon wood. The body of cavalry was passing over a wooden bridge.

A wooden bridge... The Duke tried to find the reason of consciousness – tried desperately to escape sleep's suffocating restraints. He must wake up. He must...

The wooden bridge...it crossed the little river...not five hundred yards from the house.

A yelp of alarm was superseded by a low growl, menacingly filling the night-darkened bedroom of the Duc d'Enghien. Involuntarily the young man's body lunged upwards, his arms flinging aside the bedclothes as he leapt from the phantom terror of his deeply disturbed sleep. Instantly he was awake, laying a restraining hand on the quivering head of the growling dog. The massive animal was transfixed, listening to a sound as yet unheard by the Duke. The ears alertly pricked, twitched occasionally, as its concentrated attentions remained accompanied by the threatening sound from its throat.

The Duke, exhausted by his restless attempts at sleep, moved warily towards the window. He could see the moon high in the sky, not yet full. The stars were clear and bright, some already disappearing in anticipation of the approaching dawn. As he looked towards the dark shades of the wooded landscape outside, he was suddenly engulfed in a wave of terror, the sick premonition rising from a churning throb deep within him. The innocuous shapes of the trees seemed somehow to be moving in a sinister, silent undulation. He could make out no actual evidence of physical movement, yet an eerie atmosphere of a growing encircling presence emitted a strange feeling of advancing pressure.

The dog grew more agitated, his whole body now tense and alert. The growls rising in his throat suddenly erupted into an angered bark as both he and his master swung their attentions from the window to the door of the Duke's room, thrown open without warning by a petrified servant screaming hysterically.

'Master!...Master...!'

The terrified woman was incoherent, unable to find articulation in the grip of her uncontrollable hysteria. In one stride the young man was at the side of the elderly woman whose maternal love had cared for him throughout the duration of his thirty-one years.

Looking up into the light blue eyes of her adored master, the nanny gasped, almost inaudibly: 'My Lord, the house is surrounded...'

She paused, her voice choked in disbelief. Other servants had begun to build up behind her at the doorway, mostly clad in their nightshirts, huddled together in a collective state of stunned terror. Desperately, they stared at their master as the elderly nanny, now also supported by the venerable valet, tried to express her frightened incredulity.

'S-s-soldiers...' she stammered uncontrollably, feebly pointing towards the window, tears flowing freely down her ashen face.

The Duke was suddenly calm. Soothingly tightening his arm around the old lady's shoulders, he glanced reassuringly at the confused group of servants crowded together at the door. His voice quiet and commanding, he enquired kindly of the woman, 'Where, my dear...? Where are...?'

Suddenly a collective scream from the small group interrupted his question. The dog became frenzied, barking hysterically, protectively standing before his master, poised to pounce.

The small group at the door fell back, a shared shudder of fear rippling through their ranks. The Duke felt a bitter twist of sick realisation as he stared into the gimlet eyes beneath the French military hat that he had seen in his dream.

The soldier, flanked by four others, strode through the retreating spasm of the group of household staff, his grim stare fixed on the golden figure of the Duc d'Enghien.

The young Duke gave the old lady a final squeeze of reassurance, casting a silent plea for calm to both her and his faithful old valet. The dog was now snarling at the soldier, his teeth bared, the menacing growls rolling louder and more threatening as the soldier advanced towards the Duke. Restraining the large animal by taking a firm hold on its collar, and administering a light touch of control, the Duke drew himself up to his full height, his tall, noble presence commanding a halt to the swaggering advance of the soldiers' uncouth intrusion.

He had now lost all semblance of fear. He was composed and in control, the confirmed reality of his recent hours of apprehension now before him. An actuality – finally.

Lifting his chin slightly, the light blue eyes bored into the burning animosity of the soldier's swarthy scowl. With cold politeness, the Duke crisply demanded, 'What do you mean, sir, by this unwarranted intrusion into my house at this unearthly hour?'

The soldier stared back defiantly into the cool, aristocratic gaze. Raising one corner of his mouth in an approaching sneer, he paused before replying harshly, 'I am instructed to arrest you that you might await trial on the charge that you have conspired to overthrow the government of your native France, and to inflict fatal harm on the person of the First Consul. We shall proceed to Strasbourg, there to await further orders.'

The soldier signalled to his assistants to escort the Duke. A liquid growl rose from the quivering animal, which was being firmly controlled by his master. The dog's guttural snarls rose ferociously as he sensed that the movements of the soldiers indicated a physical threat to his master.

'I am innocent of this charge, as you well know, sir.' The Duke exerted considerable effort in restraining the angry animal as he flung this biting retort to the officious soldier.

'I have orders to escort you to Strasbourg, sir.'

The soldier was impatient to complete his unpleasant task. Exasperated, he looked at the snarling animal, its savage straining against his master's hold daunting the soldier's attempt to approach the Duke.

The Duke looked at the company of dumbfounded staff, his eyes finally resting on the crumpled figure of his distressed valet, whose arm encircled the distraught housekeeper. Quietly, the Duke addressed them. 'Do not concern yourselves, this is clearly some sort of mistake. I am innocent of any such charge.' He paused, indicating to a servant to take the dog's collar. 'I shall go with these gentlemen, to clear up the misunderstanding. And I shall return shortly.'

Once more he paused as he passed control of the squirming animal to his man, his eyes falling tenderly on the valet who was now helping him dress hastily. The soft plea of his voice calmly entreated him,

'Pierre…inform my lady…'

Roughly he was pushed. Suddenly two soldiers, now unhindered by the dog, violently propelled him towards the door. The Duke's attempts at maintaining his dignity were forbidden by the coarse shoving of his surly escorts.

Now, as the soldiers marched the young man through his own house, out into the grey shades of early dawn, so too the huddled group of servants were herded unfeelingly. They too were under arrest. Behind him the Duke could hear the hysterical fury of his dog, incensed by the separation from his master, wrenching at the weakening restraint of the servant.

As they reached the courtyard, the young Duke was violently dragged towards the first of four black carriages that were lined up, and accompanied by a silently waiting cavalry guard.

The realisation that members of his household were also being arrested had induced a frantic struggle of protest that the soldiers should take only him, leaving these innocent people who clearly had no interest in the affairs of politics. But his shouts and efforts of protestation were cruelly silenced by brutal physical assaults and, as they reached the open door of the carriage, the young man, already dazed by his beatings, was bodily thrown into the carriage, the soldiers bundling his sprawling legs through the door. The dog, finally uncontrollable, hurled himself free with a ferocious yelp, howling from his frothing mouth, his teeth and eyes flashing venomously as he knocked the soldiers aside in his flight into his master's carriage.

Slamming the door shut, the soldiers stood away from the contained fury of the savage animal, as their commander clicked a signal to the driver of the coach.

The small group of servants, paralysed with fear, watched in numbed silence as the coach bearing their master and his barking protector was driven off at speed in a cloud of dust and a clatter of hooves. Obediently, they filed into the coaches, frightened and confused. Whatever was going on…?

* * *

Napoleon stared unseeingly at the carpet of spring flowers before him. Motionless, his eyes remained unblinkingly aware of the purple, yellow and white bulbs that swam in his unfocused vision. The park at Malmaison was bursting with new life on this fresh March afternoon. Vaguely, the fevered twittering of busy birds chirped happily at the back of his consciousness but he was aware that in this vital atmosphere of growth and spring excitement, he alone was still, paralysed by the internal wrestling of his conflicting thoughts.

His head buried in the stiff collar of his uniform, his hands clasped behind his back, Napoleon pondered his tortuous dilemma. He had never been in such a situation before. It was very odd indeed. This whole situation was becoming quite out of hand. He couldn't really understand it.

Even his own family: first Josephine; then Joseph; now his mother. It really was quite ridiculous. Surely it was a routine matter? After all, the damned conspirators had tried to kill him. Why then these endless emotional appeals from all these people? Basically, this was an affair of the state. An attempt on the life of the First Consul had been made, and the conspiring assassins must be punished.

He felt a twinge of disgust at the methods the plotters had chosen. Was he a dog that he should be hunted down in the streets of his own capital? Let them lead Europe against me, he thought, and I will defend myself. At least such an act would be legitimate. But no – instead they tried to get me by blowing up a Paris street, succeeding in killing or injuring a hundred people. And now – *now*, they send forty brigands to assassinate me…

His knuckles turned white as he clasped his hands tightly in anger at the very thought. Narrowing his sightless eyes, he bitterly told himself, 'I'll make them shed tears of blood for that. I'll teach them to legalise murder...'

Shaking himself slightly as he felt his anger rising, Napoleon looked around, taking in the beauty of the peaceful scene around him. How lovely it was. He sighed sadly. This place reflected the gentle nature of his beloved Josephine.

All at once he was engulfed by a sensation of affront. How *could* she? How could *she* quarrel with him over that Bourbon wretch? Why this sudden outcry, simply because this Duc d'Enghien was a Bourbon? The repeated question in his stricken sensitivity made him flush, and momentarily he felt his blood race.

Bourbons! Who did they think they were? They held this archaic view that the concept of Monarchy was their 'divine right', regardless of the will of the people. They felt that they owned France! It was madness, a pre-Christian idea, wholly unacceptable to post-revolutionary France. The hearts and minds of the masses were what mattered. And *he* represented them. He, Napoleon Bonaparte.

All these damned Royalists were was a party. An out-of-date party at that. Led by a few decadent aristocrats who claimed the throne of France through their *blood*. He smiled a bitter, mirthless smile to himself. These Bourbons fancied that they would shed his blood like that of some vile animal. But his blood was quite as valuable as theirs. Never would he suffer such an affront from any prince on the face of this earth. He would deal appropriately with any scheming aristocrat who fell into his hands – just as he would with any ordinary individual. How were they any different from any other scoundrels of similar ilk? Were the leaders of 'Royalists' any different from those of Jacobins or Liberals? They were not. Quite simply, they were just another party.

He tightened his lips. These 'Royalists' stood in need of a warning. It would be better to make one stern and striking example than to punish ten minor tools. After that he could afford to be merciful again. But they had to learn he would not stand for such conspiracies from *any* party, Royalists no more, no less than any other. He was the man of no party; that much had always been clear to everyone from the outset. To govern through a party was to become dependent upon it sooner or later.

Well, they would never catch him at that. Never! He had to make it plain to all the opposition factions – especially those errant Royalists in their deluded world of self-importance – he must make it clear that he would not tolerate such flagrant acts of terrorism.

'D'Enghien…' He moved as he repeated the name to himself, at last seeing the delicate flowers of spring emerging innocently from the green blades of grass that held them. Youth… He smiled to himself as he began to stroll slowly along the pebbled path. Spring recalled the innocence of youth.

And now his brow creased as he remembered the dreams of his own youth, as he recalled his heroes. The Great Condé! He had always been one of his heroes. Why else did he honour his bust in a gallery at the Tuileries? What a great soldier – what Honour had he brought to France. But now he had to decide upon the fate of that noble General's descendent, the Duc d'Enghien; the last remaining direct issue of the great man's line.

Napoleon felt a twist of pain. The conflict of his emotion and intellect contracted. He must not allow sentiment to deter that which he knew to be the right and proper course. It mattered not who or what this Duc d'Enghien was. What mattered was that which he had been found to be doing: namely, conspiring with General Demouriez to effect an invasion through the Alsace region of France, following a fatal attack on the person of the First Consul. The man was guilty of treason. He must be tried accordingly.

Napoleon paused, looking down into the rippling reflection of a small stream, which he had come upon. He halted at the tiny bridge that forded the water. The gentle gurgling seemed to fruitlessly attempt to balm his aching head. He stared into the glistening water. His task was to govern France that she might grow strong once more. These past few years he had begun that massive and great mission that was his destiny. But now the activities of these fanatics were endangering his great vision. They would end up by killing him, and what would happen to France then?

He stared thoughtfully, motionless once more. Where government was concerned, justice meant strength as well as virtue. He must be seen to be strong, not intimidated by these arrogant simpletons.

'Sir! I bring a message from General Savary.'

Slowly, Napoleon turned, taking in the figure of the soldier with dazed surprise, still preoccupied with his conflict. 'I beg your pardon?' He collected himself quickly, pulling himself from his thoughts as he asked the nervous soldier to repeat his statement.

'General Savary, sir. He sends you this message, and says he awaits further orders.'

The soldier bowed, handing Napoleon an envelope. With characteristic speed, Napoleon broke the seal, quickly reading the contents of the brief document.

'When did they arrive in Strasbourg?' Napoleon issued his brief enquiry with terse intensity.

'Yesterday, sir.'

Napoleon nodded, his brows knitting together in a deep frown. 'Tell Savary I must have all the papers. All of them, do you understand?' His grey eyes looked compellingly at the young soldier.

'Y-yes, sir, but...he awaits further orders. He-he can't keep the Duke in the citadel for much longer. He...'

'Yes, yes.' Napoleon interrupted the soldier's stammering discomfort. Turning away, he returned his gaze to the bubbling stream. Putting his hand on the rail of the little wooden bridge, he stepped onto it, his gaze fixed on the rippling water.

The soldier stood silently, watching the deep meditation of the First Consul. Slowly, Napoleon lifted his head and looked across the park towards Paris. For a long time he stared thoughtfully into the distance.

'Vincennes.' Napoleon's low voice was inaudible in the light spring breeze.

'Sir?' The soldier jumped slightly, blushing to have to ask the First Consul to repeat himself.

Napoleon's gaze remained fixed in its distant projection, then he spoke quietly, deliberately. 'Tell Savary to have him brought to Vincennes.'

Respectfully the soldier bowed, thanking the First Consul and making a hasty retreat from the motionless presence of the preoccupied Head of State.

Napoleon remained still. So General Ordener had arrested d'Enghien, and they had taken him to the citadel. Strasbourg. He felt a sudden shudder of foreboding involuntarily overtake him.

Now – he must decide…

* * *

The doleful eyes of the large, motionless dog took on a quizzical expression as he pricked his ears forward. As the joint-less stealth of the hairy rodent moved towards the scattered remains of stale bread which lay on the plate nearby, the dog's ears twitched on his unmoving head, its chin resting comfortably on his beloved master's thigh. Now the liquid brown eyes moved upwards, observing the sunken head of his unshaven and dishevelled master, buried in the folds of his tattered and dirty clothes pulled close across his chest to ward off the bitter cold of the damp dungeons in the castle of Vincennes. Tempting though it might be to frighten the hideous rat, he nonetheless would not disturb the brief respite of sleep at last awarded to his exhausted master. The animal could sense a feeling of despair and dejection about his usually exuberant master. He couldn't really quite understand what was going on, all he knew was that these past days had been an endless stream of strange events. Travel; being locked up in small rooms; more travel; and now finally this hollow cavern deep in the ground, bitterly cold and almost pitch dark, lit only by the weak filtering incandescence of the daylight or the moon. His master had shared with him each tiny morsel of the near-inedible food that was periodically delivered. And that which even the starving pangs of their stomachs found impossible to absorb was quickly relieved from them by some member of the considerable rat population that infested the stinking recesses of this horrible place.

Periodically those dreadful people had questioned his master – aggressively. Continually, they manhandled and harassed, with cruel malice, that precious person. A few times he had been kicked in his face by the sturdy boot of occasional individuals as he had tried to defend his master from their brutal assaults. But he had wreaked his revenge and demonstrated his anger at their behaviour towards his beloved master by sinking his teeth into any available part of their repellent bodies whenever the opportunity presented itself.

A low growl rose in his throat now as he heard the approaching footsteps of one of those dreaded individuals. The familiar sound of the steel key being inserted in the cage-like door, followed by the clanking whine as it swung open, woke his master. He felt the fraternal pressure of a much-loved hand upon him as they both watched the looming silhouette of a thick-set soldier descend the stone steps from the relative light of the moonlit evening into the foul depths of the thick darkness in which they languished.

He felt his master shudder, a deep sigh of tired despair catching in his throat as he lethargically moved his body in anticipation of the coming command.

And even as his master moved he could hear the savage shout erupting from the surly lips of the big man. How often had he heard that now familiar, uncouth sound these past days?

Now standing, he licked the hand of his master, who had resigned himself to the tired struggle of rising to his feet. The gentle response came as the young Duke tenderly stroked the furry head. Together they slowly followed the broad figure before them.

What this time?

* * *

'You are a child, Josephine. Go away, you don't understand public duties.'

Napoleon was flushed with anger. This was becoming quite

intolerable. An endless succession of people pleading for clemency for the Duc d'Enghien. Again and again they kept approaching him — even such people as Madame Rémusat! What sort of spell did the Bourbon name exert on these people?

'But darling, you know now that the documents have been falsified. Everyone knows there was no conspiracy between Demouriez and the Duke, that indeed he knew nothing at all about the plot by Georges and Pichegru...' Pleadingly, Josephine looked at her husband, wringing her hands in anguish. 'He..he was just living peacefully at Ettenheim...'

'*Peacefully?*'

Napoleon roared his interruption, his face puce with anger. Rounding on the shrinking figure of his wife, he tried to compose himself.

'The man is in the pay of the English, Madame. I am assailed from all sides by conspirators who are in the pay of the English, Madame. They raise up all manner of enemies against me for the "Bourbon cause"...' His tone was terse, almost arrogant. 'I am threatened with air guns; with infernal machines; with deadly stratagems of every kind, Madame. No Bourbon lives "peacefully"...'

He paused, catching his breath after his bitter speech. Looking into her eyes, he suddenly softened. Moving slightly towards her, he smiled appealingly. 'My dear, if he goes unpunished, factions will thrive again, and I shall have to persecute, deport and condemn unceasingly...' He paused. '...The House of Bourbon must learn...'

Josephine's eyes swam with tears as she looked into the face of her husband, seeing no compromise. She was engulfed in a dull sense of foreboding. She knew that no one could change his mind. She knew, too, that things would never be the same again...

Searching the face she loved so much, she had a strange sensation that she was seeing the face of the man she had married — the pale, handsome conqueror of Italy — perhaps for the last time...

Dropping her head, defeated, she whispered, 'It's late, Bonaparte darling. I'm going to bed.'

Napoleon nodded. Already he had turned away towards the

fire. Already, she thought, he had forgotten her, and her plea…

But he had not forgotten. As he heard his study door close behind her, he sank into his chair, staring despairingly into the orange flames of the fire. His head throbbed with the echoes of the pleas for the life of the Duke that he had heard these past few days:

'The Royal houses of Europe will never forget…'
'He's buried in the bowels of Vincennes, a Bourbon prince…'
'Remember the bloody killing of Louis Capet…'
'…The Bastille…'
'He's innocent…'
'…It will recall the horrors of the Revolution…'
'He's innocent…'
'…don't do it…'
'He's innocent…'
'*Innocent…*'

The turbulent echoes churned in his throbbing head. Josephine, Joseph, his mother; Madame Remusat; Pauline, Hortense – even Désirée… The different sounds of their voices seemed to strike a ghastly cacophony in his head, he could somehow feel them all shouting at him unmercifully, refusing to understand his point of view; indeed his obligation to France. He had to defend himself. He felt as though he was shouting his protestation back at their insensitive condemnations. He *was* the French Revolution – the embodiment of the Statutes thereof. He must defend France from the English plot to restore the Bourbon dynasty, only for their own ends. He must…

He dragged his hand across his brow. He felt as though a terrible weight was bearing down on him. As his head tilted, his eye fell on the document that lay on the floor near to his chair.

'*My name, station, my mode of thought, and the horror of my situation inspire me with hope that he will not refuse my request…*'

The words stared up at him in the flickering light of moving flames from the fireplace. It was the Duc d'Enghien's request for an audience with the First Consul. He had refused.

And even now, he knew, somewhere in the Castle of Vincennes, the military tribunal was performing the court martial against the young Duke. On his orders.

He felt a sudden convulsion of pain. What else could he do? What else...?

Talleyrand agreed with him, at least...

He rose and walked to his desk. There was the document he must sign to command the punishment for the inevitable outcome of d'Enghien's trial for treason. Numbly he stared at it, unable to move. It was said he was a handsome young fellow, this Duc d'Enghien. A true Condé...

A knock on the door invaded Napoleon's tortured thoughts. Mechanically bidding entry, he silently stared at the respectfully bowing soldier.

'Sir...' The soldier hesitated, he had made his request again and again these past hours. 'Sir...they await your orders – they won't...'

'Yes...yes.' Napoleon waved a tired gesture of irritated dismissal. 'You must wait...'

As the soldier left once more, he returned to the fireplace. This was the moment, then...

As he resumed his stare into the orange furnace he fancied he could hear the sound of 'La Marseillaise'. How often had he heard the voices of Frenchmen unite thunderously in that great anthem of Liberty? He had given them the self-respect to sing those honourable words with dignity, proudly articulating the Glory of France. Not long ago he had visited the Military Academy at Brienne where he had been schooled. He had heard the treble voices of the small boys raised in uninhibited passion as they sang that hope of their Future. That Future was his charge. No Bourbon would ever challenge that. Never...

* * *

'You are aware of article two of the law of October, 1791?'

The repeated monotony of the questions was inducing a dull response from the severely fatigued Duc d'Enghien. Wearily he nodded yet again, looking at the silky ears of his faithful dog, as ever by his side. He supposed that this was how so many of his relatives had felt not long ago at the 'Revolutionary Trials'. It was a fruitless endeavour to argue or try to reason with these people. Their minds were made up. They were simply going around in circles.

'What did you say?'

The savage shout from the officer in charge of the Tribunal momentarily jerked his wandering thoughts. He looked defiantly at the row of seven colonels. He smiled to himself, a sham attempt at legitimising this farcical 'trial'. They knew full well he was innocent of this charge.

'I said that I do.'

His reddened eyes, ringed with the dark evidence of sleeplessness, looked steadily into the soldier's glare across the tops of flickering candles.

There was a sudden uneasiness amongst the officers, and momentarily there was an awkward silence. Recovering from his discomfort in the face of such proud dignity from the beautiful young man, the soldier gruffly continued, 'Any conspiracy aimed at disturbing the State by civil war will be punishable by death...do you understand? It is a treasonous crime for any Frenchman to take up arms again France, d'Enghien...'

'Yes, sir. We have been through all this before, I believe.'

The steely politeness of the Duke's interruption stunned the soldier into silence. Dumbfounded, the members of the tribunal commission stared at the stately young aristocrat before them.

'Sirs, I have answered your questions. Repeatedly. You know my reasons for living in Baden – you are aware of my ignorance of any conspiracy by Georges Caduodal and General Pichegru against the First Consul. You have refused my request to see the First Consul himself, that I may protest my innocence to him in person. However, to you I give my word, as a Bourbon: I am innocent of this charge.'

He paused, gently stroking the head of his dog, looking quietly at the soldiers before him. One of the soldiers cleared his throat, uneasily looking at the man seated next to him. One or two fidgeted nervously. All were aware that the Duke's words were true.

'It is past midnight, gentlemen. Surely…'

The exhausted Duke's plea was interrupted by the sudden entrance of General Savary, bursting into the room carrying a white sheet of paper. Striding to the officer in charge, he demanded to see what they had been doing. Glancing quickly at the papers on the desk, he cast a look at the young man seated across the small room, his faithful dog tensed beside him.

Returning his attention to the desk, Savary shuffled through the papers, without close attention.

'Very well, gentlemen. Thank you.'

Arrogantly, Savary dismissed the startled officers, silencing the beginnings of a protest from the chief officer by shouting an order to his adjutant who was standing at the door.

'Summon Harel. Quickly.'

Snatching a pen from the officer in charge of the tribunal, he scribbled his signature on a piece of paper, and as another officer entered the room, beckoned impatiently.

Like the officers of the commission, the Duke had been startled by the unexpected eruption of Savary's presence. But as he watched the succeeding actions of the General, he felt a sinking feeling of sick realisation in the pit of his stomach, inducing a numb acceptance of that which he had feared. Now, as a small guard of armed soldiers marched into the room, directed to escort him, he knew what lay in store…

* * *

The forbidding walls of the Castle of Vincennes stretched above him, looming into the clear sky beyond. How incongruously this hideous monstrosity of man-made structure contrasted with the celestial beauty of the glistening firmament! The stars shone so clearly that he felt almost as though he could touch them were he to stretch his hand into the crisp night. The moon, full and white, seemed to hang like a comforting friend high above, casting its silver light on the Duke's upturned face, illuminating his golden hair.

Suddenly, he felt a great surge of relief, almost of joy. It would soon be over. For a Bourbon, danger was the post of Honour. He trusted that he had not deserted that post, however brief his tenure of defence had been.

The frightened whimper of his dog suddenly cut through his romantic delirium. Comfortingly, he put his hand on its head, imbuing him with a courage he now felt, and which had been upheld by the fortitude and affection of this faithful four-legged friend. Fleetingly he thought of his household – faithful too – now happily released from detention and returned to Ettenheim – safe. He thought of his father, his grandfather… Charlotte…

'Are you ready, sir?'

The halting enquiry of a soldier, clearly ill at ease, interrupted his thoughts as he pulled at the small finger on his left hand.

He and his dog had been marched through the disused moat of the castle. They had stopped near a shallow-dug hole, and the Duke had been asked to stand near the wall. As his gaze passed over the grave, he felt a dull thud of momentary fear. But now, as he handed his ring to the soldier, the fear passed. Returning his hands to the quivering animal's head, he smiled quietly at the soldier. 'Could you give it to the Princess de Rohan-Rochefort…'

The soldier swallowed as he took the ring, admiring the composure of this young man whom he knew to be innocent. 'Of course, sir.' The soldier paused uneasily. 'W-would you like a blindfold, sir?'

The Duke looked across the narrow space of the moat. Seven soldiers with guns were positioned, standing to attention awaiting their orders.

Increasing his comforting pressure on the large animal beside him, the Duke shook his head. 'No thank you. Let us get on with it.'

Raising his head once more to the welcoming moon, the Duke felt his animal friend commune with him as they tensely braced themselves in noble dignity.

The silence of the night was shattered by the burst of gunfire. And as it lapsed again into silence the crumpled remains of the Duc d'Enghien lay still in the smoke, entwined within the limp embrace of his faithful animal friend.

* * *

The hiss of dying embers was the only sound in Napoleon's hot study. A sudden wave of cold sweat seemed to overtake him, inducing a violent shiver. He buried his head in his hands. Beads of perspiration glistened from beneath his fingertips on his broad brow. Now as the sticky sensation was succeeded by a wave of nausea, Napoleon dragged his hands down over his face, pulling his eyes open in a wide stare of terror.

He felt alone. Terribly alone. He knew that it was over. But now he wondered what he had done…

The red glow from the fire enveloped his face, heightening his already deep flush. As he stared into the smouldering embers he felt a rising fear deep within him. He couldn't define it, for it was of a haunting, ephemeral quality.

And now, as the burning ashes hissed their dying protest, he seemed to see the face of a Condé. The golden ghost of the Duc d'Enghien appeared to rise before him out of the smokeless embers, smiling serenely. He blinked frantically, but still he could see the steady smile of the blonde Bourbon.

Suddenly, he felt gripped by an irrational fear. He would never rid himself of the sight of that face. He knew that it would forever haunt him. He had never experienced such a feeling of paralysis before. He felt helpless. And in his panic he felt that old feeling of chilling isolation creeping in to mingle with his fear.

Did nobody understand him? He had to…

The face smiled on at him from the shrinking ashes. He fell back into his chair, utterly exhausted, the conflict in his mind reaching a horrendous climax that was beyond the capacity of tolerance.

Unable to resist the pressure of his raging internal emotions, he seemed, unaccountably, to lose his physical strength. Submitting to the pressure of struggle, his mind went blank. He was in black oblivion. But as he slipped into the temporary solace of that enveloping refuge, he knew that when he woke from it, his life would have changed entirely. Nothing could ever be the same again...

Chapter XI

He had been unusually silent and thoughtful during our journey back to the Tuileries from St Cloud. Perhaps he had been thinking of that other coach journey almost five years before when he had passed this same route on his way to begin the fulfilment of his destiny.

Following those extraordinary events of Brumaire, I had told a friend that if Napoleon Bonaparte lasted a year as First Consul, he would have gone far. Now, five years later, with a majority of three and a half million votes, with only two and a half thousand against, the young Corsican General had surprised – even myself.

France had made him Emperor!

The execution of the Duc d'Enghien had, in my view, been worse than a crime. It had been a political blunder.

For my own part I could not see what all the fuss had been about, frankly. The fellow had clearly been involved in some sort of conspiracy to overthrow the Republic, even if it had transpired that he was innocent of the particular one of which he had been accused, which was perhaps a little unfortunate. When consulted at the time about the matter, I had agreed with Bonaparte that some severe demonstration of warning must be indicated to the Royalists, indeed to all factional agitators. France was on a course of recovery, expertly and brilliantly guided by its First Consul. I had felt, as always, that my first loyalty was to that which would ever be my life's dedication: France.

But the most extraordinary outcry had followed the unfortunate mistake of executing the young Duke. The Royal houses of

Europe had seen it as a personal affront. Indeed, Tsar Alexander of Russia had put his court into mourning for a week. Moreover, the man had had the temerity to 'demand an explanation' for 'such an act'. With some irritation I had replied that we in France had not enquired of the events surrounding the assassination of his father, Tsar Paul. Since it was widely believed that he himself had been the architect of that particular episode, the somewhat caustic nature of my response to his arrogant 'demand' succeeded in silencing further expressions of outrage, from that quarter at least.

However, the rippling repercussions of the international reactions to the execution continued, and I began to feel that the final consequences of this action would not be met for some time. Moreover, I experienced an uneasy sense of inevitability of what those repercussions would become.

Amongst the people of France, however, the incident had induced a very different reaction. The primitive magic of the Bourbon name had lost its spell for those who had lived the nightmare of a decade of Revolution. The memory of those bloody years, which they wanted to consign to oblivion, had become dulled by the brilliant years of the Consulate. The spectre of past bitterness, which the masses had believed to be receding with the annals of history, was yet too immediate for them to feel unthreatened. Thus the vulnerability of Napoleon Bonaparte became a cause of deep concern for the people. Something would have to be done to introduce the principle of heredity, that the achievement of the First Consul might be preserved – and that the activation of conspirators against him might be deterred.

The Senate suggested the changes in the constitution, and following a series of consultations with Napoleon it was moved that a monarchy by the Will of the People should be created, very different from the monarchy of divine right. Overwhelmingly, the people had exulted '*Yes!*'

Napoleon Bonaparte was now Emperor of the French Republic. Thus it was that Napoleon's blackest deed had resulted in his ascension to the pinnacle of his success.

I had watched his face as he had received the Senatus Consultum. He had been moved. Deeply moved. Yet once more I was struck by that odd look of detachment, and afterwards by the strange absence of delight or animation. For a man who was capable of displaying so much enthusiasm and passion, it – once again – seemed such an odd contradiction. Each rung of his ascent he had accepted with the composure of confirmed expectation. Yet every idea that had built his edifice of power he had helped with the wholehearted thrust of his vigorous, towering imagination, driven by an uninhibited joy in his dedication to their realisation.

He was a strange man. An enigma. To me he was a man composed of weakness, as well as of supreme strength; a man of consummate courage, yet oddly displaying occasional moral cowardice. He was a man who knew the dizzy euphoria of success and adulation. Yet too, he was a man who knew the bitter anguish of despair. He was a man who was somehow – and increasingly – always alone.

He was a genius.

* * *

His appearance had recently begun to change. Now, seated with him by the pleasant fire in his study, I had a chance to observe him closely as he studied some papers I had given him outlining the procedures required for the creation of an Imperial hierarchy to protect the sovereign. He was now almost thirty-five, yet he looked a little older. The transformation from the thin, long-haired, handsome romantic military hero into this almost solemn figure of maturity had been quite sudden. The gaunt features now found their striking sculpture swelled by the beginnings of a puffy, sallow complexion. And the untidy locks of dark hair that had so appealingly framed the boyish face were now clipped into short, meticulous order.

So too had his girth undergone a little expansion, and the new style of his clothes seemed to accentuate the corpulent inclinations of his slowly thickening physique. The grey eyes, however, remained the same, though they too had perhaps lost something of their shining lustre. Behind their sharp, intelligent alertness there lurked some fleeting shadow of melancholy, which, though too elusive and infrequent to actually discern, was nonetheless, on occasion, dimly apparent.

It had struck me that this change, which had inevitably begun by the natural processes of time's ageing, had been accelerated in these past weeks since the execution of the Duc d'Enghien.

The evidence of his remorse during the days that followed the execution, when he had remained in seclusion at Malmaison, refusing to see anyone, had been only too evident when he had appeared quite unexpectedly at a sitting of the Council of State. Pale and haggard, he had defended his action, and at the same time justified his reasons.

And afterwards, when we had been alone, he had turned his tired grey gaze upon me and said, 'Remember, my dear Talleyrand, that a man, a true man, never hates. His rages and bad moods never last beyond the moment like small shocks. A man made for public life and authority never takes account of personalities; he only takes account of things, of their weight, and their consequences. A statesman's heart must be in his head…'

I had understood then how deeply wounded he had been by the storm of critical reaction that had resulted from the decision that he believed had been necessary – indeed imperative – for France. The international demonstrations of outrage had shocked him due mainly to his feeling that he had been misunderstood with regard to his motives, and that the Royal houses of Europe had apparently believed that it was a direct attack on the Bourbon Dynasty.

Now, on this warm spring evening, in the pleasant comfort of his study in the Tuileries, I felt a twinge of apprehension as he slowly raised his grey eyes from the papers he had been studying. His smile was warm and friendly, but somehow it lacked the filial affection that I was accustomed to from him. Without comment regarding the documents, he silently rose from his chair.

'I must show you the designs for the emblems I have chosen...'

His simple statement as he approached his desk surprised me. His own preparation for the assumption of Imperial status had clearly been well advanced.

One of the functions of diplomacy is often to subtly manipulate situations in order to temper the ambitions of one's masters. Moderating Napoleon's zeal had long been my endeavour during the Consulate years. Indeed, it had often been a point of much humorous debate between us, and the First Consul had found a source of teasing amusement in my varying manoeuvres employed to restrain his often excessive enthusiasm. The question of Napoleon's personal ambition had never really been a preoccupation for me; I had always seen his dedication to France as his undoubtedly overriding characteristic, and whilst he had always been possessed of a profound awareness of his own individuality, as well as an intellectual self-confidence, I had never been especially aware of any overwhelming desires in his nature to subjugate the will of others to his own — excepting in its necessary context as a military commander.

His family, of course, were constantly locked in petty squabbles about position and relative status to their famous brother. And indeed, most of us highly placed individuals within the government — not least myself — had benefited profitably from the material rewards of power. But for Napoleon, somehow, these mere mundane facets of success had seemed to mean little. Indeed, he had always shunned the advantages of his position, retaining an intellectual detachment that approached introversion and a preferment of books to people.

Latterly, however, some slight change had been taking place. I believe, though, that the shift in his attitude — as yet barely perceptible — resulted from a defensive mode of thinking. He had absorbed the early slights to his dignity with apparent disdain, following initial outbursts of anger. However, the recent d'Enghien affair had somehow penetrated hitherto unknown depths in the man's sensitivities, and he had acquired a mask of self-protection, which reflected an approaching pugnacity.

I recognised the unmistakable hand of David, that able chronicler of first the Revolution, and latterly the Consulate. Now his exquisite talents were already recording the beginnings of yet another era.

'This is to be the emblem of the Empire.'

Napoleon thrust the powerful image of the eagle before me. For a moment he stared thoughtfully at the other piece of paper still in his hand. Then, with an almost rueful expression, he hesitatingly pushed the other drawing before me, turning away immediately towards his desk once more with a perfunctory 'The personal emblem.'

Awkwardly he indicated the title of the artistic representation on the page I now found myself holding. He busied himself with some papers on his desk, apparently disguising some odd embarrassment.

It crossed my mind, as I looked down at the gold bee so finely drawn by David, following painstaking research, that Napoleon was clearly a little ill at ease with the requirements of the assumption of his new title. Yet I knew it was not from any reluctance of intellectual aspiration, or fear of the task.

'It's a copy of the metal bees they found in Chilpéric's tomb…' His explanation for his choice of personal emblem filtered through my thoughts.

And suddenly I understood.

Chilpéric had been a sixth century pre-Capetian King of the Franks. Napoleon badly wanted to ally himself to the past, to the roots of French Monarchy. He craved legitimacy, and the respect of mutual equality from other reigning sovereigns. That was why he was going to such lengths to create a respectable and traditional influence for the foundations of his Empire. Yet there was something deeper too: to his awkwardness; to his mild embarrassment.

And at that moment I knew what it was. Napoleon had been drawn into competition. Unwillingly he had found himself having to compete with not only the Bourbons, but with the other Royal Houses in Europe. Strangely enough, Napoleon Bonaparte was not a man who was 'competitive' in the sense that the term is broadly comprehended. If he felt a need to compete, then it was with his own ideas, and his own conception of challenge. His belief in himself, his destiny, and his own vision was such that he recognised no worthy contest to that which he believed was supremely important, and moreover only partially comprehended by all others involved in his cause – himself alone understanding the entirety of that vision. That others sought to induce him into direct competition he found not only irritating, but contemptible; he was disgusted that they could imagine that his fine thoughts could be thus reduced to such petty vanities. The fact that his undisguised disregard for the importance of the ideas of others could be construed as arrogant entirely escaped him, for he was wholly absorbed in his own world, the knowledge of his own intellectual superiority expecting others to do his bidding without question.

Competition, quite simply, did not occur to Napoleon Bonaparte, for he recognised no challenger.

And thus he found himself ill at ease, drawn into a situation that he neither understood, nor liked. The natural nobility of his mind and spirit had been deeply wounded by the aristocratic nobility's rejection of the social reality. And now he found himself striving to reconcile his naturally abstractionist nature with the requirements of that very reality. Napoleon knew how to compete with an idea, but he was groping with the unknown in this new situation.

As I pondered this realisation, I felt an uneasy presentiment. Such frustrations in a man containing extreme passions could lead to disaster and the manifestations of those frustrations into something very dangerous.

'General Bernadotte, sire, is waiting outside.'

I felt a start of surprise at the announcement from the doorway that suddenly cut through my thoughts. I had not been told that Bernadotte was expected, and had been under the impression that this discussion about the ceremonial procedures to initiate the formation of the Empire was to be between the young Emperor and myself.

Struggling to pull my wretched limb into submission that I might rise, I moved to absent myself from what might be a private meeting. Momentarily a flash of the young Bonaparte animated the stern young man as he smiled that boyish grin of old, affectionately amused at my ineffectual attempts to elicit a disciplined response from my stubborn leg.

'Stay where you are, Talleyrand my dear.' The deep tones were sympathetically warm.

For a moment he looked oddly vulnerable. 'Later I shall be receiving all my Marshals – but I gather from Madame Bernadotte that the General has been strongly opposed to the recent proposals of the Senate, and the decision to create an Empire status for France…' He paused, his face tense and apprehensive, his words almost a monologue, his voice low and barely audible, oblivious now of me or any company. 'I must be sure of Bernadotte…' He finished with a tentative expression of determination, his chin jutting forward as he nodded at his Secretary, inviting the entry of the waiting soldier.

Bernadotte's tall frame seemed to loom into the room, his dark silhouette fleetingly darkening the doorway with what seemed an ominous moment of suspended animation. Napoleon was motionless, standing very straight and taut in front of the fireplace, his hands clasped behind his back, his legs slightly apart. Without flickering his eyes fixed on the advancing General, remaining expressionless as the tall man bowed low with almost comic exaggeration. Something that I had already become aware of, and that I was to notice increasingly as the subsequent days unfolded, was that if Napoleon himself had changed – and that as yet but slightly – certainly everyone else had too. The etiquette and ceremonial involved in addressing an Emperor were quite distinct from those required for a mere First Consul, and I found much amusement in observing the often absurd displays of servility from the newly grown ranks of sycophants that fawn with sickening numbers around any Sovereign, most often composed of those who have most vigorously intrigued in opposition some time past against the very one to whom they now so hypocritically pay homage.

Bernadotte, however, was no sycophant. Indeed, if he appeared exaggerated in his greeting to his Emperor, it was to do with his own peculiarity of nature. In contrast to the young Emperor, his vanity was such that he was constantly in competition with others, ever eager to demonstrate his undoubted gifts of intelligence and personal magnetism, gifts with which, he well knew, he was generously endowed.

Silently, Napoleon watched him, appearing to be collecting his thoughts as he stared at the back of the bowing head.

'How is Madame Bernadotte?'

The formality of Napoleon's pleasant greeting betrayed no hint of that which I knew already: namely, that the Emperor was quite aware of how Madame Bernadotte was. Indeed, that his apprehensions regarding this handsome soldier had directly been raised following exchanges with that charming lady at a time unknown to us all!

'She is well, sire. Very well.'

The dark Gascon flushed slightly. I was not sure why. Napoleon's penetrating gaze remained on the handsome features, his powerful presence dominating the momentary silence, somehow stultifying even the other soldier who was so superior in height.

'You see, Bernadotte, that the question has been decided in my favour...?' The grey eyes remained fixed on the General's bemused face. 'The nation has chosen me, not the Bourbons...' He paused, choosing his words carefully. '...But France needs the cooperation of her children. Will you march forward with me – and with all of our country?'

There was an uneasy silence between the two men. Understandably Bernadotte looked somewhat dumbfounded. I was quite fascinated by this extraordinary deviation from the plans. Later Napoleon would receive the entire newly created Marshalate, of which Bernadotte would be part. Napoleon was according that body the appropriate honour of being the first to be received by the new Emperor in recognition of the debt of gratitude he owed them for his ascent to power. Thus Bernadotte was understandably surprised that he had been summoned on his own before the forthcoming ceremony. However, it was clear that the events on the morning of the coup d'état, when Bernadotte had so dramatically refused to join the other Generals in their support of Bonaparte, still festered in Napoleon's mind, and he did not want to risk a similar debacle on this most important of all the proceedings in his inaugural ceremonies.

Bernadotte's dark complexion was again heightened with a deep flush. Whatever his thoughts about the creation of the Empire – confided only to Lucien, Napoleon's exiled brother – Bernadotte's ambition had clearly disallowed, on this occasion, any possibility of non-participation. The proud Gascon was surprised, no doubt flattered, that Napoleon should consider him to be formidable enough to entreat an 'alliance'.

Clearing his throat, Bernadotte began, his tone betraying a slight nervousness. 'Sire, that which I say to you now, I shall repeat later, when you hand me my Marshal's baton, for the benefit of my brother Marshals…' He paused, looking respectfully and with open admiration at the dominating figure of the smaller man. 'For a long time, sire, I believed that France could not be contented under anything other than a Republican form of Government…' Again he paused briefly. 'You must attribute my conduct toward you during that time, Your Majesty, to the sincerity of that conviction. However, enlightened by experience, I feel much satisfaction in assuring you that my illusions have been dissipated. I beg of you to be persuaded of my eagerness to execute any measures that Your Majesty may prescribe for the good of France…'

Suddenly the man appeared to become confused, his emotional disposition clearly about to transport him into expressions that he had never anticipated uttering to the small man before him now. Abruptly, he ceased his speech, the curtailment of its gathering momentum creating an uneasy hush in the room. The characteristic mask of cold impassivity that Bernadotte employed to disguise his emotional propensity had now assumed its habitual expression as, straightening himself, the soon-to-be Marshal stared past the steady gaze of the Emperor.

The grey eyes betrayed no hint of emotion whatsoever but as the deep voice broke the awkward silence, its warmth indicated that Napoleon was relieved by the acquiescence of the unpredictable General.

'I am aware that your tongue has ever been the faithful interpreter of your heart, Mon Géneral, which renders your avowal which you have had the goodness to express of infinite value to me...' Napoleon's words were spoken softly. '...Only by a thorough union can we hope to complete the glory, tranquillity and prosperity of France...I hope you will henceforth consider me your friend, as well as your Emperor...'

For some reason, into my mind came the memory of the remark made by Napoleon following the attempt on his life with an infernal machine: 'Like Anthony, he would have presented to the people the blood-stained robe of Caesar.'

Now, as I watched the tall General bow once more to his Emperor as he made his proud exit, and as I watched Napoleon's face cloud momentarily at the softly closing door, I saw the true implication of that strange remark.

And now another seemingly involuntary utterance from those now Imperial lips struck further sinister portents into my heart.

'I must have a strong Marshalate...' He was still staring at the closed door as he breathed his thoughts into dim audibility. 'Power...my power is dependent on my glory, and my glory on my victories. My power will fall if I do not base it on still more victories...Conquest made me what I am; conquest alone can keep me there. I must have a strong Marshalate for *that* reason...'

And so already the thirty-five-year-old Emperor was voicing the insecurities of all Empire builders. The insecurities that inevitably led to the destruction of those very ideas held sacred by them. The reason for the selection of the title of 'Emperor' by the Council of State had been due to the fact that the far-flung territories already belonging to France had for some time past been loosely referred to as the 'French Empire'. But was there now taking place in this young man's mind the new intention to expand the existing 'Empire'? Was he taking refuge in that which he knew himself to be supreme – military conquest – in order to avenge his injured pride afflicted so deeply by the insults of the Royal Houses of Europe? Were aggression and exploitation to be the degenerating courses that the greatest genius the world had seen for centuries was going to take?

I found myself recalling some lines from the English Bard: 'The abuse of greatness is when it disjoins remorse from power…'

Indeed…

* * *

The crowds had begun to accumulate early in the chill of the crisp December dawn. No heed, however, was paid to the winter temperatures as the humming excitement of anticipation gradually grew, its buzzing sound rising as the density of the milling crowds swelled.

'Just imagine, the Pope himself, all the way from Rome to crown our Emperor…'

The radiant face of the plainly clad woman shone as she deftly emptied the large basket clutched to her ample body, efficiently transferring the contents of bread and rolls on to a growing pile on the street vendor's stall.

'Charlemagne was crowned by the Holy Father too…'

The cheery owner of the stall proudly imparted his knowledge to the excited woman, busily taking money from one of the already pressing customers who were rapidly diminishing the fresh piles of food, even at this early hour.

'Last night the Emperor and Josephine were married in the chapel in the Tuileries…the Pope wouldn't crown them unless they were properly married in the eyes of the church…'

All eyes turned to the woman who had uttered the astonishing news, a buzz of speculation immediately rippling out from the source of this new information.

The pressure of the thronging crowd increased around the little stand, as indeed it did around countless other similar groups of people. As the morning drew on, and the multitudes grew, the circulating stories and chattering excitement rose to a fevered pitch. The route from the Tuileries to Notre Dame Cathedral was thick with humanity, and as the sun climbed higher on this cold bright day, so ascended the spirits of the masses, an atmosphere of carnival breaking out as the moment France had waited for approached.

A surge of excitement reached the waiting crowds at Notre Dame, carried in a wave from those pressed outside the Tuileries. The procession had begun.

'The Pope...!'

A hush fell as the frail little man made his way in dignified state to the cathedral, there to await the arrival of the Emperor.

Napoleon Bonaparte was about to be crowned Emperor of the French.

* * *

Napoleon was standing alone in his dressing room, the faithful Constant temporarily absent from his busy attentions on some hurried last-minute errand. From outside he could hear the distant rise and fall of cheering as the crowds showed their appreciation of each newly appearing section of the long procession of dignitaries in the new Imperial Hierarchy.

He gazed at the reflection staring out at him from the full-length mirror. He was dressed entirely in white silk, and across his shoulders was slung a purple cape, lined with ermine, and embroidered with hundreds of tiny bees in gold thread.

How strange it was, he thought. It was like looking at somebody else. He was experiencing that familiar feeling of detached isolation. The apparent chaos around him, outside and in the adjoining rooms, didn't seem to touch him. He felt as though he was a spectator himself, a spectator from some distant corner of the Universe. He didn't seem able to feel any excitement, any nervousness. He didn't seem able to feel anything... It was all a little like a dream...

Mechanically he responded to a knock on the door. 'Enter.'

His numb gaze moved dispassionately to the opening door, and the man who stood there. Napoleon could recognise the similarity of their features. And it seemed to him today that Joseph-Giuseppe also reminded him of his father. He had been thinking a lot about his father this morning. 'Carlo the Magnificent!'

Yes, it was probably the clothes. Joseph was almost as exquisitely attired as himself. Napoleon smiled as he recalled how dearly his father had loved clothes, and how much care he had taken about his appearance. How he would have appreciated the splendour of these proceedings!

Now Joseph's kind face was smiling at him, timidly entreating him to hasten his preparations. He was fond of Joseph, though he did irritate from time to time. But at least he didn't cause him any trouble and just did as he was bidden. Again the familiar rankle as the reminder of that other brother stabbed at his thoughts. Lucien... How much trouble that young man had caused him. Even today he had cast a shadow over these glorious proceedings by keeping their mother in Rome.

A cloud seemed to pass over Napoleon's face. He was saddened that his mother would not be here to witness this great event. Deeply saddened.

Through the open door he could hear high-pitched giggling, and an occasional burst of petty quarrelling. They were at it again. Even today! He felt a paternal indulgence regarding the perennial squabbles of his brothers and sisters. He knew now that it would never cease, and acceptance of that fact had curbed his former irritation with them. Let them get on with it! Joseph handled them very well, and Napoleon knew that his brother could ultimately keep them all in line. All, that is, excepting...

'It is almost time for the family to proceed – and then...'

Joseph was more than a little agitated, worried by his brother's casual attitude. Napoleon smiled affectionately at him, ignoring his anguished protestations. Putting his arm around Joseph's shoulders, he looked him up and down approvingly, glancing at the reflection of the two handsome Corsican brothers in the mirror.

'If only our father could see us now, Giuseppe...'

Napoleon spoke softly, his tone not attempting to disguise its melancholy sentiment. Joseph wrung his hands involuntarily. Really, Napoleon was so strange. Everybody was in a panic worrying about the ceremony, and here was Napoleon, entirely unconcerned.

'Sire...they are waiting...the Pope...he has been in the church for...' The sudden appearance of an aide at this moment irritated Napoleon's sentimental musings.

'That will do!' He snapped his annoyance at the confused young man whose protesting mouth closed abruptly. 'We shall begin when I'm ready!'

Napoleon's sharp reprimand was received with a blushing retreat. Turning to Constant, who had now returned, Napoleon indicated that he would take his gloves. Then, clapping Joseph on the back, he beamed, 'Well, my dear brother, let us see how the ladies look!'

As they passed into the adjoining room they were met with cries of delight from their sisters and brothers. The girls were beautifully dressed for their privileged tasks of carrying the train of the Empress. Louis and Jerome displayed the elegant attire suitable to their newly ennobled position. Napoleon was pleased, expressing his pleasure by pinching the cheek of his favourite sister Pauline, who exclaimed in protest at this rough inducement of blood to her carefully powdered cheek. Eager with excitement, laughing with nervousness, they began to move towards their great day.

Suddenly a hush fell upon the small crowd. The white figure of the Empress Josephine had appeared suddenly at the door. The impact of the small, slight figure was breathtaking. As always in white, she seemed to sparkle both with her own animation and that of the diamond diadem that encircled her head, setting off the gentle curls of her dark ringlets.

Josephine had been apprehensive about Napoleon becoming Emperor, fearing he would divorce her in order that he might find a woman who could give him an heir. But last night he had demonstrated his love for her when he had married her in a religious ceremony that the Pope might recognise their union. Her fears had been dispelled, and she now felt secure in her position as Napoleon's wife. Today he himself would confer upon her the supreme accolade by crowning her Empress. Josephine's happiness was complete.

Murmurs of appreciation rippled through the admiring Bonapartes as, suddenly hurrying, they prepared to leave. Josephine's eyes were locked with Napoleon's as they gazed at each other across the room. They appeared to be oblivious of everyone else, each absorbed entirely in the other. As she glided slowly into the room, he felt a lump come into his throat, his eyes watering slightly. How he loved this good woman. His lucky talisman...

Taking her hand, he bowed low, his lips lingering on the white fragility of her delicate fingers. 'My dear...how beautiful you are...'

His voice was husky, its deep musicality thick with the surge of his emotions. She looked up at him, her kind smile playing softly about her lips, her wide eyes searching his. Gently she kissed him on the cheek.

For a long moment they stood, silently looking at each other. They were alone now, the Bonapartes having melted through the door to find their respective coaches. Placing the backs of his fingers on her white cheek, he pressed it affectionately, the fine lines of his face creasing into a loving smile. Placing her hand in his she now gently pulled him towards the door.

'Come, Bonaparte...' The simple words breathed softly.

Bonaparte, he thought...

* * *

'Vive l'Empereur! Vive l'Empereur!'

The roar of the Paris crowds filled Napoleon's ears. As he passed through their ranks on his way to Notre Dame, he felt as though he were seeing them for the first time. Men and women of all ages; of all types of appearance. And children... thousands upon thousands of children...

These were the people who had elected him; these were the

people who had entrusted their Future to him. Suddenly he felt very small sitting in the luxurious equipage that, drawn by eight magnificently plumed horses, was taking himself and his wife to their coronation. The close proximity of the cheering multitudes – stretching back through the Paris streets as far as the eye could see and beyond – somehow presented Napoleon with a reality he had not been prepared for. They loved him. All these people, countless millions that he knew stretched across France – they actually loved him. Moreover, through their vociferous demonstration, all these faces, whose homes and occupations, whose lifestyles and problems he would never know – nonetheless, they were exhibiting their feelings for him without reservation. He felt deeply humbled. As his eyes scanned their faces, he felt suddenly alone. For a moment the cheers blended into a raw sound that felt like a rushing wind in his ears. The beaming faces, their mouths moving, seemed to momentarily float in blurred and disembodied slow motion. He felt a little dizzy. How awesome was this task…

He felt the reassuring squeeze of his wife's small hand in his. He looked at her as she graciously smiled and waved at the rippling crowds. Somehow, even though she was not looking at him, she seemed to sense what he was thinking. He felt a sudden sense of calm check the uncustomary swell of rising panic within him. He breathed in deeply. He must carry that precious Trust of the People with care.

Proud Frenchmen! He would make them even more proud…

* * *

The long ermine robe felt heavy on his shoulders. He could feel the warmth of the midday sun pouring through the stained glass window above him, bathing him in a white warm glow. He had heard the strains of music by his favourite composer, Paisello, playing softly in the cathedral from the robing room where he had been donning his coronation robes. Now there was a momentary hush in the vast nave of the sacred building. He could feel each eye of the packed congregation turning towards the anticipated viewing position of his processional route. He looked at the countless backs before him. Distant, in the chancel, he could see the small figures of Josephine, and of the Pope. Each had made their progress along the aisle some time earlier. He could see the motionless blue body of the Marshalate; the still figures of his family and of the Imperial dignitaries.

The opening chords of 'La Marseillaise' rang out. As he moved he could feel the taut respect of the spectators. The moment had arrived.

He felt quite calm as he made his slow progress behind the stately escort of his paladins. Indeed, he took his time to look around, to observe the faces of the privileged guests. How infinitely preferable were the faces in the streets outside! Sourly he thought how any one of these people, he felt sure, would stab him in the back without remorse, were his actions not in their interest. It was sad that human nature made it necessary to construct such hierarchies of 'courtiers'. They were usually composed of weak-willed sycophants.

Now, as he approached the altar, he looked at the Pope. He was an innocuous little man, very concerned about breaches in tradition. And as he kneeled and the Pope began to intone the Mass, Napoleon thought of those other coronations in Rheims Cathedral. Well, he had broken with that Bourbon tradition anyway.

The Mass had finished, and the crown had been handed to the Pope by one of the Marshals. The small frail man was standing on the step above the kneeling Emperor, holding the crown high above his head, waiting for him to bow his head to receive it.

But now Napoleon was staring at the wizened face of the Holy Father. He seemed unable to wrench his eyes away from the wrinkled white skin. Now suddenly he saw a red glow on that face. He thought he saw the glow slowly turn into the smouldering ashes of a fire. He had seen that fire before; he knew those ashes. And even as he knew what it was that would now come before his eyes, the ghostly smile of the Bourbon Duke took its form in front of him.

He shut his eyes, his reason telling him that it was his imagination. And yet he could not rid his vision of that haunting face, smiling its serene, aristocratic smile. A cold fear seemed to grip him inside. Would he never rid himself of this Bourbon ghost? Would the Duc d'Enghien forever dog his conscience…?

He felt his arms stretch up. And even as his hands pulled the crown down upon his head, the nightmare vision vanished. He heard a faint hiss of surprise sweep through the congregation. He smiled to himself. He was no Bourbon to be crowned by some Roman priest.

* * *

'But I do not want you to remove it from your beautiful head just yet, my love. I just want to look at you…'

Napoleon's voice had a liquid lovingness as he gazed across the table through the flickering candles at his wife. Outside the Tuileries windows the rise and fall of the fireworks could be seen, accompanied by the distant sounds of merriment and music. Paris was celebrating the birth of its new Empire.

Napoleon and Josephine were alone. Throughout the sumptuous dinner Josephine had been wearing her crown, the jewels dazzling and sparkling in the moving candlelight, her ecstatic face creating an aura of complete happiness.

Napoleon had been indulging himself in his wife's reflected radiance. Her complete femininity fascinated him; as usual he found it utterly charming and captivating. Tilting her head slightly to one side, she opened her dark eyes wide, an expression of mock pleading flirtatiously entreating him. 'But Your Majesty, it's…'

Napoleon seemed to stiffen, his soft expression vanishing. His voice carried a hint of harshness as he interrupted her. 'Retain your usual term of endearment for me, Josephine…' He paused, softening once more as he smiled at her and finishing gently, 'I am always the same. My kind never changes.'

Josephine, momentarily discomfited by his strange reaction to her innocent address, found herself lost for words. Nervously she reached for her glass of wine, drawing it towards her with a slight tremble. Napoleon, knowing he had barked at her unfairly, now drew his glass towards him also. As he raised it to his lips he suddenly stopped, turning to look out at the fireworks, which flared brilliantly against the crisp, black sky.

'Vive la France...' He stared long and thoughtfully out into the night.

'Vive la France...' Josephine's gentle voice echoed him with hesitation. How strange was this husband of hers, she thought. How very strange...

* * *

But Napoleon Bonaparte, Emperor of the French, was changing, despite his endeavours to assure others that he was not. I had made every effort to prevent the inevitable. Alas, in vain. My vigorous attempts were ill rewarded.

We were at war with England. And now an even greater threat loomed as Napoleon placed yet another crown upon his head: that of Italy. As I stood close to my Emperor in the Cathedral of Milan while he placed the Iron Crown of the Lombard Kings upon his head, I knew that this blatant demonstration of expansionism would alarm the European Monarchs. How I had urged that he return the State of Piedmont to its legitimate sovereign. The Republic that had been created at that time had now been turned into a Kingdom – with Napoleon its King.

Even as the coronation procedures were being enacted, England was courting the outraged European Monarchs as potential allies. The Tsar of Russia seemed unable to forget the murder of his Bourbon cousin, and Austria watched with alarm as the French touched the very borders of Venetia.

By September of 1805, I knew my dream of peace was shattered. War with Austria was inevitable...

Chapter XII

The fresh breezes of the English Channel were blowing briskly in the face of the French Emperor.

English Channel, he thought as he stared at the choppy expanse of water stretching out before him. Typical, was it not, of that nation to name this narrow strait between England and France 'The English Channel'? He felt a surge of seething anger. How he hated the English with their supercilious airs and graces! Who the hell did they think they were? Perfidious Albion! His face twisted in a bitter smile to himself. Well, he was about to teach those haughty bastards a lesson.

Turning his head, he cast his eyes along the sprawling encampment of bivouacs. From his position high on the Boulogne cliff he could see the full extent of the military settlement. 'Settlement!' His face twisted again in a grim contortion. They were getting bored, his Grand Army. Some of them had even started to make gardens around their tents! It just wasn't possible to keep such superb soldiers in permanent training mode. The men wanted action. The plan was to invade England, and take London. They had to get on with it before morale waned altogether. Preparations were complete.

Napoleon knitted his brows together, beginning to pace the grassy bluff, his head bent in deep concentration, hands clasped firmly behind his back. Where in God's name was Villeneuve? This interminable wait was demoralising. The original plan had been that, having assembled the French Fleets in the West Indies and carrying out diversionary tactics, Villeneuve would return with the combined armada to arrive in June at Boulogne, smashing the English blockades. Thereafter the invasion of England would begin.

But what had happened to the man? Napoleon glanced up at the setting summer sun. These interminable days of waiting were becoming intolerable. Moreover, it seemed that English gold had finally persuaded the Tsar to consider joining forces with Austria, and reports had recently indicated that they were in the process of forming a coalition to advance on France. Talleyrand would visit him within the next few days to brief him on that situation. Damn those English...

Today was his birthday; August the fifteenth. He was thirty-six years old. He lifted his eyes once more across the water, golden in the light of the setting sun. He fancied he could see the laughing flash of those sinister white cliffs jealously guarding that elusive land. All at once he experienced a premonition: Villeneuve was not going to arrive. The painstaking preparation of training troops, building flat-bottomed landing craft, careful strategy — even the sale of Louisiana to pay for it — was all going to come to nothing.

He gritted his teeth, savagely dismissing the thought from his mind. Nonsense! It couldn't come to nothing. He had to teach England a lesson, or else they would continue to slowly chip away at the supremacy of France on the European mainland. And then... No, he could not contemplate it. He was tired. It was the strain of all this waiting. These damned sailors, they always blamed winds and tides and all that business. In truth, they just lacked the iron resolve that a soldier must have. How infinitely easier it was to deal with the precise calculations of land warfare. How infinitely preferable. He twitched slightly. How irritating. He almost felt as though he were out of control, not knowing where the fellow was...

He pulled out his timepiece. It was late, and he had promised Berthier he would join them to partake of a glass of wine. He supposed they were honouring his birthday. Lifting his head, he faced down the Channel, narrowing his eyes against the rushing breeze. He felt that odd pang once more. Villeneuve was not going to sail up that stretch of water...

With sudden purpose he signalled to the distantly waiting adjutant who was holding his horse. Unleashing, for a moment, his anger, he wildly dug his heels into the animal, propelling it into a furious gallop. But Marengo was a horse who knew his master well. He hardly needed the painful digs to know that his long-time friend needed the balm of speed to neutralise the racing pulse of his thoughts. The two had been together for many years – luckily for Napoleon, who was not one of the world's natural horsemen. Together they streaked along the dusty road towards the camp.

* * *

'A-August the fifteenth, sire...'

The young soldier was shaking uncontrollably, quaking at the enraged figure before him with its beads of sweat breaking out on the dirty forehead, which was caked with the grime of his hasty journey. The marble grey eyes of the Emperor ruthlessly penetrated the shifting glances of the exhausted soldier. Fleetingly, Napoleon remembered it had been his birthday.

'Are you certain?' The icy demand masked a seething anger within the Emperor.

Swallowing hard, the young man nodded. 'Y-yes, sire, they anchored off Cadiz on...on the...20th...'

Abruptly the Emperor turned away in the thick silence that followed. Walking to the window, Napoleon stared out at the sea, his thoughts in tumult as he stood there, motionless. So, his worst fears had been confirmed. Villeneuve had left his course on the fifteenth, and now the French Fleet was anchored off Cadiz. The surge of his anger was almost overwhelming. And so it was finished. The invasion of England was impossible. He could hardly believe it. After so many months of preparation...

'Sire...' Berthier was anxiously addressing the still figure at the window. 'Er...sire...?'

'What a Navy...What an admiral...What sacrifices for nothing! My hopes are frustrated...'

The roar of anger seemed to erupt from the Emperor like some violent torrent, unleashed by the quiet trigger of Berthier's voice. Rounding on the small group of startled officers in the room, Napoleon flailed his arms in vigorous gesticulations, his eyes blazing as he yelled his bitter reproaches.

Berthier swallowed hard, his anxiety seeming to increase at the sight of the Emperor's fury, his awkward movements indicating that the source of his apprehension was perhaps more than this tirade from his master.

'Sire...' His quiet voice tried again as Napoleon paused for breath after his violent outburst.

Looking at him, the flushed Emperor attempted to contain his anger as he snapped, 'What is it, Berthier?' With an irritated wave of his hand he dismissed the travel-worn officer and two others who were standing nearby.

'Sire, an urgent despatch has just come from Talleyrand...' Berthier extended a sheet of paper towards the Emperor. '...The Austrians are mobilising for war...'

Napoleon snatched the piece of paper. Reading it quickly, his mood seemed to suddenly transform into an eerie calm. There was a long silence. Lowering the paper, he looked out across the expanse of sea once more. Narrowing his eyes he hissed inaudibly, the bitter words spoken with menace: 'I shall return...'

For a long moment he stared. The room was silent. Then, without warning, he savagely scrunched the paper in the palm of his hand as he turned to Berthier. 'Get my horse ready. I must go to Paris. Make haste.'

As Berthier left to carry out Napoleon's orders, the small figure turned for the last time to look out at the sea. Yes, I shall certainly return. His thoughts took the form of an internal snarl.

Finally he turned his back on the hated English Channel. He must turn his thoughts to war with the Austrians. At least he could rely on his Grand Army. On land they were invincible. Depending on those damned sailors was always a waste of time.

Mounting his horse, he wondered if he felt a small sense of relief...

* * *

I admit to having always been attracted to the glamour of Politics. Indeed, most of my life had been spent in the more opulent locations customarily associated with such 'games'. But when one is Foreign Minister of an Empire, and when the Emperor happens also to be commander-in-chief of the army, it is the unhappy misfortune of that Foreign Minister to find himself suffering that most unpleasant form of discomfort: travelling through battlefields in the wake of the Empire's military forces.

Never did I attempt to disguise the fact that I hated such sojourns. My lameness gave me considerable pain when in cramped conditions. Moreover, the nauseating sight and smell of the thousands of dead and wounded that inevitably resulted from battle was an experience I cared little for, inducing as it did a sickening sensation of revulsion at the bestial displays of mankind's more unattractive tendencies. How infinitely more civilised are intellectual methods of diplomacy at achieving agreement between nations.

Nonetheless, it was my duty to travel with Napoleon. And thus travel I did, enduring the cold and discomfort with as much fortitude as I could, assisted by plentiful supplies of wine. To ensure the Peace of Europe was the commitment of my life, and nothing was too great a sacrifice for that cause. And besides, I was growing attached to this Empire of the young genius!

And so once more the dusty roads of Europe shook under the marching soldiers' boots. The Emperor led his men with a feat of unprecedented speed, promising from the outset to repeat the unique display of military genius that he had shown at Marengo. Within a month he had reached the Rhine. The corps commanded by Bernadotte in the north and those of Davout in the south, joined with those of Soult, Lannes and Ney to surprise the Austrian commander, General Mack, who had been successfully fooled by the diversionary tactics of Murat's cavalry in the Black Forest.

Whilst I awaited the outcome of the unpleasant manoeuvres

of war – sensible to the inevitable probability that the courageous Austrians would be forced to surrender – I found myself in the relative peace of Strasbourg, having time, in a happy respite from travel, to draw up a memorandum for the Emperor on my ideas regarding French policy following the forthcoming Austrian capitulation.

Central to my view of balancing power in Europe was the thesis that Austria must be the ally of France. In order, however, to ensure a stable alliance it would be necessary to separate their territories from adjoining. Italy was clearly the stumbling block, and it was my feeling that Austria should renounce her claims on Venice, restoring to that ancient republic its Independence. However, to compensate the Hapsburg Empire for relinquishing its Venetian possession, she should be given eastern territories such as Moldavia, Wallachia, etc, that her power would not be diminished. Indeed, it would be increased, but Venice would stand as a buffer zone between France and Austria to reduce the possibilities of hostilities. Austria, therefore, would be placed to protect western civilisation from the aggression of Russia who, in the event of expansionist inclinations, would find themselves facing Austria on the west, and Great Britain in the oriental east. Thus Russia would find themselves locked into potential conflict with Great Britain; and Europe, protected by Austria and France, would remain in peace. But my endeavours to curb the hot blood of a victorious army – especially when it was composed of soldiers who had won an almost bloodless victory – were in vain.

To be fair to the Emperor, he had at first been sufficiently enamoured of these ideas to call a special meeting of the Council at Munich. But even as the debate began, he had yielded to the temptation of pressing his military advantage against the Austrians, and occupying Vienna. News of Villeneuve's defeat at Trafalgar by the British Navy, fought on the very day of the surrender of General Mack at Ulm, had strengthened Napoleon's resolve to teach the 'English hirelings' a lesson.

I watched my dream of a just peace crushed under the familiar sound of tramping boots. The Grand Army pushed on, singing the glorious spirit of triumphant France along the narrow roads of the wintered Teutonic terrain while they marched to Vienna, and thence to Moravia...

* * *

The Emperor was standing on a low hill, entirely engrossed in the detailed study of the topographical features of the surrounding countryside through his spyglass. Oblivious to the small group of officers who stood nearby beside a camp table strewn with maps and notes, Napoleon's concentration was extraordinary as he took in every minute characteristic of the woods and streams, hills and flat pieces of land that stretched before and around him. In the distance he could see the camps of the enemy Alliance. During the past few days, he had tirelessly carried out endless such reconnaissance missions. Roaming the countryside here between Brunn and Austerlitz, he had watched the bivouacs of those enemy encampments spread, swelling the ranks of their already formidable numbers as more and more divisions arrived.

Napoleon was uneasy. He was concerned about his men. They were hungry and their boots were wearing thin. Before Ulm, feeding had been no problem as they had been able to requisition at will. But as they had progressed east it had not been so easy as the Austrians had cleared the land of everything, and that which they had not wanted they had burned. That fellow Kutusov seemed to have a fixation with burning land. What odd behaviour! He was a slippery individual, this Kutusov; his strange retreat had made the Emperor wonder if he was ever going to stand. Napoleon wanted a confrontation, to have the chance of a decisive victory – and soon. But he hadn't wanted it to be on a ground of their choosing, which could lead to disaster because of their numerical advantage. That was why he had been feeding them with false intelligence, which had led them to believe that he was nervous of their strength –even that he was considering seeking a negotiated peace! Savary was doing a good job of bluffing the enemy. Meanwhile, he had summoned Bernadotte and Davout to bring up their forces in preparation for the coming battle. From the look of the enemy it seemed that time was fast approaching.

Napoleon smiled grimly to himself. They were in for a surprise, these English marionettes. They would soon learn that in war it is not numbers that count, it is the spirit of the army. His smile softened as he thought of his 'Grande Armée'; his 'children'. With what purpose and enthusiasm did they march and fight! Never had the world seen such soldiers as these, animated with the spirit of la Belle France, determined to bring more honour to their noble cause. They were invincible – he knew that, and he was proud.

And yet for all the faith he had in French valour, he had equal faith in his lucky star. He knew his destiny. That was why he could never count positively on victory unless he was in command himself. He thought ruefully of Trafalgar…

But here he was in command – himself. And he was going to win a decisive victory over the Austrian and Russian Alliance. Three Emperors, he thought: himself against the other two!

Once again he smiled grimly, lowering his spyglass and snapping it into its compact collapsible form. He glanced up at the sky. It was cold, very cold, but it was fine, and this weather would probably hold over the next few days.

Slowly, still deeply concentrating on everything he had been looking at, he walked to the table, surrounded by the silent group of officers. Studying the map on the table, he moved his fingers here and there, a deep frown knitting his brows together. The sound of hastily approaching hoof-beats broke the silence of the small group, though Napoleon appeared not to notice.

'Sire!' The breathless young officer jumped off his horse before it had halted. 'Sire! Marshal Bernadotte has arrived!'

The Emperor continued staring down at the map, his hand now lifting a pin. 'Thank you.' His perfunctory answer was accompanied by a fleeting smile at the young man.

So Bernadotte had Corps I in position. Good. Suddenly he stabbed a pin into the map. 'Here! Austerlitz!'

Looking up, he glanced round at the expectant faces of his

men. Turning away from the table, he looked down at the plain below them and at the small village of Austerlitz in the distance. Then, with a wide sweep of his arm, indicating the direction of his gaze, he addressed his officers.

'Gentlemen – examine this ground carefully; it is going to be a battlefield. You will have a part to play on it…'

Silently they all looked at the beauty of the peaceful winter landscape. In only a few hours this rural haven would be transformed into a burning inferno, a hell on earth…

* * *

The grey-coated figure of the Emperor Napoleon was moving slowly through the bivouacs of his Grande Armée, accompanied by a small group of officers. There was an icy chill in the breeze on this exposed part of the encampment, and the light was already growing dim with the shades of approaching night, even though it was yet early afternoon on this first day of December. But nobody seemed to notice the bitter elements as, in the hiving activity amongst the orange fires, each soldier was fully occupied in his own particular part of the busy preparations for battle.

As the Emperor passed through them, he observed with satisfaction the quiet professionalism of his men as they deftly performed their tasks. His nostrils were filled with the familiar aromas of camp cooking. He had always been amazed at the ingenuity with which these soldiers concocted meals of an inviting quality under the most adverse conditions, and with only the diverse ingredients of their scavenging endeavours. To him it was a reflection of the improvisational talents of the typical French soldier; those talents that manifested themselves so well in their fighting spirit. How he admired these men.

He glanced about him. He could see men brushing horses, cleaning muskets, hauling wood, building fires; some talking and laughing, others quietly performing their tasks, engrossed in their own thoughts. All were united in spirit and cause.

Fleetingly he flicked his gaze across the darkness of the empty plains to the distant spots of intermittent fires. These were the bivouacs of the enemy encampment, sprawling into the horizon. One thing was for sure – unity was not an atmosphere that prevailed in that camp! He had heard reliable reports of considerable disagreements between the Russian and Austrian commanders. Moreover, the soldiers themselves had distinctly incompatible views of war, and there had been much quarrelling amongst the rank and file. Napoleon smiled to himself sourly. Well, tomorrow they would be good and properly beaten, and what was left of them could go back to their own respective countries – for good!

What arrogance from the Russian Tsar, who had sent a spokesman to demand that France should 'give up all Italy at once'! Even more laughable that he should further threaten that if it was to be war, then France would be forced to give up Belgium, Piédmont, and Savoy... How ridiculous! They couldn't even get us out of Vienna! he thought. Still, at least it meant that the ruse was working, and they really believed the French to be loath to fight. All the same, Napoleon had found it difficult to control his temper with the haughty Russian emissary. It was commonly rumoured that the Tsar was unable to forget the affair of the Duc d'Enghien. Really! How delicate were the sensibilities of these European 'monarchs'!

Involuntarily, he shrugged to himself, dismissing the prick to his pride that that episode provoked as he recalled the outrage that had been expressed throughout Europe. He had heard that they called him 'the Corsican usurper'. A warm flush spread up from his neck. How dare they? Well, he would show them...

Forcing the unpleasant thoughts of the European monarchs out of his mind, he approached a group of soldiers busily occupied around a bivouac fire. As the small figure in the grey coat and black bicorn hat approached, the soldiers hastened to their feet, bowing their greeting to their Emperor with undisguised adoration.

As he approached, Napoleon had leaned towards his aide, enquiring about the names and any other personal information regarding these particular men. He liked the soldiers to feel that he personally knew each of them, and that he was aware of and interested in everything they did.

Passing some comments about their cooking to responsive raucous laughter, Napoleon now looked warmly into the weather-beaten face of a particular man.

'Ah! Girot! I hear your wife has borne another son for La Belle France? Congratulations, man!'

The rugged soldier was overcome with delight and confusion. With a deep flush of embarrassment, he took in the powerful presence of his Emperor, momentarily speechless at the astonishing fact that this great man not only knew him by name, but was aware of his domestic situation back home in France. Napoleon's warm and sincere smile enveloped him as, stammering, he finally replied, 'Th-thank you, sire…I-I am honoured…my wife will be…'

Napoleon laughed suddenly, boyishly, his face alight with a youthful beam of delight. Clapping the confused man on the back he kindly relieved him of his perplexity. 'I like to hear of the birth of new recruits for the Grande Armée!'

As all the men laughed, Napoleon moved to the next group of soldiers. His presence brought an atmosphere of charged emotion and high spirits to the mesmerised men. The Grand Army loved their Emperor. To them he was like some supernatural being who had given a meaning to their lives following the demoralising disarray of the Revolutionary years. He had some intangible magic that gave them a sense of immortality. Willingly would each man in the army die for this diminutive man in the little black bicorn hat, whose balance of sternness and compassion made them feel secure and content, whatever their condition.

Now, as the Emperor moved on from group to group, exchanging personal words with each one, the spell of his presence bound them in an exultant resolve that they would defeat the enemy on the morrow. And even when, as he expertly inspected the muskets and tasted the gunpowder, severely chastising, with crude eruptions of bad temper, those who had made lax preparation, he nonetheless recovered his humour with a suddenness that rendered the incidents painless, inducing only the response that such negligence would not be repeated to cause further regrettable distress to the benevolent Emperor.

Thus for some hours the Emperor continued his inspection of his troops. By the time he returned to his own bivouac, the soldiers were in an inspired frame of mind as they settled under the clear evening sky to consume their evening repast. Napoleon glanced up at that clear sky – the first stars of the crisp night were already twinkling faintly. Having placed many of the guns himself, and completed most of his dispositions, it remained for him to make out his proclamation for the soldiers. Now, as he strode towards his tent, he could hear occasional shouts echoing through the groups of men nearby.

'Vive l'Empereur!...Vive la France!...Vive l'Empereur!'

In the distance he could hear some soldiers singing 'La Marseillaise'. He smiled to himself.

Vive la France indeed! he thought.

Napoleon was in a relaxed and ebullient mood as he entered the small thatched cottage where the Marshals and Generals were meeting for dinner. Already he seemed to emanate the exuberance of a victor. That sometimes imperious manner that surfaced every now and again these days was entirely absent. In its place, once more, were the boyish enthusiasm and charismatic charm of the conqueror of Italy.

As they sat down to the sumptuous dinner prepared by the Emperor's cooks, the table magnificently adorned with silver candelabra whose flickering light danced on the glinting crystal of the wine glasses, the scene was more appropriate to a dinner party in Paris than a meal on the edge of a battlefield, on the eve of the battle itself.

'Tell me, Junot, news of Paris?'

The Emperor's dazzling smile rested on the face of the trusty General who, though he had served at Napoleon's side for many years with loyal devotion, had nonetheless not been honoured with the Marshal's baton, to his deep disappointment. Now, as the soldier most recently arrived from Paris, the Emperor was graciously inviting Junot's conversation.

'Well, sire, as you know the financial crisis has sent some of the bankers into bankruptcy. Indeed, Monsieur Recamier...'

The expression on Napoleon's face darkened momentarily, his brows drawn in a fleeting frown as he twitched at the earnest General's remarks. He did not wish to be reminded of the domestic crisis in Paris at this moment.

He abruptly cut into Junot's words, his voice sharp. 'I expected you to inform me about lighter matters, sir...'

His pleasant expression as his grey eyes looked steadily into Junot's now uneasy gaze belied the sharpness of his tone, which indicated that he was displeased with the mention of bankers on such a night.

Flushing slightly, Junot swallowed a little as he continued: 'Ah... Well, sire, "Don Giovanni" by Herr Mozart has been a great success. Paris society talks of nothing else...' His confusion was apparent as he blurted out this gross exaggeration. The Emperor's enveloping presence could be overpowering and intimidating without him saying anything at all; a mere stiffening of his body or tightening of a facial muscle was enough.

But the Emperor was in far too good a mood to allow anything to disturb him this evening, and he launched with alacrity into a eulogy about Mozart and music, his animated comments and witty anecdotes about musical experiences inducing much laughter and amusing responses from the relaxed gathering of Marshals.

As the subject of the conversation passed from the appreciation of classicism such as Mozartian composition to a bemused speculation on the recent radical musical expressions of Herr Beethoven – who was said to have been inspired by the very spirit which they themselves personified – Napoleon's grey eyes came to rest on a silent figure seated tall and erect, quietly eating. The man was Jean-Baptiste Bernadotte.

As some ribald exchanges from the wine-loosened tongues of the soldiers filled the small room, accompanied by bursts of laughter, the grey eyes twinkled with mischievous amusement at the tall Marshal.

'But wait, gentlemen! I hear that this composer, Herr Beethoven, is a good friend of my cousin Bernadotte!'

The eyes remained, in steady amusement, fixed on the Gascon, who continued cutting his food without immediate response to the slightly sarcastic tone in the Emperor's silky voice. The laughter and merriment of the other Marshals was temporarily subdued as they sensed that the Emperor was making a purposeful point to the proud Marshal, with whom, they were aware, he had a somewhat ambivalent relationship.

'Indeed, sire...' Bernadotte's cool answer fell upon a sudden silence in the room, accompanied only by the sound of the movements of his knife and fork. '...I have the honour of being acquainted with the Maestro...'

The rest of the Marshals tensed as suddenly all attention was focused on the two men. Napoleon leaned back in his chair, his eyes dancing playfully as he sipped from his wine glass. He paused, glancing round at the other soldiers before returning his grey gaze to Bernadotte.

Pleasantly he continued in a casual tone, apparently addressing everybody, though his eyes remained fixed on the cool Marshal. 'I hear he is a genius! A man inspired by the cause of Liberty...' Napoleon paused, smiling now with a hint of malice.

The soldiers were uneasy now, stealing sidelong glances at each other as the sound of moving cutlery on plates clattered in the heavy silence.

'His music is certainly passionate and full of fire...' continued the Emperor, 'but perhaps a little...undisciplined?' He was grinning, apparently enjoying himself. Bernadotte, however, remained impassive, his attention firmly fixed on his food.

'Yet I have heard that he fails to find a clear grasp of the men who create such Liberty...' Napoleon paused once more, his face taking on a slightly harder expression as he pressed his point home to Bernadotte. '...Indeed, I believe he was with you, my cousin, when he dramatically demonstrated this lack of comprehension...'

Napoleon was still smiling at Bernadotte who had now lifted his head, having finished his meal, and was looking with cold impassivity into the Emperor's relentless smile.

The Marshals were becoming increasingly uncomfortable, knowing Napoleon was referring to the famous incident that had been related throughout Europe, when Herr Beethoven had, upon learning of the declaration of Empire, savagely defaced his newly completed Symphony, 'Eroica', which had been dedicated to Bonaparte, First Consul of France. The musical genius had announced that he had been betrayed by the pretensions of a man who had proved himself to be insincere.

Somebody dropped a spoon, and one or two of the Marshals found their throats to be somewhat dry, endeavouring to clear them with nervous coughs, drowned by vigorous gulps of wine.

Napoleon appeared pleased with himself, and looked expectantly at Bernadotte with good-natured amusement. He enjoyed these little baiting games with Bernadotte. The fellow was so serious!

In the silence that followed Napoleon's provocative remarks, the atmosphere was charged with apprehension, the Marshals fearing that Bernadotte's reply would unleash an eruption of the mercurial Emperor's renowned and volatile temper.

'Perhaps he understands better than you think, sire.' Bernadotte's voice was quiet and brittle as he stared defiantly into the grey eyes of the Emperor. 'Music has an odd way of expressing the subtle changes that we human beings seem destined to go through…'

He paused briefly. All attention was almost breathlessly focused upon him.

'To write a great Symphony he must employ rigorous self-discipline to temper and balance his passions, so that the music may not become overbearing, and therefore assault the sensibilities of the listener.' Once more Bernadotte paused, choosing his words carefully as he steadily returned the Emperor's unblinking stare. 'Perhaps we too should think more deeply about tempering and controlling the passion of war; and the reason for waging war. Maybe then we could achieve a greater balance of contentment amongst individual and neighbouring cultures.'

A chorus of involuntary coughs of embarrassment burst out

amongst the Marshals as they steeled themselves for the expected outburst of rage.

But Napoleon's expression remained unchanged as, still looking at Bernadotte, he completed chewing a mouthful of food uncharacteristically slowly. Taking a leisurely sip of wine, the Emperor looked round at the other Marshals, raising his eyebrows slightly.

'It seems we have a philosopher amongst us, my friends!' His pleasant tones feigned amused surprise. Pausing, he signalled to a footman hovering at the back of the small room. 'More wine for the Marshal that he may shake off his serious preoccupations!'

With exaggerated sincerity, he now addressed the uncomfortable Marshals. 'It is said that Bernadotte's men consider themselves to have the fairest and most just commander in the army… Perhaps his secret is that he conducts concerts of the music of Herr Beethoven?'

As the grey eyes opened wide in pretended wonder at the possibility, a burst of nervous laughter came from the small gathering, quickly diminishing as the Emperor continued with his sarcastic wit.

'Perhaps Corps I is a body of philosophers, not fighting men at all…?'

As the laughter erupted again, Napoleon looked once more at Bernadotte, concluding provocatively, 'Perhaps we could defeat the Russians with music, my dear cousin?'

The loud laughter from the Marshals at the ludicrous suggestion quickly died as Napoleon and Bernadotte remained motionless, their eyes locked in a long, silent stare, the Emperor's hard and challenging, the Marshal's cold and impassive. Both were unsmiling. For a moment the small group around the flickering candelabra seemed poised for a violent outburst from the Emperor.

Then abruptly, Napoleon's fixed stare transformed into a genuine beam of affection. His face creased into a warm expression as he spoke quietly, in deep, kind tones. 'The people of Hanover are well pleased with the fair and just administrative genius of our relative, Marshal Bernadotte. He is an example for all. Such talents are invaluable to the Empire…' He paused, lifting his glass to Bernadotte. 'You have the respect and gratitude of your Emperor – and of France, my dear friend.'

As the affectionate gaze of Napoleon silently acknowledged respect for the proud, still impassive Bernadotte, his fellow Marshals lifted their glasses with a little too much alacrity, the tension seeming to tangibly drain from the room as they realised the moment of danger had passed.

Murat took the opportunity to change the subject as the servants cleared the plates from the first course, and good humour was restored once more as the Emperor was encouraged to speak of the enemy and his plans to drive them into oblivion. Heartily, the soldiers rekindled their camaraderie with the powerful presence of their commander-in-chief. And at the other end of the table, the tall Gascon Marshal bent his head with concentrated interest towards the contents of the plate that had just been put before him.

Smoke filled the small room as the soldiers slipped into a more serious mood, sensing the approaching end to the evening, which would leave each man alone in the night with his thoughts about the morrow. The candles, burning low, cast a golden light on the dark brown liquid of the brandy that now filled their glasses

The Emperor had remained in good humour, happily relating anecdotes from other battles. Suddenly a voice cut through the relaxed hum of conversation.

'Sire, my conscience obliges me to tell you that the army will not do much more. If you lead it further it will obey, but against its will. The enthusiasm it displays tonight is due to the fact that it counts on completing the campaign tomorrow and returning home thereafter.'

Every eye in the room fell upon the face of the speaker of these words – the Emperor's aide, General Mouton. A shocked silence and frozen, appalled expressions greeted the General's insensitive provocation, inevitably destined to induce an angered response from the Emperor.

Napoleon's face hardened into a mask of icy arrogance as his suddenly cold grey eyes bore into the young man's face. Slowly he stood up, viciously throwing his napkin down on the table. In low, menacing tones he bit out his words, his eyes now blazing as he attempted to control his anger.

'The army, Mouton, will follow their Emperor *wherever* he believes necessary, *whenever* he believes necessary – for the glory of France!' He paused, looking round at the other Marshals and aides with cold meaningfulness. 'Even if they must die, what matter? Death is beautiful in the cause of Glory…'

His voice was rising now, and with a passionate outburst he finally roared, '*I AM FRANCE*! Through me, the greatest army the world has ever seen brings glory to the world…'

His voice trailed off as his eyes, slightly glazed with the delirium of his statement, narrowed slightly. The silence was thick with the anxious unease of the Marshals, breathlessly anticipating his next words.

Leaning towards General Mouton, Napoleon hissed through his clenched teeth, his low voice seething with cold anger, 'Never presume, General, to underestimate the spirit of my Children.'

Abruptly, the Emperor turned and strode out of the room as the soldiers clumsily struggled to get to their feet. In silence, they looked at each other following the sudden exit of their commander.

As the gathering broke up and the subdued hum of conversation broke out once more, Marshal Bernadotte silently donned his hat and cloak, and left unobtrusively.

* * *

Anger died in Napoleon as quickly as it grew. Now, as he stepped out into the cold crisp night air, he felt the rage ebb out of him, leaving him with that odd sense of isolation once more. He regretted having allowed himself to be rankled by Mouton. Stupid man. He just didn't know what he was talking about.

It was yet early, and he felt he would like to visit the hospital now, both to see the soldiers already in there, and to ensure that sufficient preparation had been made for the inevitable influx of wounded on the morrow. Momentarily he frowned to himself. The medical facilities were not as good as he would like them to be

As he stood reflecting upon this thought, he was aware of a tall man leaving the cottage behind him, exchanging a goodnight greeting with his two adjutants who were respectfully waiting for his instructions. Turning, he saw the tall figure of Bernadotte move silently and quickly into the night towards the looming silhouettes of the waiting Marshals' carriages. As he caught the shadowy movement of the figure, Napoleon felt a sudden sense of foreboding. What was it about that man? They could be such a formidable alliance together, and yet there seemed always to be some strange barrier between them, put up by Bernadotte.

He smiled to himself, recalling the little game he had played with the serious Marshal earlier. Bernadotte's musical inclinations were well known, and he took seriously his friendship with Herr Beethoven. Still, it was all in jest. After all, he too had a profound respect for music. Of all the Arts, music exerted the most influence on the passions, in his opinion. Indeed, he had always advocated that a legislator should encourage this Art the most. It seemed to him that a piece of moral music, composed by a master, could not fail to affect the listener's feelings, and would have much more influence upon him than a treatise on morals, which convinces only our reason without changing our habits. But then, Napoeon wasn't really very sure that Herr Beethoven's music was especially 'moral'. Perhaps it was a matter of taste. Personally he preferred the melodic composition of Paesiello, or the sound of good martial songs.

Suddenly he thought of Eugènie. How sweetly she had sung when they had been young. It occurred to him that he had not heard her sing for years. No doubt she sang for Bernadotte, he thought with sudden sourness. A surge of possessiveness rose within him.

The sound of a horse whinnying wrenched him from his thoughts. Looking out across the black expanse of plain, he could see the red pinpricks in the darkness that indicated the enemy encampment. Before tomorrow night, he thought, this army will be mine. For a long moment he stared at the vast spread of those bivouac fires. Then, turning abruptly, he signalled to his two adjutants that he would proceed to the field hospital, deciding to walk rather than be transported by carriage, since it was nearby.

Silently he passed through the countless orange bivouac fires. There was an eerie quiet in the crisp night, interrupted only by the crackling of the logs, and the occasional whinnying and stamping of cold horses. The soldiers were mostly lying down, many already asleep. All were entirely engrossed in their own private thoughts. Occasionally, as a soldier recognised the small moving figure, he would attempt to scramble to his feet from the many folds of his makeshift endeavours to ward off the bitter chill of the night. More often than not, the restraining hand of the Emperor would end his difficulty, the kind smile silently acknowledging the soldier's courtesy and urging him to continue his rest.

'Vive l'Empereur!' came the sleepy murmurs of those who drowsily observed the tireless passage of their Commander.

And as he approached the clearing for the field hospital, passing a huddle of veteran Grenadiers not yet asleep as they completed a game they had been playing, the rugged men stood up, smiles animating their battered faces as they looked at their beloved leader of so many campaigns. As he inclined his head towards them with a warm smile, one of the men stood forward, quietly addressing the Emperor.

'Sire, you won't have to take any chances with your person. I promise you in the name of the Grenadiers of the army that you won't have to fight with anything except your eyes and we'll bring you the flags and the guns of the Russian Army to celebrate the anniversary of your coronation tomorrow.'

Napoleon felt a strange prickling sensation behind his eyes; a slight lump came into his throat. Silently, he put his hand on the man's shoulder, uncharacteristically lost for words. As he looked into the leathery face, he felt suddenly humbled. It was men like these that mattered; men like these for whom he worked so hard; and it was because of men like these that he had achieved what he had achieved. He must never let them down.

'Thank you, man.' The gruff reply came in a husky voice, betraying his emotion to the small group of adoring Grenadiers.

Clapping the man on the back, Napoleon moved on hurriedly towards the large tents of the hospital.

The initial sight of the inside of the field hospital always induced a sense of revulsion in Napoleon. Hardened though he was to the horrors of battle, the pathetic sight of suffering men – partially limbless and bandaged with bloodstained linen, unconscious or moaning with uncontrollable pain – whatever their condition, Napoleon found it appalling and somehow degrading. His own preference was to die in battle rather than face the torture of these emaciated victims of war. To be killed in battle was a glorious death; but to survive to face this prolonged defeat of the human condition was less than glorious.

Doctors and their assistants hurried from their tasks towards the unexpected figure of the Emperor, Napoleon glanced around the neat rows of supine, suffering men. His stomach heaved at the faint smell of congealed blood. His efforts to control his sense of revulsion were masked by his crisp demands from the medical administration as to the state of their affairs. After a brief exchange of words with the doctor in charge, and just as the frustrated man was beginning a complaint to the commander-in-chief about inadequate medical supplies, Napoleon's eyes wandered back to the rows of wounded men. And as he cast his gaze along them, he noticed that those who were well enough were struggling to make a bow of acknowledgement to their Emperor by attempting to shift on to their elbows, or however else they could raise themselves.

Touched by their pathetic attempts, Napoleon moved towards them, speaking to each one as he passed through the rows of men. With those most severely injured, whose pain-filled eyes were the only means of expressing their happy recognition of their Emperor, for whom they gladly suffered their pain, Napoleon kneeled down to speak. Tenderly and softly he attempted to ease their suffering.

'Your pain is suffered for the Glory of our Great France...it is an Honour...you have the gratitude of your Emperor...'

And whilst he knew he could give them no physical respite from pain, he nonetheless saw their bloodshot eyes, glinting in the dim light with the tears of their weakened state, assume expressions of unspoken pride and unrestrained adoration as their cracked lips, dumb with pain, accepted the drops of brandy from the cup held to their mouths by the Emperor himself.

Napoleon spent a long time with these men, his earlier sense of revulsion gone as he communed with them in their quiet world of suffering. And as he was leaving, casting a troubled glance backward, a young man, his face torn and a bloodied stump of bandages in the place where a leg had once been, struggled to his elbows.

'Vive l'Empereur!'

The brave shout sounded strangled as it issued from the purple lips in the distorted face. Murmured echoes rang out from around the room. Tomorrow night, thought Napoleon suddenly, these survivors of Ulm would be joined by...

He felt sick. All at once he felt he must leave this place. With a last smile at the suffering soldiers, he put on his hat and left the tent quickly, leaving behind him a renewed sense of struggle and purpose.

* * *

Feeling drained, Napoleon pulled off his hat as an aide began to help him take off his coat. As he sank heavily into his chair, another aide began to pull the boots from his tired legs.

Outside the tent he suddenly heard the clatter of approaching hooves. Immediately alert, despite his exhaustion, he looked up expectantly at the entering soldier.

'Sire...Davout has arrived...'

A sigh of relief escaped the weary Emperor's lips as he silently nodded his smiling thanks and dismissal.

Leaning back in an exhausted slump, he looked at his two aides. 'Ah-h...We are complete...' His tired voice held a note of satisfaction. Softly he mused, as if to himself, 'It has been the finest evening of my life…in a few hours three Emperors will fight…'

He paused in tired reflection. 'The fate of the world may depend upon this day…'

Moving slowly to his camp bed, he lay down. And even before his aide had drawn the green folds of the surrounding hangings, the exhausted Emperor was asleep.

* * *

'Sire! There is heavy musket fire reported in the area of Telnitz!'

The urgent voice of the young officer wrenched Napoleon out of the deep sleep. Instantly he began to pull on his boots. Glancing at a clock, he saw he had slept only a couple of hours. Nonetheless he did not feel tired any more. Hurriedly shrugging on his coat, he rushed out into the darkness, mounting his waiting horse and galloping off into the night.

The freshness of the midnight air was brisk and invigorating. Napoleon felt satisfied with his preparation for the battle as he rode slowly back towards his camp, observing with the acute expertise of his watchful eyes the shifting movements of the enemy's lines to the south. Smiling to himself with satisfaction, aware that their manoeuvre was intended to try to cut off the French lines of communication to Vienna, the Emperor made a mental note to shift emphasis in his own attack to apply maximum pressure to the inevitable weakening of their right centre. Yes, they were behaving as he had hoped and anticipated. The incident of the small skirmish with a patrol of Austrian Hussars had, by waking him earlier than anticipated for his midnight reconnaissance, given him more time.

Issuing an order to an aide to summon Marshal Soult to a conference at once, Napoleon then asked another the time.

'About 3am, sire.'

Napoleon looked across the plain, a slight frown of satisfaction creased his brow. The mist seemed to be gathering…

Entering his tent, he briskly greeted the waiting Marshals, and immediately set about examining the maps, changing slightly some of the orders, and shifting the attack on the Pratzen Heights to the north that it might exploit the weakness of the enemy's right centre. As the meeting came to an end and the soldiers dispersed, Napoleon stretched himself, preparing to snatch a further short sleep.

Walking to the entrance of his tent, he noticed that the mist outside was beginning to thicken considerably, and was fast becoming a dense fog. He walked outside for a moment, looking with a little concern at the enveloping shroud, hoping that it would dissolve early. Whilst the expected fog was part of his plan, he needed it to clear.

'What time is it?' he asked the young guard outside his tent.

'Shortly before 4am, sire,' came the swift reply.

Napoleon glanced around at the fog. Well, he would just have to wait and see. As he turned to re-enter his tent he heard a movement from a group of men nearby, vaguely discernible in their huddled mass in the thick mist.

'C'est l'anniversaire...' The deep voice of the soldier cut through the dense silence of the foggy darkness. 'C'est l'anniversaire...Vive l'Empereur...'

The announcement seemed to ripple from group to group into the distant fields of the approaching foggy dawn.

'Vive l'Empereur...Vive l'Empereur...'

All at once, the strange mist seemed to be animated by the gathering momentum of the intermittent shouts, the rippling quiet echoes from near and far seeming to assume a supernatural mystery, fading up from the shrouded distance.

The Emperor stopped dead in his tracks. So they had remembered the anniversary of the coronation – just as his Grenadiers had earlier. Turning, he looked out at the moving shapes in the fog as they issued their greetings.

Suddenly he felt his face was wet.

* * *

'Soldiers! The Russian Army is presenting itself before you in order to avenge the Austrian Army defeat at Ulm... The positions we occupy are strong, and as they advance to turn my right they will expose their flank to me...'

'Soldiers! I shall direct your battalions myself. I will hold myself from the firing if, with your accustomed bravery, you carry disorder and confusion into the ranks of the enemy. But if victory should for a moment be uncertain, you will see your Emperor expose himself to the first blows...'

'Soldiers ...We must defeat these hirelings of England who are animated by so great a hatred for our nation...'

'Soldiers! This Victory will end the campaign...'

The dawn proclamation from the Emperor rang out to each division across the three mile front.

'Vive l'Empereur!' rang out the frenzied response of the cheering multitudes, 'VIVE L'EMPEREUR!'

And as the sun finally broke through the dense fog, the roar of the French Army rose as they launched themselves with abandoned ferocity into the battle against the Allied armies of the Russians and Austrians.

The Battle of Austerlitz had begun.

* * *

The scene of battle defies description.

For my part I needed no verbal portrait of the grim horrors of war. The vivid picture of smoking artillery, bloodied men, shrieking horses in the fevered pitch of battle was all too imaginable, and the ghastly convulsion of aftermath a reality I had often had the misfortune to witness.

But Austerlitz was an intoxicating victory for the Grand Army of France, and the flowing tide of success for them rapidly induced a form of worship from the soldiers for their Emperor. And as the adulation of the army grew, so too did Napoleon's belief in his own invincibility...

Once more I wrote from my waiting position in Vienna to plead with my Emperor, urging the same policy that I had pressed six weeks before. I pointed out that the Austrian Monarchy was a combination of ill-assorted states, differing from one another in language, manners, religion and constitution. Yet they had one thing in common: the identity of their ruler. Such a power was necessarily weak, but nonetheless an adequate bulwark against the barbarians. Moreover, a necessary one. Now, crushed and humiliated, she required that her conqueror should extend a generous hand to her. By making her an ally, a restoration of confidence could be brought about.

I implored His Majesty to refer once more to the memorandum I had sent him from Strasbourg. I was certain now, following the Battle of the Three Emperors, that it was the best and wisest policy.

But Napoleon would not heed my advice, the momentum of success too pungent, too sweet, to look beyond to the potential consequences. Magnanimity in victory was an alien concept to France's Emperor.

Thus I was instructed to negotiate a treaty at Pressburg. It deprived the Emperor Francis of almost three million of his subjects, and one sixth of his revenue. Such insensitivity and lack of compassion for the defeated enemy disgusted me. The Treaty went against all my instincts.

And when I learned that the Tsar had been seen on the smoking battlefield of Austerlitz amongst his dead and wounded soldiers, seated beneath a tree on the ground, tears of despair streaming down his handsome face – I knew that the humiliation of these two proud Monarchs would bode ill for Europe.

But for now, France was victorious; and Napoleon, Emperor of the French, was the undisputed Master of Europe.

Chapter XIII

The small figure was motionless in the luxurious cushioned interior of the large Imperial carriage. Opposite, a concerned lady-in-waiting looked at the silent silhouette of her mistress, outlined against the Paris streets, its still presence rocked gently by the movement of the stately equipage. How strange it was that the Empress was so quiet these days. Especially odd when Paris was so gay, still in the euphoria of celebration which had begun when the bells had first rung out the news of the great victory at Austerlitz, back at the beginning of December. France had triumphed, and her people had loudly proclaimed their gratitude to the leader they so proudly admired. For weeks now the victory celebrations had not ceased throughout France.

The day after Christmas a treaty had been signed with the defeated Austrians at Pressburg, and the triumphant Emperor had then joined his gracious Empress in Munich for the marriage of his stepson, Prince Eugène, to Princess Auguste, daughter of the King of Bavaria. Subsequently the sovereigns had returned to Paris, stirring even greater revelries in the streets, and glittering official receptions. What possible reason, then, could the Empress have for her withdrawn behaviour, so uncharacteristic of the gay, pleasure-loving Creole?

The young lady-in-waiting looked at the skilfully made-up face of the ageing woman as her large dark eyes stared unseeingly out into the snow-covered Paris streets on this clear winter evening. The girl was suddenly uneasy. Was the Empress aware of something that others were not? The silence deepened as the young woman's thoughts began to race. The sound of the muffled hoof beats on the snow-whitened cobbles struck a strange harmony with the chiming bells. For some reason, she thought, those bells seemed to chime ceaselessly these day; whatever was it for? She looked out at jubilant Parisian bystanders as they recognised the Imperial Arms on the passing carriage, immediately emitting jubilant shouts of 'Vive l'Empereur!'

The young woman experienced a sudden chill as she saw a muscle move in the mask-like face of the Empress, who involuntarily responded with a start as an exultant shout penetrated the dark silence from a fleetingly close proximity. How strange. How very strange. Even this mysterious response from the Empress was odd.

How odd, too, to order her carriage at such an unusual hour. And why inform no one save the driver of her destination? Indeed, thought the young woman, had it not been for her own chance return to Her Majesty's boudoir to inform her of some forgotten triviality, she doubted that anyone would have known of the Empress' intention; much less have accompanied the troubled woman.

Her Majesty had appeared quite disconcerted when, upon re-entering the room after her dismissal, the lady-in-waiting had found the Empress dressed in her hooded sable cloak, prepared to depart through the private passages of the Tuileries. And upon the confused exclamations of surprise and dismay that the Empress was not to be attended by anyone, the young woman had been appeased by an impatient gesture of preoccupied concession to Imperial Etiquette. Josephine indicated that the girl could accompany her, but that it was the Royal wish that *no-one* should know of the outing – not even Madame de Remusat, the Empress' senior lady-in-waiting. And now here they were, sitting in the swiftly moving carriage, their destination still unknown to the bemused lady-in-waiting. It was all very disconcerting.

Now, as they turned from the busy streets of Central Paris into a quiet residential area, the Empress seemed to tense even more. The frown of concern deepened on the young girl's unfurrowed brow. She loved this kind and gracious person who was her mistress, and it hurt her to see the older woman so obviously anxious. She felt helpless, and strangely inadequate, aware that she was unable to comfort the gentle Empress in whatever secret agony she was suffering.

Just then, they passed a small group of young people, each carrying a blazing torch as they huddled into the warmth of their voluminous outer clothing to protect against the chill of the January night. The flickering flames from the torches cast their moving light on to the faces of the merrily singing crowd, and as the carriage passed, the young woman leaned curiously to the window to look at the strange, high-spirited group.

'Your Majesty! They're wearing masks...!'

Her spontaneous utterance, following her initial intake of breath at the bizarre sight, caused her to forget that she must not address the Empress until invited. Realising instantly her breach of etiquette, the girl's hand flew to her mouth, her deep flush hidden by the darkness. A tired smile of indulgence came, for the first time, to the older woman's face as she observed the typical behaviour of youth. Momentarily she was distracted from her melancholy preoccupations.

'Indeed, my dear? Party revellers, no doubt.'

The low, gentle tones of the Empress' slightly accented voice relieved the embarrassment of the young woman, the grace of her famous smile seeming somehow to warm the inside of the carriage.

The melancholy gaze of the Empress lingered for a long moment on the fine features of the young woman before her. She was the daughter of an aristocrat from the 'Ancien Régime'. Napoleon had insisted: all lady-in-waiting attendants to his wife must be of aristocratic families... The Empress sighed deeply,

'Party revellers...'

The whispered repeat of her words was barely audible as the carriage now slowed, and the sound of the horses' hooves struck a different surface. It hadn't been very long since she too had been a 'party reveller', dressed in strange masks, participating in another victory celebration: the fall of Robespierre at Thermidor...the end of the Terror. Josephine shuddered at the memory of her imprisonment in the prison of Les Carmes, wherein the revolutionaries had executed her first husband, Alexandre de Beauharnais, and where she herself had so narrowly missed having to take her place on the tumbrels to meet the icy blade of Madame la Guillotine. How sweet had the revelry been after that ghastly nightmare. And now...she was an Empress.

As the motion of the carriage slid smoothly to a halt, the young woman noticed that her Royal mistress' face had returned to its serious preoccupation with the mysterious masked anxiety. So too did the young smiling face return to its previous expression of concern as the girl prepared to assist the Empress, hurriedly gathering into her hand the small gold parcel that Josephine had earlier entrusted into her keeping, and which had lain on the seat beside her during their journey. The icy blast of the winter evening air hit them on their faces as the girl moved towards the opening door in preparation to assist her mistress to descend from the carriage. Yes, it was all very strange, she thought.

'Y-your Majesty...' The stammered gasp of disbelief exhaled in deep confusion from the throat of the middle-aged woman as, hastily wiping her reddened hands on her apron, she sank her ample frame into a deep curtsy before the heavily cloaked figure. 'We-we didn't...'

'Is your Mistress at home, Marie?'

The kind voice of the Empress cut short the flustered apologies of the astonished woman. Casting an enquiring glance about the large, dimly lit circular hall, she proceeded to answer her own question as she fixed her gaze on the closed double doors that imposingly dominated the tastefully decorated reception area, off which other doors and corridors fanned.

'Indeed, I believe she is...' Josephine did not need a reply from the servant. The Empress paused, her smile deepening into a soft expression of rueful tenderness. 'I would recognise that sweet singing anywhere!'

There was a momentary hush as the three women listened to the soft strains of a beautiful singing voice coming faintly from behind the heavy doors. Then, as the Empress moved to divest herself of her cloak, the young lady-in-waiting instantly sprang to assist her mistress.

'No, Marie...' The quiet tones of the Empress checked the movement of the maid towards the double doors. Taking the small gold parcel from her lady-in-waiting, she continued. 'Perhaps you could find this young lady some refreshment, Marie?' The Empress gently beckoned to the young woman to accompany the flushed maid. 'I shall announce myself.'

Her quiet authority refuted any further protestations of assistance, and she watched with benign grace as the two women, one heavy and middle-aged, one slender and young, silently obeyed the Royal instruction, leaving the Empress alone in the pleasant hall as they disappeared down a corridor, exchanging uneasy glances of shared incomprehension.

For a long moment the small figure remained motionless. Then, lifting her eyes towards the large portraits that hung on either side of the double doors, Josephine looked into the handsome face that she knew so well. Bonaparte! How extraordinarily good-looking he had been in those days. Her eyes travelled over the entire painting of the thin young man, clothed in the crimson uniform of First Consul of the Republic.

She smiled, returning her gaze to the lean features of the handsome face, framed with its long dark locks, its blue-grey eyes staring with that familiar intensity, arresting the attention of any onlooker – with or without resistance, as she herself knew only too well. How his appearance had changed in a few short years.

Her smile vanished. She cast an admiring glance up at the other portrait, of the woman so well known to her. Moving lightly towards the doors and lifting her hand to the doorknob, she paused, bending a little as she listened to the singing, accompanied by the sound of the piano, which came from inside the room. She could hear it more clearly now.

'...no matter where we go, the image of this love is always new...'

Quietly, Josephine turned the handle, silently entering the room, unbeknown to the singer whose attention was entirely absorbed in the melancholy strains of her song, her eyes fixed on the fast falling snow as it silently shrouded the garden beyond the long bay windows, as yet un-curtained for night, revealing an eerie sight of whitened ghostly shapes of garden landscape blending into the winter darkness.

Josephine remained still by the door, watching her friend at the piano across the pretty room, lit only by the warm flames of a blazing fire and occasional candles. The Empress was moved by the sadness of the song, and by the lonely figure of its singer bathed in the deep pink and orange hues of the moving firelight. There was something magical, almost ethereal, about the serenity of the atmosphere she had just entered, and Josephine felt strangely comforted as she listened to the sad resolution of the beautiful song. As the harmonics of the final chords died away into the flickering recesses of the now silent room, stillness fell.

Désirée Bernadotte jumped as a light clap came from the direction of the doors behind her. Swinging round, her eyes opened wide in disbelief as she failed to disguise her surprise at the sight of the small figure now approaching from the door.

'Bravo, Désirée! How beautifully you sing…'

Désirée swallowed, temporarily lost for words as she realised that the Empress had been listening to her song. Rising from her piano stool, she moved towards her visitor, delight infusing her astonishment as she greeted the unexpected figure whose triumphant return from Germany she had only just read about in the 'Moniteur'.

'Why Jos…Your Majesty!'

In the confusion of her surprise Désirée had forgotten the protocol nowadays required in greeting this particular friend. Sinking into a hasty curtsy, she blushed slightly.

With a light laugh Josephine moved towards the other woman, embracing her with affection, and kissing her on both cheeks, giggling in girlish delight at the surprise she had sprung.

'Chérie, please… No ceremony – we are alone…'

The older woman laughed with the feminine camaraderie of youth, her face momentarily shedding its recent haunted expression of tiredness. Linking her arm through Désirée's, she moved her towards the warmth of the fire, stooping to place the small gold parcel on a table nearby.

'It's a little gift for the Emperor's godson, my dear…' She paused. 'He is very fond of your little Oscar, you know.'

Though her expression had returned to its normal smiling composure, a hint of melancholy indefinably hovered about her

'How thoughtful you are, Josephine. Thank you.'

Désirée was touched by the characteristic kindness of this unusual woman, whom she had come to know, and indeed to be fond of despite her early reservations.

During these past years since the coup d'état of Brumaire, the two had become friends. Yet Désirée felt sorry for the strangely beautiful Creole, knowing the entire Bonaparte family to be united in Madame Letitia's opposition to her daughter-in-law. Napoleon's mother — now known as Madame Mère — had taken an instant dislike to Josephine. Indeed, her condemnation had begun even before they had met in Italy, the matriarch deeming the widow to be a flippant spendthrift who cared only for the pleasures in life, contrary to everything the Corsican woman had endeavoured to instil into her children, not least her most famous son. But whilst in Josephine's youth there might have been an element of truth to such a charge, and notwithstanding an inclination towards extravagance which undoubtedly characterised her, in latter years Josephine had, nonetheless, proved to be a good and loving wife to Napoleon whose influence, reflecting her kind and generous nature, had often tempered Napoleon's impulsive caprice in sometimes potentially dangerous situations. Thus Désirée had felt that the ignorant behaviour of the Bonapartes towards the woman Napoleon loved was both unfair and unjustified, and she had determined that she, at least, would never behave in such a manner towards this gracious woman. Besides, she liked her; a sentiment she knew to be shared universally by the people of France.

'That was a beautiful song you were singing, my dear. What is it? I don't recall hearing it before.'

Josephine was seating herself on a sofa near to the fire as Désirée, taking a taper to light more candles, tugged on the bell-pull to summon her maid.

Blushing slightly, Désirée lowered her head for a fleeting moment, before turning to light her taper from a nearby candle. 'It's called "First Love"…'

Désirée's slightly embarrassed answer as, busying herself with the candles, she avoided the enquiring gaze of the Empress, was suddenly interrupted by the entrance of her maid.

'Yes, Madame?'

Turning to Josephine, Désirée thankfully changed the subject. 'Your Majesty, will you take chocolate? Wine…?'

Josephine's face melted into a mischievous grin as she twinkled her reply, returning to the humour of their earlier girlish camaraderie.

'My dear Désirée, I think we must have champagne…!'

The Empress rolled her large eyes, her small mouth pursed in a playful expression of mysterious amusement. Smiling at the happy sight of the Empress' relaxed mood, Désirée spoke quietly to Marie, her shining eyes locked with those of the Empress.

'It seems that Her Majesty has some good news! Champagne, Marie!'

As the maid closed the door behind her large exiting form, Désirée sank onto the sofa beside Josephine. Putting her head on one side, she inquisitively searched the soft features of the Empress, her excited anticipation clearly expecting a particular answer.

'Do we have a happy event to toast, Your Majesty?'

Her knowing smile faded as she saw a troubled look, almost a stab of pain, suddenly cloud Josephine's humorous expression.

'How sweet you are, Désirée…' Josephine's voice sounded suddenly tired as she realised the implied reason for delight in Désirée's question. 'Thinking of the happiness of Bonaparte and myself, always…'

Her voice trailed into a sigh that echoed of despair as the door opened once more for the entry of Marie, bearing the champagne.

There was a silence as the woman carefully placed the silver tray on a table and, following an awkward curtsy to the Empress, moved heavily out of the room once more, leaving the two women in a moment of uncertain silence, warmed by the friendly crackle of the blazing fire.

Realising that she had somehow cast a damper upon the conversation, Josephine wrenched her thoughts from the melancholy preoccupations that lurked beneath the surface of her mind. Assuming a gentle expression, she looked into Désirée's questioning eyes.

'It is for you we celebrate, Désirée; for your sister…and…'

'For my sister?'

Désirée was astonished. Her relationship with her sister, Julie Bonaparte, was very close, and she felt she would know already if there were any particular cause for celebration.

'Indeed…' Josephine's low voice smiled '…and perhaps, because of her good fortune, soon for you too, my dear Désirée…'

The Empress was aware that her friend, initially curious, was now confounded, and she was enjoying her little game as she watched Désirée pour the champagne.

'It seems that this Empire is becoming quite a family concern!' Josephine stopped for a moment, casting a quick glance at a nearby bust of Napoleon. 'Your sister, Désirée, is to become a Queen. Bonaparte has decided to make Joseph King of Naples…' She paused again briefly. '…It will soon be official.'

Désirée felt her mouth drop open as she looked at the Empress in wide-eyed amazement, almost spilling the golden bubbling liquid from the glass, which she had been handing to the now animated Creole.

Lost for words, Désirée stared at her friend. Had she thought about it, of course, she should have guessed that something like this would happen. But it had never really occurred to her to think about it. That she and Julie were the ordinary, middle-class daughters of a businessman from Marseilles, and always would be, had somehow precluded any illusions of grandeur. Now, as Josephine continued, Désirée found herself doubly shattered.

'Bonaparte has plans to bequeath the titles of the conquered territories on to all the members of his family...' The Empress paused '...though probably not Lucien... 'Her voice took on a weary tone as she added her remark doubtfully. How tired she was of the continual bickering and squabbling that went on within this temperamental family.

'Anyway...' Her eyes grew warmer as her mouth softened into the seductive smile for which she was famed '...I doubt he will forget his little Eugènie in the distribution of his acquisitions...'

There was a faint hint of sourness in this last remark, though her warmth towards Désirée was not diminished. Increasingly, however, Josephine was given to fits of jealousy regarding all Napoleon's objects of affection, and in the past there had been disputes between them over the subject of Désirée Clary, and the special affection he had always retained for her. Yet in spite of this, Josephine found herself unable to dislike Désirée, and indeed had come to feel a strange kinship with her for some inexplicable reason.

'It seems first loves never do forget each other...' She laughed, attempting to put the embarrassed and confused Désirée at her ease. '...and besides, your fine Marshal has quite distinguished himself as Governor of Hanover, as well as in battle at Austerlitz...'

Désirée was utterly confounded at the somewhat nervous chattering of the Empress. 'Your Majesty! I-I don't understand...?'

Her bemused question was answered with a kind laugh from the Empress who looked into Désirée's eyes and replied softly, 'My dear, the Emperor intends also to honour your Marshal with a suitable title.' There was a fleeting silence. 'Though as yet he has not decided which one... He...' She flicked her glance around the warmly glowing room. 'He says that the sister-in-law of the King of Naples must also be titled.'

Shrugging her pretty shoulders, the Empress looked into the

fire, drinking slowly from her glass as a silence fell between them.

Désirée was nonplussed, unsure of her own reaction. She was aware that Josephine was imparting information to her that was probably known only to a few people. Moreover, she was certain that the Emperor was probably unaware of Josephine's transgression of confidentiality – not that it was exactly an important breach of security. And yet, she couldn't help wondering why Josephine had come here this evening; why she had told her in advance of these forthcoming honours. Why did she appear to be so tense? For whilst they were friends, they had never been especially close, meeting mainly through the somewhat dynamic gatherings of the Bonaparte family, and official court receptions. Occasionally they had shared conversations about Josephine's passion for flowers. And indeed the Empress had shown a generous and keen interest in Désirée's own attempts to cultivate her garden. Nonetheless, it seemed to Désirée that there was some other reason for Josephine's visit.

'Y-your Majesty…I am overcome…I do not quite know what to say. The Emperor…is very generous…'

Désirée's faltering response was interrupted by a hard laugh from the Empress, who rose abruptly, walking towards the fireplace. Désirée's eyes followed the small woman's back as she moved quickly into the more intense light of the dancing flames.

'Indeed! He is generous…'

Josephine's voice seemed to have a catch in it as her almost harsh words faded into the crackling sound of the fire. Désirée remained silent as she looked at the small figure who was gazing thoughtfully into the orange furnace. There was a long silence, the room animated only by the sound of the fire.

Suddenly a stifled sigh escaped from the motionless Empress as, taking an agitated sip from her glass, she abruptly turned to look into Désirée's eyes. 'Désirée…sometimes I think that you and I are the only two people in the whole world who actually know our Bonaparte…' She broke off, twitching slightly in irritation as something appeared to agitate her. 'Those wretched bells. Whatever is it now? They seem to ring interminably these days…'

Désirée rose, seeing the Empress was severely agitated. The sound of the bells was indeed incessant, but their distant chimes were hardly intruding. Lifting the bottle from the tray, Désirée refilled the Empress' glass, warmly smiling into the dark eyes that seemed now to hold an expression of real panic.

Soothingly, she attempted to calm the older woman's mood of rising agitation. 'Napoleon has taken France to the great heights of Power, restoring its glory as he always said he would.'

A memory of the thin young General's belief in destiny, proclaimed under a Mediterranean sky, flitted through her mind involuntarily.

'The Austrians…'

'That is precisely it, Désirée. The Austrians. It is not as grand as it seems…'

Josephine's interruption of Désirée's calm words induced the younger woman to hastily drink from her glass as she seated herself once more on the sofa, her head a little dizzy at the force of Josephine's unexpected remonstrance. The Empress broke off, the dark eyes in her unusually pale face intently staring into those of Désirée, who was reluctantly compelled to return the gaze.

Moving from the fireplace, Josephine returned to seat herself on the edge of the sofa beside Désirée, her taut body leaning slightly towards the younger woman.

'Désirée…the Treaty that was signed at Pressburg is not all that it is loudly being proclaimed to be…'

Désirée caught her breath, her eyes opening widely in surprise. She could hardly believe her ears. Paris had talked of little else these past weeks save the magnificent achievements of France through this Treaty. Why was Josephine now appearing to contradict this?

'Bonaparte has humiliated the Austrians…and especially the Prussians…' Désirée's face creased in horror as the ashen-faced Empress spoke quickly with a near incoherence. '…There have been violent disagreements between Talleyrand and Bonaparte about it…Talleyrand was forced against his judgment to conclude the Treaty…but he believes it will result in eventual catastrophe for France.' Josephine took an agitated drink from her glass. 'I-I have witnessed some of their quarrels…' Josephine shook her head. 'I fear their friendship will never be the same…and that will affect France. Bonaparte won't…'

She broke off, seemingly paralysed by her frustrations. Casting a wild glance at Désirée's astonished face, she rose suddenly, starting to pace the room in distress.

'Talleyrand tried and tried to persuade Bonaparte to be generous to the Austrians. They…they are an old Empire. Proud. They need the identity of their ruler to maintain their dignity. Talleyrand believes that their constitution must be maintained to preserve their confidence.'

Placing it absently on a table as she moved towards the fireplace, placing both hands on the mantle as she looked deeply into the now quietening flames.

She finished her outburst in a low, despairing voice. 'God knows what the repercussions of such injury to a proud people might be…'

The small figure of the Empress seemed to suddenly droop as the hissing sounds of the fire drowned her words. Désirée felt numb. She looked at the distressed form of the Empress outlined against the fire, unable to quite absorb the entirety of the woman's outburst.

Without warning, she became aware of the unrelenting ringing of the distant bells. Josephine was right; they were irritating. As the implications of Josephine's words induced a delayed reaction in Désirée's suddenly aching head, she felt overcome by a strange wave of compassion for the older woman. She knew that Josephine had many worries to contend with being Napoleon's wife, and she admired her courage for the way she overcame her many difficulties. But her feminine instinct told her now that Josephine's expressions of fear were more than simple, unfounded apprehension. The Empress was intuitively aware of a profound change that was taking place, and she was voicing a hitherto unspoken presentiment of doom.

Rising silently from her seat, Désirée moved to the fireplace. With a sisterly tenderness she put her arm around the older woman's limp shoulders. As she looked closely at the face, which possessed a strange beauty, in defiance of the irregularity of its features, Désirée noticed that beneath the thick make-up the lines around the Empress' now watering eyes had deepened. How unusually quickly she had aged since the day of her coronation.

Désirée looked appealingly into the glistening eyes as she spoke softly. 'Are you certain of this, Josephine? Jean-Baptiste is at Ansbach...I know nothing of...'

Josephine nodded sadly, her kind voice interjecting Désirée's helpless utterances. 'He no longer heeds advice, Désirée. Even Talleyrand... His victories are changing his character. He has forgotten... Sometimes I wonder if he remembers how it all began...the Revolution...even though he claims that he is carrying the message of "The Rights of Man" into foreign lands...'

She fell silent, closing her eyes for a moment. An involuntary shudder seemed to fleetingly grip her fragile body. Feebly she shrugged, failing to finish the sentence. Désirée pressed her hand on Josephine's arm as a helpless wordlessness fell between them. She knew that there was some further burden on Josephine's mind.

Now, as she looked at her with a genuinely pained sympathy and shared sense of foreboding, the Empress lifted her eyes once more to meet those of this woman whom she barely knew, and yet to whom she was confiding her deepest fears.

'I-I know he wants to divorce me...so that he may have an heir...I-I understand...' Josephine's choked words seemed to bite into the charged atmosphere. Désirée blinked as the haggard Creole forced a bitter laugh. 'Like you, my dear friend Désirée, I shall be a pleasant memory of love...' She swallowed. 'But I fear for him... He doesn't realise how much he needs me... Talleyrand...you... What will happen when he has rid himself of those of us who understand him? Who know best how his strange mind works?'

Suddenly she threw her hands in the air. 'A woman, especially you and I, Désirée, who love him...we can feel these things coming...something...something dreadful is going to happen...I'm sure...'

Tears were falling from Josephine's large eyes in a steady flow. Désirée guided the distraught, now almost incoherent Empress to the sofa, assisting her to sit down, vainly trying to soothe her as, now unable to stop, she continued to blurt out her pent-up emotions.

'The reason I...you...France...the reason we love him is because along with that great genius and vision which is beyond the comprehension of us all...his character is basically generous...magnanimous...compassionate...' She dragged a hand across the already smudged make-up on her wet eyes. 'He has always shown concern for everyone...he-he's almost childlike at times...'

Her body was heaving as she painfully struggled to take in a deep breath through the taut muscles of her aching throat. Her blurred gaze wandered to the small gold gift on the table as she continued in an almost inaudible croak: 'But if that beautiful nature that we love should harden, should he become inflexible, intolerant, as...as he showed himself to be at Pressburg...if he drives away the only man who can moderate his sometimes excessive enthusiasm for power, the only man who dares to challenge him...'

Her voice was rising now, her eyes looking at Désirée with an almost crazed look of fear. '...If his talk of confederation and economic blockades as moves against England make him insensitive to the people of Germany, of Holland...'

Suddenly she buried her wet face in her hands. 'Oh God...his hatred of the English frightens me...'

Her muffled words gave way to violent sobs. Suddenly she gripped Désirée by the shoulders, her nails digging painfully into the younger woman's soft flesh. With a wild look of horror she held Désirée's horrified attention as she shouted with an uncharacteristic shrillness, 'Désirée! What's happening to him? What will be the outcome...?' Her voice broke as she finished, 'I-I have a terrible feeling...'

Tearing herself away from Désirée, she threw herself across the sofa, burying her head in the cushions, her bitter sobs wracking her body as she cried without control. Désirée stared at the violently shaking body before her. Without thinking, she put a pacifying hand on The Empress' back, her feelings numb from the emotional outburst with which she had been faced. She could hardly believe it. Josephine, who loved him so much, even Josephine could see the change that was taking place in Napoleon's character. She felt a twist of pain as she realised that this moment had crystallised the feeling she had herself experienced, but had not really allowed to surface. A wave of dizziness overcame her as she realised how much it hurt her to think of what might happen to the man to whom she had once been betrothed. How lonely he would become.

A lump came to her throat as she checked the surge of compassion for him. What mixed emotions did that enigmatic genius induce in those who cared about him.

Her eyes fell once more on the quivering body. She felt her own eyes water as she helplessly patted the small back. How strange that Josephine had come to her to share her pain. It was true then. That love, real love, transcended the barriers of social friendship. Such 'social friendships' were simply frameworks for convenient and necessary communication behaviour – they didn't really penetrate the real meaning of 'love'. And yet, when two people, ordinarily performing the empty charade of 'social friendship', were confronted with the mutual pain of a deep concern for a loved one, such barriers were swept aside.

With a jolt Désirée realised how deeply she still cared about the lost love of her youth. And yet it was a strange affection, somehow deeper in her maturity and from the security of her own happy marriage to her beloved Jean-Baptiste. How odd, she thought, that Josephine should have recognised that. Her eyes burned as she looked at the pathetic form of the weeping Empress. Poor Josephine, she had never known any real happiness for long. And now, did she sense something that was inevitable? For both her, and her Emperor?

Suddenly Désirée felt cold. She wished that Jean-Baptiste were here... But then she knew that even if he were, he would never understand. And now she felt even colder.

She rose, moving to the fireplace to stoke the smouldering ashes. The Empress' sobs were subsiding into a low moan. Oh Napoleone, she thought – what are you doing with your destiny?

The ashes hissed as she dropped a log on top of them. Wearily she placed the back of a hand on her forehead as she weakly tugged the bell-pull with the other. She must get some warm refreshment for the Empress, who had now ceased crying and was attempting to regain her composure in between sniffs.

'Oh Napoleone...Napoleone...' Désirée said to herself once more before turning her tired body towards the Empress.

Chapter XIV

August is a month I find tiresome. The heat seems to sap at one's energy, and insects appear to breed at a disgustingly accelerated pace, adding a nauseating contribution to the sticky discomfort by the irritating presence of their buzzing multitudes. It is, indeed, a month when I have a preference for even the boredom of the country rather than the repellent odours of the hot Paris streets, and it is usually my wont to spend extended periods at my country house at Valencay, where my health finds a welcome improvement during such unpleasant conditions.

However, the August of 1806 was one such disagreeable summer month when I was denied my customary respite from the acrid atmosphere of the capital city. 1806 was a year in which events of change occurred in rapid succession.

News of the Peace of Pressburg, concluded on the twenty-sixth of December 1805, had opened the year for France with a renewed sense of triumph. For my part, I had been forced to contain my misgivings relating to that particular event. But I was certain that it would not be long before my determined Master would be compelled to face the consequences of his insensitive actions. Even at that time I had momentarily thought of resigning, but I felt that I would be better placed to act in the interests of France, when the inevitable reactions became manifest, if I retained my position in the Government.

The Emperor's brother-in-law Murat was now known as the Grand Duke of Berg and Cleves, and his brother Joseph had become a King. The new monarch of Naples and the former Marshal were promoted to their illustrious positions in March, beginning the rapid flow of noble elevations bestowed by the generosity of the Emperor, in expression of gratitude for services rendered to the Empire. But whilst I was myself to be a beneficiary of the Emperor's distribution of states and principalities, I was nonetheless aware that in most cases, especially relating to those more important positions which would be held by members of his family, the rule of each particular state was in actual fact being made into an effective satrap of France, its people being subjected in a subtle way to the edicts of Napoleon's philosophy.

June saw the accession of a new King of Holland: Louis Bonaparte. And this same summer saw the death of the Holy Roman Empire, which had existed for a thousand years.

The Emperor of the French gave the German people, in its stead, another form of identity in a Treaty signed in Paris in June: the Confederation of the Rhine. The Emperor was himself to become the President of the new Protectorate, and the members of this new composition of small German states were expected to both provide the Emperor's growing army with troops, as well as play an active role in his proposed economic plans for Europe.

Naturally I was the principal negotiator for the Empire in the complex negotiations that were required for the restructuring of the conquered territories. At that time I believed that their individual cultural identities would be preserved, and that these were, in fact, important steps in the organising of a modern Europe, wherein the major powers would administer their states in peaceful co-existence. I did not, of course, hesitate to avail myself of the considerable opportunities that my duties afforded, enabling me to make lucrative fillips to my personal fortune. I have always considered it important to ensure the standards of one's comfort. Poverty does not appeal to me.

But my central preoccupation at this time was the possibility of peace with England. The death of Pitt in January had changed the mood in certain English political circles towards the long-standing disputes between England and France. The influence of the new Foreign Minister, Charles Fox, encouraged the English Coalition Government to begin negotiations for peace, and I detailed the faithful Montrond to seek out certain information from his personal friend, the English intermediary, Lord Yarmouth.

But whilst the intentions of both Fox and myself were united in our earnest desire for a Peace, the aristocratic arrogance of Lord Yarmouth, displaying a deep-seated mistrust of the French, continually frustrated the smooth progress of our negotiations. Moreover, the Emperor entirely compounded the difficulties by capricious behaviour, making promises of ceding Hanover to the English, when he had already promised it to Prussia. Lord Yarmouth relished the chance to meddle. He informed the Prussians of the Emperor's misguided actions, knowing that their already injured pride would be outraged. Thus peace negotiations with England faltered and Prussia erupted into open anger.

As I arrived at the palace of St Cloud, where the Emperor now held his Court, my mind was filled with thoughts of the recent months. And while I lethargically made my way through the luxuriously furnished rooms and corridors, observing the dark green and gold bees that dominated the carpets and curtains, firmly burying any reminder of past occupants of this Bourbon Palace, I contemplated the possible reactions that would result from that news which I was about to impart to the Emperor.

'Two million gold francs to be distributed to senior officers; an extra fifteen days' pay for each member of the Guard; pensions for the widows of the fallen...'

I could hear the Emperor's authoritative voice dictating as I passed through the busy ante-room to the Emperor's office, my presence barely noticed by the numerous young clerks whose attentions were entirely absorbed in their respective tasks relating to their Master's vast correspondence, and General secretarial demands.

As I was announced to the Imperial Presence, the small, now thickening, figure at the window waved his hand with a casual arrogance as he looked down across the Courtyard of the Palace of St Cloud, continuing his dictation.

'…Battle orphans may be permitted the name of Napoleon to be added to their Christian names…'

There was a pause as Claude Meneval, Napoleon's secretary who had succeeded the now disgraced Bourrienne, cleared his throat before repeating my name to the still back behind which the imperial hands were clasped.

A momentary silence elapsed, during which time the eyes of the clerk taking the dictation, those of Meneval, and indeed my own, gazed expectantly at the compelling figure who, even when viewed from behind, commanded a submissive respect from those in its presence.

'…I shall formally adopt them myself.' The words were spoken with a pleased flourish.

Abruptly, the Emperor turned to face the room, the conclusion of his dictation accompanied by a beaming smile at me, and an impatient gesture from his arm indicating to the others that they were dismissed. As the young clerk scuttled thankfully towards the doorway, followed quickly by the conscientious secretary, Napoleon's eyes remained fixed on my own, his now rounded cheeks stretched by the broad animation of his expression.

'And how is the Prince of Benevento, today?'

His smiling tone was genuinely affectionate, the twinkling relish of addressing me by my new title reflecting his good humour. Napoleon was in high spirits today.

'I am in good health, thank you, Your Majesty.'

My polite response was perhaps a trifle terse due to my acute discomfort caused by the stuffy heat of the room, and my aching leg forcing me to lean awkwardly against the nearest chair.

'Good! Good!' The Emperor moved purposefully from the window towards his desk, waving his arm generously at me as he reached it. 'Sit down, sir! Sit down.'

He had always shown consideration for my disability. The ebullience of his mood was today reminiscent of that exultant dreamer of old – the First Consul. And as I heavily lowered myself into a chair, I smiled to myself as I experienced that familiar feeling of being disarmed by the boyish charm of the man, a sensation I had not felt for some time.

'Do the revenues of your new Principality satisfy you, sir?'

I could feel the penetration of the Emperor's sidelong glance as he enquired with mischievous curiosity as to my response to his recent generous bequest.

'Indeed, sire, you have been most generous. I shall endeavour to administer the Principality with justice and compassion.'

I am a man of few words at all times, but today my brevity was exacted both by the uncomfortable heat and the serious nature of the news I was about to give him. That I had stressed the words 'justice' and 'compassion' in a mild allusion to our recent discussions about such ethical consideration in relation to the Treaty of Pressburg did not escape the notice of the closely observing Emperor. His smile abruptly vanished, to be replaced by a sharp look, followed by a short silence.

Unperturbed, I settled myself into a position of comfort, carefully placing my cane against the arm of the chair.

'I detect a seriousness in your disposition today, Prince?' The imperious tone so often adopted by the Emperor these days had returned to his voice. He paused briefly before continuing with a sardonic tone: 'Unfortunately I have to distribute Honours in a Military Review so I have little time to relax your mood…'

He had seated himself at his enormous and cluttered desk, and was leaning intently over some large maps spread out across it. As his eyes scanned the maps he went on, '…and besides, I wish to show you my plans here for blockading the Continental ports…' He broke off with a hard laugh. '…The lucky winds of Trafalgar will not protect that nation of shopkeepers from defeat forever. There are other ways to defeat the English swine…'

His eyes narrowed as he paused once more, his arm making a sweeping gesture over the map he was looking at as, with a dramatic flourish, he concluded, 'We shall crush them economically.'

I remained silent as he finished, a grim smile on his face as his gaze stayed fixed on the map before him.

Suddenly he pushed back his chair with a violent thrust, rising with an exasperated sigh of impatience exhaling from his lips. His tone was irritated as he strode back towards the open window.

'Come Prince…whatever is the matter?'

My silence was agitating him as he sensed that I had something important to say. The room grew quiet as the Emperor resumed his preoccupation with the outside activities of his soldiers. I could hear the distant shouts of military orders accompanied by the steadily increasing sound of horses' hooves and marching soldiers. The Imperial Guard was assembling for its Review. The short figure in the simple green and white uniform, free from embellishment of any sort, was motionless. I felt an odd twist of emotion as I looked at his back once more, outlined against the blue sky through the large open windows. It occurred to me suddenly that he was strangely vulnerable. How much he had achieved, both for France as well as for himself and his family. How young he still was, and how badly he craved the respect of his European counterparts.

Unexpectedly my mind recalled the meeting in the sleazy Paris slum with Sieyès and Ducos – so long ago now, it seemed. 'Sword of France'! We had sought a *sword* to restore order to our country. Napoleon Bonaparte had indeed succeeded in doing that. Moreover, he had brought a growing prosperity, and had given the People back their confidence. But now the whole glorious dream was in danger of going wrong.

Napoleon half turned in surprise as he heard my cane scrape. I was summoning its assistance in my struggle to rise from the comfort of the chair.

'Sire…'

His expression grew oddly defensive as I limped slowly towards him. Questioningly he looked at me as I joined him by the window, glancing down at the immaculately symmetrical pattern of men that was growing beneath us. I looked into his blue-grey eyes, detecting a hidden expression of apprehension behind their impassivity. Slowly I began, attempting to display as best I could the consideration I felt for this unique young man before me.

'Sire – your genius has brought France glory such as it has not experienced since the time of Charlemagne. Our territories extend beyond the dreams of most Frenchmen. France is indeed great once more...' I paused, noticing an uncharacteristic expression of embarrassed discomfort on the Emperor's face. 'You have so made it.'

Twitching slightly, casting his gaze once more out of the window, Napoleon remained silent, correctly anticipating that I was making preparation for a particularly momentous statement.

'However...' My own eyes followed his out of the window to attend the scene below. '...Military glory is not all there is to greatness, sire. The sign of true greatness lies in the degree of magnanimity a victor is prepared to extend to his defeated victim...'

I paused as I observed that the Emperor's face was hardening into a stony mask. I could see a muscle move in his jaw as – his eyes still fixed on the soldiers below – he listened for my continuation.

'I have spoken thus to you before, Sire. Following Austerlitz I urged you to extend some generosity to Austria, to Prussia...' As I paused, carefully considering my next words, the still handsome face twisted round to look at me with a fierce expression of impatience on its dark features.

'What are you saying, man?'

His irritation was followed by the arrogant contempt that I found so disturbing, and was a facet of his character that displayed itself more and more frequently these days.

'What are you talking about? Frederick William? That Prussian weakling is *finished*!' His sneering words broke off momentarily as he laughed a short, harsh laugh. '...For all I hear he has a spirited and beautiful Queen who rides in battle like a man.'

He broke off once more, his eyes narrowing in a cold, unseeing gaze into nothingness as he thoughtfully murmured his next phrase. 'And in spite of his bizarre meetings with fellow blue-blooded monarchs...'

I knew his bitter words were a reference to the somewhat macabre gathering that had taken place inside the tomb of Frederick the Great just before Austerlitz, when Frederick William had, with his Queen, Louise, met with Tsar Alexander to pledge their united endeavour against Napoleon Bonaparte.

'The man is...'

'Sire.' I interrupted what I knew would be an increasing flow of abuse against the Prussian King. 'Let not your contempt for your victims lead you to underestimate their courage.'

My cold words seemed to sting the Emperor into silence. Uneasily his eyes returned to the assembling soldiers as he waited for me to tell him that which he knew I had come to say.

'It seems...' I too was looking at the soldiers in the courtyard below '...that those gentlemen will see a battlefield once more, sooner than they might have anticipated.' The Emperor swung his gaze to lock with mine as I continued in my low, measured tones. 'That "Prussian weakling", sire, is massing his troops in preparation for war...' I paused briefly. 'He has the support of the Tsar.'

Napoleon was thunderstruck, seemingly lost for words as he stared with wide-eyed disbelief into my steady gaze. The silence of the room was charged with the feeling that an explosion had just erupted. Outside, the rhythmic sound of the assembling troops went on. Somewhere distant, some birds seemed to be singing, and the buzzing of the infuriating insects appeared to become deafening.

'Have they lost their heads?'

The Emperor's bemused question was almost comically feeble. He appeared strangely deflated in his numbed daze of shock. After a further silence he looked at me with an imploring expression of sudden vulnerability.

'But – we cannot go to war now. I-I have too much to do here in France. The domestic situation needs my attention. Joseph can't...his Regency fails to understand my vision for...' Suddenly he broke off from his bewildered bemusement, and the curious petulance transformed with abrupt rapidity into a savage, blazing anger. 'I don't want to fight Prussia and Russia now!' His furious roar rose in irritated frustration. 'I don't *want* to fight them.'

His eyes blazed as they defensively remonstrated. He paused, searching in vain for an appropriate articulation of his feelings.

With a wild look, his eyes wandered for a moment before finally he threw his arms wide in frustration.

'And anyway, the true enemy is England.'

As he shouted his final words he turned, grabbing the window on each side with his hands, his knuckles turning white with the intensity of his grip.

He lapsed into a morose silence after his frustrated outburst; his short body seemed to suddenly droop. Moodily, he stared down at the soldiers, his face set in an expression of sullen anger. I too gazed down at the soldiers below.

Finally he broke the heavy silence. 'Look at them. They wait for me to confer the Legion of Honour on the Heroes of Victory...' Napoleon's words were muttered slowly in low, bitter tones, scarcely audible to me. 'It is with such baubles that men are led...' A deep sigh muffled his last quietly spoken word: 'Ambition...'

As he hunched across the window, I thought I discerned a slight shudder that seemed to momentarily grip his body. He closed his eyes as if recalling some ghastly horror.

Then, in a low husky voice, he murmured in a sad despairing tone that moved me, 'It's more than simply revenge for defeat that fills these Royal cousins with such foolhardy courage...' He paused, almost whispering his next words. 'Will they never accept me? Will they never forget...?'

His words were uttered to himself; indeed I believe he had become oblivious to my presence, locked as he was in the private nightmare of his own fears. As I looked at the pain-filled face, drained of its colour to an eerie white, I felt a sudden alarm. Without knowing it, he was keenly displaying his vulnerability to me, voicing his secret fears. I felt embarrassed, as though I had witnessed something I should not have seen. Moreover, my admiration for the young genius, as well as a sudden sense of compassion, made me feel sorry for the man. Pity was an emotion I did not wish to feel for him, as indeed I knew he would despise any such contemplation. But in that moment I felt I had witnessed the unlocking of a secret: his remorse for the execution of the Duc d'Enghien, and his full realisation of the hostile attitudes of the

Royal Houses of Europe towards him because of it.

I could bear the silence no longer. Gently, I placed my hand upon his shoulder, speaking softly to the sadly preoccupied Emperor.

'Come, sire, let us honour the proud Nobility of France, the France of Napoleon the First, Emperor of the French.'

Slowly he withdrew from the window. Looking into my face, he smiled a soft expression of gratitude. Silently he moved to pick up his little black hat from a nearby table. Together we left the room to attend the Review where the Emperor was to distribute his own special honour.

* * *

I was confused by the man. I need hardly add that I was more than a little baffled by myself, which doubly confounded the problem for me. 'Love' is an odd emotion.

As a child I had seen little of my family. This was not an unusual situation amongst children of the nobility, but my disability had resulted in me being made into a virtual outcast, depriving me of the little contact that would have been normally available. Thus I had become an isolated child, confined to the company of the servants designated to care for and, in my early years, educate me. Naturally they had no particular affection for the crippled son of an unconcerned, unseen master.

Although I was an elder son and therefore by convention destined for the army, my parents had seen little future for me in such a career, suffering as I did from the deformity that had been thrust upon me by a careless servant. I had thus been cast into the position of a second son, my younger brother being elevated to become heir to the titles and wealth that went with the traditions of eighteenth century nobility. And so, whilst my brother was proudly sent to join the King's Army, my parents decided to dedicate their disabled liability to the church, no doubt believing themselves to be ensuring a place in the Elysian fields, which would be equal in privilege and comfort to that which they enjoyed here on this earth. If, however, they were reliant upon my agency to further this end, they were to be disappointed, and where they now languish I do not know.

I knew no parental love. Nor did I encounter love in any other form when I found myself in the grip of the bleak institutions of further education and Religion that were to entrap me for so many unhappy years in their insidious clutches. As I passed into manhood I had grown disillusioned of the hope of encountering the reality of affection. My witness to the behaviour of human beings was one of basic disgust at the limited vision brought about by a singular preoccupation with pursuits of self-interest, excluding the possibilities of participation in that which was not of a direct concern to the individual. People, I found, were stultified by the rigid rules of the social criteria by which they lived, and they actively curtailed the potential of their imagination, believing a freedom of expression to be inviting unseemly displays of emotion that approached madness. Thus the world seemed to me, as a young man, to be populated by institutionalised vegetables, who appeared to fear their own shadows. I despised them.

Later, of course, when I had finally broken free from the suffocating constraint of their hypocritical existence, I was to meet the very antithesis of such colourless specimens of humanity in the form of the Revolutionary leaders, whose raw energy and crude simplicity of purpose and belief in Ideals excited me. That was until their methods degenerated beyond my capacity of toleration...

Thus, human beings in general had tended to disenchant me, and I found the single solace for the emptiness of my disillusion in the pleasurable, if intellectually unchallenging, company of women, whose animal guile seemed to be the true organising factor behind the progress of the human race.

It is a strange thing to say, perhaps, but I had never encountered the sheer excitement of innocent youth in the 'dreamer of dreams' – dreams that were, I believed, the essence of the thrust in human progress.

Until I met Napoleon Bonaparte...

Perhaps it is the intrinsic nature of genius, that peculiar ability to retain a childlike vulnerability? I am certain that each person who came into close association with this strange man found himself subject to the same confused emotions in varying degrees.

The complexity of his character was bewildering. His outbursts of arrogance; of petulance; his fits of rage, and later his displays of outright tyranny. These violent explosions were equalled in their intensity only by the sheer gentleness, generous consideration and genuine care that the man seemed to sincerely feel for people, especially at the beginning of his career, and particularly for those close to him. And whilst his methods of displaying his affections were inevitably unorthodox due to his natural disposition placing him apart from ordinary men, the depths of those affections were undoubtedly undiminished by such.

But as time went on, the extremes of his moods had become more pronounced. His introspection had grown, even as his apparent extroversion seemed to support his enormous stature in the world. As his responsibilities had increased, his time discussing his 'dreams' with those of us close to him had become limited. His boyish enthusiasm and excitement at the prospect of a new idea had ceased to exude their energy, and eventually he had become almost unable to communicate his visions at all. Increasingly he rejected even my own challenges to his imagination, and I was aware that nowadays I was the only person who was still able to elicit some form of visible response from the isolated genius. He lived, these days, in his own world. Those around him were mere pawns in the great game, which he now played only with himself. I shall always believe that it was this inversion of that extraordinary imagination that resulted in his tragedy…

And so, once more, I had found myself responding to the 'childlike' Napoleon. I knew full well in my mind that his insecure impulses were leading France down a road to destruction. Yet I allowed my heart to rule my head. I loved the man – the son I had never had. Once more the strange emotion of deep affection overcame my intellectual perception.

Now, on the evening of the twenty-fourth of September, as I found myself seated in a carriage departing Paris for Germany, I knew that I was not alone in my dilemma. Seated beside me in this uncomfortable rattletrap was the woman who understood him even as I did; who loved him, even as no other.

* * *

Josephine too was travelling with the man seated opposite us for the last time, though she was not yet aware of it. She was a woman with whom I had experienced an odd relationship. On the surface, and in social intercourse, we remained distant, and I knew that like so many she was critical of my penchant for increasing my worldly comforts, a characteristic that had always amused her husband.

However, beneath the limiting perspectives of our apparent responses to each other, both Josephine and I instinctively understood that the other was entirely necessary to the tempering of the Emperor's excesses of caprice, and I was aware that the natural kindness and goodness of this gentle woman, and her sustaining, steady influence, had retained the sensitivities of the man we both cared so deeply about.

But her time with him was yet short. I knew him to have resolved to divorce her in the interests of his Dynasty.

Actually I myself had a conflict of opinion about this inevitability. I knew it important that the Napoleonic dynasty should be secured in the interests of France. Yet I wondered what the effect would be on the isolated Emperor when he lost the constancy of the woman who knew him so well…she whom he had always referred to as his 'Talisman'…

That time would reveal all, I doubted not.

* * *

'…for the mobilisation of integral elements…'

My ears had grown quite inured to the unending sound of the

Emperor's dictation as one exhausted secretary succeeded another on the seat beside him in the rattling carriage that was hurtling us at a perfectly appalling degree of haste towards Mainz.

'Bernadotte must be ready to march at Nuremberg by October the second; Ney must have his IV Corps assembled at Ansbach on the same day – confirm also that Augereau is informed that he must reach Frankfurt by that date.'

The Emperor's untiring attention to confirming each detail had never ceased to impress me. It was clear that in his mind the entire campaign was worked out with perfect precision, and each facet of his plan was of integral importance and observed with close scrutiny by its architect. I smiled to myself as I recalled how, following his initial reaction to the imminent war with Prussia, Napoleon had, upon accepting the fact that they had indeed 'lost their heads', sprung immediately into action, mobilising his troops with a speed that only he could muster. Moreover, my amusement had increased upon the discovery that he had, in fact, many of his divisions already conveniently placed in southern Germany, and I wondered if perhaps the realisation of an early war with Prussia had not been as entirely surprising to him as he had indicated. Certainly it was uncanny serendipity – if serendipity it was!

The carriage lunged in an uncomfortable jerk, unexpected in this instance as we were on one of the best and most recently modernised roads in Europe. Like myself, the Empress, seated beside me, was thrown forward, and I felt the pain in my uncomfortably cramped leg sharply increase as I twisted myself to assist her to restore whatever measure of maximum comfort was possible in this jiggling box.

The Emperor ceased his dictation, breaking from his concentration with an indulgent smile of affection at the struggling efforts of the Empress and myself to regain our composure from our state of disarray.

Josephine burst into a girlish giggle. I noticed that she frequently did this these days, and I detected a faintly nervous tenor to her laughter. This however was a spontaneous reaction to the ludicrous result of the coach's lurch. I attempted to settle myself, having ensured the Empress' comfort, and the Emperor resumed the drone of his dictation.

Suddenly I heard Josephine giggle once more and, as I looked sideways, could see her looking up at me, her hand attempting to suppress the laugh that had once more interrupted the Emperor. I glanced with quick apprehension at Napoleon's face. These days he was intolerant of any uninvited address or interruption of any sort. Indeed, I knew that I still retained some sort of privileged position with him, for I still enjoyed a reasonably normal rapport, which I knew was not the privilege of anyone else. Yet now I could see that he was not only smiling at us once again, but it was evident that his humour was such that he wished to relax for a moment, leaving his dictation.

'Prince Benevento, you look decidedly ill at ease!'

I could see that Josephine too sensed that the Emperor desired an easing of the atmosphere. Evidently my facial contortions expressing my discomfort were of some comic value to the now often melancholy Empress, and thus I endeavoured to appease the attempt to lighten the mood.

With a further grimace I replied, 'Indeed, Your Majesty. The requirements of loyalty to one's Emperor are certainly demanding!'

I cast a brief look at the Emperor, conveying my amusement in my eyes whilst retaining an expression of feigned agony. The gurgling sound of the Empress' laugh seemed genuinely happy, and Napoleon appeared relieved to see the white face of his frequently tense wife relax into the happy expression of old.

Leaning forward, Napoleon patted me on my knee, his face beaming broadly as, winking at Josephine, he spoke in the warm musical tones so reminiscent of days gone by.

'Come, come, my dear old friend! An Emperor cannot be without his right hand as he rides to defeat the King of Prussia...' He paused. '...And the Tsar of Russia!'

His teasing tones were succeeded by those more meaningful, as he added his last words. But now he smiled at me once more with boyish affection, and I felt myself once again succumbing to his familiar charm.

'I have not the physique, sire, for a man of arms.'

As the Emperor and the Empress both laughed, I looked out of the window at the moving lines of soldiers whom we were passing. There was a long silence, as the rattles of the carriage seemed to impose a relentless encroachment on our efforts to converse. It was a tiring business, this coach travel through battlefields.

'I hear this young Tsar believes himself to be an instrument of God!' A hint of sarcasm tinged the tone of amusement in the Emperor's voice. '...That he is a mystic?' His smile was wry as he raised an eyebrow at me in an enquiry that expressed, at the same time, incredulity.

I frowned, thinking before I replied. I had an instinctive feeling that it might be possible that we were all underestimating this handsome young Tsar, whose performance at Austerlitz had been disastrous, resulting in his collapse in tears under a tree on the smoking, stinking battlefield. Nonetheless, the man was young and intelligent, and I did not doubt that he would learn well from his mistakes.

'Certainly, sire, he appears to be a complex character...' I paused, anxious to convey the crux of my unease to the Emperor. 'His youth has been absorbed in the study of Rousseau's gospel of humanity...' I broke off as I felt Napoleon's keen attention to my words. 'They say he mounted the throne over the body of his dead father...' I shrugged.

A sharp exclamation of shock came from the lips of the gentle Empress, as opposite a loud guffaw erupted from the Emperor's thrown-back head.

'A man with a sense of the absurd!' The Emperor was laughing as he spoke, apparently finding this image extremely amusing.

Suddenly, and without warning, he became serious, and with a dry irony in his voice he added, '...Or perhaps a sense of priority...'

I looked into the blue-grey eyes, which had lost their momentary air of relaxation. I knew he had understood my veiled message.

* * *

Napoleon was riding through the smoking battlefield near to the village of Jena. Dusk was beginning to shroud the late autumn beauty of the surrounding, thickly wooded landscape. But the Emperor did not notice the darkening shapes of the silent, distant observers of nature. His tired attentions were entirely preoccupied with the sprawling evidence of the bloody encounter his army had just experienced with the Prussians. The dead bodies of Prussian soldiers were being silently moved into long piles.

For a moment he felt a sense of revulsion at the sight before him. Never had his army inflicted such carnage; the ground was literally carpeted with the bodies of soldiers from the enemy army. Still, he thought, resuming his grim dispassionate appraisal of the day's events, the battle was going satisfactorily, despite the few problems in swift reorganisation that had been necessary when it had become apparent that it would be impossible to engage on the date he had projected; and as the enemy's plan had been revealed to him he had been forced to respond to their challenge earlier than he had anticipated. However, at least the Russian threat of reinforcement was removed. They were still too far away. His own 96,000 men, he thought – looking round at the tired movements of the countless groups of men interspersed across the landscape for as far as his eye could see – had certainly fought well today, and he believed they had all but defeated the main body of the enemy. Tomorrow the Prussians would be finished off, and Bernadotte and Davout were well placed to attack their lines of retreat.

As his horse halted outside his bivouac, Napoleon wearily allowed himself to be assisted to dismount. He felt very tired, lacking his usual sense of elation in battle. His nostrils twitched. The smell of a battlefield was never particularly pleasant, but this evening, in the dampening approach of night, he found it almost nauseating. He preferred clean victories, with as few casualties as possible. Nobody enjoyed the stench of death.

Nodding in curt silence to the group of officers gathered around his tent, he walked quickly into its dimly lit interior, casting a brief glance at the bunched set of captured standards that had been erected outside his headquarters. Inside he wearily sank into his chair, dragging his hat from his head.

'Sire.'

Silently, Napoleon acknowledged the dirty-looking officer who had just entered the tent.

'I have come from Marshal Davout, sire. He has won a great victory, defeating the main body of the enemy at Auerstadt.'

The Emperor seemed almost to jump, unable to believe his ears. For a moment his exhaustion was forgotten, his grey eyes bore into the grimy face of the young soldier with a relentless penetration.

'What are you talking about?' His voice was arrogantly enquiring. 'Your Marshal must be seeing double,' he snapped at the young soldier with imperious irritation.

'N-no sire...'

Napoleon listened intently as the soldier proceeded to describe how Marshal Davout, with only 27,000 men, had indeed confronted the main body of the enemy, Brunswick's army of 63,000 men.

To his chagrin, the Emperor discovered that he had, in fact, carried out his own engagement with the Prussian flank, a body of greatly inferior numbers to his own. Whereas his Marshal had fought successfully against odds three times as great. Swallowing, he realised the full implications of his errors in calculation. But as he strode to the table, which was thickly draped with maps, his thoughts immediately turned to the forthcoming events of the morrow. Sinking his chin into his chest he intently studied the maps before him. Finally, summoning Berthier, he began to issue orders.

'Tell Davout that if Bernadotte is with him they can march together. But the Emperor expects Bernadotte to already be in the position assigned him, at Dornburg...'

* * *

Marshal Bernadotte looked at the small slip of paper in his hand. His dark handsome features in the light of the single flickering candle betrayed no expression of his feelings. The whinnying of a cold horse, followed by the impatient sound of its stamping, penetrated the damp silence of the small, bare room.

Uneasily, the young officer who was waiting expectantly for a response from the silent Marshal glanced through the cottage window. Poor animal, he thought, it must be tired after such a hectic day and now this hurried journey bringing Marshal Davout's message to Marshal Bernadotte at four o'clock in the morning. The officer felt tired, and hungry. But there was much travelling yet ahead for both himself and the horse. No doubt, in the light of the exciting events of Marshal Davout's victory today, there would be a complete change in plan for this division, and that would doubtless mean further travels. Still, it was exciting! The French would show those Prussians…

His attention returned to the motionless figure of the Marshal. His young brow creased in a troubled frown. Whatever was the matter with the man? It was all quite simple. Marshal Davout needed his support. The French Army was in the process of winning a glorious victory, and it was obvious that Davout needed extra reinforcement to complete his splendid feat. Why then was Bernadotte taking so long about ordering him to do the inevitable?

The silence continued. Finally the young man could stand it no longer. Clearing his throat, he addressed the Marshal. 'W-will there be any reply for Marshal Davout, sir?'

The Marshal's tall frame remained motionless, his eyes now looking through the window into the foggy night, still expressionless.

'A-any orders, sir…?' the soldier anxiously persisted.

Turning his head slowly, the Marshal looked at him. Ignoring the young soldier's questions, he suddenly shouted a summons to his adjutant in the adjoining room. As the bespectacled assistant, instantly responding to his master's call, appeared at the door, the tired messenger began again, his agitation mingled with annoyance at the arrogant attitude of the Marshal.

'S-Sir…!'

'No reply.' The snapped words from the Marshal struck the young man with a stunning force.

He blinked, unable to believe his ears. 'B-but…'

His stammered protestations were coldly silenced by the Marshal's command to his adjutant. 'We shall proceed to Dornburg at dawn as planned. Make necessary preparations.'

As the Marshal turned towards his desk, the young messenger from Davout, apparently forgotten by Bernadotte, stepped forward, his confused face flushed with disbelief. 'B-but, sir, this is not…'

'Thank you, sir.' The cutting words silenced the protest once more, and with a note of disdain the Marshal added, 'My orders are to proceed to Dornburg.' And with an arrogant wave of dismissal, he turned his back on the shattered young man.

Opening his mouth to attempt his protest once more, the tired officer knew it was hopeless as he watched the tall figure of the proud Marshal sit down at the table, and immediately engross himself in the maps and documents before him. Awkwardly he turned towards the door, his head bowed in dejection. How very confusing. What did it all mean…?

Quickly he un-tethered his horse, urging it into a gallop, even as he mounted the confused animal. At speed he rode off into the gathering fog of the hour before dawn.

What could Marshal Bernadotte be thinking of? he wondered, as his thoughts raced with a rhythm complementary to the thundering sound of the horse's galloping hooves. So far in this, his first battle, he had witnessed only the demonstration of heroism and of honour – for the glory of France. But now he had encountered something else, something more complex and personal. He couldn't quite understand it, but he felt it was to do with some sort of excessive pride.

The horse galloped on. Well, it was not for this young officer to decide what cause Marshal Bernadotte had for his odd decisions. But it seemed that he was disobeying orders and refusing to assist Marshal Davout. No doubt he would be court-martialled for it – well, that was what happened on such occasions, or so the officer had been taught at the military academy. Time would tell, he supposed. Meanwhile, he had to inform Marshal Davout.

* * *

The fog did not seem to be quite so thick this morning, thought the Emperor. He could make out quite clearly the dark shapes of the receding clumps of trees, merging into the murky dark of approaching dawn. Napoleon stared at those distant shapes, his eyes deliberately travelling past the vast open spaces that he knew to be scattered with the dead flesh of men. Behind him, inside the tent, he could hear the drone of the report being made to him by an exhausted officer, the latest in a succession of reporting officers from each respective section of the battle areas. He had been listening to such reports all night following the second successful day of fighting.

'And the roads around Apolda are in a state of confusion from the retreating Prussians. The troops of the Corps of Marshal Lannes, Soult and Augereau are in a state of exhaustion following their heavy engagements, but Corps I of The Prince of Ponte Corvo are…'

The clasped hands of the motionless Emperor seemed to involuntarily stiffen into a tighter grip behind his back, as the mention of the name reached his attentive ears. His eyes maintained their distant, unseeing stare as he felt the sudden surge of familiar anger at the thought of the recalcitrant Marshal. How many times in the past had he experienced this same turbulence of angered emotions towards this man?

The recollection of the morning of the coup d'état Brumaire flitted momentarily through his memory, recalling the expression of insolent opposition on the face of the dissenting General in the small room at the Rue Chantereine. Nothing had changed, it seemed. He felt a thud of disappointment. How he had tried. He had even extended to him, before all the other Marshals – excepting his own brother-in- law, Murat – one of the first bequests of the conquered territories. Yet honours and recognition seemed to mean nothing to him. What did the man want? His throne...? The Emperor knitted his brows, his tiredness seemed to overcome him.

The drone of the soldier's voice ceased as Napoleon turned from his position at the open entrance of his tent. Bowing, the soldier prepared to depart following the completed delivery of his report.

'Send Marshal Berthier to me.'

The Emperor's voice was weary as he issued the order to the departing soldier. Sitting down heavily, he leaned back in his chair. He felt an odd sense of hollowness. In vain he tried to summon the elation of Austerlitz; the sweet sense of victory from Marengo. But he could not rid himself of this strange feeling of anti-climax. Was war becoming predictable? Had he lost his crusading spirit? Or was it just that he was losing his respect for human beings, knowing that they would continue to provoke wars against him until they defeated him?

Bitterly he thought of the European monarchies. The Tsar, the Hapsburgs, the English... They would never acknowledge him as 'one of them'. Whatever reforms he made; whatever good he did; they would never really accept him. With a tired sense of despair, Napoleon faced what he knew to be true, despite the superficial charades of politics. In 1799 he had been the embodiment of the Revolution, the salvation of the French dedication to the Rights of Man. And now, in 1806, he remained the embodiment of the Revolution – a Revolution that the crowned heads of Europe wanted to forget lest it happen in their own country and displace their comfortable crowns. In the end he would always be a revolutionary to them, never a monarch. He smiled sourly to himself. The only thing these people understood from him was conquest. They had laughed at his peaceful overtures for cooperation. Instead he would have to compel their 'friendship'...

His eyes wandered to his desk, resting on a sheet of white paper placed neatly for his attention. He stared at it, transfixed. Lifting it, he brought it closer to his eyes, reading it again and again in the bad light of the waning candles. The blood suddenly drained from his face.

'Forgive me, sire, I was delayed.'

The entry of Marshal Berthier jolted the engrossed Emperor. Silently Napoleon nodded as the Marshal began his transmission of information regarding the troop positions. Alert now, the listening Emperor rose, returning to his earlier position at the tent entrance.

There was a long silence following the conclusion of Berthier's statement. Napoleon's eyes scanned the dark silhouettes of the trees against the lightening sky.

'What time is it, Berthier?' The Emperor's tired voice was strangely abstracted.

'It's almost 5am, sire.'

Napoleon heard the reply dimly in the melee of his racing thoughts. Lifting the document he still held in his hand, he stared once more at it. He swallowed. For some reason the bleeding face of the Duc d'Enghien seemed to materialise indiscernibly on the paper.

A damp sensation of cold fear seized his body. Clasping his hands abruptly behind his back, still holding the document, he suppressed a shudder as he strode purposefully into the room. Briskly he began to issue orders to his chief of staff.

'Today we will begin the pursuit of the fleeing Prussian Army...' He launched into his crisp instructions without trace of his earlier tiredness.

Earnestly the Marshal made notes as the Emperor paced up and down the length of the tent interior, speaking with his customary authority. Abruptly he paused, momentarily fixing his eyes on the ground. Berthier's expectant look was succeeded by a surprised raising of his eyebrows as the Emperor continued with his instructions.

'The Prince of Ponte Corvo will proceed with the initial encircling movement...' The Emperor's face betrayed no emotion as he ignored the expression of surprise on his chief of staff's face. 'And now I shall take a short rest, Berthier.' Napoleon's face relaxed into a smile as he finished dictating to the Marshal. 'Ask Constant to attend me. Thank you.'

The warm tones of the Emperor's voice betrayed at last the exhaustion he was fighting.

As the Marshal left, closing the entrance behind him, the tired Emperor sank on to his narrow camp bed. Slowly he lifted the crumpled piece of paper he had been holding. Once more he scanned the words written on it.

He knew they had expected a court-martial. Indeed, he knew that the bitter words exchanged between Bernadotte and himself were the object of discussion throughout his entire army. Bernadotte had claimed that he had received no direct orders from the Emperor instructing him to assist Davout, and he had acted in accordance with the original instructions he had received. The note he had read from Davout had indicated that the Emperor had indeed expected him to be at Dornburg, and it was only due to the exhaustion of his troops, who had been subjected to long, forced marches over the previous five days, that he had been delayed in arriving there. And when he, the Emperor, had pointed out that the Prince had been at Naumberg when he had received instructions to change and assist Davout, the insolent Marshal had insisted that he had received no such direct order, only a vague note that was not even addressed to him.

Napoleon sighed deeply. The man was too sensitive by far, it really was so irritating. Supposing they had lost the battle just because Bernadotte had been ambling along a road in the opposite direction to the battle...?

He stared at the paper in his hand. Suddenly he tore it in half, savagely ripping it into shreds as his angered momentum grew. He couldn't court-martial him. He couldn't. The man would be shot, he knew that...

Lying back on his bed, his fury spent, Napoleon closed his eyes. For a moment he saw once more the bleeding face of the

Duc d'Enghien before his eyes. He would not subject Bernadotte to the same fate. Or his own conscience...

His thoughts faded into the welcome embrace of sleep, even as his faithful valet quietly appeared. Looking at the exhausted body of his beloved master, the valet smiled. The Emperor would have to sleep with his boots on, for it was too late to disturb him.

Bending down, the valet picked up the untidy fragments of torn paper scattered around the floor by the camp bed. He had better tidy up all this rubbish before the Emperor woke and they prepared to leave this dreadful battlefield.

Quietly he swept away the fragments that had been an order for a court-martial...

* * *

I know that I am not alone in thinking it one of the great mysteries of history, this strange ambivalence Napoleon seemed to have in his behaviour towards Jean-Baptiste Bernadotte. Indeed, had he acted in the manner that would have undoubtedly been justified by Bernadotte's outright disregard of orders, the manner in which the rest of the Marshals clearly expected, the course of later events might have had a very different outcome. Yet once more Napoleon saved Bernadotte from the arm of his own justice at Auerstadt. Why?

That is a question that has been much conjectured, and I suppose no one can ever really know that which is in another's mind. All the same, I have often thought that some of the more apparent reasons that clearly contributed towards his decision indicated, at least to me, an interesting insight into the strange complexity of Napoleon's mind, and the extremes of his emotional nature.

It is certain that the marital tie of Napoleon's first love, Désirée, to Bernadotte was an innate factor. There is little question that Napoleon had always been deeply attached to the young woman, and was to remain so all his life, considering her part of his family – as indeed she was, being the sister of Julie Bonaparte. I was not indifferent to the charms of this delightful young woman myself, and am not surprised at the Emperor's continuing affection for the woman whom he had so nearly married, and to whose son he was a fond godfather.

But though this strong relationship undoubtedly had some bearing upon the Emperor's decision to spare Bernadotte from the force of law, I do not believe that it was by any means his sole reason for behaving thus.

As I have already suggested, Napoleon was a man who inspired deep loyalties and love. Perhaps one of the reasons for this extreme response from people was the fact that he himself was capable of these same emotions. Characteristically, once he formed such attachments, they were deeply implanted in his generous nature, and loathsome above all to Napoleon was the betrayal of loyalty. He was possessed of a deep medieval sense of honour, and he regarded loyalty to friendship as one of the most important features of human behaviour. That he had formed one such attachment to Jean-Baptiste Bernadotte was probably not as peculiar as it might seem.

Bernadotte was different from Napoleon's other Marshals. Reserved, even cold, he was nonetheless polite in the extreme, emanating a charismatic presence and displaying a quiet reticence, which spoke of a deep moral integrity. A fanatical Republican, his early rise through the ranks of military service had taught him, in practice, the real meaning of 'The Rights of Man'. He had only succeeded in gaining a commission because of the fall of the Ancien Régime, whose rules had forbidden soldiers to progress beyond the rank of sergeant major unless they could prove noble blood. Thus he had always felt he owed the opportunity to begin his extraordinary ascent to the position of a General in the Revolution to those very tenets. Indeed, as a young man he had had himself tattooed with the revolutionary phrase 'Death to Tyrants.'

The soldiers under his command had always been fiercely loyal to their brilliant General, from the early rabbles he had commanded in the Revolutionary wars, to the proud Corps I of the Grand Army of the French Empire. Recently he had proved that he could inspire loyalty and trust from another position, that of administrator, and during his period as governor of Hanover he had become a paragon of Justice, admired and respected by both occupiers and occupied. 'Fair' was the word most often attributed to Bernadotte. He was a just, considerate, 'fair' man.

These were qualities Napoleon liked and admired, but his own impulsive nature often blinded him to the necessary reserve that is required to make coldly objective judgements in emotional situations, particularly of a personal nature. A fact of which he was inwardly aware.

In so many ways they were 'in concert' in their ideals, and it always seemed to me that co-operation between these two men would have created a powerful working complement. But perhaps the contrasts in their highly individualistic personalities were too extreme, for Napoleon's emotional extroversion succeeded only in inducing the stiff mask of Bernadotte's natural self-restraint, and the result was that each man reserved a wary suspicion for the motives of the other, which was, nonetheless, tempered by their mutual admiration and respect.

Napoleon had a fascination for that which he could not conquer. And in this man, Bernadotte, for whom he felt a deep loyalty and friendship, and perhaps a sense of almost brotherly affection – in this man, nonetheless, he found one whom he could not conquer.

So once more Napoleon had allowed Bernadotte to escape the consequence of disobedience. The recalcitrant Prince was now to redeem his behaviour at Auerstadt by a display of heroic achievement, and no one would be more relieved or delighted than Napoleon.

But the Emperor was not to escape for long the necessity of reprimanding the disobedient Marshal...

* * *

His troops well rested, the Prince of Ponte Corvo now threw himself with an almost crazed vigour into the hot pursuit of the tattered Prussian Army. North, and east marched the relentless forces of Bernadotte, Murat and Soult. And as they swept through the heart of Prussia, crushing the retreating victims of the Grand Army's ardour, the Emperor made his way to Berlin, pausing at Potsdam to visit the tomb of Frederick the Great, whose bust he displayed in his gallery of heroes at the Tuileries.

By the end of October only Blucher, that intrepid Prussian General whose renowned pugnacity would one day find full expression for the hatred he bore Napoleon, was fighting back. Eventually Bernadotte, Murat and Soult had him entrapped under siege in the Hanseatic fortress town of Lubeck. It was the fifth of November.

At two o'clock on the morning of the sixth, Bernadotte led the attack that stormed the fortress, and with only 12,000 men captured Lubeck, defeating Blucher's force of 20,000. It was a daring and audacious assault, which even the Emperor was later to marvel at. Bernadotte knew, as he opened the gates to Murat and Soult, that he had more than atoned for his behaviour at Auerstadt, and when in due course the Emperor received the standards from the Prussian surrender, he made an immediate order of the day commending the brilliant achievement of the three Marshals for their conduct in the pursuit and capture of the Prussian enemy. The campaign of Jena and Auerstadt had ended, and France was once again victorious. Bernadotte had redeemed himself – for the last time.

But the atrocities committed by the French troops against the citizens of Lubeck were appalling. Without delay, the Marshal set about using his administrative and military skills in combination. Imposing a strict discipline on the troops, now rampant in the elation of victory, the Marshal gradually created order in the occupied city. With his characteristic fairness he now ensured the comfort and safety of citizens, occupying troops, and prisoners. And it was his attention to a particular group of prisoners in that captured city of Lubeck that was to change his life completely...

* * *

News of Napoleon's triumphant entry into Berlin following the defeat of the Prussians had been received in Paris with little enthusiasm. The French were tiring of war in 1806.

But the Prussians were re-arming, and the incensed Austrians and Russians were refusing surrender or compromise. Within a few months the Grand Army was once more on the march – to Poland.

For me the endless journeys through the carnage of battle were becoming a nightmare. The sound of marching feet hammered in my mind continually, and time seemed interminable as the months dragged on. Endless uncomfortable journeys in cramped conditions, through the bleak landscapes of eastern Europe, were already depressing me, and now had come the grimmest phase of all.

Napoleon had sensed that a threat from an English-financed Russian intervention was imminent, so he had launched his carefully laid plan to cripple the English economy. The issuing of his 'Berlin Decree' meant that all continental ports were to cease to allow entry of any British ships, and all British commerce was outlawed. Characteristically, the British were to turn the situation to their advantage, creating a black market that provided much lucrative potential for them. But for now Napoleon believed, despite the disadvantaged European economy, that he could defeat the British through crippling their trade.

However, in order that his plan would succeed it was necessary to compel the one remaining British ally, Russia, to conform to his 'Continental System', and thereby blockade the Baltic ports. Thus he decided to approach the resistant Russians through Poland. And in the process he would reconstitute Poland, creating a new French ally in the east.

Any influence I might once have had with Napoleon had now ceased to exist. I found myself compelled to assist in events which were both alien to my philosophy, and clearly courting disaster for France. Napoleon was rapidly losing sight of any recognition of identity of his conquered territories. To him they had become simply a part of an ever-expanding France. His France.

His growing ambitions for sole superiority seemed now to lash him on. Battle followed battle…My worst fears were realised.

As I travelled those broken roads to Poland, I knew that my heart could no longer rule my head. Napoleon had become a victim of his own genius. The realisation of his early constructive dreams had created the means to pursue a growing vision of domination; a vision that he mistakenly interpreted as 'liberation'. Napoleon believed that he alone knew the answer to the stability of Europe. Indeed, he believed he *was* the answer.

I resolved to have done with this empire of his, and with the man himself. I could no longer tolerate his flagrant disregard for human dignity and cultural identity.

But the Polish wars were yet to continue, and my release was not yet imminent…

Chapter XV

Rain was impeding the progress of the small travelling coach. Frequently it became entrapped in the thick river of mud which passed for a road, and the small group of soldiers from the French Imperial Guard who were accompanying it were obliged to assist the coachmen in the slippery task of freeing the paralysed wheels. It was a dirty business, and the soaking soldiers, their uniforms browned with mud, were not enjoying it.

But the real reason for their unease was not the simple if tedious work of heaving the cumbersome coach from the grip of the slimy mud. Nor indeed was it the driving rain, or the frustrating realisation that so little distance was being travelled in a day due to Nature's intervention. Rather, it was the gory reminder of recent bloody days that had induced a sense of sickened revulsion from the young soldiers, whose normal duties were of a more formal domestic nature at the Imperial palaces in Paris.

But now they were faced with the reality of war. Before them here, stretching across the bleak, rain-swept terrain on either side of the slippery track, was the horror of glory's aftermath. A few hastily erected crosses showed how the compassionate amongst the survivors had attempted to give their mutilated compatriots dignity. But it was clear that the relatively few awry Christian symbols scattered across the landscape were in no way related in number to the amount of dead bodies buried just beneath the surface of the ground. The thousands of small muddy mounds, their surfaces already pitted with the force of relentless rain, indicated the reality.

Despite their attempts to resist, the eyes of the young men were compelled to witness the ghastly horror before them. And even as they desperately busied themselves with the task of mobilising the encumbered carriage, the irresistible magnet of the unimaginable gore around them hampered their actions. For days they had been passing through such battlefields. Some, further back, had already been partially embraced by the passage of Nature that had begun to grow grass and motley weeds across the grim surface undulations.

But now, as the road turned north toward Marienburg and Tilsit, the remains of battle had become sickeningly recent. The young men looked at each other, their fresh faces running with water flowing from their rain-soaked hats. And perhaps, too, ran tears on one or two occasions, shed from young eyes that had just witnessed nearby the unbelievably terrible sight of a stiff, thickened, blue hand, stretching its still reaching arm out of the small slimy mound that struggled to hold its rigid captive in a shifting embrace. Everywhere such escaping, decomposing flesh demonstrated death's petrified rigor mortis. And as the soldiers' eyes gradually took in detail from the landscape, they saw more and more protruding limbs and staring faces thrusting their ghastly decaying presence from the trampled ground that had buried summer's green attempts in its churned brown torpor. The inflated bellies of dead horses had already burst open to release their running entrails to the crawling armies of maggots, and the once mighty limbs of the rotting animals stretched proudly to the sky in a gruesome salute above the muddy shrouds of their masters. War held no glamour; glory no meaning; honour only hollow desolation, here in this place of hell. And the high-pitched sound of an eerie wind, lashing the searing rain, played the savage anthem of death to the still bodies in their shallow graves, whose silent screams seemed to strike an hysterical cacophony with the thoughts of onlookers who stared in numbed disbelief at the unimaginable horror around them.

Suddenly the young officer in charge of the small group was lurched out of his mesmerised state by the sense of frozen terror behind him. Abruptly he turned attention towards that petrified presence. And as he looked into the carriage through the streaming water which ran down the window, his eyes met the fixed, dark stare of the woman inside, whose contorted face was expressing an aghast fear and revulsion, while the white bloodless fingers of her shaking hands stretched the skin from her shadowed, quivering eyes, dragging reluctantly from their failed attempt to shield the focus of that terrified gaze upon the horror outside.

As their eyes met, they exchanged a look of helpless enquiry, these two people – one, the woman in the Imperial charge, the other, protector of that privilege. Both were bearing witness to the futility of that now seemingly empty principle that respectively governed their lives: the 'Honour of War'. Where was the 'honour' for these savagely mutilated young men? Where was the abstract glory for their mothers and wives, for their fatherless children? What strange force was it that drove young men of the same age from differing cultures and distanced territories to fight each other, and willingly face the agony of death in places such as this…side by side…and for what…?

It was beyond their comprehension, these two. It was beyond the comprehension, and indeed the contemplation, of everyone they knew – because it was so to all men…Yet even as they suffered this assault to their sensibilities before the gruesome reality of the recent carnage here, in this desolate place, these two knew that time would create an amnesia for their wracked sensitivities, and the subtle manipulations of language would work its somnolent spell upon their torn emotions, imposing the tidy musicality of thought and reason on their grim memories. They would be persuasively seduced back into the safe embrace of the intellectual articulation of those ordered, abstract principles that claimed to justify the bestiality of human behaviour.

They would forget that here they had witnessed hell. They would forget that they had known a moment when they had been certain of the futility of conflict. They would return from that moment of enlightenment to the captivity of the intellectual influences of those whose eloquence of language invoked the alliance of the Almighty to justify the weak-willed trust of their followers.

And yet, perhaps, despite the claims of their leaders, these two would always know that a true concept of the creator of this strange Universe, with its extremes of beauty and ugliness; of goodness and of cruelty; such a concept was impossible for the perception of the human mind. And just as it was impossible to take in the single facet of horror before them now, so it was an ever more remote impossibility to absorb or understand the balancing extremes of Nature, and human behaviour.

But somehow it was important to believe, despite the possessive assertions of bellicose men, that they were themselves the 'agents', that somewhere beyond this vacuum of hell there was an Almighty. And that it was a benevolent force, with some great vision prohibited from the view of men. How else was it possible to accept the sight of such savage destruction of soldiers and animals, if not by believing that death was somehow dignified by something much greater…? Perhaps, after all, that was the meaning of 'Honour' – but how did any man have the right to claim to be its defender? And yes, perhaps the irresistible rush of men towards each other in conflict was inevitable, because pursuit of 'Honour' was pursuit of God. But we would never find it manifest – though it would leave its bloody signature in fields such as this throughout time.

As the soldier saw the tears begin to flow freely through the woman's fine fingers, he turned in worried haste to his stricken companions. Shouting at them, he urged their attentions to the stationary coach. And as they sprang into action, heaving, to their very physical limits, the heavy wooden vehicle, the woman suddenly buried her face in her arms, her face receding into the dim interior of the coach in a sinking convulsion.

The soldier looked up at the window once more, as a hand from inside pulled a curtain across the rain battered window. At that moment the coach wrenched itself free.

* * *

'Enter!'

From the depths of a large comfortable chair the resonant tones of Jean-Baptiste Bernadotte's deep voice gave a preoccupied response to the sharp knock at the door. The Marshal was entirely engrossed in the study of some papers, his massive head sunk into the thick white bandages that encircled his neck, while his long bulky form sprawled from its cushioned support in front of a large crackling fire. Light, gradually dimming, filtered faintly through the narrow window into the small stone room of the medieval castle of Marienburg, where the wounded Marshal of France was reading his despatches.

It was not late on this June evening, but the wet weather had made these latter days unseasonably cold, and the darkness had crept into the rather depressing interior of the bleak castle earlier than usual. The steady orange flame from a single candle, accompanied by the joyful blaze of the warm fire, were the only means of light in the small room, and the deepening shades of approaching night were already casting their dark shadows over the sparse furnishings of the Marshal's quarters. The cluttered table at the window, as well as the narrow bed nearby, were already engulfed in the folds of darkness.

'Yes?'

Bernadotte's voice was suddenly weary as he enquired with lethargic uninterest the reason for the entering officer's visit.

The wound in his neck had been troubling him today, and the acknowledging incline of his head to this messenger from the Emperor had reminded him of the painful task any movement of his neck had been these past ten days since a musket ball had wounded him in action at Spanden.

'I bring a message from the Emperor, Your Highness.'

The young officer was straightening himself from the somewhat exaggerated formality of his bow. The Marshal blinked his attention to the young man, not risking a further inducement of pain from his neck. His polite smile held a hint of wryness. There was often an almost comic display of self-importance from some of these young men who carried messages from the Emperor.

How different were things nowadays in the 'Imperial Grand Army' to the conditions he had known as a young soldier, when he had been this boy's age. The Prince of Ponte Corvo fleetingly recalled the bitter memory of his early struggles as he looked enquiringly at the youth before him.

'The Emperor sends you his sympathy for the wound you received at Spanden, and bids you a speedy recovery...' The soldier paused, lifting his chin as he rather pompously launched into the delivery of his message. 'He expresses pleasure at the display of spirit by your troops, inspired by your own zeal to defend and preserve the Honour of France...'

Bernadotte looked away from the irritating affectation of the young man's verbal delivery. His gaze resting on the orange flames in the fireplace, the Marshal listened while the messenger continued.

'Following his great victory at Friedland, the Emperor will discuss peace terms with the Tsar of Russia at Tilsit on the 25th June...'

Bernadotte breathed in heavily. All this he already knew, earlier despatches having reached him already with news of the outcome of the recent manoeuvres in the north. However, he did not interrupt the young man as he droned on.

'Subsequent to these proceedings you are ordered to assume your new command of the occupying forces in the Hanseatic cities: Hamburg, Bremen, and Lubeck, which are engaged in enforcing the blockade of British ships attempting to trade with Europe...'

The Marshal raised his eyebrows, a sudden expression of keen interest spreading over his face as he awkwardly turned his head to focus his attention to the soldier's face, wincing briefly at the sharp pain from his wound. With close scrutiny, he listened intently to the young man.

'...And following your recovery you will proceed forthwith.'

Abruptly the young soldier ended his delivery, an expression of satisfaction on his face as he bowed unnecessarily once more to the large figure of the Marshal, extending with an almost comical formality a heavily sealed envelope to the rising Prince. With a wry twitch, apparently approaching a smile, the Marshal stretched his hand forward to receive the document.

'Thank you.'

The polite words indicated dismissal to the stiffly attentive soldier, whose subsequent exit was then performed with a degree of dramatic, almost comic courtesy equal to his earlier extreme displays of formal etiquette.

As the door closed behind the departing young soldier, the Marshal breathed a sigh of relief, swiftly crossing the room to the table by the window. Finding an implement that would assist him to open the large envelope, he also lifted a taper from the thick profusion of writing materials which were scattered amongst the numerous maps, books and documents that littered the table's surface.

Returning to his seat by the crackling fire, he lit a few more candles on the table beside his chair before sinking heavily once more into its ample embrace.

As he began to break the seals on the bulky envelope, his attention was momentarily disturbed by the sudden clattering sound of a coach entering the stone courtyard beneath the window. Surprise at the unusually loud noise of the coach and numerous horses fleetingly passed through his mind, but his eager impatience to examine the details of his new orders quickly dismissed any further interest as he unfolded the thick wad of documents, his concentration becoming immediately engrossed by their contents. Sinking back into his chair he became oblivious to the rest of the world.

'Jean-Baptiste!'

The soft voice from the doorway spoke its whispered words unnoticed. Quietly pushing the door a little further open, the small, cloaked figure moved gracefully into the silent room, closing the door as noiselessly as it had been opened. For a long moment the intruder remained motionless in the darkened shadows near the unlit door. From beneath the hooded cloak it appeared to be regarding the large back of the chair in which Bernadotte sat, his long legs stretched out in front of the huge fire, his attention entirely absorbed by the papers he was reading. Then once more the silent observer spoke, the quiet tones a little louder this time, audible through the merry crackling of the fire.

'Jean-Baptiste…?'

The small figure moved forward a little.

Suddenly the large form of the Marshal seemed to leap out of the chair, turning as he rose, an expression of uncontainable astonishment and delight on his face as he paused, unable to believe his eyes as the cloaked figure ran across the room towards him.

'Jean-Ba…'

The choked repeat of his name was drowned as he crushed the small form in a tight, almost desperate embrace.

'*Désirée*!' A note of disbelief sounded in his shout as he buried his mouth in her soft hair, knocking the enveloping hood from her head. 'Désirée, my darling, how…?'

He had picked her up, unable to hold her tightly enough in his unexpected rush of emotion. Hungrily he kissed her face and neck, the more usual bounds of his self-restraint unleashed as he hugged to his body the most precious thing in his world, hardly able to believe it was really her.

Désirée was laughing now, the soft musical tones filling the austere room with their gentle femininity.

'Jean-Baptiste…' she laughed 'put me down, darling!' Her face was radiant as she looked into his dark, handsome features. 'I can't breathe!'

Lovingly she gazed at him, kissing him on the forehead once more, before he lowered her to the ground. Her hands remained stretched up to his shoulders, her fingers gently touching the thick white bandages.

'Doesn't it hurt, darling?' Her large eyes were filled with a troubled concern as she lovingly searched his. 'I-I was so worried…'

For a moment the dreadful memory of the battlefield passed through her mind. What if Jean-Baptiste had been one of those?

He might have been…

Now she put her arms around his waist, leaning her head against his chest as he folded his arms around her and, after his initial frenzied embraces, he moved her in a deeply tender rocking rhythm, his mouth buried in the soft hair on top of her head. The wound in his neck was throbbing after its exertion, but his sense of elation, and sheer disbelief, at seeing his beloved wife here, in the field, without warning or expectation, had been so overpowering that the unpleasant sensation of pain was a mere annoyance.

'It's alright, darling…'

He took the small hands that were touching the thick bandage into his own. Lovingly, he pressed his lips to the slim fingers as his eyes, suddenly moist with emotion, gazed deeply into the expression of worried enquiry in his wife's face.

'Truly – it's almost better!' His voice held a hint of amusement. Then, as he continued, his expression turned to startled amazement. 'Désirée, my love, did you come all this way, to this dreadful place, just because I was wounded…? To nurse me…?'

He was suddenly incredulous as he realised the enormity of her undertaking, knowing her conditions of travel would have been unpleasant and uncomfortable.

Now, as Désirée gazed up into the face she loved so deeply, tears began to flow down her lovely face.

'I-I couldn't bear to stay in Paris when I knew you were ill…it-it was terrible not knowing how you were – how…how bad the wound was. I-I wanted to take care of you…'

She paused, burying her head in the massive chest of her husband, sniffing at her running tears, absorbing the familiar warm smell of her beloved Jean-Baptiste, that comfort she had yearned for so badly during the long months since he had been in Paris.

'I-I managed to get a special pass from the Emperor to come…'

All at once she felt weak. The tiredness from her journey seemed to suddenly overcome her, and she sank limply into the strong embrace, unable to support herself any longer.

As she closed her eyes she could feel him lift her, and her head rolled on to his shoulder, her forehead touching the thick bandage. She could hear the warm crackle of the fire, and feel the tender pressure of his lips on her face as he sank into his large chair, the small form of his wife cradled in his embrace. She had succumbed to her exhaustion and fallen asleep in his arms. He could still hardly believe she was actually here as he looked down at the deeply loved face. He felt slightly dazed as he fully grasped the realisation that she had come. She has come, he thought, to me... To me – not to him...

Thoughtfully he studied the sleeping face closely. How much he loved her. How much...

* * *

'Here, put this round your shoulders, Your Highness.'

Désirée's maid, Marie, was fussing as her mistress seated herself at the imposingly set dinner table, whose magnificent candelabra lit up the room with a soft dancing light, glinting on its silver with tiny myriad sparkles. The clean table linen and heavy cutlery gave the Spartan room a domestic feeling, and as the room filled with the delicious smell of steaming dishes being brought in by Bernadotte's faithful batman, the place seemed transformed from its earlier austerity.

Placing a shawl around her mistress's shoulders, Marie looked at Bernadotte, her kind face creased in a frown as she sternly proceeded to rebuke the tall form of the Marshal of France.

'This is no place for a lady, Your Highness. The princess will catch her death of cold here in this damp...'

As she berated her master, the Marshal and his wife were regarding the broad figure of the elderly woman with amused indulgence. Gesticulating, the woman continued, 'It just won't do. There's nowhere suitable for her to sleep...the place is crawling with insects and mice, and there's probably rats, I wouldn't wonder...'

From his position by the fireplace the Prince now moved forward, kindly putting an arm across the elderly woman's shoulders, his face alight with a broad beam of amusement as he soothingly interrupted her fussing protestations, gently guiding her towards the door as he spoke.

'Now, Marie, don't worry. The Princess will be all right. We will make her quite comfortable, but some suitable furnishings have to be requisitioned from the town – and such a feat cannot be accomplished in five minutes, you know…' He winked mischievously back at Désirée. 'After all, it was a little bit of a surprise, you know Marie! We didn't know you were coming…' His amused voice continued with gentle patience as the woman shook her head, protesting that she had known all along that it was a bad idea. 'I think the Princess had better have her food now before it gets cold, don't you, Marie?' The Prince's tactful politeness silenced the woman. 'She must be very hungry after such a tiring journey…'

The woman glanced suspiciously up into the good-looking face of the Marshal. Grudgingly she nodded, her concerned gaze returning to her radiant mistress as she regretfully moved to go through the door that the Marshal was courteously holding open for her. Awkwardly the woman heaved herself into a cumbersome curtsy as the object of her affectionate concern spoke softly to her from her place at the table.

'Thank you, Marie…I have everything I want.'

Désirée's glowing eyes travelled lovingly to the figure of her husband as he held the door calmly for the two departing servants.

Closing the door behind the hurried exit of the man, Bernadotte leaned against it for a moment, gazing at the beautiful vision of his wife. For a long moment, they gazed deeply into each other's eyes, the silent room tranquil and glowing with the love between them. Quietly he moved from the door and sat down opposite her.

'Thank you for coming, darling…'

His voice was husky as he tried to reflect the depth of his feelings. There was a silence, and then the air seemed to fill with the soft sound of her laughter as she picked up her knife and fork.

261

'Come on Jean-Baptiste. It really will get cold!'

Happily they began their meal.

The small room had grown very warm from the heat of the fire and the many candles. Désirée leaned back in her chair, dreamily smiling at her husband's efficient batman, Fernand, as he cleared away the dirty dinner dishes. A combination of the wine, the food, the warmth, and the deep sense of contentment at being with her husband once more, had made her slightly light-headed.

During dinner they had exchanged, with eager excitement, news of the recent months when they had been separated. To him she had related the antics of their son, and the intrigues of the Paris court; and to her he had described the recent battle movements as the Grand Army had made its advance across Germany into Poland, and the exciting news of his new appointment at the Hanseatic cities. They had talked and talked without ceasing, each one anxious to share with the other every moment that they had been separated. Then, as they had finished their meal, Jean-Baptiste had rung for his batman to remove the remains of the food and the dishes, while he himself had moved to the fireplace to pile more logs on the dark red smouldering furnace, poking the hissing heat underneath as the rekindled orange flames began slowly to lick the long brown pieces of wood.

Bernadotte turned to his batman, smiling happily.

'Thank you Fernand.'

His eyes returned to his beloved wife's face. As the door closed, he drank in silent contentment.

Désirée's dreamy gaze was staring at the pale gold liquid in her glass. She was aware of her husband's loving attention on her from across the room. There was a long silence between them. Only the sound of the fire filled the air.

'It's as though we've never been apart...' Her voice was low, her words almost involuntary as she voiced her thoughts, still looking at the glistening gold wine.

Jean-Baptiste smiled. How gentle she was, his little Désirée.

'Yes, it's wonderful to be alone together, my darling. It happens so seldom...'

His happy voice was silenced as Désirée continued, apparently not hearing his words, her voice seeming to become somehow melancholy and tense.

'The other Marshals…they-they seem to send for their wives, and yet you…' Her face had clouded with a sad expression. Now she turned to look across at her husband, inclining her head slightly, her eyes blinking a little with sudden nervousness. 'You…' She paused, before continuing uncertainly, 'You never seem to want…me…'

Tears welled up in her eyes as she looked at the tall man, he whom she loved so deeply. Unable to finish her sentence, she abruptly picked up her glass, drinking from it quickly and thoughtfully.

The smiling expression vanished from the Marshal's face. Dropping his gaze, he stared for a long time into the fire.

'I thought you liked being in Paris, Désirée…' The words seemed to rasp, as some sudden constriction in his throat appeared to make Bernadotte's deep voice oddly brittle. He raised his head to look meaningfully at her as he went on, his voice quiet, and suddenly cold. 'Your presence in Paris seems to be important to…' He returned his attention to the fire. '…the demands of the Imperial Family.' As he spoke his bitter remark, he turned his back to the room, spreading his long arms to grip each end of the wide mantelpiece.

'Whatever are you talking about, Jean-Baptiste?' Désirée's sharp words, raised in an indignant tone, cut across the room.

His broad back remained unmoved as his bent head regarded the increasing flames in the fireplace. As the sound of her words faded, a heavy silence fell.

Désirée's face creased into a troubled frown, her shocked indignation transformed into a confused concern as she stared at the motionless figure of her husband. Deliberately setting her glass down on the table, she rose. Slowly she walked across to stand by Jean-Baptiste's still form. Gently she reached her hand up to touch his shoulder.

'Jean-Baptiste…?'

She waited for his response, her own sad gaze followed his to observe the vigorous blaze of the fire beneath them. He remained silent, lost in some troubled, incommunicable thought. Glancing upwards, from underneath his stretching arm, she could see his face, its chin buried in the thick white collar of bandages. He seemed tired, deep shadows, accentuated by the now leaping flames below, shrouded the contours of his face, and Désirée noticed lines she had never seen before etched in fine patterns around his eyes and across his forehead. Sighing deeply, he moved backwards from the fireplace, sinking with exhaustion into the large chair. Momentarily he closed his eyes, fingering his throbbing neck.

'Forgive me, my love. I did not mean to speak in such a way to you.' Jean-Baptiste paused. He was looking apologetically at his wife, who was still standing by the fire. 'I-I'm tired…this wound has given me such pain these past few days…'

He stretched a long arm towards her and, taking her hand, pulled her down to him, his troubled eyes lovingly searching her face. Responding to his touch, Désirée sank with liquid grace on to the floor at his feet, taking both his hands in hers as she now looked up at his massive form above her. Leaning against his legs, she rested her chin on his knee, their hands locked together on his lap. The flickering light from the fire threw moving shadows across them as they searched each other's faces in the silence. And as she realised that Jean-Baptiste's pain was more than just the physical result of a battle, Désirée's voice was sad as she began in a low, gentle whisper, 'What is it, Jean-Baptiste?' She hesitated briefly before going on. 'It's…the Emperor…is it not?'

She could feel Jean-Baptiste's body stiffen slightly as she mentioned Napoleon, and with a sinking feeling of confirmation, Désirée turned her head towards the fire, staring unseeingly into the orange blaze. Knowing that inevitably she must discuss the subject that seemed to be so sensitive to her beloved husband, she resolved to continue. Her voice sounded dejected as she spoke her next words in almost a monotone, pleading for understanding.

'Is it because he shows such generosity? Because he bequeaths us lands and titles? Is it because he gave us Moreau's house…?'

Her husband's body stiffened. Poor Moreau. The Emperor had exiled him to America because of his part in the plots against the Sovereign's life. Then Napoleon had bought the General's beautiful Paris house – and given it as a present to the Prince and Princess of Ponte Corvo.

Désirée knew how sensitive Jean-Baptiste was to the mention of his exiled friend. And yet, as she had reflected upon the strange workings of Napoleone's mind, she had nonetheless pondered the fact that, despite his resentment, Jean-Baptiste was a willing recipient of the Emperor's generosity. On what principles, then, did one defend one's moral values? But discussions on ethics always confused her. People were always so hypocritical.

Now her eyes searched her husband's tense face imploringly. 'Jean-Baptiste – he is Oscar's Godfather – he is my sister's brother-in-law; Jean-Baptiste, why...?'

Her urgent pleadings suddenly ceased as she felt her husband's expressionless stare. Involuntarily her narrow shoulders drooped, and taking in a deep breath she turned her head away from his gaze, looking sadly into the fire. 'Alright, Jean-Baptiste...' Her toneless murmur fell thickly into the heavy silence. 'I – I... have a deep affection for the Emperor...'

But even as her words thudded their admission, she swung her head back quickly, clasping her husband's large hands tightly, and her eyes, wide and pleading, flashed their urgent accompaniment to her now rapidly spoken words.

'But darling, you don't understand the nature of my feelings for him. It's...it's not what you think...You and Oscar, *you* are my family, my life... I love you...more...more than life itself.'

She stopped, a lump coming to her throat as she looked into his bemused face, her eyes filling with tears. Wordlessly Jean-Baptiste lifted a hand, gently brushing a hair from his wife's brow, silently waiting for her to continue, knowing she was struggling to control her confused feelings which he knew, at last, were going to be explained to him.

Shifting her position slightly, so that she was now facing her husband squarely, kneeling as she sat on her feet, she stretched her arms across his lap, looking with love at his hands clasped inside hers. Bathed in the orange glow of the fire, she began.

'Napoleone...' She smiled to herself, a soft expression of affection ruefully touching her gentle face. Her voice was quiet and steady. 'I have known Napoleone since I was a little girl...' Again she smiled, remembering her youth in Marseilles, and the thin handsome General with the untidy long hair. 'How I loved him – and he me...' She nodded slowly, her smile soft and melancholy as she added with faint audibility, as though to herself, '...He loved music...'

As her murmur faded into the crackling sound of the fire, she thoughtfully looked into space. Suddenly, pulling herself from her preoccupations, she turned once more to look into Jean-Baptiste's face, her expression smiling in amusement.

'You Marshals! You see Napoleon, Emperor of the French – the mighty conqueror, following in the footsteps of Alexander and Caesar, strong and invincible...' She laughed. 'Oh, my darling, you do not know the man beneath that arrogant façade. You do not know how deeply vulnerable, how sensitive and insecure a child exists beneath that charade he subjects us all to...'

A thought seemed to occur to her. Inclining her head slightly, she spoke more seriously, half to herself. 'Perhaps that's the very reason he has become so unbearable and uncompromising...so that no one will ever see what lies beneath...it's all some strange sort of mask...'

Once more she fell silent, this time for a long moment, apparently pondering her own last statement. Jean-Baptiste studied her face as she reflected, oblivious to all but her thoughts. How odd it was, he thought, that she was so utterly certain of her statements; so almost possessive about the man who had subjected Europe to his will. He could hardly believe that she could speak with such pragmatism about the man who had already become a living legend. How strange was the mind of a woman...how very different from that of a man. Women were somehow more worldly.

Her eyes returned to meet his as she continued. 'His brothers and sisters don't understand him. They only support him because he showers them with gifts and honours. They don't even try to understand how extraordinary is his nature – that he is unique. They even have the temerity to believe that they are possessed of the same qualities!!' She laughed harshly. '...Which shows how ignorant they are. Can't they see that...'

Abruptly she broke off in agitation at the thought of the Bonapartes. Finally composing herself, she continued sadly, 'They don't really love him. Except perhaps Pauline...' Reflectively she added, once more as though to herself, 'And Lucien...he was different. It's a pity...'

As her sentence trailed off unfinished, she looked steadily into her husband's eyes. Lucien and he were still good friends, she knew. They had remained in close and regular contact, even though Lucien had lived in exile in Rome for some time now.

'Jean-Baptiste...' She had pulled herself back from her musings, and was looking intensely into her husband's eyes, gripping his hands hard. 'Jean-Baptiste...he is completely alone. You – you have me, Oscar. You have Fernand, and the friendship of your officers. Lucien...' She shrugged and sighed, her face involuntarily falling into a sad smile, which instantly vanished. 'And even though so many people misunderstand your reserved nature, you know that you have the respect and admiration of everyone...No-one...*no-one* laughs at you behind your back.'

She halted, uncertainly this time, her face creased in troubled pain. It was so difficult to explain what she felt to Jean-Baptiste. It was difficult to understand it herself. Her voice was thick as she continued slowly.

'Napoleone always had so much vision. He really believed that he could bring glory, peace, prosperity, happiness – to France, to all human beings. He-he believed he was translating the real meaning of the Rights of Man for all the world to see, that he was the heir of the Revolution which so many French men and women died for...He really believed that what he was doing was his destiny...He – he had always believed that. I-I know...'

She stopped, drained of emotional energy.

Jean-Baptiste was concerned as he looked at the woman he

loved and knew so well, and yet who was revealing a facet of her understanding that he had never before witnessed, or even known to be there. He pressed her damp hands, unwilling to interrupt her labouring words, which he knew had to come out. And now her eyes searched his, pleading with an urgent request for understanding.

'But he's not like other people, Jean-Baptiste…' She shrugged. '…And because of that, no one else really understands him. And because of *that* no one else can share his complete vision. They can only see part of it… By nature he is energetic and enthusiastic, and when he fails to communicate his ideas, he becomes impatient and isolated. Language does not seem able to afford him an appropriate expression for that great imagination - for that great mind.'

Désirée was now shaking Jean-Baptiste's hands in a plea for comprehension. 'Jean-Baptiste…he is terribly, *terribly* frustrated. He believes himself misunderstood by all. He…he is so…alone…'

She was trembling as she tried to express her uncertainties. Jean-Baptiste was alarmed as his wife broke off once more, a sob in her throat thickening the words, which seemed to be giving her so much pain. Reassuringly he squeezed her hands as she stared at the floor, gathering her strength for the final thrust of her impassioned plea for understanding.

A dawning perception was taking place in his mind. Slowly he was becoming aware that his wife looked at things in a different way from him, and that therefore her sensitivities responded to aspects of character and realities of circumstances that he would not generally perceive. Once more he was struck by the basic observations that characterised feminine perception.

He was used to being in the company of men, and sharing the natural camaraderie of soldiers in the united pursuit of honour and glory. Certainly ambition, and the desire to excel, were factors in the proud career of a soldier, but the essential thrusting drive was the principle of the integrity of honour itself, for its own enigmatic sake. His life, therefore, was dedicated to an abstract principle. And the consequence of circumstance was entirely related to his obedience to that presiding dedication. His fellow soldiers he knew to be the same, and thus his relationship with others of an equivalent rank and responsibility was one of rivalry and natural masculine competition in the field of honour. To him Napoleon Bonaparte had always been one of those rivals who, though undoubtedly possessed of outstanding military abilities, had nonetheless attained his position of supremacy through the expediency of luck.

Désirée, on the other hand, addressed herself to an entirely different order of priorities in her perceptions: a feminine perspective. To women, it seemed, honour and glory were nonsense, the stuff of childhood fairy tales and dreams. The reality of home and children, of material security, these were the concerns and preoccupations of women. And as they indulged their children with stories of knights and wizards, so they indulged their husbands by listening to their dreams of honour and glory on the battlefield. With wise intuition they allowed the strutting posturing of masculine pride, whilst shrewdly they organised the practical mechanics of order, effortlessly tempering the excesses of male dramatics with apparent submission. Men lived by dreams – and women used those dreams to create comfort and ease within reality. Women saw beneath the glitter and glamour of men's glorious crusades. Yet they skilfully encouraged male participation in such quests, knowing the practical results to be the basis for their own procreative spirit.

Jean-Baptiste was dumbfounded by this revelation. As he looked at the demure figure of his wife, her head bent meekly as she stared at the floor, he felt suddenly naked. He knew that her feminine wisdom looked deep into his soul, seeing things that even he could not understand. So too had she seen into the inner vulnerabilities of Napoleon Bonaparte, and she had understood something that men could never see.

Suddenly he felt ashamed of his jealousy, knowing that he had felt such an emotion towards the Emperor because of his wife's devotion to him. Jealousy was such a petty emotion, not worthy of challenging such great spiritual insights. Unexpectedly he felt a strange sensation of dawning admiration for Napoleon. Perhaps the great man had recognised this quality in women? That was why, perhaps, he revered the position of women and family. And perhaps too it was why he remained so close to Bernadotte's wife. He understood the real strength of the female sex, knowing that to them men always remained small boys, forever playing romantic games.

Jean-Baptiste blinked at his own confusion. His breast swelled with a protective surge for the frail figure of his pale wife as she looked up at him, tears glistening in her eyes, her beautiful face lit magically by the orange glow of the fire behind her. How gentle she was, how deep, how lovely, how strong...

Now the wisdom of her words struck him with profound intensity. 'His isolation is growing, Jean-Baptiste. He is somehow lost in the maze of his own great mind. As time goes on fewer and fewer of the people around him attempt to even try to understand him, they're content to exploit his generosity, and appease his wilfulness for their own ends.' Her voice was contemptuous now. 'They don't care about him – or France. Deep down he knows that, and it makes him less able to communicate with people like Talleyrand who *do* care. But his pride won't let him. And so his actions will become more reckless, reflecting the desperation of his feelings...the way they were when he failed to make the Bourbons understand him...and he killed the Duc d'Enghien.' She broke off, a note of despair in her voice. In a low tone she continued, almost inaudibly, 'I am quite certain that no one suffered more deeply for that dreadful deed than Napoleone himself. I-I know he is haunted by guilt...'

Returning her gaze to her husband, Désirée once more pleaded with her eyes. 'Darling, there are two people in this world who understand Napoleon: myself and Josephine. No one knows that better than he.' She smiled sadly. 'Poor Josephine. Even now she waits for the inevitable divorce, and bears the humiliation of the reports of his new affair with the little Walewska. Yet, as with me, he will try to retain 'possession' of her, because he needs to know that our affection is constant…so that if – when – this great empty empire he has built suddenly collapses, there will be two people who will know what it is he really wanted; what it was he really tried to do – and why…'

Jean-Baptiste was moved, feeling the backs of his eyes prick with the impact of her quiet words. Adoringly she now gazed into his eyes as she lifted his hands to her mouth, pressing her lips tenderly upon them before continuing, her voice breaking slightly as she spoke.

'My strong Jean-Baptiste, how much I love you. How much…' Her voice was husky as she continued, stopping to wipe away one of the tears that were beginning to fall. 'Please understand, my darling, you know no competition from Napoleone. But never ask me not to feel the deep affection and care I have for him. If- if I cannot stand by him, then he has no friend on this earth…They will trample him into the ground should the tides of fortune change… How…' The control she had managed to maintain seemed to burst. 'How would I feel if it were my Oscar…?'

While the constricted words tumbled out, her body crumpled as the shaking of a tearful convulsion now swept over her, defeating her halting speech.

Jean-Baptiste was horrified as his wife broke down, and leaning forward he hastily gathered her up in his arms, pulling her wracked form up on to his lap, cradling her wet face to his cheek.

'Désirée…Désirée…my little Désirée…' He felt exhausted himself as he murmured her name in his endeavour to pacify her despairing sobs. 'I understand…'

His large arms enfolded her tightly to him as he kissed her face, desperately trying to stop the pitiful sound of his wife's crying.

Yes, he did understand, as well as a man could ever understand a woman. Love was many-faceted for a woman – it wasn't as straightforward as it was for a man. For a man it was love of an idea, and of conquest. For a woman the love of the perceived reality, and the maternal need to nurture… But no, it was much more complicated than that.

He felt hot and confused, and his thoughts were in turmoil as he clasped to his body the precious form of his beloved Désirée. He was ashamed that he had caused her so much pain, and that he felt helpless to comfort her.

Suddenly he buried his face in her neck. His voice was thick and muffled as he blurted out his incoherent thoughts.

'Destiny is cruel to our tormented souls...Admiration; jealousy; respect; love...' He swallowed hard, his throat felt so dry. 'How roughly does life pitch us into the turbulence of our emotions...' He stopped for a moment, rubbing his forehead against the soft skin of his wife's neck, the fragrance of her body making him feel light-headed, unable to discern his thoughts properly. 'But how can we learn to temper them?'

His voice was choked as he felt Désirée's trembling stabilise to a quiver as she lay against him limply. Tenderly he kissed her, gently stroking her head with one hand, the other clasped around her body. His cheek brushed against the top of her bent head, as he looked sorrowfully into the now dying fire. They were both exhausted as they clung together in the orange glow, their energies spent. And as they stared – unblinking – into the fire, he suddenly heard himself voice his apprehensive thoughts.

'Perhaps it is better to distance oneself from the grip of the destructive forces of emotion... Who knows what catastrophes can be released when they become uncontrolled...'

Abruptly he stopped. But perhaps it was only men who were ever really carried away... He looked at the still silent form of his beloved wife as she lay in his arms. Her eyes were fixed on the thick white bandages around her husband's neck. And as she envisaged the bleeding wound beneath them, she stared into a recent memory: the sight of a blue decomposing hand, reaching out to her from a sodden battlefield...

'Destructive forces...'

Faintly he heard her echo his words with chilling tonelessness.

He stood up, still holding her to him tightly in his arms. In a few strides he carried her to the bed...

Chapter XVI

He had ceased to smile with his eyes.

I suppose it was an odd thought to strike me on that historic morning at Tilsit on 25th June 1807.

Notwithstanding the fact, however, that Napoleon, Emperor of the French, was certainly engaged upon a considerably vigorous exercise in smiling that day, perhaps it was not so altogether strange that I had made such an observation during the somewhat absurd proceedings of this particular occasion.

I had wondered, as I saw the short erect figure of the Emperor outlined against the background of Holy Russia itself, what exactly had been going through his mind. Certainly his fixed smile, and gracious condescension, were no indication of his thoughts as he stepped into the boat that would row him out to the raft that had been moored in the middle of the River Nieman. But as he turned his head to face the distantly approaching Tsar, similarly flanked with his floating guard, I saw his chin lift slightly, and I knew that the smell of supreme power was most agreeably penetrating his nostrils.

I smiled somewhat sourly to myself, as my eye scanned the mathematically precise patterns of the thousands of French and Russian soldiers that lined each respective bank of this natural border of the Russian frontier. For hours they had been standing to witness the historic meeting of the two most powerful men in the world upon this odd looking construction in the middle of the river.

I smothered a sigh of boredom as the slow ritual proceeded midst the rapt anticipation of thousands of stilled observers. How he loved these ridiculous displays of dramatic spectacle. I suppose they appealed to his sense of *destiny*. Personally, I find such exhibitions ostentatious and disgustingly vulgar. Furthermore, the long hours of standing cause me considerable discomfort in my leg, as well as a tiresome headache induced by the seemingly interminable tedium of the formal procedures involved.

But the French victory at the battle of Friedland had certainly ensured Napoleon's supremacy of power in Europe, and now, eleven days later, the Tsar was seeking terms of peace with Napoleon. And thus it seemed that the Corsican General had at last reached the pinnacle of political and military authority. But as I looked at the small receding figure in the boat, I felt I hardly recognised him as the young First Consul of Brumaire. Those grey eyes had indeed ceased to smile.

I shifted my weight slightly, leaning heavily on my stick. Confound these charades. I felt as though I was witnessing, indeed participating in, some sort of absurd comic opera. Though perhaps the eccentricity of this exercise was beyond the limits of exaggeration for even those flippant ephemera of Art.

The boats were approaching the raft now, and I pulled my eyes away from following the sanguine sight of the Emperor. I was feeling a trifle sickened by his excessive display of self-confidence. It was not a sensation that was strange to me any more.

Perhaps with men of destiny it is their profound faith in themselves, and what they thereby claim and aspire to do for the common good, that exacts the devotion and worship of ordinary people. Perhaps, therefore, that supreme self-confidence of those who hold such faith in themselves inspires some sort of feeling of an imparted self-assurance for those who place their trust in them. Perhaps then, the whole phenomenon of 'hero worship' is a strange form of acquiring self-esteem through proxy. I know not! Nor indeed did I care as I stood on the banks of the River Nieman. What I did know was that in this moment I could somehow discern the shadow of impending disaster.

These past months in Poland I had witnessed the final transformation of his character, from earnest and benevolent First Consul to selfish and insensitive Absolute Ruler of Europe. He had now ceased entirely to heed my advice, and though I had hoped for a flicker of the old Napoleon in discussions about Poland when I had urged the return of its own sovereignty, I was to be disappointed.

To my dismay I observed that he was changing with an alarming rapidity, not only in his mental attitudes, but also in his physical energies – and though he would never become indolent, he had nonetheless lost much of his vigour and capacity for attention to detail. His growing rotundity reflected this physical degeneration, and he appeared to be ageing prematurely.

Only the night before this spectacle at Tilsit had the final blow been dealt to my former faith and admiration for the man. Indeed, I was still suffering from a state of shock due to the sheer lunacy of such a preposterous determination. He had confided to me that it was his firm intention to bring about the destruction of the Spanish Bourbon dynasty, and that he would embark upon his plan immediately following his return to France.

I was appalled. I had known of his earlier vague references to such a dreadful possibility, indeed he had frequently referred to it in Berlin. But now he had formulated a plan, and I knew him to be intent upon his folly. Thus my resolve was confirmed. I would resign from his service upon my arrival in Paris.

My eyes were now resting upon a beautiful face. Her melancholy gaze mirrored my own feelings of apprehension as it followed intently the slow passage of the Emperor of France to the raft. I am not a man much given to the wrenching consequence of emotion. But as I looked into those exquisite features amongst the rows of dignitaries ranged along the bank, I knew that what I saw was not simply the face of a beautiful woman, but that it was also the expression of tragedy in the most profoundly dignified sense. I was deeply moved.

Queen Louise of Prussia was a woman whose courage and bravery matched her beauty. I knew that she had come to Tilsit in the hope that she would be able to exercise her unequalled charm and considerable intellect for the cause of her beleaguered country, by trying to soften the heart of her oppressor, thereby salvaging some meagre degree of dignity for her already crushed people. But even as I looked at her I knew that her hopes were in vain, for Napoleon was not disposed to be conciliatory towards Prussia, whatever the charms of its beautiful Queen, and I was certain that he would not hesitate to further humiliate these proud people and their magnificent champion.

The succeeding days would confirm my sad certainty, and I would be forced to witness the young woman suffer the most degrading rebuffs from the insensitive conqueror, which she bore with a dignity that equalled her beauty and courage.

I had the honour to become closely acquainted with this extraordinary woman, and I would forever regard the memory of her friendship as a privilege. Three years later, aged only thirty-four, she would die – it was said from a broken heart.

But in these two weeks at Tilsit, as she vainly fought for her country, she was a commanding figure for admiration, and it was more than I could endure to watch the callous humiliation of Prussia that took place. Frederick William was thus compelled to lose half his territory, and suffered the reduction of his population to little over five million. And as the Prussians bore this final assault to their dignity, I knew that such injured pride could never be healed, save by revenge. Their hatred of Napoleon would fester until one day…

Roars from the cheering ranks of soldiers were now rising into the clear midday sky: 'Long live the Emperor of the East!' Long live the Emperor of the West!'

The cheers rang out joyfully from both banks of the river as the two Emperors, having set foot on their raft at exactly the same moment, had at last met.

'Sire, I hate the English as much as you do.' Thus spoke the Tsar of all Russia, finally forced to reject his former alliance in the face of the formidable French conqueror.

'Then all can be arranged. Peace is settled.'

And upon Napoleon's ready reply the two young men fell into an embrace, which delighted the spectators, and sealed the acquiescence of the Tsar to Napoleon's wishes.

In subsequent days they would sign treaties agreeing peace, and ensuring Russia's full participation in enforcing Napoleon's Continental System in the economic war of attrition with England.

The blond, handsome, thirty-year-old Tsar, whose sense of *destiny* ominously equalled Napoleon's own, was, for now, utterly seduced by Napoleon's charm. The two retreated into the incongruous pavilion that covered most of the raft, and we, the onlookers, were obliged to wait a further two hours before the historic meeting ended and we could at last disperse.

Napoleon returned to the west bank of the Nieman, justifiably pleased with himself. He had placed the Tsar of Russia under his spell. He was now indeed the Master of Europe.

* * *

It was the year 1808, and France was at Peace with Austria and Prussia. Their Emperors were the reluctant allies of the Emperor of France.

Only England continued to thwart the will of the French conqueror, and it was thus towards the methods and means of defeating that country that Napoleon now fully directed his obsessional energy.

I now found myself addressed as 'Vice Grand Elector'. The splendid ring to this somewhat pompous sounding apparent distinction, however, in fact belied its true nature, for it was a position as empty in substance as its vulgar title deserved.

Upon our return to Paris from Tilsit I had, as indeed I had determined, submitted my resignation. I was astonished, and flattered, to discover that my action had been received with a considerable degree of consternation by the French people.

Napoleon, however, whilst accepting in principle that I no longer wished to continue in the position of Minister of Foreign Affairs, nonetheless refused to relieve me of the advisory aspects of my work. Therefore, after much debate, we agreed upon a compromise. I was to be apparently promoted to the lofty office of Vice Grand Elector, but whilst I would remain an advisor to the Emperor, I would no longer be in a position of active authority. Napoleon was a man who refused to part with possessions – even when they were people!

The arrangement suited me most agreeably since there were considerable financial assets associated with the title. Moreover, being essentially a lazy fellow, I was delighted to find a position that, whilst still involved, did not overtax my strength. However, my real reason for delight in my relative freedom was that I was now in a position whereby I could work with more constructive vigour, unhampered by restriction, for what I considered to be the real interests of Europe.

Much of my time I now spent with the Austrian Ambassador, Clemens Metternich, a young man who shared my views on the necessary balancing of the European powers, and held a deep distrust for the ever expanding objectives of the French Emperor.

Napoleon, I suspect, was secretly better satisfied with the new arrangement. He had often displayed a certain displeasure at the esteem I had recently been fortunate enough to have extended to me from leading statesmen all over Europe. His increasing self-confidence and autocracy no longer required a Minister who held views of his own. My successor, Champagny, was a more malleable individual, disinclined to challenge the Imperial perspective, and therefore more to the new Napoleon's liking. Thus I found myself at relative ease to observe the events unfolding before me, for in my view potential disaster was looming for a man who owed his success to the army.

One subject was commanding an ever-increasing interest from me...

I had noticed that many of the Marshals were beginning to display a certain disenchantment with continual warfare. They had acquired great wealth and lands, many of them had titles, and they were tiring of battle, wishing to enjoy their rewards.

Amongst the Marshalate there was one individual who had long fascinated me: Bernadotte, the Prince of Ponte Corvo, whose principality neighboured my own of Benevento. This reserved and intelligent Marshal seemed to be destined for something unusual. His talents for administration were most impressive. And, as a Marshal of France, he commanded always an unusual degree of loyalty from his soldiers. As an individual he had, from the months preceding the coup d'état Brumaire, presented Napoleon with his single most formidable challenge, and I had always seen him as something of a Mark Anthony – as indeed had Napoleon himself. Strange it was too that this tall, proud Gascon was known in military circles as 'the last of the Romans'!

At this time he was once more proving his worthy talents as a governor while he controlled, through his administration of the Hanseatic ports, the enforcement of the Continental Blockade.

Amongst my other preoccupations thus, I found myself observing closely the behaviour of this man with considerable interest. He who had himself so nearly become the 'Sword of France'...

* * *

The building that housed the governing French administration in occupied Hamburg was an imposing specimen of architecture. Ugly and commanding, it would never be known for its beauty. But then beauty was far from the minds of those who worked inside it, ensuring the obedience of the occupied inhabitants of the German ports to the conditions of the Continental Blockade. Few dared to flout the new French laws, and it was a daring smuggler who attempted to run the gauntlet of the Prince of Ponte Corvo's efficient patrols. Efficiency was the key word in this administration, and all who were engaged in its employ were mindful and respectful of the supremely efficient example of their commander, whose scrupulous sense of order would tolerate no relaxation from the standards he insisted upon maintaining.

He was, nonetheless, a fair ruler, even towards those to whom he was cast in the role of oppressor. Painstakingly he concerned himself with even the most minor of problems. And characteristically, he used his authority with meticulous justice, whose equitable results met with the respect and admiration of oppressed and oppressors alike. Thus, as in Hamburg, he proved himself to be a liked and respected governor by all.

The building was the centre of permanent comings and goings. The soldiers who guarded its gates were continually scanning passes and documents from visiting dignitaries, officials, military envoys, and people with countless other occupations that necessitated visiting the French Government Headquarters. People ascending or descending, busily engrossed in their business, were constantly traversing the long wide steps that led up to the high portals of the imposing building. The place was a hive of activity, seemingly swarming with people.

It was a particularly warm day on that June of 1808, and the busy scene was being closely observed in the shining midday sun by a tall, very thin young man, whose hair was almost as yellow as the stripes on his pale blue uniform, which in turn matched the paleness of his extraordinarily light eyes.

For a long time the young man stood motionless, intent upon his observations through tall bars that formed the barrier protection around the building. Suddenly he moved, plunging his hand into an inside pocket of his uniform, and pulling out a document. Then, with a resolute stride, he moved towards the military checkpoint at the gates to the building, presenting the document to the presiding guard who, accompanied by others, examined the credentials of all those wanting to enter the building. Following a brief perusal of the papers, the soldier nodded his head with curt formality, and beckoned to his colleagues to let the young man pass.

Moving inside the enclosure, the handsome face of the young man scanned the building as he paused momentarily. Then, once more with resolution and an apparent sense of purpose, he walked quickly towards the steps.

* * *

'Yes, yes…inform the British through the normal channel, you must know the procedures by now…'

Jean-Baptiste Bernadotte, Prince of Ponte Corvo, spoke with a good-humoured impatience over his shoulder to the appealing face of a young man who was struggling for the attentions of the French Governor from the midst of a noisy and jostling crowd.

The tall Marshal was surrounded by a tight group of secretaries, aides and numerous others of a less defined role, all eagerly clamouring for his attention. The sound of their chattering voices, seemingly all speaking at once, filled the wide corridor along which he was walking. Nodding indulgently as he responded to certain anxious faces amongst the group, he repeated again and again hurried promises that he would attend to each grievance or petition in the course of time.

Tactfully trying to extricate himself from their pressing protestations, he thankfully extended his hand to open the large double doors of his office as he at last reached the threshold of his personal haven. He smiled to himself with amused good nature as the pitch of the chorus rose at the sight of his imminent disappearance. It seemed that the whole world required the personal attentions of the French Governor himself! Whatever were the rest of the staff doing? Oh well, he would see to their problems – they knew that. But for now he was grateful as the expert diplomacy of his personal secretary fended them off with consummate tact. With relief his hand closed around the handle of the door.

'Sir, a despatch has just arrived from Spain…'

A young breathless soldier had materialised beside him, seemingly from nowhere. The pink fresh face beneath its hat was flushed and wide-eyed with excitement. Bernadotte raised his eyebrows, astonished by the erupting presence of the young soldier, which had silenced the group of people and frozen the hand of the Marshal on the door handle with its unorthodox breach of etiquette.

'The Emperor has stabilised the internal conflict in Spain. At Bayonne he has accepted the abdication of King Charles IV…'

Bernadotte's face remained expressionless, save for a slight movement of a muscle in his jaw, as the young soldier blurted out his news. But on the handle of the door, unseen by the crowd, his grip tightened. So, he thought, he has finally done it. He has dethroned the Spanish Bourbons...

The familiar surge of repugnance seemed to rise up inside him. Even without yet knowing details, he knew that the 'abdication' of the Spanish king would have been forced in some way by Napoleon. Had he not boasted of Spain being his next conquest? And yet, too, Bernadotte felt a strange and frightening sense of envy within him, from which he recoiled in horror. Why ever would he feel envy for a man who defied the very principles of what he had always stood for? He had always had a profound respect for the presiding, properly constituted authority, whatever it was. And thus he had always believed that any violent or ill-directed movement towards it must necessarily be fatal to liberty. That was why he had not joined in the coup d'état Brumaire. He had told Lucien, his friend, at the time that he was convinced that the abuses of power always increase when the will of an individual is substituted for the law of the land. Yet Napoleon had gone on to create a fair and just law himself. One, moreover, that had been wholly acceptable to the people. And so he had decided to throw in his lot with his rival after all, because that was the government that embodied the will of the people. Perhaps then his envy was because Bonaparte had managed to achieve the impossible: he had made the people believe that his will was theirs – no man could fail to admire such supreme audacity!

But there was a point at which continued displays of audacity became detrimental to the real interests of the people. Instinctively, Bernadotte knew that, whatever his reasons for performing a 'coup d'état' in Spain, Napoleon had passed the limits of the indulgence of fate upon that audacity. And as this presentiment passed through his mind, Bernadotte's mild sensation of envy subsided. Instead he felt a sudden feeling of pity.

'Thank you.' Stiffly he nodded dismissal to the young soldier, and with a curt smile cast to the small group of people pressing still around him, he roughly twisted the handle of the door, entering his room with an arrogant flourish.

Bernadotte's dark eyes opened wide as in frozen disbelief he stopped, still holding the door, staring at the person who was sitting in a chair near to the Governor's large cluttered desk.

'Y-your Highness... Sir...' Surprise at the suddenness of the Marshal's abrupt entry into the room had confused the visitor, who was now hastily rising from the chair. Bowing as he found his feet, the tall, thin, yellow-haired man apologised before speaking again. 'Forgive me...I-I asked to wait in an ante-room, but I was directed straight in here...' He shrugged now, moving hesitantly towards the door. 'I'll return when...'

'Why, Baron Morner! I am delighted and honoured to welcome you to Hamburg...' Bernadotte was striding forward, his hand outstretched as he beamed his astonished utterances in effusive delight. 'A pleasant and unexpected surprise, my dear friend! What brings you to Hamburg?' He was shaking the young man's hand with jovial alacrity. 'Come, seat yourself, my dear Morner.'

The Marshal spread his arm in a gracious gesture of welcome, his towering presence warmly easing the hesitant shyness of the young man.

At the doors, which were still wide open, the group of people who had earlier accompanied the Governor were staring into the office in mesmerised curiosity. Who was this tall young man who was receiving such a warm response from the charming but more usually reserved Prince of Ponte Corvo? Looking at each other, some raised their eyes in enquiry.

'Bring some wine.' Turning suddenly to his secretary at the door, Bernadotte issued his command crisply, indicating with an irritated gesture that he required privacy.

Hastily closing the doors in the straining faces of the onlookers, the Secretary swiftly passed into an adjoining room, reappearing almost immediately with some wine and two goblets. Bernadotte, meanwhile, still enthusiastically displaying his welcome, had moved to his chair behind his desk as his now relaxing visitor had once more seated himself.

'Tell me, my friend,' Bernadotte repeated his earlier unanswered question as he poured wine into the two goblets, 'what brings you to Hamburg? I had believed you to be in Stockholm...'

Smiling in genuine delight at the Swede, Bernadotte extended a glass to him, as the sound of the door closing quietly behind the departing secretary seemed to accentuate the question.

The light blue eyes in the fine features looked intently now into the French Marshal's face. He paused, drinking briefly from his glass, before replying.

'I have business for King Gustavus in France. When I learned of your immediate proximity to my travel route, I could not resist an opportunity to renew our friendship...' He paused once more, smiling warmly at Bernadotte. 'I have been curious to know of your whereabouts and present occupation...' He was silent for a moment, becoming more serious as he looked deeply into Bernadotte's eyes with a gentle expression of gratitude. 'De la Grange, Flack, Leijonhjelm...the others...we often speak of you, recalling our meeting when we were your prisoners at Lubeck...'

Morner hesitated, his blond good looks momentarily thoughtful as he continued, voicing a mysterious tone in his singing Swedish accent.

'Such kindness as that which you extended toward us in those unhappy circumstances, when you could so easily have been insensitive to our needs and our position as Swedes...' He paused again, meaningfully continuing as his translucent blue gaze held the dark Frenchman's. '...Such kindness is never forgotten, Your Highness. Sensitivity to the vanquished in victory is a true sign of greatness...'

He broke off; his blond skin flushing slightly as he hastily drank from his goblet.

Leaning back in his chair, Bernadotte threw his head back, laughing with mild embarrassment. 'Come now, my dear friend! I dare say you would have shown me the same consideration had the circumstances been reversed!'

Still chuckling, he took a sip of his wine, becoming serious as he placed the goblet on his desk, his eyes thoughtfully looking at it.

After a short silence he continued in a low tone, still staring at the goblet.

'To find oneself in a position of authority over an innocent victim is one of the more distasteful sides of victory…the situation could so easily be an opposite one…' He stopped briefly, reflecting. 'To befriend such innocents seems somehow to act as a palliative to the natural responses of guilt in such a situation…'

He broke off, remembering the countless times he had been faced with organising the fates of people who had found themselves, through no fault of their own, at the mercy of an alien occupying force.

Lifting his head suddenly, he looked into the handsome features of the admiring man before him. Flashing a brilliant smile, he concluded, 'So you see, Morner, how even natural justice has its selfish needs to the conscience of man!'

As he laughed, drinking uneasily from his goblet once more, Bernadotte was aware that the young man had been closely observing him. Now, as he returned his slightly embarrassed gaze to the intense young man's pale face, a silence fell between them. The young Swede had apparently forgotten his shyness and earlier nervousness as he now spoke with a brittle emotion in his voice, his blue eyes searching the Marshal's face with a profound expression of admiration.

'Sir, I am now assured of that which I, and my friends, have felt from the outset of our acquaintance…'

Bernadotte was perplexed by the hypnotic seriousness of the earnest young Swede's tone and expression.

'Your talent for administration with fairness and justice is animated by a deep insight into the complexity of men's minds, be they ordinary men or great Marshals of the French Empire…' Suddenly Morner's voice saddened. 'Indeed, even if they be kings…'

The Swede fell silent for a moment, as he unblinkingly looked into Bernadotte's eyes, displaying, without inhibition, his open admiration for the tall, dark Prince. 'Your Highness, you have a strength of character that is unique.'

Bernadotte swallowed. He was more than a little taken aback by the emotional words of respect and admiration from the aristocratic young Swede. Yet despite his embarrassment, and even as he laughingly responded with polite dismissive modesty, he felt a surge of pride and pleasure at the flattering words spoken by the young man. He had felt a special affinity with the polite group of Swedes from the beginning, when he had first concerned himself with their plight following the surrender of Lubeck. Now he saw that the affinity had been reciprocated, and he was strangely touched. They were a charming people, these Swedes. He liked and admired their polite manners, and the natural reserve that seemed common to their northern character. He knew that he possessed similar qualities of reticence, and was therefore able to understand what appeared often to others to be a form of arrogance.

Changing the subject, the two conversed for a further few minutes, a new understanding now easing further their already good rapport. Happily they agreed to meet later and dine together. And then with relaxed friendliness, the Swede took his leave.

As the door closed behind Morner, Bernadotte turned towards the window, looking down on the busy scene below. He had a strange feeling... It was ludicrous, he knew, but he felt as though his life had suddenly changed. He blinked at the sheer irrationality of such a thought, but all the same he could not rid himself of the sensation. Earlier he had experienced a presentiment about the Emperor. Now, inexplicably, he was feeling an extraordinary sense of expectation about his own life. How strange... His thoughts appeared to be in a sudden racing turmoil that he could not untangle, and yet his emotions were somehow rising in some wholly absurd sense of excitement – for no reason.

'Sir, here are the details of the despatch from Spain.' The voice of his secretary interrupted his thoughts. 'Oh...and this letter has just arrived from Paris.'

Burying his preoccupations, Bernadotte returned to his desk, smiling kindly at his secretary as he took the documents from his hand. Seating himself, he placed the military despatch on the table as he saw, with delight, that the letter was from Désirée. Eagerly he opened it, scanning the news of his son and beloved wife with a loving ruefulness. Suddenly his happy expression froze as he reached a paragraph halfway through the letter. Re-reading the lines, his face assumed a hard mask of displeasure.

Amongst her vivid descriptions of domestic life and court intrigues, Désirée had told her husband of an unexpected gift that had been given to her by the Emperor. It had been known that the Tsar of Russia had, following their meeting at Tilsit, given the French Emperor three priceless fur cloaks. Now, it seemed, he had given one of them to Désirée, keeping another for himself, and giving his favourite sister Pauline the third.

Bernadotte flushed as once more he re-read this news. He was aware, of course, that it was a great honour for his wife. And he knew it to be perhaps typical of the Emperor's generosity to those he loved. Bernadotte's blood seemed to rush to his head, making him feel dizzy as he felt a familiar anger rise from within him. Indeed – it was typical of the Emperor's generosity to 'those he loved'

He was unable to curb the sensation of jealousy and rage that overtook him now. Why? Why did Bonaparte still always single out Désirée for special favours like this? Why...? Bitterly he looked now at the portrait of the stern-looking Emperor that hung on the wall of his office. In vain he struggled with his feelings, trying to remember the things that his wife had told him at Marienburg. But even as he tried, he could not free himself of his jealousy.

Suddenly he stood up, picking up his hat. He felt he must get away from this Imperial claustrophobia. He cast a last bitter look up at the portrait.

Would he never be rid of Napoleon Bonaparte?

Chapter XVII

'If a gentleman commits follies, if he keeps mistresses, if he treats his wife badly, even if he is guilty of serious injustices towards his friends, he will be blamed, no doubt; but if he is rich, powerful and intelligent, society will still treat him with indulgence. But if a man cheats at cards he will be immediately banished from decent society and never forgiven…'

Thus I explained my attitude to Napoleon with regard to his forcible seizure of the Spanish Bourbons. Had he chosen instead, as indeed I had vaguely suggested to him once, to effect a coup in the Spanish Province of Catalonia – even without justification or indeed provocation – I doubt that he would have offended, to such an acute degree, the sensibilities of the established ruling Monarchs of Europe. And whilst it might be that such behaviour from an Imperial Power might eventually find acceptance from peoples used to such political dynamics, the traditionalist sentiments so jealously guarded by the ancient Dynasties of European Royalty could never accept or forgive what they considered to be a personal affront.

The forced abdication, and subsequent detention, of this innocent family was an offence, in the eyes of Europe, almost equal in horror to the unjustified murder of the Duc d'Enghien. In carrying out the coup at Bayonne, and placing his brother Joseph on the Spanish throne, Napoleon was breaching the bounds of the superficial tolerance barriers, which were stiffly observed by the ruling hierarchies of Europe. The monarchs and governments were outraged, and Napoleon's rash petulance was to define the future movements of his already reluctant allies in a very different light from that which he had intended. Far from being the step towards ensuring the blockading of the Peninsula ports in his economic war with England, thus strengthening his power, it was, in fact, to spell his doom. His hasty action had sealed his fate. Napoleon had indeed 'cheated at cards'.

As for me, I found myself unable to condone such emotionally charged politics. As I had realised at Tilsit, the limits of my endurance regarding Napoleon's rash behaviour had long since broken. Napoleon was probably the person I loved most in my life. But when I saw this great genius fading, indifferent to France's interests, or his soldiers' lives, my heart, which had already cooled, turned to ice.

I was deeply saddened, but my lifelong commitment and dedication had been to what I believed to be the well being of France, and the stable balance of European co-operation. Love for a man who I felt had finally become blinded by his own power could no longer interfere with what I knew to be my duty.

The Spanish Bourbons were to live their six years of exile under my own roof at Valencay, happily spending their captivity engaged in the pursuits of hunting and dancing, in between their devout observation of the requirements of Religion. The triumph of hatred over judgement had resulted in Napoleon's interference in the very bases of European tradition, and the humiliation of this Bourbon family was a catastrophic political blunder. The very premise of the balance of powers was being severely threatened by this man, and I now found myself entirely preoccupied with contemplating the horrifying implications. I knew now that I must do everything in my power to free Europe from the unrelenting grip of Napoleon Bonaparte's will.

Thus, in September 1808, I found myself pondering deeply the potential for recovery from the headlong descent into disaster that I knew France and Europe were facing. Once more, I travelled uncomfortably to the second meeting of the two young Emperors, Napoleon and Alexander. This time it was in a bizarre location: Erfurt.

As my conveyance finally arrived, my thoughts were of both hope – and fear. Perhaps the fate of the world would be decided here…

* * *

'Highness! The Emperor asks that you immediately conduct yourself to his presence; he awaits you in his rooms. He is expecting the ceremonial visit of the Tsar, who arrived this afternoon – in one hour's time. He…'

I silenced my fussing assistant with an expression that conveyed my displeasure at his irritating attempt to admonish me to make unnecessary speed. I dislike being bustled at all times, but most particularly following a long and tedious journey which has induced extreme degrees of discomfort.

As the face of my anxious helper looked with earnest dismay at my laborious attempts to extricate my painful limb from its cramped position, I impatiently instructed him to assist me out of the tiresome carriage in which I had been incarcerated for so many unpleasant hours. Slowly I began the difficult business of descending the steps of the vehicle, employing my customary efforts to ignore the throbbing resistance of my crippled leg.

I smiled briefly at the young man as I felt the bolstering strength of his arms while he supported me. Poor fellow! He was often the victim of my somewhat terse responses to annoying situations. But he was a good and honest worker, and I knew that he was aware of my true appreciation of his qualities. Today, however, I was generally vexed, and the delays of the journey had exacerbated my irritability.

As we slowly ascended the imposing steps to the entrance of the typically German building in which the French delegation would be housed for the duration of the conference, my earnest companion informed me of the morning's excitements as Napoleon had ridden out to meet the Tsar on the road, and, following fraternal embraces, they had entered the small German town – which for the moment was the focus of all Europe – with a display of the triumphant harmony of Tilsit.

I smiled dryly to myself as I heard the descriptions. Perhaps the uncomfortable necessity to travel elsewhere on business had been worthwhile after all. At least I had been spared that vulgar sight!

Well, at least they were all here now. The two self-satisfied Emperors, and the eager congregation of the petty sovereigns of Europe, who had come to crave the indulgence of the mighty Corsican conqueror who so casually held the key to their destinies. Once more I was reminded of the absurd travesties of comic opera. My Emperor seemed to be acquiring a penchant for such grotesque displays of ostentation. Indeed, he had urged me to ensure the attendance of as many monarchs and princelings as I could muster, presumably that he might assert his supreme presence with the maximum degree of impact. Small wonder he had been the author, in his youth, of some exceedingly dramatic novels! Certainly he comprehended the full implication of exaggerated theatricality, and moreover was a master of the art of manipulating such pretentious situations to his advantage.

However, my own resolve remained undiminished. I had determined that even were he to succeed at a superficial level, he would fail in his prime objectives. To ensure this end I now directed my entire energies.

'Sire! His Highness the Prince of Benevento.'

Yes, the opera was in full swing! The deep bow of the flunkey, whose appearance would not have been out of place at the court of Louis XIV, did nothing to muffle the ringing tones of his dramatic heralding. And as the harmonics of the pompous announcement died away, a heavy silence fell upon the vast room. Only the sound of my stick striking the floor, accompanied by my laborious shuffle, punctuated the listening silence.

Napoleon was standing at the window, his motionless back towards the sumptuously furnished room. He appeared to be entirely preoccupied with the inconsequential activities of the many people circulating in the formal gardens below.

I was aware, however, that he was acutely attentive to every sound of my laboured approach, and as I neared him I smothered a smile as I recognised the familiar symptoms of a calculated display of displeasure. I had always been amused by Napoleon's propensity for histrionics. Indeed, I confess that I found it an oddly endearing characteristic, if a little tedious at times.

Leaning against a chair, I now patiently waited as the silence continued. Curiously I looked around at the luxurious furnishings of the room. No expense was being spared at this conference to impress Europe!

'Your arrival is somewhat delayed, Prince.'

The snapped reprimand bit into the thick silence. It seemed to me that the knuckles of his hands, which were firmly clasped behind his back, appeared momentarily to whiten.

Shrugging, I replied politely, informing the Emperor that he was no doubt aware that the methods of travel, which we were obliged to employ, were not conducive to speed. Nor indeed did they conduce to comfort, I felt impelled to add with profound regret.

Perhaps it was my unrepentant tone, perhaps it was that the Emperor had temporarily recovered the response to humour that we had shared of old. Whatever it was, I was astonished when his tense shoulders suddenly relaxed, and he turned to bestow upon me a brilliant smile of genuine welcome.

Confound the man! Why was he always so unpredictable? He always appeared to resurrect his erstwhile charm at the very moment when one least expected it. Moreover, the memory of his former attractive and enthusiastic nature was, inevitably, potentially disarming. But I was aware of the tricks of his mercurial charisma, and my inner resolve had hardened me against the seductions of his powerful personality. Politely I returned his smile.

'Sit down, Prince. You look tired.'

Despite his consideration for my disability, the Emperor's tone was aloof, betraying the now permanent arrogance that he was attempting to mask with his smile. I knew that he had no real concern for my tiredness for he had long ceased to hold any affection for me. But he had need of me at this conference, and thus it was necessary to humour me.

As I seated myself, he began to pace up and down the room, his chin buried in his chest, his eyebrows knitted together. He was deeply preoccupied.

Briskly now he began. 'The Tsar has arrived. I met him this morning on the road. We have not of course met officially yet...'

He stopped abruptly as he observed my nodding head. Raising his eyebrows, he looked at me enquiringly, apparently irritated that I should already know the news he was imparting. While I now told him that I had already heard of his meeting with the Tsar earlier in the day, I thought how extraordinary it was that, having performed the dramatic greeting for the very benefit of the people, he should be so surprised that I had heard of the event through the descriptions of an impressed onlooker! How strange he was. Sometimes it was as though the mass of the people was some distant phenomenon to him, entirely devoid of human characteristics. He seemed to forget, nowadays, that the cheering multitudes were people with feelings – and moreover quite accessible to Imperial communications, should he wish it. Alas, he no longer did.

Incredulity at the change in the man struck me once more, as it did so often these days. I was, too, continually surprised at my own continued surprise!

'Have you prepared the draft for the Treaty?' He did not wait for a reply to his sharp question as he continued with dramatic intensity, his expression fixed in a hard, determined mask. 'I must secure an assurance from the Tsar that if Austria decides to give me any trouble he will...' He broke off, clenching his still clasped hands behind his back. Once more he was looking out of the window, his back towards me.

'We must defeat the English in Spain...I have to ensure their total destruction through the annihilation of their economy...' His voice was rising quite menacingly. The very thought of the English seemed, these days, to induce some sort of almost pathological snarl of hatred from the Emperor. His preoccupation with this island nation was becoming injurious to his powers of reason; everything else was merely incidental to his central objective: to defeat England.

Lowering his voice, he turned to face me again. Repeating himself, he now resumed his instructions to me, insisting that it was for me to urge the Tsar's cooperation through my diplomatic talents. With an arrogant gesture of disdain he ordered me to 'humour the Tsar with talk of the partitioning of Turkey, Alachua, Moldavia...' Flicking his hand at the mention of each unfortunate nation, he forcefully instructed that '...Russia can keep the Austrians in check...the important thing is to unite against the common enemy – England.'

He seemed to hiss the hated name.

* * *

To be aware that one is about to commit an act of treachery is an awesome realisation. It was not a prospect that I regarded with any pleasure, contrary to the judgements of the misinformed.

It will be clear by now that I had, after all, long had deep feelings of affection for the Emperor, and though the interests of France dictated a course of betrayal, I did not relish the idea of destroying the genius who had contributed so much to the restructuring of France following the Revolutionary years.

Perhaps it is the wont of such constructivism that it will eventually invert upon itself and retard into destruction. Perhaps any forward thrusting impulse of any consequence must, through its very nature, regress, unable to sustain the forward concentration of energy. Whatever the reason, France had ceased to grow, and her young men were dying unnecessarily on battlefields all over Europe. If treachery can never be wholly justified as an act, then perhaps some understanding of the reasons for that act must be attempted.

As I looked at the Emperor's intensely penetrating eyes, I knew that I would strive to ensure that he never received that assurance of support from the Tsar. I could never entertain the possibility of Austria's destruction. This noble Empire was an integral part of Europe, and had been so for hundreds of years. I would not see it destroyed.

Unacceptable to me too was the idea of the destruction of the English constitution. The English race was possessed of a tolerant liberalism, peculiar to their own national character. Whilst I could never identify with such people on a basis of temperament, I nonetheless held a deep admiration for their broad vision of society, and had always felt it to herald future inclinations in the rest of Europe. The English were certainly a difficult and aloof people, hard to understand in many ways, but nevertheless an essential part of the fabric of Europeanism as a whole. Their steady beliefs would always ensure that revolutionary fervour would never be allowed to sweep aside completely the basic values of European Tradition. I would not see them crushed either.

And so I listened to the Emperor – with every intention of pursuing my own course...

'His Imperial Majesty: Alexander, Tsar of all Russias.'

The operatic displays had begun once more!

As the liveried footmen ranged themselves dutifully in their appointed positions for the imminent approach of the Tsar, the chosen attendants from the French contingent hurried into the room, bowing in profuse apology to Napoleon for their rushed entry, pre-empted by the Tsar's early arrival. Quickly, the harassed individuals joined me as I moved to a respectful distance behind our Emperor. Expectantly we waited in silence for the entry of the tall blond Tsar.

I cast a look at a nearby clock. It was my fervent hope that this business would not be too prolonged. Such ceremonies I found to be an irksome bore. Furthermore, long periods of standing severely tried my leg.

At that moment the youthful presence of the tall sovereign erupted powerfully into the room. The ceremonial visit of Napoleon's subservient ally had begun, and the Emperor of the French had assumed his expression of gracious superiority.

But as I looked into the fine features of the handsome blonde Tsar, I noticed that he had lost that expression of bewitchment in addressing Napoleon – that which he had displayed at Tilsit. Here was a young man who had grown up considerably since the emotional scenes upon the raft on the River Nieman. His actions were sublimely gracious and formal, but gone was the vulnerability that had characterised the impressionable young victim of Austerlitz. Here, instead, was the self-possessed sovereign of Russia, the grandson of Catherine the Great, who had instilled into him a sense of destiny to relieve the burden of the oppressed. His sudden maturity had now settled that sense of destiny, and he emanated his spiritual awareness with an unconscious confidence.

Napoleon, however, was not disposed to notice such a change in the young man before him now, too busy was he effusively exhibiting his gracious condescension.

With close attention I now observed the formal exchanges between the two sovereigns. I found much to interest me beneath the veneer of the ceremonial procedure – from both participants.

* * *

'We shall meet again, sire?'

I inclined my head expectantly in addressing the Tsar. It was apparent to me that he was anxious to pursue a conversation away from the inhibiting presence of the French delegation. Doubtless he had sensed my willingness to be forthcoming in such a private exchange.

Napoleon had unwittingly provided the Tsar and myself with the fortuitous opportunity to speak personally, as he had asked me to accompany the visiting Sovereign to his waiting carriage. The handsome young man was looking, with a deliberate intensity shining from his light blue eyes, profoundly into my face. Without apparently answering my question, he instead delivered a friendly statement with a calm serenity.

'I believe, Prince Benevento, that you will shortly receive an invitation from my cousin, the Princess of Tours and Taxis…'

His casual courtesy belied entirely the forcefulness of his magnetic blue stare. 'I find her gatherings quite stimulating!'

He smiled warmly at me as I again inclined my head, this time as an indication of comprehending his veiled message.

We were descending the wide semi-circular staircase into the large circular hall. Hundreds of eyes from the formal gathering of patiently waiting dignitaries and officials below watched our stately progress. The young Tsar had a commanding presence, and a sense of quiet theatricality that made good use of his impressive natural attributes. He was an earnest young man, of that I had no doubts. Moreover, I knew that he was imbued with a sense of mission, and that mission was rapidly becoming the Peace of all Europe. He was also a deeply religious young man, and this devotion, combined with his belief in his destiny, meant that he had an inclination to see himself as some sort of saviour. Here then was my key…

After the formal farewells, and the irritating business of all the pomp and ceremony that was necessitated, I was thankfully able to return to my own apartments. As I sank gratefully into a comfortable chair, I accepted with alacrity the glass of wine that my sensible secretary had already poured for me. The good man then held out a silver tray upon which a small white envelope, of exquisite quality, had evidently arrived in my absence. Upon opening it, I found myself invited to the salon of the Princess of Tours and Taxis.

* * *

Napoleon had always found himself ill at ease in the jungle of diplomacy. The physical requirements of the necessary formal rituals were, in themselves, alien to his impulsive nature, for although he revelled in impressing the masses with his theatrical techniques, the restrictions of etiquette in the stiff frameworks of diplomacy were frustrating for him. And so, although at the outset of the proceedings he appeared to enjoy the sensation of dramatic spectacle as he surrounded himself with almost the entire sum of ruling princes of Europe, these ephemeral feelings of satisfaction soon began to pall, and Napoleon became eager to conclude satisfactorily the negotiations for which he had travelled to Erfurt. The nightly dinners surrounded by the aristocratic flatterers, each vying to surpass the other in their efforts to impress the great Emperor and elicit some favourable response from him, basically bored him. And though each night at the theatre he displayed an expertise of drama that exceeded that of the most celebrated actors of the performing Comédie Française, it was blatantly evident that Napoleon was not only wearied by the apparently adoring entourage, but was inwardly despising of the sycophantic behaviour. Napoleon had never been very good at masking his contempt for those whom he did not respect. Erfurt was no exception.

Perhaps, though, his general irritations were exacerbated by the fact that he had gradually become aware that the attitude of the Tsar had changed towards him since the heady days of Tilsit.

As the conference progressed, Napoleon was increasingly exasperated by the cautious and non-committal responses from Alexander during their long daily discussions, and in private betrayed signs of extreme frustration with the young man whom he had erroneously believed to be his admiring slave.

The Tsar had assumed an aloof posture from the beginning. It was undoubtedly a fact that he had himself been seduced by Napoleon's magnetic charm at Tilsit. And certainly, at that time he had genuinely been personally anxious to accede to the wishes of the French Emperor. However, his bewitched response to the magic of the seemingly invincible conqueror had not been shared by either Alexander's family, or the Russian court.

Upon his return to St. Petersburg in July of 1807, the young Tsar had been met by an atmosphere of cold disapproval. The people, who had been ordered to celebrate the success of Tilsit, performed their duty without a spirit of joy, internally maintaining their harboured resentment of Napoleon Bonaparte who, from being the hated enemy of the Russian people, was now suddenly a man they had to look to as a beloved ally. At Court the resentment was less disguised, and Alexander's strong-minded mother, the Empress Dowager Maria Feodorovna, made no secret of her disgust at her son's behaviour towards the man who had murdered the Bourbon prince, the Duc d'Enghien. Her powerful example inspired other leading members of the nobility – who had always feared an infiltration of the revolutionary ideals that had stripped their French cousins of their lands, wealth, and indeed lives – to join in open condemnation of Alexander's new-found friendship with 'the parvenu'.

Now, the golden sovereign of the Russias, hitherto beloved by his people and society, had found himself facing a bitter barrage of criticism that increased as the months went by, and finally reached expression of supreme outrage as yet another Royal family of Europe, the Spanish Bourbons, were humiliated by the Corsican usurper. Ally or not, the Russian people and society hated Napoleon. Alexander was now forced to accept the inescapable truth: that the Russian people and the powerful nobility, who shared their snobbish dispositions unashamedly with the threatened nobilities of the rest of Europe, would never tolerate the prospect of becoming subservient to the will of a man they considered to be an illegitimate ruler.

In the months that had followed Tilsit, Alexander had acquired a degree of unpopularity that he had never imagined was remotely possible, and he had found himself severely shocked and necessarily obliged to remedy the situation. Thus he had agreed to the meeting at Erfurt, and he had arrived with the vigorous exhortations of his family and advisors to display no compromise with the French Emperor, and to assert Russian superiority.

The contingent of Russian diplomats and Imperial entourage were quite amusing in their displays of apprehensive distrust towards Napoleon. Inspired by an absurd fantasy – dreamed up, I believe, by the Empress Dowager – that the 'parvenu' might attempt to appropriate a similar tactic toward Alexander at Erfurt as he had effected at Bayonne towards the unfortunate Bourbons, the Russians exercised a protectiveness towards their sovereign that exhibited such unnecessary zeal as to be comical to the

French participants at the conference. But their Head of State, and Emperor, was wholly unamused...

The meetings were thus stiff and inconclusive, finding no agreements for firm resolution. Napoleon, of course, attempted with his full capacity for passion to convince the Tsar of the necessity to limit arms to Austria, and stressed that it was in the interests of Russia to accede to his policies. But the Tsar maintained his position of reserve, and refused to submit to the persuasions of the French potentate.

Napoleon then proceeded to moot another proposal. This was a most sensitive subject to the Tsar, and one in which the French Emperor entreated me to conjoin with him by advancing persuasive arguments in its favour to the Russian.

Napoleon had long been concerned with the issue of appointing his successor. Upon becoming Emperor his earlier ideas of nominating a Bernadotte, or some such candidate, had receded as the preoccupation with the founding of his dynasty had taken precedence in his mind. He was, however, aware that none of his brothers or sisters was appropriate for the position of heir, and he had been deeply disappointed at the inability of his wife Josephine to give him a child. Moreover, this failure had been compounded by the fact that his Polish mistress, Marie Walewska, had recently presented him with a healthy son, and any doubt he may have previously entertained regarding his own capabilities for procreation were laid to rest.

Thus his thoughts had once more turned towards the possibilities of marrying a young woman who would strengthen his position in the eyes of the European monarchs, and provide him with an heir. To him the obvious answer to his problem was one of the Tsar's sisters, and I was despatched to discuss the matter with Alexander.

I, however, was less than enthusiastic about such a proposition, my reason being that, were there to be any remote possibility for the salvation of the Napoleonic reign, I felt it would be better that the alliance should be with the Austrian house of Hapsburg, rather than the Romanovs. My natural tendency was always to favour the Austrian potential in a matter such as this. My insipid representations, however, were entirely inconsequential, as the Tsar's own reaction to the proposal that he become Napoleon's brother-in-law was startlingly explicit.

With maximum employment of his royal discipline, the Russian endeavoured to conceal his dismay by adopting a posture of unconvincing uncertainty. It was evident, however, that such a proposition had caused him to recoil in distaste. Postulating – and not without some truth – that his sisters were entirely under the control of their mother, and that therefore his own suggestions were entirely irrelevant to their marriages. Alexander's response nonetheless betrayed an excessive display of repugnance to the suggestion, and his rejection was swift and unequivocal. Again, Napoleon was thwarted.

Accord, however, was eventually reached as they drafted a joint appeal to George III, to agree Peace for the World. This empty gesture of agreement gave credence to the pretence that Erfurt was a splendid affair, expressing the goodwill and concord of the two great potentates.

But behind the pomp and ceremony that created the façade of Erfurt, there was a very different reality.

Each night, following the official revelries, other meetings took place. And from the first visit I made to the salon of the Princess of Tours and Taxis, the sister of the beautiful Queen of Prussia, it was clear that the die had finally been cast, and Europe had embarked upon a new course. I confess that I was the architect of that direction...

And, necessarily, Napoleon was entirely oblivious to my scheme.

* * *

'Good evening, my dear Prince. Your delayed arrival had me quite concerned that we might be deprived of your charming company. The Tsar has enquired several times as to your whereabouts, my dear. Come...'

The Princess of Tours and Taxis was a woman of much charm

and grace who, though she lacked the sublime beauty of her sister, the Queen of Prussia, was nonetheless as astutely aware of the ways of politics.

In the tradition of many past formidable members of her sex, the Princess most skilfully endeavoured to employ her feminine talents to satisfy those political needs – by creating suitable conditions in which the necessary processes of intrigue associated with diplomatic affairs might flourish. So it was that in her salon, during the conferences at Erfurt, the real political developments were to take place.

I had indeed been a little delayed on that first of my nightly visits to the tastefully furnished rooms of the Princess, and I felt a little tired as I gratefully accepted a glass of wine from the charming creature. Willingly I allowed her to slowly guide me through the pink and white surroundings, which were thickly populated with beautiful young people who, whilst relaxed in the warm atmosphere, had nonetheless retained their manners, and I was greeted with amiable courtesy from all sides as I passed through their midst.

Russian society was less 'modern' than French, and I was charmed by the old-fashioned reminder of pre-revolutionary France. I had never regretted the passing of that era, and yet I was filled with a warm nostalgia for the more 'civilised' aspects of it, which had now largely been forgotten in France. There was a marked lack of subtlety at the Napoleonic court, which seemed to deprive it, somehow, of the glamour it was striving to attain. Undoubtedly, though, it had been a vast improvement on the gross vulgarities of the Revolutionary Directory, and the decadent ways of the Ancien Régime had inevitably outlived their usefulness.

Nonetheless, the civilities of these Russians recalled for me a lost refinement. And perhaps a proclivity for etiquette that had always been a constructive contribution to discipline in the upper echelons of society...

I dismissed the thought, and declined to entertain the ramifications of my sentimental musings. One is often tempted to reflect upon the memory of one's upbringing, often imbuing it with some merit that it did not in fact possess. Time tends to dull the harsher aspects of life. All the same, there is a certain ease with which one responds to situations that recall the familiarity of youth. For me this was one such moment.

'You are looking a little pale, sir. Are you feeling quite well?'

The handsome face of the Tsar was creased in a frown of genuine concern as he stood up to greet me. I was oddly touched. He was certainly a deeply sincere young man, this beautiful golden Russian.

He had been surrounded by a bevy of lovely young women when I approached. All of them had been eagerly seeking to attract his good-humoured attentions, and gales of happy laughter rose periodically from around the sofa upon which he was so comfortably ensconced. I had been struck by how different the young sovereign was in this relaxed informal atmosphere. His good looks were positively alight with the animation of laughter as he conversed with his female companions. How different from the serious sovereign who stiffly attended the daily conferences with his fellow potentate.

Now, however, as he invited me to seat myself beside him, politely bowing to the giggling group of obediently departing women, his expression returned to the grave portrait of the responsibility of his office.

Momentarily I closed my eyes as I sank into the comfortable sofa. The pain ebbed from my leg with a throbbing farewell as I relieved it from its burden, and extended it to a position of respite. It had been a tiresome day filled with the petulant outbursts of my frustrated Emperor. Such fatigue invariably induced more pain to my crippled limb.

The Tsar now seated himself once more on the sofa, his expression still enquiring after my health as we both drew upon the liquid from the exquisite crystal of our wine glasses. Relaxing, I smiled at him, aware that my face was probably displaying a somewhat unpleasant paleness.

Involuntarily I expelled a weary sigh as I looked into the pale blue concern of his eyes, replying to his enquiry, 'Sire, sleep, alas, escapes me these nights...' I was endeavouring to establish with tact the full implications of my concerns. 'I confess to an unhappy preoccupation of the mind.'

I glanced about the room as once more I sipped my wine. I could feel the fixed stare of expectancy penetrating my unease.

'Divulge to me the source of your conflict, my friend...it troubles me to see you thus disturbed.'

The perfectly spoken French was voiced in the low concern of a friend. The thought suddenly struck me that here was the Emperor of Russia speaking French with accent-less perfection, when the Emperor of the French spoke the native tongue with an acute foreign pronunciation that had never found its ease. How strange it was that the thought had never occurred to me until now. For some reason my observation deepened my sense of sadness, for it reminded me of the ebullient enthusiasm of the young conqueror of Italy whose very foreign-ness had been one of his many sources of charm. Could it be that I was really going to bring myself to betray him?

'Europe.' I interrupted my own racing thoughts, pausing before I repeated the word that must transcend all else in importance to me. 'Europe, sire – the preservation of our great culture and traditions – this has been my lifelong dedication.'

I was speaking as much for my own benefit as for that of the Tsar. It seemed to be necessary for me to hear my own reaffirmation of my life's commitment. I was experiencing an odd sensation, for though I was aware that most who knew me would have cynically regarded my life's activities as mercenary, the truth of the matter was, in reality, that which I was stating now to the Tsar. And the enormity of the implications – of what might be seen by some to be perhaps pretentious – startled even myself. The sudden revelation of actually seeing oneself objectively, comprehending in an instant the actuality of that which is taken for granted as being one's philosophy – but which one never really examines or totally understands – such a revelation is an extraordinary experience.

At this moment I had perceived a deep insight into my most

profound beliefs, and to my astonishment, I had realised that my commitment to European civilisation was much more than a purely intellectual exercise, but was indeed composed of a deeply emotional love for my heritage.

I was utterly confounded. I, who had made a career out of cultivating the suave cynicism that had carried my dubious reputation – in which I had delighted, due to its ability to exercise unpredictability – I, nevertheless, suddenly had found myself to be imbued with some 'sense of mission' too… How preposterous! Yet in that moment I knew myself to be the victim of my own commitment.

Moreover, in that instant I had become wholly aware of the meaning of *destiny* – that word that was used so often, yet which I knew few people really understood. Indeed, I myself had never fully grasped its real significance, though I might have imagined I had. Indeed, I was acutely aware that so many things I had complacently believed myself to understand, I had in fact never fully fathomed, and had instead accepted the superficial view of such things, like most other people. Life is so much simpler if one does not delve too deeply.

I knew that I had come to this moment of realisation because of the suppressed emotions I was carrying regarding the dreadful deed of treachery that I was about to perform. And it was strange that in this moment, when I had been forced to understand myself, I had also come to understand finally he whom I was about to betray. Perhaps that is the necessary requirement of conscience, and of real love between people. I had at last understood his sense of destiny. Really understood it. Furthermore, in understanding it I now knew that what I was about to do would, in the end, be for his own redemption. In a strange way I would be saving him from himself, rendering him the destiny of tragedy that his mighty genius had to have, for he was no ordinary man.

I had been cast in the role of Brutus, and it fell to me to save Caesar – by destroying him.

The Tsar was looking at me. I knew he could have no inkling of the tenor of my turbulent thoughts. He was nodding, confirming the fact that he knew me to be a man dedicated to the cause of Europe. I glanced around the room, eyeing with my customary appreciation the charming beauties of the Russian Imperial entourage. I mused aloud now as I gazed at the ladies with a preoccupied languor.

'Even the pursuit of such exquisite creatures pales into insignificance beside one's dedication to the great cause of our cultural heritage...!'

The light blue eyes were staring at me as I smiled into them. I was attempting to relieve the atmosphere of expectation for a moment before continuing with the serious discussion. The eyes smiled back. He was aware of my reputation with the fairer sex.

'Sire...'

I wrenched myself from the uncustomary confusion of my thoughts. Intently now, my eyes held the blue unblinking stare, and with the fullest assertion of whatever commanding presence I possessed, I began.

'A lifetime of active participation in the machinations of political games has assured me of one thing: namely that the prevailing characteristic of superficial judgements, as practised by most people, fail entirely to comprehend the true nature of a political thinker...' I hesitated, for I knew he was aware that I was making a reference to the many diverse opinions perpetrated about me. I shrugged as I added, 'Material rewards are part and parcel of the intrigues of politics...'

He smiled at my dry observation, becoming once more serious as I now began to speak my words with the slow deliberation that endeavoured to accentuate the imperative of my thought.

'But the essence, sire, the fundamental integrity of one's loyalty to the basic principles of the constitution – these are beyond material interests, beyond ordinary value judgements...' I paused, leaning slightly towards him as a note of urgency crept into my voice without conscious inducement. 'Those principles cannot be...must not be...tampered with. Civilisation depends upon their preservation...'

I broke off. I was aware that the intelligent Tsar was transfixed by my intensity, attentive to every word I was saying. As I searched his face, I could feel that I was asserting the visual severity allowed me by my superior age, even towards an Emperor. I was trying to control my tone of urgency, but as I continued I failed to prevent the inflection of passion from affecting my quietly spoken words as my eyes locked with his.

'Sire, it is within your power to save Europe, and you will do so by refusing to give way to Napoleon. The French people are civilised – their Sovereign is not. The Sovereign of Russia is civilised – his people are not. The Sovereign of Russia should, therefore, be the ally of the French people…' A slightly startled expression had come to the Tsar's face, but as I continued I knew that he understood that I was speaking about philosophy, and I knew that he respected my words. 'The French people have but one desire – to have done with war. They wish to be able to enjoy the fruits of conquest. They are tired…'

I paused once more, maintaining my demand on his close attention. 'Nobody else, sire, is in a position to give the people of France what they want. Without liberation they will be dragged as victims into yet more wars in the wake of their increasingly autocratic leader…' I stopped, searching for words strong enough to express my inexpressible fears. 'It will be their ultimate destruction…'

I broke off, overcome by my own passion, and frustrated at what seemed to me an unaccustomed inability to express the full force of my words. Lowering my head, momentarily feeling an almost overwhelming tiredness, I drank deeply from my glass. I could feel the rigid presence of the Tsar sitting tall and still beside me.

After a few moments, I raised my eyes once more to look at his face, expecting to see his earlier expression of astonishment. It was, however, I who was to experience bewilderment.

He was staring into the distance, his handsome features relaxed in an expression of angelic serenity. The gold of his hair, and the pale tranquillity of his face with its light blue, sightless eyes, gave an almost eerie feeling of mystical detachment. He remained silent, apparently oblivious to everything around him. It was now my turn to become transfixed. His emanating serenity forbade my interruption, for such would have been an audacity.

After a few moments he spoke, though I did not feel it was to me. Rather he voiced his awesome thought, his face displaying the humility of those imbued with the spirit of religion.

'It seems that God has given me a mission...' His voice trailed away as his expression deepened into one of entranced wonder. Alexander, who had always been a devout and ardent Christian, and had long sought to find the true expression of that zealous faith, had finally found himself to indeed be the instrument of God...

I was dumbfounded by the degree of intensity that suddenly animated that angelic face. The power of religion had never ceased to amaze me. Now I was witnessing the most profound manifestation of faith that I had ever seen. Indeed, it was more concentrated than I could ever have imagined.

Eventually he broke from his trance, and a soft smile came to his lips. With a newly born expression of gentle saintliness, he now looked at me.

For some reason, a cold shudder seemed to wash over my body. I knew that the power of sublime religious faith had taken hold of Alexander, and that nothing could ever shake that elevated crusade upon which the young man was now embarked. He had, in the course of a few minutes, come to see himself as the Saviour of Europe, as indeed I had foreseen. But I had not envisaged that which I now knew: the power of his faith was such that he was now invincible. He had assumed some extraordinary quality that rendered him unconquerable because of his utter belief that he was God's instrument.

My thoughts wandered to Napoleon, that unmatchable genius. His fate was sealed. I knew that Alexander would defeat him.

'Do you know what I admire most in this world, Talleyrand? It is the total inability of force to organise anything. There are only two powers in the world: the sword and the spirit. By spirit I understand the civil and religious institutions – in the long run the sword is always beaten by the spirit...'

Napoleon's words from long ago were ringing in my ears. I felt a sweat begin to break out on my body. Did he know? I wondered. Did he know that I would turn upon him the very force that he knew he could never defeat...?

I felt a little sick as I tried to smile back at the Tsar's expression of saintliness. For a moment I thought I saw Napoleon's face materialise in front of my eyes: 'Et tu, Brute...'

The words were softly spoken from the lean dark features of my Sword of France.

* * *

The closing months of that year of 1808 were filled with an intense activity.

Following our return from Erfurt, Napoleon had hastened to Spain where English support for the resisting Spaniards had forced the occupying French into a retreat from Madrid. The insurgent factions in that country had been increasingly active, and the recent arrival of the English General, Arthur Wellesley, had raised a new spirit of confidence amongst the Spanish opposition to French domination. Also, the defeat of Junot in Portugal had been an added fillip to their strengthening resistive inclinations.

* * *

Meanwhile, in Paris, whilst the Emperor was sorting out the disarray of his Spanish strategy, I busied myself in organising my own affairs in accordance with my plans.

In the pleasant environment of the balls and receptions of the Imperial Court, and through the appropriately subtle devices for which I hold a partiality, I now endeavoured to make known to the political establishment my profound disapproval of the Emperor's policies, and indeed my active opposition to them. It was, of course, immediately assumed that I was conspiring to effect an overthrow of the Government, and I listened with enjoyment to the diverse rumours that were reported to me, reflecting the varying speculations upon my methods for such an action. I am often amazed at the imaginations of men. Such fantasies that were related provided me with hours of amusement!

As it happened, though, I was not participant in any active plot to displace the Emperor. I was confident of the eventuality of another, international outcome. However, I did nothing to dispel the rumours since their circulation suited my purpose – as well as providing me with entertainment!

Circumstance did, however, dictate a necessity that I could never have foreseen earlier in my career. Strange are the quirks of fate.

I had always held a particular dislike for Fouché. His underhand, back-street methods frankly disgusted me, reminding me all too graphically of the more bloody events of our recent history. Indeed, I had long taken pains to associate as little as possible with this clever but deceitful man. I had nothing whatsoever in common with him.

But France's political structures were taking on new characteristics, and it was becoming necessary to employ every constructive contribution to the strengthening of the constitutional defenders, for I was not alone in my dissatisfaction with the Emperor. Plots were beginning to breed in embryo form. Indeed, there was even a conspiracy to replace Napoleon with Murat in another military coup.

However, the way I saw things at this time was that France had broadly divided into two factions: the Emperor – and his People.

Napoleon remained at the head of the military, still commanding their loyalty, though with a growing disenchantment from some of the Marshals. Napoleon saw only himself and his family in Europe, it seemed, and he sought to extend his influence through force.

The other contingent was the mass of the Nation. The great, trusting French people, who were now denied their inherent power of action, and who, tired of war, watched helplessly as their sons, at younger and younger ages, died in the bloody battlefields that had long ceased to account for Glory.

I felt that I was the representative of this latter, helpless party. And my political instincts informed me that my natural ally in this cause would seem, inevitably, to be the Minister of Police: Joseph Fouché.

Thus it was that some meetings took place between myself, and Fouché. I took no pains to conceal the friendly nature of these discussions, and indeed I ensured that we were seen in public places engaged in deep conversations.

Naturally, and as I had expected, news of the new accord between myself and Fouché was reported to the Emperor who was in Valladolid, directing the military operations in the Spanish Peninsula. To my profound amusement, Napoleon appeared to be disconcerted to such an extent that he returned to Paris, declaring that the forming of an alliance between Fouché and myself was a more formidable opposition than that of the Austrians, whose mobilisation had been reported to him at the same time!

Upon the Emperor's return to Paris, I was summoned to the Tuileries for a meeting of the Privy Council. Together with some others, I was ushered into the Imperial presence, and an apparently routine meeting began. However, within a few minutes it was obvious that the Emperor was endeavouring to control his rage as he informed us as a whole that Grand Dignitaries and Ministers were not at liberty to think for ourselves, and personal initiatives were out of the question. To disagree with the Emperor was the onset of treason, and the individuals who believed themselves to be governing France were thus informed that they must cease to aspire to personal expression.

Leaning against a small table, I raised my eyebrows at this new departure of the excitable Emperor. His autocracy had never extended itself hitherto quite so far. Clearly he was masking some deep fury. Indeed, a tremor of anger had already begun to raise the ringing tones of his voice.

My anticipations were correct, for at that moment of my speculation, the grey penetrating gaze, now so cold, turned upon me. With cool resignation I stared back, awaiting patiently the onslaught I knew was coming.

For the next half hour I was subjected to an uninterrupted flow of abuse from the now openly enraged Emperor as he paced up and down before me, never taking his burning eyes from my expressionless face. Beginning by attaching to me the undignified labels of thief, coward and traitor, the temperamental Corsican continued with the impassioned accusations of my deceptive dealings with everyone I had ever encountered, including, indeed, God himself!

Stirred to near madness, his hot blood induced him to lay at my feet the responsibility for the murder of the Duc d'Enghien, the Peninsular War, and most other of his more unsavoury deeds of violence. Finally, in a fit of uncontrolled rage, he taunted me about my lameness, my character, and the infidelities of my wife. His voice now rising in an undignified, salivating scream, the puce Emperor, incensed at my expressionless impassivity, most unpleasantly shook his fist at an alarmingly close proximity to my face, and informed me in language of the camp that I was nothing more than dung in a silk stocking.

I was amused at the expressions of horror on the faces of the witnesses to this ill-bred tirade. Myself, I had become weary of Napoleon's displays of temperament. Rather, therefore, than allow my offended feelings to animate a reaction to this disgusting invective, I decided instead to contain my anger, affecting a mask of unperturbed impassivity. Time, I knew, would avenge me of my hurt dignity. Thus, following the shocking outburst from the Emperor at this meeting, I determined, nonetheless, that I would not be deterred from going about my normal business. Resentment is a feeble emotion. And so I continued with the normal motions of court procedures as though nothing untoward had ever happened.

For a few days the Emperor maintained a stiff antipathy to my presence, and persisted in entirely ignoring me. However, within a short period the normal pattern of life resumed. I believe that Napoleon regretted his behaviour. Indeed, I knew that if even a shadow of his former character remained, he probably suffered more from his appalling display of temper than I did.

But now, three years after the humiliations of Austerlitz, Austria was actively preparing for her revenge, as I had always known she would. Rumours of a mobilisation of their army under the command of the Emperor Francis' brother, Archduke Charles, had been filtering into Paris for some time. Through a combination of my own close associations with Clemens Metternich – and Fouché's close attentions to his correspondence – we were aware of the progress of their preparations, and Napoleon was now forced to divert his preoccupations from his attempts at correcting the calamitous blunders of his brother Joseph in Spain. Duly, in April 1809, without an official declaration of war, Austria began her advance.

And so the marching feet of the Grand Army once more accompanied their patriotic singing in central Europe, even as their superior regiments sang theirs in the arid wastes of the Spanish Peninsula.

But in 1809 their rendition of 'La Marseillaise' had lost the vigorous lustre they had exulted at Marengo and Austerlitz. And some of the voices singing it in the swelling ranks of hastily recruited conscripts were too high to belong to grown men...

The crusade to spread the message of the Rights of Man had long since died, and the soldiers fought for the glory of the Emperor, not the Honour of France. But then, he *was* France, was he not...?

Nonetheless, the fighting expertise of the French soldiers was still unmatched in Europe. The long years of discipline and experience had ensured that they maintained their dominating supremacy as fighting men, despite their waning enthusiasm for war.

Chapter XVIII

Marshall Bernadotte pulled a dirty hand across his already smudged face, which was caked with the smoky grime of battle. The deafening sounds of drums and marching feet, of battle cries and excited horses, of echoing gunfire and rumbling artillery, assaulted his ears with a roaring relentlessness. His face was creased in an expression of grim determination as his towering figure, astride his massive horse, shouted crisp orders interspersed with commanding cries, rallying the surging Saxon troops of his command.

The anxious Marshal glanced up at the heights behind the town of Wagram upon which his corps was advancing. Rank upon rank of Austrian troops still lined those hills, and a steady stream was ominously pouring down into the town below. And in the narrow streets of that town, and all around it, the steaming struggle of hell was taking place as men locked in hand-to-hand conflict. Screams from the victims of savagery are no different, whatever their uniform.

As he directed his troops in the midst of the bloody melee, their mechanical obedience beyond the sensations of fear, Bernadotte squinted his eyes upwards to the sky, peering intently through the black smoke of spent gunfire. The light was already fading on this late evening of the fifth of July.

In helpless exasperation, Bernadotte looked around him at his Saxon soldiers. They fought valiantly. But they had no discipline and, as usual, were not responding to orders. Moreover, the Austrians seemed to be flooding into the town in ever-increasing numbers, and ominously looked as though they were fresh troops.

Bernadotte wrenched at the reins of his whinnying horse with excessive irritation. He was angry. Very angry.

'Lebrun ..!'

He yelled into the tumultuous roar, summoning his aide-de-camp who was attempting to coordinate the action against an approaching Austrian offensive. As the clash of swords and bloodcurdling yells drowned the colonel's directions, the harassed man, his anxious face running with perspiration, moved his protesting horse to Bernadotte's side.

'Sir…' he puffed, attempting to breathe properly through the acrid smoke.

'Where is my reserve? They should be here by now.' Bernadotte's blackened face was puce with rage as he spat his questions at Colonel Lebrun amidst the surrounding furore.

Shrugging his confused ignorance of the whereabouts of the promised reinforcements, the vexed aide thrust his body aside as he narrowly escaped a passing musket ball.

'We *must* have those reinforcements…we can't hold the town without them…this is a massacre…' Bernadotte was shouting his uncontrolled anger with an uncharacteristic lack of discipline, the intensity of his rage consuming him. Wildly he lashed his sword at an approaching Austrian, who fell back in wise recognition of certain defeat by the Marshal who always exposed himself to the dangers faced by his men with zealous determination.

At that moment, as the momentum of battle moved the locked group of men away from the Marshal and his attendants, a wild-eyed soldier galloped up to Bernadotte.

'Sir…' He pulled his panting horse to an attempted standstill. 'Sir, the Archduke has rallied the Austrian Corps I. He has fresh troops.' The almost incoherent young man was staring in agitation at the Marshal, who had now regained control of his emotions, and was peering up at the hills through his spyglass.

'What is the exact position of Prince Eugene?'

As Bernadotte barked his question, he scanned the ranks of advancing soldiers from the heights above. Just as the young soldier was about to try to answer, he was interrupted by the sound of another messenger approaching at a gallop, breathlessly shouting, 'Sir – the Italians have broken ranks...they are retreating...'

Abruptly Bernadotte lowered his glass, his shocked eyes penetrating the flustered soldier. He felt a bitter thud of disappointment. Without Eugene's Italian troops pressing on his right, he knew that they could not hold Wagram in view of the fact that the Archduke had launched a new offensive. It was a painful blow, for he and Eugene had done well to breach the Austrian line, and he knew they could have won the day if the reserves had been sent. A seething surge of anger rose within him. Berthier... How he loathed that bastard! That man never failed to try to discredit him...

Messengers were approaching thick and fast now. General Oudinot too had penetrated Wagram from the other side, and in the growing darkness, which was thick with the bitter pungency of smoke, the confused French troops from Oudinot's corps were firing upon the Saxons by mistake. Chaos had been unleashed in Wagram.

Regretfully, Bernadotte looked around him, his mouth twitching in his mask-like face. How damned infuriating it all was, he thought.

'Fall back to Aderklaa.'

He issued his tense command with a biting attempt to control his anger. Arrogantly he turned his horse into the forced retreat.

* * *

'The Emperor directed affairs badly today...'

Bernadotte was sprawled in his camp chair, his long legs outstretched towards the bivouac fire into which he was staring. His face was deeply thoughtful in the flickering light as he drank deeply from the goblet he was holding.

The faithful aide-de-camp, who was seated beside the Marshal, remained silent as he listened to the sour remark of his Commander. The Prince was not himself these days. Ever since the beginning of the campaign back in April he had been behaving with less than his usual perfection of manners. It was very unusual, and most unlike him.

'Had I been in command I could have forced Archduke Charles by means of a telling manoeuvre to lay down his arms without combat...'

Bernadotte's bitter tone held a hint of arrogant bravado as he voiced his thoughts. Uneasily his aide-decamp looked at him. He was really quite concerned for this man for whom he, like so many, held enormous respect and admiration. Marshal Bernadotte was, after all, the man they called 'the last of the Romans', the one who was most fitted to challenge the position of the Emperor himself because of his popularity with the rank and file of the army. Why then this uncharacteristic behaviour? It was almost as though the man had reached the end of his tether.

'Sir, a messenger from Headquarters.'

Out of the darkness had emerged one of Bernadotte's staff, closely accompanied by the shadowy figure of another soldier. They had been standing there for some time.

Bernadotte turned, looking at the man with a haughty expression. After a long, stony silence the Marshal sourly launched into a bitter list of complaints, including a belief that he had been the victim once more of Berthier's treachery, and that his Saxon troops had suffered unnecessarily because of it. Finally, the delivery of his grievances exhausted, the Marshal made an irritated gesture of dismissal, and the messenger melted back into the shadows of the night.

Turning to his aide, he now instructed him, with more kindness, to seek the brief respite of sleep. Still agitated, he felt unable, despite his own exhaustion, to avail himself of that same opportunity just yet. Instead he filled his goblet once more and, now alone, settled again into his thoughtful repose.

In his solemn solitude, Bernadotte's thoughts began to calm. Looking around at the dark shapes that were the exhausted bodies of his sleeping Saxons, scattered between their dying fires, he smiled wryly to himself. It seemed ironic that these poor undisciplined fellows, who did their best to please him, were the very roots of his annoyance. Yet it was not them personally, rather the fact that they were foreign troops.

Foreign troops! He sighed bitterly to himself. How long, how very long, had that subject been a bone of contention between himself and the Emperor. Time and again he had begged Napoleon to let him have a command of French troops. But always the Emperor had failed to respond to his requests, despite promises that he would. And yes, once again, in this campaign, the same thing had happened.

Looking at the slumbering soldiers as he drank once again from his goblet, his mind recalled the beginnings of this campaign.

He had been summoned from his happy administrative position at the Hanseatic Ports in March, and told to repair to Dresden, there to await orders. Regretfully he had followed the instruction and in Dresden he had waited for what had seemed an endless period of time for his orders. From that town he had sent the Emperor a stream of letters beseeching him to let him command French troops – or else retire. He had anticipated that he might be given the Saxon command, a prospect he dreaded, and in the course of time his apprehensions had been confirmed. Berthier… The thought made him seethe as usual.

Naturally he had accepted his disappointment with as much grace as possible, and for the next few months, from the commencement of the engagements with the Austrians, he had endeavoured to improve the performance of the undisciplined Saxons, and his diversionary mission in Bohemia had been very successful. But all the time he had pressed for French troops who had more experience as well as discipline. And upon each occasion he had been promised them. But the promise had never materialised.

In May he had become alarmed as the rumour spread amongst his troops that Dresden was threatened with a possible attack. Many of these men were from that city, and they became discontented and disheartened.

Repeatedly he wrote to the Emperor, warning him of the Saxon attitude of resentment at having to fight for a foreign cause, under foreign commanders. But still there was no response, even when he sent his own aide, Colonel Lebrun, to warn headquarters that the ninth corps was composed entirely of Saxon troops who were decidedly disinclined to fight.

Bernadotte's eyes scanned the thousands of sleeping men. He felt sorry for them. They were an army in captivity, forced to fight against their will. He had tried to instil into them some positive sense of fighting vigour, but he knew they were an unhappy force, though they had shown, as best they could, a considerable degree of loyalty, and indeed affection, for him personally. That was one of the reasons he had felt so disappointed about having to retreat from Wagram. To have held it would have been a considerable boost to the morale of his troops. If only those reinforcements had come. He sighed again deeply, his eyes narrowing as the inevitable thought of Berthier came into his mind.

Suddenly he felt tired. Terribly tired. But it was not simply battle fatigue. It was a deeper exhaustion. He was tired of fighting. He was tired of the army. He wanted to retire, and spend time with his wife and son. Ruefully he smiled to himself as he thought of Désirée, and Oscar.

His loving reflections settled a sense of calm upon him. Yes, he *would* retire. He had been talking about it for some time anyway. He smiled as he remembered the startled expression on the face of one of his Swedish friends when he had spoken about his intention. The poor fellow had only come to Dresden to tell him about the overthrow of their King, Gustavus IV, and the election of the Duke of Sudermania as King Charles XIII! Actually, it was a bit of a predicament, he had gathered, for Charles was old and had no children. Still, they were in the process of electing the Prince of Augustenburg as his heir, so their problems would soon be solved. He smiled. Nice people, those Swedes. He had grown very fond of his friends from that country.

He shook his head. He must snatch some moments of sleep. Tomorrow there would surely be another bloody battle. He sighed.

God willing it would end this war, at least...

Looking at his watch he saw it was almost midnight. Yes, he had time to have a couple of hours' sleep. He had ordered his men to leave Aderklaa at 3am. He was anxious to close up with Eugène, who was on his right, and Massena on his left – thus shortening his line. Perhaps his Saxons would perform better when bolstered by that support.

Stretching himself, Bernadotte rose and moved into the ramshackle barn in which his camp bed had been prepared. He was not aware of his head coming to rest on his pillow as sleep overcame him.

* * *

'*What...?*'

The Emperor's roar could be heard some distance away as the blinking bearer of the unpleasant news stepped back involuntarily at the force of the blast.

'At what time...?' Napoleon barked his question brutally at the frightened officer.

'B-between three and four o'clock, sire...he-he has closed with Prince Eugene and M-Marshal Massena,' stammered the young man, his fresh features pink with fear at the Sovereign's rage.

The face of the Emperor was reddened with anger as he looked penetratingly at the trembling young man. He could barely contain his disbelief at the news this messenger had brought him. Casting an angry glance at the group of aides and assistants standing around him, Napoleon suddenly threw up his hands in an expression of exasperation.

'What is Bernadotte doing?' he shouted. 'I gave no orders. Doesn't the man realise the importance of Aderklaa?' He broke off, choked with enraged disbelief.

'H-he...intended...'

'SILENCE!'

The young soldier's attempt at an explanation was buried forever by the Emperor's thunderous roar. There was a long, charged hush amongst the group of men crowded around the Emperor's map-covered table. Only the sounds of the endless columns of soldiers moving out to attend their positions interrupted the stormy dawn contretemps at the Emperor's headquarters.

Suddenly beckoning to Berthier with an impatient gesture, Napoleon broke his fuming silence. 'Instruct Bernadotte and Massena to re-take Aderklaa.'

Snatching up his spyglass, the Emperor strode from the table and, lifting it to his eye, absorbed himself in studying the terrain before him. The subject of Bernadotte's removal from Aderklaa was closed. He must concentrate on watching the right for the movement when Davout would take Markgrafneusiedl.

Bernadotte… The thought irked him. Why must the fellow persist in being so damnably difficult? Napoleon's mouth set itself in a hard line as he stared through the glass.

* * *

It was not yet nine o'clock but the temperatures were already rising steadily. It would be a long, hot day, this sixth of July. Bernadotte and Massena, obeying the Emperor's instruction, had re-entered Aderklaa. But now, just as their divisions were securing their positions, Archduke Charles descended upon them, with a vigorous assault by his Austrian grenadiers and reserve cavalry. The viciousness of the sudden onslaught had taken the inexperienced Saxons entirely by surprise and, as Bernadotte had always feared, they turned and ran for the rear, accompanied by part of Massena's corps.

Bernadotte felt as though his heart had leapt into his mouth. He had always expected something like this might happen, but even so it was a surprise in the event. In desperation he kicked his horse savagely. He must rally his men. Stop them from going into retreat. With a blood-curdling yell, he pointed his sword ahead and charged to the front of the column, defying all convention in his wild efforts to inspire his soldiers.

His crazed battle cry died on his lips as, turning his head, he found himself looking into the marble grey eyes of the Emperor. Napoleon had come to Aderklaa, in a carriage since he was suffering from a wound, to encourage the troops in action. He had stood motionless outside his battered conveyance as he had witnessed the hysterical lunge of the theatrical Marshal.

As their eyes now locked, Napoleon coldly raised his eyebrows. Bernadotte felt a deep flush rise from his neck to engulf his confused face as he pulled his horse to an abrupt halt in front of the Emperor. Automatically, he jumped down to bow to his superior officer. Around them the bloody confusion continued, but the two men were temporarily oblivious to everything else. For a moment it seemed to both of them that the history of their conflicting relationship had raised itself before them for final resolution.

'The Prince of Ponte Corvo's tactics grow increasingly...unconventional.' The Emperor's cutting words bit into the bated moment between them. Napoleon paused as an imperious smile of damming sarcasm came to his mirthless face. 'Tell me, Bernadotte, is this the type of "telling manoeuvre" with which you will compel the Archduke Charles to lay down his arms...?'

As Bernadotte heard himself gulp with surprise, a young man standing behind Napoleon lowered his head as the Emperor finished his sarcastic remark. Bernadotte instantly recognised him. It was the messenger who had come from Headquarters the night before. Dumbfounded with astonishment, the Marshal began to protest his justifications with confused incoherence. He was silenced, however, as the Emperor, glaring coldly at the Marshal, continued in slow, smouldering anger.

'I hereby remove you from the command of the Corps which you have handled so consistently badly. Leave my presence immediately, and quit the Grand Army within twenty-four hours.'

As he finished his icy speech, Napoleon turned away in arrogant dismissal. Mounting the steps of his coach, he impatiently urged haste to his driver and Guard.

Bernadotte swallowed, aware of the shocked witnesses who

were staring at him in amazed disbelief. He felt a little dazed. So it had finally happened – the great, wrenching rift. Inevitably...

He looked around at his valiantly fighting Saxon troops. What a humiliation. Here, in battle. Casting a glance at the sympathetic onlookers, he suddenly raised his chin. Smiling proudly at them, he flung himself back onto his horse, and rode off at a gallop. The soldiers exchanged uncomfortable glances, embarrassed for their commander.

Perhaps, after all, it had been appropriate that the pretence of friendship had at long last ended – on a battlefield...

* * *

'Father! Father! It must be a *monster*...!'

The small boy was convulsed with laughter as he watched the massive figure of his father struggle to pull in the fishing line. The small boat in which they were sitting was rocking violently as Jean-Baptiste Bernadotte wrenched repeatedly at the obstinate rod, his bronzed face flushed with both effort and pleasure.

He glanced in amusement at the small figure of his son beside him who, in his feverish excitement, had risen to his feet, pitching the already unsteady boat into an even more precarious motion. Water was now spilling over the sides of the craft in considerable quantities, as father and son delighted exuberantly at their difficulties.

'We've hooked the bottom!' shouted the exultant Bernadotte as he gave a final violent twist to the fishing rod.

With a loud crack, the uncompromising rigidity of the angling implement snapped, and as its balancing pressure to the occupants of the boat was released, father and son were thrown back, while their fragile craft capsized. In a great splash, the two were plunged into the warm depths of the pretty little lake, and after much thrashing of the water, and flailing of rising and submerging limbs, Bernadotte managed to obtain a firm hold of his small son in one of his long arms, whilst with the other he moved the boat into a supportive position.

After some time, and skilful manoeuvring of the small vessel by the powerful Marshal, the two were eventually able to clamber breathlessly back into the wet interior of their floating vessel, their laughter undiminished by their watery experience. Slowly, beneath the clear July sky, they rowed themselves back across the now rippling lake to the grassy bank, which was set into the rich green foliage of summer woods.

As the soaking man and his tired but laughing son glided smoothly towards the gentle slope of land, Bernadotte looked at the small white figure of his watching wife seated beneath the spreading arms of an enormous tree, a large white hat shading her face from the hot midday sun. His heart seemed to surge in his breast as he looked at her, the singing sound of his son's now shivering laughter in his ears. He felt he had never been so happy in his life. These past few days since his return from Austria, here at his country home 'La Grange', near Paris, he had experienced a peace and tranquillity such as he had never imagined existed.

Basking in the love of his precious Désirée, and entirely devoted to the sharing of simple pleasures of country life with his son, the pain and unhappiness of these past months had almost receded into vague memory. Indeed, he had lost entirely that permanent feeling of anxiety he had experienced for such an interminable period of time.

Ambition, power, the army, his pride – they were all so far away from him now. Here he had found true simplicity and happiness. Here, with the two people he loved more than anything in the world. At this moment he felt that there was nothing else in life that mattered, nor indeed that he wanted. He was utterly content.

* * *

'Your Highness! Two gentlemen have just arrived. They wish to speak with you. They await your pleasure in the house. They're very…persistent.'

The embarrassed servant stared fixedly at the thick green grass at his feet. He had been reluctant to interrupt his master and mistress during their picnic at the lakeside. But the two men had been very insistent. Their business seemed to be a matter of some urgency.

Bernadotte looked at his wife. She was in the process of rubbing the wet body of her cold and shivering son with a large towel. Ruefully she looked up at her husband as she saw the expression of disappointment transform his face from carefree happiness into a troubled look of unwanted responsibility. As he hesitated, reluctant to leave his little family, she smiled at him, her eyes large and soft beneath the flickering shade of her wide-brimmed hat.

'You had better see who they are, darling...' Her voice was gentle as she eased his unwilling sense of duty. 'It might be important.'

Turning his head, he looked up the long sloping hill towards the pretty house. He had a sudden feeling of apprehension, a strange presentiment that his idyllic rural dream was about to be shattered. He looked down as he felt the light touch of his wife's hand on his arm, gently urging him to go. And as her warm lips pressed his cheek, he felt a lump come to his throat. Happiness was so fleeting, he thought.

* * *

The drawing room of this pleasant country house reflected the personality of its mistress, I thought. It really was quite charming. Sunny and light, it was filled with elegant but comfortable furniture, and the softness of its furnishings was enhanced by the exquisite fragrance emitted by the numerous bowls of fresh flowers that were scattered across the room. There was no formality or pretension here in the country residence of the Prince of Ponte Corvo, only the simple spirit of domestic happiness in tasteful surroundings. It was quite enchanting.

Indeed, it had been a most enjoyable journey altogether on this warm day at the end of July. The Marshal's house was not far from Paris, so it had not been a daunting prospect of prolonged travel, which I so dislike. Fouché and I had left Paris at a civilised hour, after breakfast, and driven at a leisurely pace through the picturesque summer countryside.

We had not informed the Prince of our intended visit for the simple reason that it had seemed pointless to curtail his rural pleasures any sooner than was necessary. After all, the poor fellow had only returned from his humiliating experience in Austria a few days since.

In addition, it had been important to observe a delicate degree of discretion in conducting our business with the Marshal, and we had been anxious that as few people as possible should know of our visit to see him. Thus it was appropriate that we should neither send a messenger to summon him, nor inform him in advance of our visit. Instead we had chosen that cautious guardian of secrecy: personal surprise!

Fouché had displayed some quite uncharacteristic elation during our journey. He was enjoying the opportunity to display the strength of his own power – and to expose the weakness of Napoleon's – which this little mission of ours was providing. I was amused to see some positive animation in his sallow, hooded expression. Those permanently half-closed eyes seldom betrayed any hint of human emotion. It was always difficult to know what might be in the mind of this slippery individual, whom I now found to be my necessary ally. However, I had a suspicion that he had an interest in Bernadotte that was projected beyond even our immediate business.

The wounding of the Emperor at Ratesbon had caused a universal speculation as to what would happen were he to be killed in battle. His dynasty had not been assured, and the thought of Joseph as heir, or any other Bonaparte, was distasteful to everyone.

Those who conjectured such matters had considered two contenders: namely, Bernadotte and Murat. But the latter, though a glamorous and charismatic soldier, who undoubtedly commanded loyalty from the army, nonetheless lacked Bernadotte's considerable intellectual talents.

Thus it was that, as in 1799, he was again Napoleon's principal challenger. Paris was once more rife with plots and intrigue. But the master of all the conspiracies, Fouché, I knew to favour Bernadotte as a possible replacement for Napoleon.

Bernadotte, though possibly aware of being the focus of such possibilities, was, I felt certain, in no way participant in any form of intrigue. His basic integrity, and loyalty to the elected government, refused such treasonous co-operations.

Napoleon, ensconced in the Hapsburg Palace of Schonbrunn in Vienna, was meanwhile acutely aware of the hatching conspiracies in Paris. Indeed, it was his fear regarding these proliferating plots that was now to push him towards finally ending his marriage to Josephine in order to endeavour to beget an heir. My own intelligence had informed me that he had regretted his hasty actions towards Bernadotte on the field of Wagram, for the very good reason that the disgraced Marshal's presence in Paris would inevitably give potential conspirators against the Empire a figure to whom they might rally. Napoleon had ever remained wary of the challenge from the Marshal who had never fully accepted the superiority of his former fellow General of the Revolutionary Army.

Following the fracas during the battle, Bernadotte had further compounded the bitterness between himself and the Emperor by issuing an Order of the Day, which had claimed the Victory of Wagram for his Saxon troops. This was certainly audacity on a magnificent scale, and as the arrogant Marshal left, apparently to take the waters at Plombières, the Imperial Headquarters was in a state of considerable consternation as they saw the Marshal's extravagant congratulations for the unfortunate Saxons published in the International newspapers. Bernadotte's reasons for such an extraordinary claim remain obscure. But my own opinion is that he sought to boost the morale of his embattled soldiers, and the humiliation he had just suffered made him unrepentant of anything he might say, no matter how imaginative. Whatever his motives, they incurred the exploding wrath of the Emperor, who had written profuse refutations of the statement, and had instructed the Minister of War to severely reprimand the insolent Marshal. Bernadotte, however, remained unmoved.

Now, after his initial expressions of rage, the Emperor had recognised the error in his precipitant behaviour, and realised that he had thrust the Marshal into a position where he might create a very difficult problem. Thus had Napoleon tried to induce him away from Paris. First he had instructed him to visit Ponte Corvo which the recalcitrant Marshal refused to do, claiming that he would rather relinquish his titles and lands than submit to such infringements on his liberty of movement by the Emperor. The Emperor, realising he would get nowhere through exerting pressure on the proud Prince, instead then tried to appease his vanity, and I knew that he was in the process of trying to devise a way of making Bernadotte the Governor-General of Rome, where the unfortunate Pope had just been arrested by Napoleon's government, thus annexing the Holy City for France. I did not doubt that Bernadotte would refuse this offer, but at this time I did not know for what extraordinary reason he would do so.

But now, in these closing days of July, our business with Bernadotte was of a different nature...

* * *

'Prince Benevento!'

Bernadotte's surprise expressed incredulity in his voice. I was happy to note that, moreover, his response of disbelief was complemented with a warm indication of pleasure at my unexpected presence.

'Monsieur Fouché.' His greeting to the Minister of Police was polite, but less than enthusiastic.

The Marshal's astonished expression at the identity of his visitors was equalled by my own in response to his dishevelled appearance. Never had I seen the scrupulous soldier in such a state of disarray as he stood, his clothes apparently dripping with water, in front of us. How extraordinary are the pursuits of some people when in the country!

Insisting that I remain seated in the chair to which I had grown accustomed during our wait, the Prince crisply ordered some wine to be brought by a hovering servant and, assuring us of his immediate return, disappeared to divest himself of his soaking garments.

Barely had the servant appeared with the welcome liquid refreshment, when Bernadotte himself reappeared, still uncharacteristically untidy, but at least clothed in dry accoutrements. Delivering his apologies with customary politeness, he then proceeded to pour wine into the glasses, again bestowing upon me a warm and genuinely welcoming smile. I responded with equal expressions of friendship; I had always had a partiality for this intelligent man.

'Well, gentlemen!' His tone was brisk but relaxed. 'To what does a disgraced Marshal of France owe this pleasure?'

Handing us each a glass of wine, he smiled pleasantly, seating himself as he picked up his own glass from the tray. Fouché had refrained from sitting down, and had remained standing at the window where he had placed himself upon our arrival. Bernadotte, slightly uneasy at the brooding presence of the Minister of Police, addressed himself mainly to me.

'Fouché here finds himself in some difficulty, Prince,' I began. 'It appears that you alone are in a position to save France!'

I had been aware that my oblique statement would induce an interested curiosity from the Marshal. Raising his eyebrows with a humorous inclination of his large handsome head, he enquired, 'Indeed...?'

His eyes twinkled slightly as he looked into mine. But I knew he was not prepared for that which was coming.

The thin figure of Fouché moved now from the window, his heavily lidded eyes fixed on the massive figure of the Marshal. Without preamble he began, somewhat pompously: 'The Emperor is at present in Vienna, as you are aware. Distance, therefore, forbids me time to inform His Majesty that there are, at the present moment, English troops massing under the command of the Earl of Chatham. It seems they are bound for Antwerp, and will probably make a landing somewhere at the mouth of the River Scheldt in the coming days. I have reason to believe that they intend to proceed to Paris from the Channel coast, and it is my responsibility as Minister for the Interior to call up the National Guard in the interests of the safety of the country.'

He paused, majestically taking in a deep breath as he prepared to make his gracious appointment. I smothered a smile at both the self-important tones of the pale Minister for Police and the Interior, and at the bemused expression on the dumbfounded Marshal's face.

'I must ask you, Prince, as a Marshal of France, to assume command of these troops for the defence of France.'

Fouché's thin lips clamped together like a rat trap. How odd, for I had always thought he resembled a rat! His rodent-like gaze was now fixed upon Bernadotte's astonished stare.

I looked from one to the other, enjoying myself in the charged silence that followed Fouché's dramatic speech.

'But I am in disgrace…' Bernadotte was attempting to recover his stunned response to the extraordinary prospect of invasion by England.

'France, Marshal. France.' Fouché's harsh interruptions silenced the Marshal's embryonic protestations. 'The fate of our nation lies in your hands…' He hesitated before finishing sharply, 'You must depart for the Channel coast at once.'

The room fell once more into the heavy silence. Bernadotte appeared to be collecting himself as he stared into his glass. Fouché removed to the window once more, and I sipped the pleasant wine as I observed Bernadotte.

Abruptly the Marshal rose from his chair. Silently he moved to stand by the bow windows that opened out onto the beautiful descending gardens beyond. For a long moment he stared down to the small lake in the distance, so charmingly set in the woods. Watching him closely, I could see a muscle working in his cheek, and he appeared to swallow. He seemed to be wrestling with some troubled thought.

Finally, in a toneless voice, he huskily muttered, 'Very well, gentlemen. I shall accompany you back to Paris.'

He did not turn from the window. His eyes were somehow mesmerised by something beyond those trees.

* * *

The Prince of Ponte Corvo departed for Antwerp on the third of August. Fouché duly informed the Emperor of his initiative, which had been decried by his useless colleagues in the Government. They feared the Emperor's anger at an independent action. I, however, supported Fouché and believed him to be taking the right decision.

Bernadotte arrived in Antwerp to find a motley rabble of only 12,000 troops, without uniforms, arms, or enthusiasm. Within a week he had more than doubled their number. He clothed them, instructed them in the basic army disciplines, and instilled into them an ardour and a self-confidence that they had never experienced. Out of chaos, Bernadotte had once more created order. Out of a mob, he moulded an army. And, as the National Guard was despatched along the coast from Antwerp to Dunkirk, he organised a formidable line of defence that once more reflected his extraordinary gifts of leadership.

The English had meanwhile sailed, and by mid-August had occupied the island of Walcheren. But their timorous Commander, Lord Chatham, was an indecisive individual, and whilst Bernadotte was preparing the French defence, he failed to exploit England's moment of advantage. Instead he kept his troops languishing in inactivity upon the disease-infested island. Eventually, under the relentless stare of Bernadotte's ever-strengthening lines, the English soldiers began to succumb to the fevers that gripped that unhealthy place. Soon, thousands of men were dying from the ravaging diseases, and by the end of September the English were forced to accept that their invasion was a failure.

The Emperor rewarded Fouché by creating him the Duke of Otranto. Bernadotte received only silence as his reward. Not even a letter of thanks was forthcoming from the Master of Europe.

Yet this had been a moment when England might well have invaded France but for the Marshal's stalwart defence, created entirely through his own extraordinary talents.

Chapter XIX

The Paris street lighting system was certainly impressive, and one which was the subject of much admiration from visiting foreigners. But then, the Emperor had always maintained his keen attention to the latest inventions and scientific developments, and even though he no longer had the time to involve himself personally with men of Science and innovators – in the way that he had done so at the time of the Egyptian Expedition – he had, nonetheless, retained his interest and support for progress in such fields.

Paris of the Empire was not a centre for Art and Literature, and Napoleon held a deep suspicion of the small groups of intelligentsia who claimed their distinction mainly in exile. However, though the Emperor did not encourage writers and artists, those with inventive talents were supported, and they flocked to the busy hum of Paris in their droves. The city was positively teeming with eccentric individuals displaying their often bizarre innovations, and the results of some of the more practically advantageous were to be evidenced in all sorts of subtle ways, from the flickering of the gas street lamps, to food preservatives, ostensibly devised for the appetites of the shifting legions of the Grand Army.

He had brought order. He had brought prosperity – before he had started to deprive France of her young men. He had also brought the spirit of change, and the anticipation of a new type of society with emphasis on different priorities of the human talents. He had achieved so much, yet the cracks in his Empire had already begun to weaken its structure.

I looked at the streetlamps through my carriage window. They always fascinated me, these still sentinels of night. There was something oddly beautiful about their serene detachment from the bustle of Paris.

Moving my leg very slightly, I settled into the comfort of my slowly moving conveyance. I fingered my high collar, easing it from its irritating pressure on my neck. How I lamented the passing of the lacy elegance of bygone fashion. However, I endeavoured to wear the new clothes with some degree of panache. One's style must not be inhibited by the limited imagination of those who call themselves 'designers' of fashionable clothing. My new carriage was extremely comfortable. Surprisingly! These rattletraps are normally conducive only to excruciating discomfort. Perhaps some new device in design had contributed to its smoothness. Or perhaps it was the street. Such things were a mystery to me! I was fortunate, actually, to have a new means of transport, since I had been experiencing a period of most distressing financial difficulties. Indeed, I had not been alone in my problems.

Many of the prominent banking houses had been forced to close due to the economic difficulties created by the continental system. My association with one of them had been the source of my distress as I had faced the catastrophic loss of an enormous sum of money. So bad were the results of this disaster that I had been obliged to sell my library, which caused me acute vexation. I had appealed to the Tsar to relieve me of my financial embarrassments, but he had politely declined his assistance, thus forcing me to divulge my dilemma to Napoleon. A property transaction with the Emperor, who knew my distaste for poverty, thus fortunately relieved my dire situation, and I had been able to resume my accustomed standard of living. I was aware that the eyebrows of many of my acquaintances had been raised at my acceptance of money from the Emperor, in view of our strained relations and my open opposition to his policies. But, as I have said before, I have never seen any merit in poverty. It does not conduce to the sharp performance of the mind. I see no point in suffering such degradation when it can be avoided, albeit through mildly doubtful means.

And so, my financial traumas resolved, I was now on my way to one of the many balls being given to celebrate the Emperor's marriage. It was barely four months from the dramas that had surrounded his divorce. Poor Josephine! How wretched was that poor creature now in her lonely solitude at Malmaison. She had been devastated at the reality of finding herself divorced from the man she had grown to love so passionately, even though it had long been a commonly held expectation that Napoleon would divorce his wife of thirteen years – not least by the Empress herself. The political expediency of a younger wife was inevitably going to eventually triumph over the sentimental procrastinations of the man who had once loved the now aging Creole so deeply. Perhaps Josephine had hoped that the weight of memory would prevail, and he would cease his preoccupations with dynastic intentions. But in the absence of the sublime passions of love, the passion of power is a consuming force, and Napoleon had long ceased to love Josephine with the former ardent zeal of his youth.

The divorce proceedings had been an unpleasant and harrowing experience for all concerned. Josephine had wept openly and dramatically, making no attempt to conceal her bitter unhappiness from those assembled to witness the dissolution of a partnership that had been loved and revered by the entire nation of the French. As I had handed Josephine her speech accepting the terms of her divorce, she had trembled in pale disbelief. Glancing across at the Emperor, I had seen, beneath the stony mask of his outward expression, an unevenness of breathing, and a sadness of the grey eyes that I knew reflected a profound sorrow at the loss of she whom he had always referred to as his 'lucky charm'. Perhaps, after all, she really had been his 'talisman'…

Subsequent to the divorce Napoleon had continued to see the broken Empress, visiting her in the beautiful surroundings of Malmaison where they had once been so happy. But as his visits quickly grew less frequent, Josephine – who had succumbed to the ravages of time by suddenly growing into an old woman – resigned herself to her melancholy fate and, in the refuge of her exquisite gardens, waited for her final release from life, accompanied by only her haunting memories. That release would come as her husband stood on the threshold of his own imprisonment.

Napoleon had been financially generous to the woman that he still loved – insofar as he was still capable. And her children were attentive to the mother who had been always kind and considerate, as indeed she had been to everyone she knew. But Josephine was shattered, and though she would not die until 1814, she lived in a brooding sadness that irresistibly drew that dark mantle prematurely towards her. Like so many, I felt a deep sympathy for the woman who had always displayed such gentle charm, and whose only misfortune was that she had been unable to bear her second husband any children. It was a sorrowful business, Napoleon's divorce.

The successor to the kindly Creole could not have contrasted more with her predecessor; indeed, day and night have extremes no greater than those two women of different generations. The empty-headed nineteen-year-old, whose youth and health would indeed give Napoleon his heir, nonetheless brought little else to the Court of Paris, despite her impeccable breeding. Josephine's quiet dignity had created a certain warmth at the Imperial centre, but though Napoleon grew fond of his new bride, she never really settled to life in France. Personally I believe that a distinct lack of intelligence in this sensual young woman was the basic reason for her inability to participate in the French way of life. However, since I was myself the interlocutor in the matter of the Emperor's marriage, and indeed the zealous advocate of this particular alliance, I should perhaps refrain from reflecting upon any impressions regarding Marie Louise, the oldest daughter of the Emperor Francis of Austria.

Napoleon had called a meeting of the Council in January following the dramas of the divorce in December. We, the Grand Dignitaries and Ministers, were asked to give our opinions as to the question of the Emperor's marriage. In contention were Russian, Saxon and Austrian princesses, and the prevailing preference seemed to be for a Russian alliance. Fouché and Murat in particular supported Cambacéré's strident advocacy for Russia.

I, however, as I have already said, had determined that were there any possibility at all of salvaging the Napoleonic rule of France, it would not be through a Russian marital tie. Indeed, such an event would inevitably prove disastrous for the Austrian Empire, possibly resulting in them being crushed altogether. For me the preservation of Austria was integral for the European balance, and their Ambassador, Clemens Metternich, and I had conjectured the Franco Austrian alliance with painstaking attention to every detail of its advantages and disadvantages. We had both concluded, and agreed, that an Austrian marriage for Napoleon was essential for the interests of both countries at the present time of France's supreme domination of Europe. Moreover, I was anxious that France should attempt to expiate her inexcusable crime of the Revolution when she had executed her Austrian Queen, Marie Antoinette.

Thus I addressed the Council, urging the choice of an Austrian princess, aware that Metternich was similarly encouraging his own Emperor to offer the hand of his daughter to Napoleon. Fortunately my powers of persuasion over my Sovereign had seemingly not entirely died, and he acceded to my advice on the matter.

On the eleventh of March 1810, Marshal Berthier officiated as proxy on behalf of Napoleon at the marriage in Vienna between Marie Louise of Austria, and the Emperor of the French.

Two weeks later the young Empress travelled to France, and found her journey interrupted by her new husband before she reached Paris. His anxiety for an heir – or perhaps sheer masculine impatience! – induced the Emperor to wish to consummate the marriage as soon as possible. And so, to her astonishment, the young woman's coach was unexpectedly halted by two men, one of whom, without warning, erupted his small rotund form through the door of the carriage, presenting himself romantically at the girl's side. Thus did Marie Louise meet her forty-year-old husband. Aided by Murat, the Emperor now dramatically diverted the Empress and her entourage to the Castle of Compiègne deep in the forests of that name. There the couple spent their wedding night. Some days later, on the second of April, the two were married formally in a religious ceremony in Paris.

Parisians will celebrate anything – anytime! It is in their nature to be gay, and coronations, royal weddings, war victories, all such occasions present opportunities to indulge their propensity for enjoyment.

The spring of 1810 was one such time. Ever since the nuptials, Paris had been celebrating. After all, it was a time for revelry. France was supreme in Europe, even the mighty Hapsburgs recognised the restored power of the 'Patrie'. And though for a while the new young Empress was not seen in public – the Emperor believing that quietude would better induce pregnancy- nonetheless, the Parisians continued to celebrate, and there were balls, receptions, and more balls.

It was now June. Fouché, now the Duke of Otranto and my uneasy ally, had finally been disgraced. Following a display from the Emperor somewhat similar to his verbal assault on me of the year before, the Minister of Police had been dismissed, and despatched to Italy. Without authority he had been found conducting negotiations with England, and Napoleon, ever sensitive to the plots of exiled Bourbons, assumed Fouché to be intriguing with his hated enemies.

The 'terrorist' was replaced at the Ministry by Savary, whose loyalty to his master was undisputed, and who had recently organised the dubious proceedings of the Spanish abdications, as well as having officiated long ago at the execution of the Duc d'Enghien. Savary was entirely trustworthy, and would never challenge the Emperor. Napoleon was now surrounded entirely by servile individuals, accepting his will without question.

Fouché had been forced to accept a gilded punishment. He had been made the Governor-General of the recently annexed Holy City, and was now, in effect, the Pope's gaoler. I did not doubt, however, that distance would never deter Fouché's capacity for intrigue at the Imperial Court. The position that he now held had, of course, been previously offered to Bernadotte, who had contemptuously turned it down.

Bernadotte – I smiled to myself. A clever fellow! Could he have known…?

My carriage was slowing down as we were now approaching the Tuileries. I straightened myself in preparation for disembarkation. Taking out my snuffbox I availed myself of a brief intake of its fortifying contents. Snapping the exquisite object shut, I returned it to my pocket. Bernadotte – the thought of it all amused me. This was going to be an enjoyable evening!

* * *

I was wondering if she remembered that her Aunt, Marie Antoinette, had probably crossed this very ballroom, in similar circumstances, only a few years ago. Involuntarily I looked at the Empress' rather thick neck. I shuddered as I recalled the barbarism of those dreadful years.

The richly robed nobility of France were pressing forward, frankly like an undignified mob, in their eagerness to examine in close detail the pretty young girl. She moved slowly through their parting ranks, graciously smiling at faces whose detail she would never even take in, much less remember. But she was the daughter of an Emperor, and such gracious displays of apparent interest were ingrained in her upbringing. Beside her, considerably shorter, strutted the Emperor. He was pleased with himself, I could see, for he had assumed what I like to call his 'mask of Caesar' – I knew so well each tiny flicker of his range of expression. As always when I looked into his face nowadays, especially when I had not seen him for a while, I was seized by the sensation of lament for times past, and my memory presented that poignant image of the young genius with his long untidy hair, and shining grey eyes.

The 'mask of Caesar' looked coldly around at the straining faces of his Nobility. I felt rather sick. Power – what a strange force. 'I believe in my star…' he had always said in those days. And now, I wondered, what did he see now? Had he lost sight of his 'star'? Or did he believe he no longer had need of its mysterious influence?

Power! It makes an insidious progress through the complexities of the human psyche, that much is certain. There seems to be no discernible specific moment when it finally assumes its control. But slowly, ineluctably, it nonetheless tightens its sinister grip, taking possession of the personality by disabling the tempering facets of reason and altruism. Surely such is Tragedy in its true form – as understood by the Greeks? For the very characteristics that once made greatness, are now transformed, with equal intensity, into the instruments of inevitable destruction. That such a transformation comes about, however, I am certain is aided – perhaps even actively induced – by the contemptible venality of weaker men, whose sycophantic fascinations render them incapable of constructive challenge to the powerful will of genius. In their stupidity, and pandering self-interest, they appease the single most sinister and festering weakness that lurks beneath the surface of the extraordinary talents of such men: Vanity. And as that vanity is fed, it grows, like a great hungry animal that eventually devours all that was once great.

Thus, for me – and I was particularly reminded of it as I looked around this brilliant gathering of Marshals, Nobles and Dignitaries – there is nothing more sickening than witnessing the enfeeblement of a once proud and formidable genius by the whimpering mediocrity of those servile parasites of greatness. History will, of course, always condemn the man himself. But in my view much of the responsibility for such horrifying change must rest with those who encourage it to come about. People exploit the isolation of leaders – and I am not at all sure that they do it innocently.

These were my thoughts as I watched Napoleon and his bride cross the floor of the ballroom to mount the Imperial thrones. And as the formality of the progress ended, and the dancing began, the tension released as excited conversation rippled through the small groups of people. I smiled wryly to myself. I did not need to be told what every conversation in that room was about!

My eyes wandered across the magnificent scene before me. Whirling ladies, dancing lights, beautiful music, it was all familiar and predictable.

My eyes came eventually to rest upon a tall figure who was leaning against a column. Nearby, his wife was engaged in an animated conversation with a group of people. But the handsome man was entirely divorced from their conversation, and was looking idly around the ballroom, sipping occasionally from a glass of wine. Jean-Baptiste Bernadotte was decidedly 'not involved' with the proceedings in this room. He was a polite, uninterested observer. I laughed to myself. He had never changed!

At that moment I was approached by a chattering group of ladies, and shortly afterwards by some serious young men. However, after one or two diversions, I eventually managed to find my way over to the still solitary Prince of Ponte Corvo.

His face broke into a warm welcoming smile as I limped towards him. He appeared to be delighted to see me. My returning smile concealed an amused anticipation of that which I was now going to divulge to him.

'I have just completed a questionnaire concerning you, my dear Prince.'

I waved my hand casually in the direction of a small group of tall, yellow-haired young men with whom I had earlier been conversing. I discerned the handsome Marshal stiffen a little as his gaze followed the indications of my arm, his intelligent eyes immediately becoming alert. I was affecting a casual air, for it suited my purpose, as I was interested to see the exact nature of the Prince's reaction to my forthcoming announcement. And besides, I enjoyed such little games, and this Marshal was always a good-humoured participant.

'Those Swedish emissaries to the Emperor's nuptial celebrations appear to have an uncommon interest in your well-being, sir!' I twinkled a little at him as I noticed a slight embarrassment appear to momentarily pass over his face. 'Indeed, my dear fellow, I believe you are acquainted with the Swedish King's representative, his relative having once been your prisoner? Baron Morner?'

Bernadotte was looking into my face with an expression of good-natured expectancy now. He knew me well enough to know I was about to make some unusual remark. He was not, however, prepared for the sort of information he was now to learn as he patiently replied to me.

'Indeed, my dear friend, I am acquainted with Baron Morner's cousin, Count Morner. We correspond occasionally.'

'Charming people, the Swedes...'

I smiled pleasantly at him as a servant re-filled our glasses, and Désirée, who had earlier departed to dance, returned to her nearby seat in an apparent state of exhaustion.

'A courteous nationality, I always find. They always strike me as having a most remarkable ability to mask their feelings with admirable displays of decorum!' As I paused to choose my next words, I could see that Bernadotte was politely nodding in agreement, clearly amused by my apparently inconsequential remarks. 'Take as an example my recent encounter with your friends. Utmost control is employed in their conversation, even though they must be in a state of considerable disarray and confusion following the unhappy accident of their Crown Prince; after all their King is old and...'

'Accident?'

Bernadotte's sharp, authoritative voice cut across my conversation. His body had become taut and attentive, and his eyes stared penetratingly into mine. I was aware, too, that his wife Désirée had been drawn from her happy observations of the dancing figures on the floor, and her eyes were now fixed upon her husband's impassive but alert face.

'*Accident?*' The Prince repeated his shocked question. 'I have heard nothing of such news, Prince. Can it be you are mistaken?' Bernadotte was clearly nonplussed. He hesitated before continuing. 'What...what exactly have you heard? What has happened to the Prince of Augustenburg?' The poor fellow was trying to control a rising urgency in his voice.

I feigned surprise as I replied, lifting my eyebrows as I spoke with the casual air of an impartial gossip. 'Why, my dear Prince, how uninformed you are! The Prince of Augustenburg is dead.'

As I looked into the frozen face of disbelief that the Marshal was unable to conceal, I shed my own posture of innocent prattler of tales. My game was over now. I had delivered my information in exactly the manner I had intended. Moreover, I had received the response I had hoped for. There was more than had been apparent in the relationship between Bernadotte and his former prisoners – that much was now obvious to me. How much more was something I intended to find out in the coming days. It was my feeling that an important change of the map of Europe could take place if carefully devised, and it was my intention to encourage that potential once I was certain of its existence.

I leaned slightly towards the stupefied Marshal now, as I knew he found himself lost for words in his current state of shock. In a low voice I spoke to him in meaningful tones. 'It appears these young men wish to converse with you, Prince…' I paused deliberately, staring into the bemused face. '…And it is my opinion that it would be of some considerable service to Europe if you were to meet with these charming young people from the north.'

I smiled now at him with a twinkling knowingness. 'I believe they have deeply valued some advice you once gave them, my dear fellow… Armed neutrality…? The ceding of Finland to Russia in favour of a federation with Norway? Why, my dear Prince, what a coherent vision you have for that important country. 'Tis little wonder that they seek your conversation. Men of vision are a rare breed anywhere. In Sweden they are extinct!'

I laughed heartily at my own joke. This had been a most satisfactory little exchange.

I looked down at the now seated Désirée, who gave me a dazed smile that was more than a little rueful. It seemed that she did not share her husband's enthusiasm for Swedes. I returned my attention to Bernadotte as I felt a twist of pity for the gentle Désirée. What a pity, I thought.

Bernadotte, meanwhile, had transformed entirely. His earlier astonished confusion had now been replaced by a brilliant smile that appeared to approach jubilance. He did not speak, but his shining eyes transmitted to me the fact that he was aware of my thoughts, and furthermore was anxious to pursue their course since the same ideas had clearly occurred to him. For a long, still moment we exchanged our silent messages. Then, as the orchestra unexpectedly changed its tempo I was suddenly jolted from the detachment as I became aware of the Princess of Ponte Corvo's melancholy observation of us both. Eager to relieve her of her growing sadness, I turned to her.

'Why Princess – You have been sorely neglected by us, I…'

'I trust that no one should ever neglect the Princess of Ponte Corvo.'

The deep icy voice momentarily froze all our actions through its surprise eruption into our midst. Collecting ourselves hastily, Bernadotte and I bowed to the unexpected Imperial Presence. Désirée, rising instantly from her seat, sank into an embarrassed deep curtsey, from which she was gently lifted by the Emperor, whose silky tones continued as he looked with genuine affection at the blushing princess.

'What subject can be so absorbing that anyone could forget this beautiful creature.' He paused before withdrawing his temporarily softened gaze from the face of his first love. Now, as he flicked his marble-coloured eyes from Bernadotte to me, he resumed his cold sarcastic voice as he bitterly sneered in astoundingly acute perception:

'Perhaps the latest gossip from the continuing saga of the mad Vasas of Sweden, eh?' He laughed, a short, harsh rasp as he looked coldly at Bernadotte. 'Hardly a fitting stimulation for a Marshal of France, Prince…' There was an uneasy pause as he slowly turned his withering glare upon my impassive face. '…Even if I can believe that such trivialities would fascinate the devious processes of thought that seem to excite this dangerous snake.'

He had breathed these last words with an almost animal snarl. However, such undignified displays of uncouth behaviour did nothing to me. Indicating my disgust at his insinuations, I simply raised an eyebrow and responded with an apparent lack of concern, stifling a yawn to elucidate my point, and equalling the Imperial sarcasm in my tone.

'How graphic are the Emperor's gracious musings this evening! It must be the effect of the Holy masses being said to give thanks for your Majesty's recent nuptials.'

There was a silence as the grey eyes narrowed slightly. I fully expected an explosive outburst of the type I was accustomed to. Abruptly he turned his back to me, entirely ignoring my remark as he continued, now addressing Bernadotte. I leaned on my stick to observe their conversation. I would not be intimidated by Imperial bad manners.

'Well, Marshal! What have you to say for yourself? You keep strange company these days...' The Emperor was attempting to exhibit some sort of cold charm, though his endeavour could not deter him from making his stinging reference to me, nor from adding sourly in his address to Bernadotte: '...But then you always did.'

There was a stilted pause, during which I noticed Désirée becoming increasingly agitated, as she looked from her husband to her former fiancé in dread anticipation.

'Do you enjoy living in the house I gave you, Prince? The house of your friend Moreau?'

'Indeed, sire, but I spend most of my time at my country house. I am unemployed, you will remember...' Bernadotte's reply was a monotone.

'Two years in exile in America must have cooled that ambitious fool.'

A hard laugh accompanied the Emperor's remark, which had entirely ignored Bernadotte's cold attempt at politeness. And now, as Napoleon seemed poised to blaze into one of his crazed tirades, Désirée, in desperate anxiety, suddenly burst out in a blind endeavour to halt the gathering momentum of the exchange.

'Sire, your Empress is most beautiful.'

She had inadvertently placed her hand on the Sovereign's arm in her desperation, contravening Imperial etiquette. Napoleon stopped, looking down at the delicate hand on his arm. As his expression softened, a strange light came into his eyes while he moved their focus onto Désirée's pleading face.

'I like my women beautiful, Eugènie. You should know…'

The low voice was suddenly tender and intensely personal. As Désirée flushed with embarrassment, her wide eyes staring helplessly into his, I glanced at the stiff towering figure of Bernadotte. He too had flushed, but not with embarrassment. Rather his expression was one of deep mortification and bristling anger. Désirée searched the Emperor's melted gaze beseechingly. How extraordinary is the power of a woman! She had succeeded in entirely transforming his mood, even at the risk of her husband's displeasure.

Placing his hand possessively over Désirée's, the Emperor now turned to Bernadotte once more, this time bestowing upon him a smile that could be described as genuinely warm. Briskly he issued in a pleasant voice, 'Prepare to assume command, Marshal. It seems that the Tsar does nothing to stop English ships approaching his Baltic ports. He must be taught a lesson. France needs the talents of all her Marshals, Prince.'

As he emphasised his final words, Napoleon returned his attention to Désirée. Bowing slightly to her, he enquired if she would do him the honour of giving him this dance. Inclining her head, the confused Princess acceded graciously. And as the Emperor guided her towards the floor she cast a fleeting glance of helplessness back towards her expressionless husband. Unseeingly, Bernadotte seemed to be staring into the middle distance. It seemed to me that in that moment, the tall Gascon appeared to assume an even deeper thrust to his already considerable ambitions.

'Prince – I see the Swedish legation is approaching us.' My announcement pulled him sharply from his preoccupied thoughts. As he smiled at me now with a sudden startling alacrity, he appeared to grow even taller.

'Good evening, Your Highness.'

I smiled to myself as Bernadotte acknowledged with grace the polite greetings from the Swedes. Yes, the map of Europe was going to change.

Chapter XX

Désirée was slumped in the back of the carriage. Her head had fallen against the solid support of her husband's arm, and she was in a dozing state of light sleep. She was tired though it was still almost light on this evening in late August. It had been an exciting evening at Court. Julie, her sister, had secretly confided to her the news of the Empress' pregnancy. At last Napoleone was going to have an heir! She felt happy for him. Poor Julie. She missed Joseph. But still she was so pleased to be visiting Paris. She hated Spain. Joseph seemed to be entirely out of control from what she could gather. All the same, Désirée was not really very surprised. He had always depended on Napoleone.

She sighed, remembering her sister's tear-filled eyes when she had asked her when she herself would have to return to Spain. Julie treasured every moment of her brief respites and could not bear to think of the moment they would end, in spite of the thought of her reunions with Joseph. Poor Julie.

The carriage jolted violently, jogging the sleepy thoughts of its feminine occupant. The solid arm of her husband moved, pulling her slightly more towards him. She smiled, snuggling into his huge side, feeling the roughness of his uniform against her cheek. Jean-Baptiste... She gave another sigh of contentment. The movement of the carriage rocked on gently. Soon they would be home.

'Jean-Baptiste!'

'Shhh... my darling.'

Désirée was restrained by Bernadotte's firm curtailment of

her astonished exclamation. She had been wrenched from her happy slumbers when she had felt a suddenly excruciating pressure from the encircling arm of her husband. Instantly awake, her eyes had widened in astonishment as she had found herself confronted by the scene upon which her husband, suddenly rigid, was focusing his mesmerized attention.

'Darling... what is it? What does it all mean?'

'I...I don't know yet.'

Bernadotte squeezed his wife's hand reassuringly as she hissed her suddenly terrified questions. Désirée could feel her heart beating with an unusual acceleration. She felt cold as she looked out of the carriage window. Frightened, she gripped her husband's hand in desperation.

A neatly parked line of carriages was standing stationary outside their large house. Torch-bearing soldiers who were dressed in a strange uniform of light blue and yellow were tending immaculate horses. The carriages carried a coat of arms that Désirée had never seen before, though she vaguely remembered having seen soldiers dressed in that uniform visiting her husband frequently over the past few days. But then so many soldiers, dressed in so many strange uniforms, visited Jean-Baptiste. She was used to such visitations.

But now, while their carriage slowed as they approached the entrance of their house, the foreign soldiers, who she noticed were mainly blond, bowed respectfully. And as the vehicle came to a halt she noticed that the inside of her house was ablaze with light, and she could see more people in the same uniforms standing inside their hall. Désirée's heart was thumping now, and she felt herself trembling. Whatever was going on?

'Jean-Baptiste...'

'Don't be frightened Désirée. Just say nothing, and stay close to me.' Once more he squeezed her hand as he yet again abruptly silenced her.

Suddenly the door was thrown open by one of the strange tall soldiers who bowed low to Bernadotte as he moved quickly to descend from the carriage. Désirée felt the blood drain from her face. A strange sense of foreboding suddenly overcame her, and she shivered slightly.

Jean-Baptiste was extending his hand to assist her in alighting from the carriage. As she looked into his face in the flickering light of the torches, she saw that his eyes were looking into hers with a steady, meaningful stare. How strange. What on earth was going on? She had never seen him like this. So tentative. So intense.

Suddenly he smiled at her encouragingly. He could sense her fear. Taking a deep breath, Désirée now lifted her skirt slightly to ease her exit. Stretching her hand she felt the warm contact of that strong grip she knew so well. Bravely she smiled. Trust him. That was what he was asking...

'Your Highness – forgive me. I-I didn't know what to do – they said that they would wait outside but... it didn't seem right, they...'

'Don't worry about it Marie, dear...'

Gently Désirée reassured the fussing maid who was in an untidy state of disarray, and still garbed in her night attire. Patting the confused woman kindly on the shoulder, the pale princess now quietly directed her to bring some wine into the drawing room, but the wringing hands of the elderly woman instead pulled nervously at her grey strands of uncombed hair as she cast a doubtful look around at the ceremonially ranged fan of soldiers, who were now formally bowing to the calmly disrobing figure of Jean-Baptiste Bernadotte.

Divested of their summer evening coats, Bernadotte and his wife slowly passed through the formal gathering of attendants in the hall. And as they entered the drawing room Jean-Baptiste once more took his wife's hand, pressing again a firm re-assurance.

'Gentlemen, good evening. Or should I be saying good morning!'

Bernadotte was at his most gracious and charming as his tall figure moved majestically into the room. Instantly, the three fair-haired men who had been seated jumped to their feet, bowing with formal politeness.

'I am honoured to welcome you to my home, sirs, though I confess surprise at your choice of hour!'

The Marshal was warm as he acknowledged their bows with an incline of his head, indicating to them that they might resume their seated positions if they wished.

'Count Morner!'

Bernadotte moved towards the man in the centre who was standing near to the fireplace. As he approached him, displaying a genuine delight to see the pleasant looking man, Morner held out his hand, now shaking the older man's with warmth.

'I have had the honour to meet with your young kinsman on a number of occasions, who has always informed me as to your well-being.'

Désirée looked at the man. She had never seen him before. Nor had she any idea who her husband was talking about when he referred to his 'kinsman'. How strange, for he seemed to know these people very well especially this one.

Marie had entered with the wine, and Désirée, having been introduced to the men, busied herself with pouring. Suddenly she heard one of them mention Lubeck.

Of course! These were Jean-Baptiste's prisoners from Lubeck. Count Morner – yes, he had been the Colonel in command of the Swedish soldiers who had fallen captive to France after the Battle of Jena and Auerstadt, at which Jean-Baptiste had been disgraced. Now she remembered...

A hush fell upon the room as Désirée handed round the filled glasses. Each of the foreign soldiers politely accepted her offering, but proceeded to deliberately place them on nearby tables. Count Morner, now removing a thick white envelope from his inside pocket, cleared his throat, instantly demanding the focused attention from everyone in the room.

'Your Highness...' His light blue eyes were fixing their gaze intently on the proud face of the French Marshal as, with a grand ceremonial formality he announced: 'On behalf of his Majesty, King Charles XIII of Sweden, and in my capacity as Grand Chamberlain, I have the honour to inform you that the Diet of Sweden has unanimously agreed to elect the Prince of Ponte Carvo, Marshal Bernadotte, as heir to the Throne of Sweden. It is the earnest desire of His Majesty to adopt the Prince as his own son – that Sweden may have the honour to address him as Prince Royal.'

There was a charged silence as the three Swedes now bowed to the tall figure of the handsome Marshal, who graciously accepted the white envelope from the King of Sweden, which Count Morner now handed to him.

Désirée was staring in disbelief at her husband. Her head was suddenly throbbing and she felt rather dizzy. Prince Royal? King of Sweden? What was this?

Her husband had remained motionless, apparently unperturbed, and certainly not surprised. She was shattered. Sweden was offering their crown to her Jean-Baptiste...! How extraordinary...! Oh, she had often heard idle discussions about him being made king of this or that country, but they had always been one of Napoleone's conquests, and so he would, in effect, have still been some sort of 'grand governor'. But this was different. Very different. These people were a proud and independent people, and their nobility was amongst the oldest in Europe. And they had offered Jean-Baptiste their crown...

Suddenly she felt faint. The room began to spin, and she could feel her body swaying uncontrollably. But now she was steady once more as she felt the familiar strength supporting her – that strong grip she knew so well. Gently Jean-Baptiste lifted her into a chair, tenderly settling her while he smiled at her reassuringly. Through the whirling haze she smiled back. And now he moved away once again, standing straight and tall before the three men.

'I am honoured to accept the nomination of the Diet of Sweden.' Jean-Baptiste paused before his deep voice concluded on a quieter note that approached a husky humility: 'And I am deeply humbled and honoured to accept King Charles XIII of Sweden as my revered father.'

He remained motionless, moved by the moment. So too were the three Swedes who seemed lost for words. Désirée stared at her husband from her cushioned support. Jean-Baptiste. He was to become a King. And she a Queen... Numbness overcame her.

'Champagne!'

Jean-Baptiste had recovered himself entirely from his moment of emotion as he issued his order with a note of jubilance to a servant who had appeared from nowhere. His face was radiant. How strange – he didn't seem to be particularly surprised at all... Désirée stared in bewilderment at her husband.

* * *

I shall not deny that I had contrived to avail myself of every possible opportunity to lend my influence in an effort to assist the appointment of Jean-Baptiste Bernadotte to the Swedish Royal family. That there should be firm and stable government in that northern Peninsular was of integral importance to the stability of Europe. I had felt it very necessary that their inclination to engage the talents of our most able Marshal, whose administrational abilities had already been most successfully tested and confirmed, should be most vigorously encouraged. Indeed, I commended the young group of Swedes for both their initiative and their active determination to see their choice of 'a strong man' realized.

Napoleon's reaction to the possibility of Bernadotte becoming King of Sweden was interesting. This was the first time that a country had, of its own accord, requested a French Marshal to succeed to its throne. That it should have been Sweden was surprising, in one respect, since the Vasa Dynasty was an old one, and it might have seemed inconceivable to some that Sweden would elect an ordinary French soldier to their throne. He did not even speak their language!

But the Swedish character, proud as it was, valued their independence and dignity beyond their Royal Heritage, and the people had tired of seeing themselves increasingly restricted by the yoke of foreign powers. The Vasas, interbred with the other northern royal families, had long been regarded as decadent. Moreover there had been speculations upon the sanity of various members of the dynasty.

The young nobility, reflecting the wishes of their people, wanted, instead of this weakening line, a strong man, a man who would restore to them their pride as an independent nation. Perhaps it was due to that national characteristic that they chose Bernadotte, for in him, there was no doubt, burned the flame of an independent spirit. He alone, of all the Marshals, had always resisted becoming the puppet of the French Emperor's will.

Napoleon, it has seemed to me, had known from the outset that Bernadotte had been selected as a candidate for election to the Swedish throne. Through my own information channels I had learned of the death of the Prince of Augustenburg even before Bernadotte. So too had the Emperor.

To begin with he had ridiculed the idea of the Prince assuming the title, and had blandly suggested that they should have Prince Eugène or Murat if they wanted a French King. Or, that if they really wanted an ordinary Marshal, he could offer them better than Bernadotte. Indeed he had generally affected a posture of treating the whole issue as some sort of joke. But beneath his flippant remarks I knew the question was of considerable importance to the Emperor, and that he was deeply pondering the real implications of Bernadotte's candidature.

The young Baron Morner, and his group of astute young nobles, was determined that they would not have a man who would simply become a vassal of the French Empire. Furthermore, they faced considerable opposition within their own country from the traditionalist party who supported the election of the deceased Prince Royal's brother, the Duke of Augustenburg. Napoleon, who understood the situation with a degree of sensitivity reminiscent of his old perceptions, knew that he would not be able to persuade the young Swedes to select any other French candidate. It is my opinion, too, that he secretly admired their choice, as did I. After all, had he not often talked about adopting Bernadotte himself as an heir to the French throne before he had decided to re-marry?

Nonetheless, Napoleon remained aloof from the situation during the period of electioneering. He was, however, through others and myself closely observing the course of events.

By the end of July Bernadotte had employed an agent, and it was through this means that Napoleon was now able to give Bernadotte some covert support, while maintaining a public distance. The main task for this agent was to organise the financial arrangements that were inevitably involved at both personal and governmental levels. Napoleon, it seems, made certain guarantees on behalf of Bernadotte, who was naturally obliged to make financial and property commitments to his new country.

The principal reason for the Emperor's reluctance to make public his contribution to the election of Bernadotte was that he feared a rupture of his increasingly shaky relations with Russia. But there was no doubt, all the same, that he actively assisted the cause of the Marshal. What it was that made him come round to the idea that the man who had rankled him so much, and so often, should indeed become a King – even though he knew he would never gain his unconditional co-operation – will forever remain a mystery.

But I had watched those two rivals from the early days of their extraordinarily ambivalent relationship, and despite their respective vanities and jealousies of each other, there was a curious form of mutual need between these two. And I was certain that each held an admiration for the other that somehow transcended their petty resentments.

Thus, when Bernadotte was finally elected as Prince Royal of Sweden at the end of August 1810, it had been with the assistance of his Emperor and rival, the man who had once been engaged to his wife.

But as the idea became a reality, Napoleon seemed to fall into an ill humour regarding Bernadotte's new position. Perhaps it was because he knew that the new Crown Prince's sense of honour would now always put Sweden above every other priority in his life, and he would never again be forced to comply with Napoleon's wishes, regardless of the power of his Empire. Whatever measure of control over the recalcitrant Marshal he had once had would now be gone forever. Bernadotte was to be a Sovereign. Of an independent country. And though that country was small, it was proud, and would never become a vassal state. His Gascon rival had indeed become his equal, as he had always claimed.

* * *

'Mama! The Emperor is very busy.'

The high-pitched voice of the child echoed around the vast room, which was the Emperor's official office. The disappointed tones of Oscar Bernadotte, the appointed Duke of Sodermanland, instantly silenced the scratching of the Emperor's pen. Lifting his head Napoleon looked at the small figure of his godson who stood between his parents in front of his desk, where they had patiently been awaiting the Imperial attention for over five minutes.

To Napoleon, the wide innocent eyes he now found himself looking into reminded him momentarily of the child's mother, who was endeavouring to silence her son, embarrassed at the breach in protocol at this critical moment in the lives of her family. Eugènie…he thought. A Queen. He cast a brief glance at his flushed first love, his heart lifting a little as his eyes lingered upon her. Leaning back in his chair as he laid down his pen, his eyes now travelled to the tall dark figure of Jean-Baptiste Bernadotte who stood proudly before him staring at something far away, and above his head. Arrogant bastard – he thought fleetingly.

There was a long silence as Napoleon looked at them. Deliberately he moved his eyes from one to the other. It pained him slightly to see that his action hurt Eugènie. Finally his eyes returned to the round gaze of the boy. Suddenly Napoleon's face broke into a broad smile – an open smile that was reminiscent of his own boyish expressions of old. Throwing back his head he burst into loud guffaws of laughter.

'My Godson appears to have acute powers of observation‘

He looked affectionately upon the boy as he spoke, pushing

back his chair and rising at the same time. Walking around the enormous desk, the Emperor now appeared to entirely ignore the child's parents, addressing himself to the little boy.

'Oscar, you have grown tall of late. How old are you now?'

'I'm nearly eleven, Godfather.'

Oscar's reply was enthusiastic in response to his godfather's attention. He was eager to talk to the small plump man who had always been so nice to him, and given him such lovely presents.

'Eleven!' Napoleon spoke the word in soft incredulity. 'Eleven years…' He looked at Désirée as he repeated the number. '.How quickly time passes.'

Turning away, he continued to address Oscar, apparently oblivious to the tall brooding presence of the Marshal. 'I hear you like music, Oscar? A very important attribute. Your mother has always been…'

'Sire!' Bernadotte's puce face now exploded from its impassivity into an expression of acute frustration, as the interruption seemed to involuntarily erupt from his lips.

'How dare you interrupt your Emperor, Prince! Have you not learnt the rules of protocol?' Napoleon too now exploded as he screamed his rebuke to his Marshal. The grey eyes of the Emperor burned into the once again impassive face of the tall Bernadotte. A short silence fell upon the room.

Oscar blinked, and held his mother's hand with a tighter grip. His wide stare was fixed on his flushed godfather as the man now stalked round his desk once more, returning to his seat, his penetrating eyes never leaving the face of the calm Marshal.

Suddenly Napoleon viciously lunged at a piece of paper on his desk. Shaking it at Bernadotte, he began to shout once more. 'What's this all about, Bernadotte?' Napoleon was beside himself with rage. 'You have been offered the Swedish Crown. All right. They are to be admired for their choice – you have brilliant administrational abilities. So, I instructed the Grand Judge to make out Letters Patent authorising you to accept this new dignity – and what is this? You refuse to accept them…'

'Sire, I cannot submit to the obligation which you propose.'

Bernadotte was calm as he quietly and firmly defended his action. 'My election as Prince Royal of Sweden makes it impossible for me to contract any engagement that would make me a vassal of a foreign country.'

'*Foreign Country?* This is France, Bernadotte, *France*. This is your motherland. Philip V of Spain was able to accept these terms from Louis XIV. My brothers Joseph, Louis and Jerome are able to accept such terms. What is so different about *you*, that you cannot?'

'Sire, if I accept the great honour that Sweden has given to me, then I must embrace it entirely. As a Swede. As you know, I wish to relinquish my French citizenship, my associations with the French Army, and my lands and titles that belong to France. The King of Sweden, Charles XIII, wishes to adopt me as his son. I cannot remain attached to France. My loyalty must be to the country that entrusts me with her Crown.'

Napoleon was silent for a moment. He was pacing the room, his hands clasped tightly behind his back. His head seemed to be bursting with rage at this coldly arrogant man. Yet, in spite of everything, he admired him. After all, had he not himself embraced a new Country? And was the question of adoption not one of his most cherished issues? Indeed, had he not himself drafted the clauses in the Code Napoleon regarding that question, believing such heredity to be sacrosanct, and necessarily requiring the total loyalty of those adopted. He knew that were he in Bernadotte's place he would do the same. Yet he could not be defeated on this matter. He could *not*.

'What can you be thinking of, Bernadotte? You wish to become the adopted son of a mad Swedish King. You wish to resign your French citizenship and that of your family. You wish to be released from your "obligations to France", which you have adhered to as a Marshal, as a Protector of France. And now you reject the simple clause that states you will not bear arms against France? Do you intend to defy France? Do you dictate terms that…'

'Sire…' Bernadotte halted the snarling tones of the Emperor's rising rage. 'Sire, as I have said: if I accept the succession of the Swedish throne, then I must become Swedish. If I become Swedish, then I must serve Sweden as a Swede. I cannot serve Sweden's interest if I am merely a vassal of France…'

'But the clause…'

The Emperor was emphatic, but Bernadotte spoke with equal force.

'Sire – you are at the moment negotiating a pact of non-aggression with Sweden. There is no reason that it cannot be extended into an accord of friendship. I can see no possible reason to suppose that I would in any way be opposing the interests of my Motherland. But Sire, I *cannot* succeed Charles XIII with *any* restrictions upon my position.'

Napoleon appeared to be temporarily lost for words. He stared with apparent incredulity at Bernadotte's expressionless face. The uncompromising words of the Marshal had thrown him off course. Bernadotte, he knew, would never be dissuaded from his resolve. He was too damned proud. And he was honourable…

'And you, Eugènie?'

Napoleon felt he had to tear his attention away from the towering presence of his Marshal who was now, suddenly, no longer his Marshal. His voice was tender as he looked into the pale face of the woman he had always cared about so deeply.

Gently he asked her as he lifted a document from under a folder, 'What do you wish me to do? Shall I sign this document making you all Swedes?' His face clouded slightly as he spoke. 'Is that what you *really* want, Eugènie?'

Désirée swallowed, her hand involuntarily squeezing her son's. Hesitating a little, she replied in a faltering, small voice, her eyes staring fixedly at the floor. 'Sire, it-it is the wish of my husband… H-his wishes are mine…'

She broke off, swallowing hard once again. She could feel the grey eyes she knew so well boring into her. There was an uneasy silence as Napoleon stared thoughtfully at Désirée.

'They're my wishes too, Godfather.'

The high eager voice of the child suddenly relaxed the uncomfortable tension in the room. Napoleon, arrested by his Godson's charm, moved to stroke the small boy's curly hair. He was a handsome child, he thought. So like his mother.

'I chose your name Oscar. Did you know that?' Napoleon paused, tilting his head slightly to one side as he remembered. 'How strange that it's of Nordic origin…'

He broke off, musing to himself for a moment. Silently he moved back behind his desk. Looking down at the sheet of paper, he seemed to be thinking deeply.

'You were always different from the others, my friend…' He raised his head to look at Bernadotte. 'I knew that at Brumaire.' He paused. 'Are you certain that you realize the implications of your course? France is your Motherland. If I sign…'

'Sire, would you make me a greater man than yourself by obliging me to refuse a crown?'

Napoleon was silenced. The two men were locked in a long silent exchange. There was a hush of bated anticipation in the room.

'Very well, go, and let our destinies be accomplished.'

'I beg your pardon Sire, I did not catch what your Majesty said?'

Napoleon looked into the dark, unrepentant eyes. Once again he felt a flicker of admiration at the proud man's insolent arrogance. Picking up his pen to sign the document he repeated: 'Go, and let our destinies be accomplished.'

As he lifted his head after signing his name, his eyes met Désirée's. Destiny… At that moment they both remembered his pronouncements upon that word, spoken under a starry Mediterranean sky.

* * *

It has been said that Bernadotte, while insisting upon the removal of all restrictions imposed by Napoleon, had already determined upon the path of treachery against the French Emperor upon which he was now to embark. I disagree.

I knew the man well, and over the years had watched him turn down other positions, which, at the time, he would have delighted in taking. But he was a man who has always weighed the possible consequences of his actions, and it would have been entirely against his principles, and out of character, for the man to assume his new position without knowing himself to be free from any restraints, whatever they were.

Thus, Jean-Baptiste Bernadotte, Crown Prince of Sweden, left France on September the thirtieth, 1810. Prior to his departure he and his family were entertained privately by the Emperor and Empress. And publicly Napoleon had honoured his new title at a formal Court farewell.

We witnessed an emotional scene as most of the Marshals sadly took leave of their former brother-in-arms. And while Davout and Berthier were less than sad at his departure, the evident affection of the others was perhaps an indication of the high esteem in which the body of the French Army had held Bernadotte. This man, who now wore a Swedish uniform...

And so, leaving his wife and son in Paris for the moment, the Prince Royal left to meet his new father – and his new People.

In Paris, certain commentators were expressing opinions that the election of Bernadotte to the Swedish throne presaged a new war between the Emperor of France and the northern Powers. And on the night that the new Swedish Prince Royal left France, the French Emperor, so he confessed, had a nightmare in which he and Bernadotte faced a storm at sea together. Bernadotte sailed away, abandoning him to the elements.

These ominous forecasts and portents were soon to find their manifestations in reality.

Chapter XXI

The bells of Paris were ringing relentlessly.

'Mama, I can't sleep. The church bells, aren't they ever going to stop?'

The lump in Désirée's throat seemed suddenly to suffocate her, as the hot tears in her stinging eyes started to flow uncontrollably down her cheeks. His voice, Oscar's little voice – it was so clear, so near... But he wasn't here...

As her breathing heaved painfully in her efforts to stop the consuming despairing sobs, her hand lovingly moved across the smooth cover of the neatly made child's bed. What was he doing now? she wondered. Who was he with? How tall had he grown? Why, why could she not stop missing him...?

Her body ached as her chest refused the efforts of restraint upon her emotion. She felt she could see his little face on the empty pillow, but as she blinked her stinging eyes she knew it was only an illusion, like the sound of his voice asking about the bells – as he had always plaintively questioned since a toddler.

Losing control entirely, the bitter sound of her weeping filled the immaculately tidy, empty child's room. No child lived here anymore. Nor would he ever again...

Her body was now wracked in hysterical convulsions. Burying her face in her hands she gave in to her despair, crying and crying, no longer able to attempt any control. Finally, in exhaustion her head fell upon her son's untouched pillow. Unable to weep any more, she closed her burning eyes, placing a tired hand upon her forehead, which hammered with an intolerable pain. And now her sobs became dry wails of sorrow. She wanted to die. Oh God, what had she done? Why was she here alone? Had the nightmare of these last months been real? And Oscar – Oscar her baby...

The stout figure of Marie was standing at the door of the darkened room. This often happened to her Mistress these days. Nobody else knew except for her, though they must have noticed the large hollow eyes in the thin, drawn face. Poor lamb. But there was nothing she, Marie, could do except be there. There was no comfort for the poor creature. Time... time would heal the memories of that dreadful country, with those horrible people.

Softly she closed the door. She'd return in a little while with a nice cup of hot chocolate, and get her beloved Eugènie out of little Oscar's room. But for now, she had to be alone a little longer. She sighed as the door closed upon the moaning sounds of her exhausted Mistress. Poor lamb, she thought again.

* * *

'Marie.'

The ample figure of the middle-aged woman started as she descended the staircase, still deep in her disturbed thoughts. She knew that voice. She knew it well. It couldn't be...She narrowed her eyes slightly to peer down into the dimly lit hall.

'Marie...'

The deep musical tones repeated her name with an old familiarity.

Now she saw him, though her failing sight obscured his features. Still, she knew that figure well – grown stout, too, over the years since she had first known him. He still wore the same shabby uniform though, despite his grandeur. And yes, always the small black hat, which he was holding at the moment. She smiled maternally. How it had all changed...

'Sire.'

Marie heavily attempted her awkward curtsey as she reached the bottom of the stairs. She supposed she should be surprised to see the Emperor here alone at this time of night, and yet she wasn't. But then nothing much surprised her these days. Life was so extraordinary, and with so many unexpected events, how could anything so natural as the reappearance of her Mistress's first love, and Miss Julie's brother-in-law, surprise her? All the same, it was odd he was alone. He seemed to always be surrounded by dozens of those smart people these days. Those awful people who chattered about nothing in their affected voices.

Well, thank goodness her Mistress didn't have much to do with them any more, at least. They were no good. She was sure of that. Look at the unhappiness they had brought poor Miss Julie. And her always so nervous…poor child! She smiled her kind wrinkled face at the Emperor. He'd been such a nice boy!

'Marie, is your mistress here?'

'Sire – I…'

His deep voice had shown its usual consideration. Napoleon was fond of the elderly woman who had always been with Eugènie. Nonetheless, his tone betrayed a hint of agitation, and as Marie wrung her hands while she began to explain that her mistress was indisposed, she could feel he was very anxious to speak to Désirée.

'Very well then. I'll wait.'

Napoleon was firm as the worried woman finished her attempt at an explanation. Taking off his coat in characteristic haste, he casually threw it over a chair, tossing his hat after it. Smiling kindly at the protesting woman, he turned to go towards the drawing room, fleetingly thinking of Moreau, the previous owner of this fine house.

'Sire…'

Désirée's thick husky tones floated down from the top of the staircase, her incredulity seeming to heighten the hush of the silent house as it echoed through the large hall. Napoleon jerked his head round, his eyes instantly focusing on the small motionless figure at the top of the stairs.

'Why Eugènie…'

He was horrified at the transformation in her appearance. How thin she was. How frail… And now, as she glided down the stairs, he could see how pale.

'Sire, I am honoured – I…'

'Eugènie please…'

He grasped the small delicate hands, curtailing the curtsy. He stared in undisguised concern at her tear-stained face as her large eyes, encircled by dark rings, tried to smile at him. Gently he put his arm around her shoulders, guiding the fragile object of his affection towards the drawing room.

'Perhaps some wine, Marie.'

His firm authority buried his surprised concern as he took control. He was no good with emotional situations, but this was different. Eugènie was suffering some unspeakable unhappiness, and now his news would probably compound it. Oh dear…

Désirée felt numb as she sank into the soft sofa. How strange – she seemed to be seeing Napoleone in front of her. But maybe it wasn't him at all. She seemed always to be imagining people these days. She squinted at his face, which was creased in confused concern. She blinked, trying to focus a little better. But her eyelids felt thick and heavy, and she couldn't really see very well because her eyes were so sore.

The bells. They were still ringing…Suddenly she remembered.

'Your Majesty – it's your son's first birthday – con-congratulations.' She felt the surge of those tears that were always so near. Oscar her son. It would be his birthday in a few months' time. But she wouldn't be with him. 'F-forgive me…'

She smiled at Napoleon bravely through her tears as she fought to stop dissolving once more into violent sobs. A pressure on her hand told her that he understood, and the grey eyes that looked so deeply into hers, in helpless concern, were soft with the light of times past. Sniffing, she wiped a tear from her cheek, tossing her head slightly as she determinedly asserted her self-control. The warm pressure of this man she knew so well was helping her. But she kept forgetting that he was the Emperor.

'Napoleone… I-I mean… S-Si…what can I do for…?'

'Was it so terrible, Eugènie?'

His tone was deep with worried affection as he relieved her from her faltering attempts at politeness. She sniffed, her large eyes staring into his. He understood... Her tears had stopped. She felt steadied by this presence from the past. Closing her tired eyes for a moment, her body shuddered involuntarily. She could see that white, relentlessly cold sky. And those blond, relentlessly cold people. Unsmiling. Staring at her.

'They...they love Jean-Baptiste...and...' She broke off, choking as she forced herself to speak her son's name '...and Oscar...'

Suddenly her tears refused to come. Her stinging eyes opened in a burning stare as she looked into nothingness. For the first time she allowed herself to feel a surge of resentment. She squeezed the hand that held hers.

'Maybe...maybe...it was because I wouldn't change my religion?' She turned her despairing, questioning eyes to meet the grey affection of her comforter. 'Napoleone – they just think of me as...as a *parvenu*...a-a middle class upstart...'

She broke off once more, swallowing as she remembered the pain of the insults she had received from the Swedish Royal Family. The King had tried to accept her, but the women...

'A *parvenu*.' His deep voice repeated the word with a bitter intonation as, taking her hands now in both of his, he turned his head away for a moment, bitterly shaking it as recollections of his own humiliations swept through his memory. How well he knew her pain...

'The Swedes, they want Jean-Baptiste to marry a Grand Duchess from Russia...' She stopped as she remembered that in a house not far away, Josephine too sat alone. Napoleon bowed his head in shame as he perceived her thought. 'No, no – it's not the same, Napoleone... Oscar. I'm Oscar's mother...'

Gratefully he looked at her as she tried to remedy the hurtful implication of her statement. No, there was no parallel really. He had needed an heir. Bernadotte already had one: Oscar, Napoleone's Godson. He smiled sadly as he recalled the last time he had seen that child who reminded him so much of his mother.

'Oscar – as long as fortune attends him he will have no lack of admirers. But I hope he will never experience adversity, that he might learn to despise his fellow man...'

As he mused his thought aloud, Désirée looked at him, wrenching herself from her own miserable thoughts. He had voiced his words with such a bitter sadness.

Suddenly her brooding thoughts of the past long months receded. All the time, these past days in her solitude, she had thought about her journey to Stockholm where Jean-Baptiste had been received so warmly, and where she, the 'common Frenchwoman', had been so utterly humiliated. That freezing place where she had eventually felt she could no longer stay, but where she had been forced to leave her son who was the heir to their throne. How she had been tormented these past months...

But now, her anxieties about her own misfortunes were suddenly put aside for the moment as she realized that the man before her, whom she had known for over twenty years – more than half her life – was also deeply disturbed. About his brow there hovered some dark thought, she could see that. But his concern for her had restrained him from confiding it.

'Napoleone...' She leaned towards the decanter of wine, which Marie had placed on a table nearby. Breaking her hands from his, she began to pour some wine. 'Napoleone – why did you come...? What is it?' Her voice, now steady, was soft as she handed him the glass. She searched the grey eyes in reciprocated concern. 'There's something wrong, I know...'

There was little point in disguising the intimacy of friendship that had endured, with much difficulty – but for so long.

The bells penetrated the silence of the quiet room. Napoleon looked quickly at her as he hesitated, taking a sip from his glass. Momentarily he frowned to himself. What he had to say was going to increase her already obviously dreadful unhappiness. But then, if he didn't tell her himself she would only learn it from the newspaper, and that would be much worse.

Clearing his throat, he looked at her gently. 'Eugènie! – I shall shortly be leaving for the Front...' He paused. 'As you probably know, hostilities have once more broken out with the Russians, who are refusing to enforce the System.' He shrugged, a grim expression passing over his face. 'Our troops are already massing on the banks of the Nieman...'

He stopped, loathe to discuss the details of his military matters when they were of no concern to her, or necessary importance. It was bad enough to have to mention politics at all. But he must. He looked steadily into her eyes.

'I...wanted to share a moment with you alone once more, Eugènie, before...'

Abruptly he stood up, falling silent for a moment as he broke off. Thoughtfully he moved to the fire that was burning quietly after its earlier attentions from Marie.

'Eugènie, Marshal Davout is at this very moment taking possession of Swedish Pomerania.'

Désirée gasped, her eyes opening widely in a terrified stare as the Emperor turned slowly to see the look of fear he had dreaded on the pale face.

'Your husband has amassed a force of 28,000 Swedish troops...'

'But they're neutral, Napoleone, Sweden is...'

'...And he has signed a treaty of friendship with the Tsar...'

'... But they will not fight, they...' Désirée fell silent, bending her head in despair.

'Eugènie...' Napoleon's shoulders drooped a little, as his chest seemed to constrict. 'Eugènie, I have reason to believe that your husband is in the process of negotiating terms with the Tsar... It may be that Sweden will not remain neutral...'

Désirée was stunned. Immediately she understood the implications of what her former fiancé was telling her. Jean-Baptiste, her husband, Prince Royal of Sweden, would be fighting France. His own motherland.

Napoleon was watching her closely. The anger he felt about the news he was imparting was almost buried by his concern for the effect it might have upon this lonely little creature, for whom he cared so deeply. Why must it be that the two women he loved the most were alone and unhappy, and he was helpless to aid them? Indeed he was the very cause of their unhappiness, which was the last thing he had ever intended.

'A-are you sure…?'

The voice was toneless, as her round red-rimmed eyes searchingly pleaded for him to say no. Swallowing he looked away.

'At the moment Eugènie it's only an intelligence report, but…' He broke off turning back to look into the fire once more. Gripping the mantelpiece, he continued in frustrated agitation. 'I offered him Finland…Pomerania…the entire Baltic Coast… but he wouldn't join me… he…'

Throwing his arm in the air in a gesture of incomprehension, he moved back to the sofa, seating himself next to Désirée, once more taking her hand.

'Eugènie, this may be the last time I shall be able to see you like this. If you are seen to be the wife of an enemy it will become politically impossible for us to meet, that's why…'

He stopped as he saw the look of dawning terror in her eyes. Suddenly she was frightened. Not only would she be shamed, she would be outcast…

'You…don't have to leave Paris, Eugènie, I'll ensure…'

She gripped his hand tightly as the tears began to shine from her dark eyes once more. Forlornly she breathed: 'He…he can't…'

Napoleon lifted her hands to his lips, and then buried his face in them. He too was consumed by her pain. Partly his impulse was because he cared about her so much, but also, because he had a dreadful sense of foreboding about this coming campaign. His army was the largest and strongest that had ever been seen in Europe. They were well equipped and in good spirits. He himself was inspiring in them the great thirst for Honour that Frenchmen could so dynamically manifest in their victories. And yet – he had this dread presentiment from which he could not escape.

He didn't want to fight the Russians…or the Austrians…or the Prussians…or the damned Swedes… The English. Couldn't they see that the *English* were the real threat to Europe? That was why he had to compel them to adhere to the System. Otherwise those bastards… Spain – look what the English were doing to his army in Spain – 50,000 soldiers a year were dying down there. Why, in God's name, couldn't the Tsar see what the real problem in Europe was? What was all this nonsense about the System destroying their economies? They'd all be rich when England was defeated and their trading monopolies were stopped. His head was throbbing as the heightened emotion of his situation with Désirée released his thoughts in a confused rush. Why was it all going so terribly wrong? he wondered as he held Désirée's hands to his beating head.

'Napoleone.'

The dark, pain-filled eyes looked like those of a hurt animal as he lifted his gaze to meet them. He sighed deeply, bowing his head to look at the hands he was still holding. He felt himself tremble slightly at the nearness of her soft, fragrant body. Fleetingly he recalled warm Mediterranean nights long ago

'Eugènie...' His voice was low and husky, barely audible to Désirée, who stared at his head sadly, numbed still by the revelations she had just heard. 'You were my first love, Eugènie...' He lifted his face again, smiling ruefully at her. 'Still now you remain closer in my heart than anyone...you and...' He stopped as they both remembered Josephine. 'You and Josephine... You're the only two who have ever really understood me...'

His voice trailed again slightly as he looked into space. 'Whatever happens, Eugènie – whatever – will you always remember...?' He was looking deep into her eyes once more, the smile in his eyes glistening in the soft light of the room. 'How many dreams we shared, Eugènie. Do you remember? Under those bright Mediterranean stars...' He paused. 'We have a Mediterranean spirit, you and I, Eugènie. Perhaps that's our bond – we're individual...'

'Don't sound so sad, Napoleone. Please...'

'Never forget Eugènie, will you? What I tried to do. And why... They won't...'

'Napoleone, what is it? You have done so much. You are the most powerful man in the world. You have a great Empire to leave to your son. You...'

'I am alone, Eugènie.'

His bitter words silenced Désirée's maternal comforting. Abruptly he stood up walking back to the fireplace.

'Alone?...The Emperor of the French..?' Timidly Désirée spoke her words as she looked in concern at the broad back.

There was a long silence. Only the sound of the hissing fire filled the room. Désirée took a hasty gulp from her glass.

'Wars. All these wars!' The bitter exclamation erupted unexpectedly from the suddenly agitated figure at the fireplace. With a sigh he fell silent once more, then murmured,.'An idea is greater than a man, you know Eugènie.' He had turned once again without warning, looking meaningfully into her eyes. 'An idea is...divine...' His voice trailed as he lost the firmness of his statement in the silence. 'But I would rather live a short life of glory, in defence of honour – than live a long life in obscurity...'

Désirée was startled as he blurted out his words, apparently without reference. He wants to die, she thought. He wants to die in battle. Why? Does he think he'll lose...But he won't, he never has...yet...

She rose, moving quickly to stand beside him at the fireplace. Taking his hands, she smiled at him with a maternal affection. 'Napoleone. France loves you. You are never alone. They...'

'Then you will always remember...?'

She stopped, troubled by his urgent interruption, which entreated her to understand. How vulnerable he was. Just as she had always known. Somehow like a little boy. He really was a genius, with all that was entailed in that gift – weakness as well as strength. How he suffered from his great talents. If people only knew how extreme he was. Perhaps then they would understand him better. The great thoughts that took shape in that mind frightened him, as much as they motivated him to act upon them. But his belief in them always overcame the fear. Yet as the ideas got bigger so did the fears, and he needed more courage to overcome them. And he had, too, to have the courage to face the fact that nobody knew his struggles, or could ever understand...

Now she too felt a sense of foreboding. Perhaps his energy was flagging. The energy he needed to build that courage. Perhaps he suddenly had doubts penetrating his beliefs – because he was so alone. Yes, he was terribly alone… she knew that. And he was here tonight because he knew that Jean-Baptiste had betrayed him, and that meant he would lose her, his Eugènie. The fact that a Marshal had betrayed him hurt, but not as much as the idea of losing her. Like Jospehine, she was a part of him that no one else knew about – because she understood a part of him that no one else knew… And now he won't have either of us, thought Désirée sadly.

She smiled at him, her soft expression loving in the flickering light. How strange that she knew every detail of that face still, even though it had changed so much. She nodded slowly.

'I'll remember, Napoleone – always…'

She knew he needed her to tell him. The great genius, whose mind could encompass such vast and complicated subjects, needed the simple re-assurance of an inconsequential woman, that his dreams *were* understood. That he was not alone in some imaginary world where nothing else existed except his ideas.

Suddenly he drew her into his arms, grasping her in a desperate embrace. Holding her with a strength that almost hurt her, he placed his cheek on her head. Would he ever see her again? And Josephine, would he ever see her…?

'Thank you…'

His voice sounded thick and strangled. He had to leave her. And she would be alone, in this silent house. Only her memories… But then that's really all anyone ever had – memories and dreams. Perhaps, after all, that was what love was… Shared memories – of dreams. Reality never matched those dreams, though. Never. Yes, an Idea was surely greater than a man, as the Greek Philosopher had said.

Kissing her quickly on the forehead, he broke away from her and strode from the room. He couldn't bring himself to say goodbye.

Désirée heard the door close as she stared, unblinking, into the fire. Perhaps, she thought, I am already dead… She felt nothing as she sank into the oblivion of her numbness.

Chapter XXII

It has often been said that the events of 1812 were precipitated by Napoleon's desire to conquer the world. Such speculators seem to believe the absurd idea that the defeat of Russia, following his already established mastery of Europe was to be his first thrust in that direction. It is my opinion, however, contrary to this mistaken, misinformed, and excessively imaginative observation, that war with Russia was a practical necessity as far as Napoleon was concerned. Moreover it can be said that Alexander had been making preparations for such a confrontation from early in 1810.

For my part, as has been already demonstrated, I had been expecting such movements for some time. However, though events had arrived at their inevitable result, as I had foreseen, I still entertained the hope that Napoleon might at last compromise with common sense. I believe that a balanced mind takes an accurate measure of human capacity, and does not indulge in the mad hope of extending its limits beyond what experience has proved practicable.

It was thus my hope that Napoleon, in the current light of affairs, would realise that he had asked too much of his European Allies, and indeed of France. Early in 1812 there was still time for him to modify his ideas, and thus accommodate his allies.

But he had begun to believe his own created image of himself to be real, and somehow lacked the courage to soften his position in this respect.

'They think I am stern, even hardhearted. So much the better

– this makes it unnecessary for me to justify my reputation. My firmness is taken for callousness. I shall not complain, since this notion is responsible for the good order that is prevailing.'

How often had he spoken these words in recent years. Always he would qualify them by claiming that he was also in possession of a heart, but insisted it was the heart of a Sovereign. His idea of what exactly that might be never appeared to be made explicit, but clearly it was something approaching stone.

It had become entirely impossible to reason with him, and it was a sadness to me that he had obviously forgotten what it was that had actually made him great, namely his insatiable energy and enthusiasm, and his unique ability to inspire the thoughts and ideas of others to meet his own extraordinary vision.

But now, in 1812, Napoleon Bonaparte, whose character, pride, youth and genius France had once loved so dearly, and Europe had admired, was feared by those same people. They, whom he had once inspired.

The principal reason for the eventual eruption of hostilities between France and Russia was the breaking up of the Continental System. But Napoleon's determination to weaken Russia's strength, by forcing the creation of an independent Poland between the two frontiers, was certainly of equal importance to him.

However, the blockading of the ports had created severe political distress. The banks had eventually found themselves in considerable difficulties, and many of them had been forced out of business altogether. The result of such financial havoc was the near economic collapse of some of the smaller countries where the people were becoming poorer, and increasingly discontented.

But Napoleon's diseased hatred of the English blinded him to the hardship induced by his theoretically brilliant, but practically impossible, policy.

The Emperor himself was, in those darkening moments of his career, surrounded mainly by people of inferior intellect and questionable integrity. Their sycophantic behaviour and lackadaisical attitudes severely undermined, and thus weakened, the coherence of the governmental hierarchy.

Meanwhile the wars in the Peninsular dragged on. The Spanish spirit of resistance, coupled with the uncompromising determination of Wellington's army, ensured that no capitulation resulted.

Perhaps too, the Spanish resentment of Napoleon's detention of the Pope remained an important element in the continuing resistance to French pressure. The poor man had now been moved from his captivity in Italy to yet another place of confinement: Fontainebleau.

And so, as legions of French soldiers died each year on the Spanish battlefields, attempts had been made to negotiate with the Tsar. But diplomacy failed as the blockade on the Baltic ports was lifted. Europe had tired of Napoleon's ideas. Now they looked to the Tsar to restore normality.

'Soldiers! The second Polish war has begun.'

As the French eagles were once more raised in battle, the advance to Moscow began on the twenty-third of June, when the Grand Army, roaring their response to their leader's rallying cry, crossed the River Nieman on to Russian territory.

There was no turning back for Napoleon now. My hopes that he might change his policies had been dashed forever. It was the beginning of the end.

Meanwhile in Sweden, the Crown Prince, Bernadotte, had found himself forced to face a situation of impending collapse. The Continental System had succeeded in entirely ruining the Swedish economy, and now he too was forced to consider his priorities. During the first six weeks of Napoleon's advance into Russia, the Tsar developed a frequent correspondence with the new Prince Royal. Finally, towards the end of August, they met: at Abo, in Finland.

* * *

'...*and* we shall annexe Norway for Sweden in return...'

The fine features of Tsar Alexander's handsome face were fixed in an expression of serious urgency as he stared intently at the tall figure sitting at the other side of the bare wooden table. It seemed to him that here was a man who, though they had only just met, had a presence that made him feel he had known him always. Unlike his initial response to that other, once dazzling French General, the Crown Prince of Sweden did not inspire in the Russian the reaction of being spellbound. Rather, this was a man who had an innate kingship, which emanated a sense of dependability. Bernadotte was a Prince for whom he had found an immediate admiration. Here was a man, astute and talented, with whom he could establish an honest relationship.

Alexander believed utterly in the Divine Right of Sovereigns, and that the defence of the Honour of God was the central meaning of that belief. In his position as Tsar of Russia he was – as he saw it – pre-eminent amongst such rulers. And so, the advent of such a clever and strong newcomer to their ranks was, to him, a sign that a new force had been added to their number in order to contribute to their mission. Thus it was up to him to engage that talent in the fight against the violator of the sacred estate of Sovereignty: Napoleon Bonaparte.

Bernadotte rose, aware that the Tsar was watching him closely. He moved to the tiny window of the farmhouse, and looked out onto the strange darkness of this northern summer midnight. He could clearly make out the still landscape, which stretched away from the farmhouse, flat and featureless. Somehow it seemed to reflect how he felt at that moment.

Averting his gaze he focused on the tethered horses nearby. He could see the waiting attendants close beside them. His – and the Tsars. How strange, he thought, to see only the uniforms of Sweden and Russia on those young men. It seemed such a long time since he had seen a French uniform…

He bent his head slightly. A soldier, or a Crown Prince for that matter, must not allow personal feelings. He must obey and observe discipline, especially of emotions. Otherwise there could be no guarantee that one could defend the nation to whom one's loyalties were pledged. This was the belief that he had always held. Now, more than at any time in his life it was being put to the test.

'My dear Prince, don't you see, you have no choice... It is in the interests of all Europe. We must rid France of this impostor. The Austrians, the Prussians – Honour requires our united action. You can remain neutral no longer. You must join me.'

Bernadotte turned as he listened to the gentle urgency in the Tsar's words. He looked into the pale blue eyes across the flickering candlelight. The golden head was illumined by the candles, which gave the royal figure a strange sort of aura. There was something slightly disconcerting about this mystical man. All the same, Bernadotte liked him. Respected him. Now, as he listened to the quietly insistent voice of the Russian monarch, the Crown Prince of Sweden already knew what his answer must be.

'The man is insatiable, Prince. His ambition already knows no bounds. He has become the flail of the world. He must be stopped.'

There was a short silence before Bernadotte sighed. 'Indeed, Napoleon must be beaten in the end,' he replied in a low, resigned monotone. 'I know we cannot stand by and let him destroy Europe because of his own personal hatred of the English.' He paused, frowning thoughtfully before continuing with steady deliberation. 'Your majesty will win because your armies can repair their losses, and must always hold superiority in numbers. While his armies are at such a distance from their base they cannot possibly count upon receiving reinforcements from Poland, or from the interior of Germany...' He broke off, as he looked hard into the attentive Tsar's eyes.

Moving quickly from the window he returned to his earlier place at the table. 'An army... an army, sire, must be guaranteed two things on a long campaign: Food and shelter.'

'Food and shelter,' repeated the Tsar, the blue eyes wandering slightly. '...Shelter...'

'Indeed, sire.'

Bernadotte was becoming characteristically intense now as the momentum of his thoughts grew. His earlier reserve now vanished, he leaned forward as he went on, the gesticulations of his hands confirming his vehement military advice.

'Drag the war on for as long as possible. Refuse to be involved in big battles. Tire out the enemy with marches and counter marches. That is the policy that is most worrying to the French soldier, and it will give you the maximum advantage over him. Then – keep harassing him with your Cossacks…and in case of a reverse, keep on. Persevere. Even if you have to retire, everything will soon right itself, provided you do not let yourself be discouraged. A retreat is more worrying to Napoleon than a stand. The answer is time…'

He fell silent for a moment, rising and walking to the window once more. Lowering his voice he finished sourly: 'Besides, when Napoleon is well beaten he loses his head. He is quite capable of abandoning everything, or of committing suicide…'

The Tsar looked at him in surprise. Bernadotte was mute once more. Motionless, he now stared moodily out of the window, his intense enthusiasm suddenly gone.

'If you join me, Prince, I will give you 80, 000 men for such an enterprise. And I shall see with pleasure the destinies of France in your hands.'

Slowly Bernadotte turned to see the pale eyes staring steadily into his. What? Could it be that the Tsar was thinking of placing him on the French throne? He felt his pulse quicken as the Tsar's expression confirmed his meaningful implication. Bernadotte felt a tingling in his veins. The throne of France – in *his* place..?

'Every friend of liberty will grasp me by the hand, and the result in France will be a constitutional monarchy, a republic, or… who can tell…?' Bernadotte spoke his ambitious thoughts aloud, his sudden realisation of the Tsar's idea exacting a note of hushed incredulity in his voice.

The Tsar smiled. He was pleased, both with himself and with this Crown Prince of Sweden. Yes, he would be a good fellow to put on the French throne. Strong and talented, but not likely to get carried away. Yes very suitable indeed. A dependable monarch for France at last.

'Come now Prince. Let us discuss this business of 'food and shelter'. Explain it to me. Do you think…'

Bernadotte returned to the table. The two men immersed themselves in their discussion throughout the night. The Swedish Crown Prince refused to take command of a Russian Army, but he agreed to relinquish his neutral position. When they emerged into the cool dawn air, they had become both friends and allies.

The destiny of Europe had changed.

* * *

The horror of the Grand Army's retreat from Moscow is a memory that will never be erased from the minds of Europeans. The straggling columns of sick and dying soldiers through the bitter torment of Russia's 'General Winter' is an image that defies imagination. I, for one, cannot bear to think about such a gross indignity to the noble fighting spirit of these brave young men who, if they survived, had nonetheless lost fingers and ears, arms and legs, that would leave them forever crippled and maimed. To me it demonstrates the utter futility of war, and is the reason why I have always advocated diplomacy.

Futile indeed had been Napoleon's journey to Moscow. The bloody victory of Borodino proved to be no victory at all, as the apparently defeated Russians drew their pursuing French victors further and further into the interior of their vast and mysterious country.

I do not find it hard to imagine the fury with which Napoleon exploded his statements regarding the barbarity of his enemy. As the ringing sound of his pacing footsteps echoed through the corridors of the empty Kremlin, he must have been experiencing some deep sense of mortification knowing that the burning buildings all around him were also empty of Russians.

For Napoleon, to capture and occupy a capital was to expect surrender. But the Russian temperament does not see things that way. Sacrifice of a city, of countless lives, is of no consequence in comparison with the dread possibility of foreign domination. The Russian people could never be enslaved by an alien conqueror. Their reserves were too great, their sense of sacrifice too innate. To Napoleon they were incomprehensible.

I have always been certain that for Napoleon the necessity to deliver the inevitable order for the Grand Army to return to France was a more crushing defeat than any he might have received on a battlefield. He had waited and waited in the empty grandeur of the Kremlin for a sign of surrender from the Tsar, but he had waited in vain. Only silence met his repeated demands for Russian capitulation. And as the army, finally in September, began its long nightmare retreat; the consequence of such a rebuff on Napoleon's warrior pride must have inflicted a deep wound. It did not, therefore, surprise me – as it did so many – when he then left his army at Smorgoni to return to Paris, accompanied only by Caulaincourt.

To a man such as Napoleon, the acute sense of failure and humiliation could only be salved by immediately addressing himself to re-building his armies, and planning his angry retaliation to the incomprehensible insult that he believed had been inflicted upon him. To him now, as his men struggled through the grip of the unimaginable cold, there was little point in him staying with them when he could serve no useful purpose, and their appalling plight was only a constant reminder to him of his mistakes.

Napoleon looked always to the future. This had been one of his great strengths. Now, at this the hitherto worst moment of his life, it was still his natural response. The future. He would rebuild; consolidate. He refused to accept that he could not defeat Russia. He must make plans, and he could not do that on the long, slow, painful march with his men.

To me, he did the only thing that he should have done. And, as I have said, his sudden and unheralded arrival in Paris did not astound my expectations. For many, though, his actions were inexplicable.

However I was indeed surprised when I saw his face as he announced to the Council that 'the Grand Army has been lost.'

So too, it seemed to me as I looked at his expressionless face, had the spirit of Napoleon Bonaparte been lost in those barren white wastes of Russia.

Yet even still, as that terrible year of 1812 closed, the howling echo of a nightmare silent scream from tens of thousands of young men, pleading with their Emperor to *stop* – still he was unmoved. Something in Napoleon's character would never allow him to cease. Whatever the consequence…

Chapter XXIII

My carriage appeared to have come to an abrupt halt. Irritated, I took out my watch. It was late in the day and I was anxious to return home to prepare for my evening entertainment. I was tired and vexed. It had been an exhausting interview with the Emperor. Frankly I was looking forward to having a glass of wine. His little tantrums irked me. He really could be very tiresome, refusing as he did to accept one's reply to his requests with grace. The road back from St Cloud had seemed long today. Whatever was this delay all about…?

For a moment the scene I witnessed as I looked through my window reminded me of those bygone days of the Revolution. Indeed, so strong was the image that I felt myself start a little. A very unusual occurrence from one who was not given to emotional reactions.

But the sight of young mothers clutching their children, their faces convulsed in stark terror, is something that no witness, however cynical of the inevitability of misfortune, finds easy to watch. Perhaps, too, it seems even more distressing when the children are in that strange period of transition from child to youth, their fresh faces still chubby atop their usually gangling bodies which have been stretched oddly by those sudden bouts of growth that happen periodically at this time of adolescence. A time in the child's life that is still so far from manhood.

The rain was pouring down on this pathetic huddle of mothers and sons who, heads bowed while looking hopelessly at the soaking grey cobbles, listened to the proclamation that was being read by the soldier, the end of which I could now hear:

'... must report to the recruitment centres in their local vicinity... They must yield themselves to the service of France and defend the Honour of the Motherland under the guidance of the Emperor Napoleon...'

The pain on the faces of the women, and the bewilderment of their clinging sons, was more than I could take. I leaned back in my seat, drawing the curtain across the window. A mild heaving sensation was taking place in my breast. Children – little more than babes, some of them. How disgusting. And the mothers? How many of those wretched creatures had already lost fathers, husbands, brothers, perhaps even other sons...? I doubted that one could find a single woman in all France who had not already suffered the loss of a male in her family.

In the country these recruitment drives were even more ferocious, I had heard. Desperate mothers hid their children, who were searched out wherever they were. Many a child had been pierced by a probing bayonet through the flimsy coverings of straw or hay wherein they attempted to hide, screaming their last agonized breaths, which echoed their pleading protests across the nation. Alas their cries were to fall only upon the ears of the insensitive pursuant, whose duty was to enlist as many able-bodied males into the Grand Army as they could find. Whether children or pensioners, it mattered not. Fight for La Patrie they must.

It seemed to rain endlessly these days. I smiled grimly to myself. Perhaps nature too cried for poor France. Over six hundred thousand men had taken that fateful road to Moscow. And only just over ninety thousand had returned. Even now, their last crippled stragglers slowly struggled to reach their own firesides. Yet still they were dying, from sickness or exhaustion. Perhaps from sheer misery. 1813 had been born in the shadow of that horror.

And even amongst the more privileged here, in Paris society, the calm pleasures of home life had ceased to exist for the majority of people. Napoleon did not allow one to become attached to them, for he thought that those who belonged to him must cease to belong to themselves.

In an atmosphere of war and political change, people found it impossible to apply themselves to personal affairs. Public life occupied so great a part of their minds that private life was never given a single thought. One felt like a stranger in one's own home. A kind of inertia seemed to hang over Paris in those early days of 1813.

I had been aware of why the Emperor wished to see me. Indeed, I knew it would be a repeat performance of the interview we had conducted some days earlier. It seemed that he was now anxious that I should resume my former position of Minister of Foreign Affairs. But though I was content to offer him advice, and indeed had continually urged him these past weeks to negotiate now – even as the Russians advanced into the heart of Europe, doubtless soon to be joined by Prussia and Austria, as well as by the formidable force of Sweden under Bernadotte – still I did not wish to become his Foreign Minister once more. How well I knew Napoleon.

For while he now urged me to join him, I knew that, in the event, he would reject my advice and follow his own beliefs. It had been a long time since the Emperor had been able to see a viewpoint other than his own. Actually, I believe something had happened to Napoleon's mind.

Perhaps it was the lack of intellectual stimulation around him. But the quality of his leadership appeared to be beginning to fail. He had ceased to trust his subordinates entirely, insisting upon attending to every detail himself. Obviously that was an impossible task for one man, and especially a man who was in command of half a million men.

Moreover, he now physically lacked the energy on the extraordinary scale of his former years. Possibly, this was due to the unreasonable demands he summoned from his own person. But he refused to accept his own fallibility, instead deluding himself with ever increasing certainty that he was, indeed, invincible. And whilst he blinded himself with his own fantasies, his perception of reality became distorted.

During the Russian campaign he had overestimated the capabilities of his own army; and he had underestimated the character and spiritual resolve of the Tsar, and of the Russian people. Yet now, as the bloody events of 1812 had dragged into 1813, and even as the allied treaties of coalition were prepared for signatures while Russia, Austria, Prussia and Britain ranged themselves in anticipation of the final confrontation, *still* Napoleon refused to entertain even the possibility of defeat.

'Negotiate while you still have something to negotiate with...' I had urged him. But the Emperor was a warrior. His name, Napoleon, meant 'desert lion'. And indeed, like an old lion he rallied.

And France, poor war-torn France, weary though she was, refused to reject her beloved Emperor, her romantic Napoleon of the Consulate. Thus did France rally, and her mothers were forced to yield up their last sacrifice: their little boys.

My coach resumed its journey as the women and children dispersed. How much tragedy, I wondered, for those poor souls lay ahead on the future battlefields of Europe? Perhaps on the very sites where the blood of their fathers and uncles had already been spilled. I shuddered. How I hate war.

But the die had been cast. Even at this moment, the re-built French Army, training as they went, marched to meet the advancing Tsar. The negotiations with Sweden, their mediation forced through the reluctant representations of the unfortunate Crown Princess Desideria – whose loyalties were painfully divided – had broken down completely, and Napoleon knew that his former Marshal would now actively engage on behalf of the enemy. That Bernadotte's treachery was now assisted by the returned exile, Moreau, was an added source of chagrin to the enraged Emperor.

It was April. Napoleon was once more preparing to depart for the Front. As I sat in my gently rocking coach, I wondered when I would see him again. Under what circumstances would it be? I had a strange presentiment that it would all be very different...

Or perhaps I would never again see Napoleon Bonaparte.

* * *

'Tell the Crown Prince to remember that he is born a Frenchman.'

The phrase repeated itself over and over again in the Prince Royal of Sweden's tormented mind. He could feel the piece of paper upon which those words were written, as though it was burning a hole in his pocket.

'A Frenchman…'

He pulled the collar of his plain coat up over his ears. It was a cold October night, somehow colder than usual for the time of year. Perhaps it was because it had just been raining. He shivered. Perhaps it wasn't for that reason at all that he felt so cold. Slowly, his reluctant footsteps moved him on through the darkness in the small hours of a new day. He felt a pain in his chest. A new day…indeed. A day like no other for him. A day upon which he would actually draw the blood of fellow Frenchmen.

Taking in a quick strangled breath at the thought, his eyes wandered about the shadowy damp darkness of the field through which he was walking. Here and there he could see movement as small groups of men moved the bodies of dead soldiers. French soldiers.

And all around, stretching into the distance, were the smouldering lights of the countless bivouac fires. French bivouac fires.

'Tell the Crown Prince to remember that he is born a Frenchman…'

He shook his head. Why could he not rid himself of that dreadful phrase? Why did Napoleon have to send him that taunting reminder now, at this moment? Did he not realise that he was already committed? There was no way out. And anyway, he was no longer a Frenchman. He was a Swede. He winced to himself as he asserted his own profound thought. A Swede. A man from the north. That was why he was the commander of the army of the north.

He bowed his head a little. It was now raining very slightly. Somehow the light drops seemed to calm his tumultuous thoughts.

He had stayed out of it all for as long as had been possible. Indeed, even now he had demonstrated his reluctance, for he had only just arrived this evening, and the opposing armies had been engaged in heavy fighting throughout the day. His heart wrenched as he looked around once more at the scattered bodies. Yes, he had saved himself from spilling French blood for as long as possible. He smiled a grimace of self-contempt. What a 'brave' commander...

Involuntarily, he dragged a hand across his aching forehead. But he had been allowed no alternative, had he? His tacit support for the Tsar had necessarily been forced to become manifest. Even as Napoleon had delivered brilliant victories for the French in the early months of summer, at Lutzen and Bautzen, the Tsar had been strongly urging support from his friends. And when Napoleon had called for an armistice in June, Alexander had continued to draw his allies more deeply into their commitments. Austrian and Prussian troops had been mobilised while other sovereigns finally signed their treaties of alliance with the Tsar. The brilliant Metternich's attempts at negotiations had led to nothing as Napoleon had utterly rejected relinquishing any part of his Empire. And finally, the hope of peace had vanished.

The war would continue. And Sweden, like Austria and Prussia, was obligated to oppose its enemy. And he, Bernadotte, must now fight.

How heavy had been his heart as he had attended the Council of War in August at Trachenberg Castle. His allies had looked to him, of course, to design their strategy. Because he understood Napoleon's military systems so well. And this he had done. It was his 'duty'...

His duty to create a plan to destroy his own countrymen. Finally, the success of that plan had brought him here, to Leipzig. The dread moment had arrived: he was going to have to face those French uniforms that he knew so well, that he himself had once worn. And it was his 'duty' to kill those who were now wearing them...

Suddenly he felt something grip his ankle. He bit back a scream, as he knew it was the desperate lunge of a dying man. Transfixed, and quivering slightly with a sense of sick terror, he looked down into the suffering Frenchman's face. Dimly he could make out the pleading eyes of the soldier. Bernadotte's heart seemed to churn as the familiar French country accent thickly begged for some water, through the congealed foam of his dry mouth.

Bending down, Bernadotte took his small flask from his pocket. Gently lifting the soldier's bloodied head, he poured some of the brandy from the tiny flask through the soldier's cold stiff lips. Temporarily relieved, the man closed his eyes, exhaling a sigh of relief. Bernadotte held him, compelled to look into the typically French face.

After a few moments the man opened his eyes and looked up into the handsome features above. Life's energy was leaving him – and both men knew it. For a long moment they held each other's gaze, these two Frenchmen on the Leipzig battlefield of death. The cold October breeze breathed eerily around them.

Suddenly the dying man smiled. His weak endeavour was genuinely warm, as he fixed his last gaze in life on the man who looked down upon him; the man in the plain coat who was not apparently a soldier.

'Thank you, Marshal Bernadotte...'

The man's wheezing words accompanied his smile with difficulty. Bernadotte remained motionless. He was stunned that the man had recognised him. As he held him, he could see that the labouring man was about to say something else as the smile now faded from his dying face.

'Vive la France!'

Bernadotte felt as though a knife had been thrust through his chest, as the brave soldier issued his last valiant shout, its rasp echoing around the dark vicinity nearby.

'Vive la France'

The words hammered in Bernadotte's head as he laid the dead soldier flat on the ground, closing his glassy, accusing eyes.

He felt dizzy as he stood up, his vision seemed to be obscured by tears. Perhaps, he thought, it would have been better if he too had died like that proud soldier – on a battlefield.

Slowly he turned. Finally he raised his head, as he began to retrace his steps. Towards the Swedish and Russian bivouac fires.

'Your Royal Highness, forgive me. I-I fell asleep...'

Fernand struggled to find full consciousness as his master walked into the tiny room, in which his camp bed had been neatly prepared. Bernadotte's face was white and haggard as he smiled kindly at his faithful friend. Wordlessly, he sank on to his bed, wearily stretching his long legs while Fernand leapt to relieve him of his heavy boots.

Lying down, he closed his eyes painfully. He felt drained. Exhausted. But it was not a physical exhaustion.

'Today we shall storm the Grimma Gate...' Involuntarily he spoke his thoughts aloud to his close companion, the low words sounding halting, and almost despairing. 'Today, I have arranged to meet the Tsar in the market place with the other Sovereigns. Today I must drive my former master out of Leipzig, out of...' He broke off, suddenly putting his hands over his eyes. The lump in his throat seemed to be choking him. He couldn't think.

Finally he was rescued from his pain by the enveloping oblivion of numb sleep.

Quietly Fernand blew out the candles. He looked at the stilled sleeping figure of his master, his brow creasing in an expression of concern. How great was the price that this man he loved had been forced to pay when he had become a Crown Prince. The elderly man frowned. How great was the price of conscience?

* * *

And now we witnessed the death of an Empire. But still the great colossus of Europe refused to give in. Still, as the Allied armies advanced relentlessly, forcing the French soldiers to fight on their own soil...still Napoleon resisted.

Eventually the retreating French soldiers were reduced to the indignity of pillaging their own native land. Cruelly they were forced to ignore the pathetic pleas of French peasants who vainly tried to protect their meagre stores of food. These simple people were left, hopeless, despairing, wondering how they would feed their miserable families throughout the remainder of the winter. And with dignity they resigned themselves to their fate of certain sickness and death in their ravaged communities. War is not simply about the struggle of soldier against soldier. It is also about starvation, inflicted upon ordinary innocents, who did nothing wrong, save find themselves in the path of fighting men. War brings no glory to such people, only the tragedy of hunger.

How dreadfully were Frenchmen degraded in those long winter months. Yet even so, they stood by their Emperor. Their Napoleon. And doggedly the now ragged, desperate army fought in the face of the unrelenting allied invasion into French territory itself.

Even as they fought, negotiations were in progress. But conferences followed conferences, and each time they were dissolved without agreement, because Napoleon refused to be humbled into becoming a mere Sovereign of a single country. He insisted that he must retain his Empire. And it was this arrogance that refused the moment when he could have salvaged France.

In November, as the fighting was dragging on into the winter of 1813, and following the disastrous and gruesome defeat of Leipzig, the Allies once more offered Napoleon the natural boundaries of the frontiers of France: the Rhine; the Alps; and the Pyrenees. His refusal of this magnanimous offer showed how extreme his distorted perspective had become. How vanity had finally blinded him to sense.

Even the crushing events at Leipzig, which had proved to the world that Napoleon was not after all infallible, had still failed to enlighten him that it was possible to arrive at a position whereby his situation would become hopeless.

Yet somehow it was characteristic of him that he should fight to the end – that he should wrestle with the fate of his destiny. And it was strange how, even now, in the battles that were fought as the Allies pushed on to Paris, the Emperor still displayed, with unmatchable panache and audacity, his great genius. Through his remarkable ingenuity and skill, he still managed to win, despite his isolation and his impossible odds.

Nothing is more painful to watch than the last panting paroxysms of greatness. Yet in those uncertain days of March in 1814, one was compelled to look on as the inexorable force of destiny exercised its cruel and unrelenting fate upon its once magnificent champion. From the north – from the south – from the east: Napoleon's enemies had been slowly pressing, pushing him back into the capital. And by the middle of that fateful month, the Prussians had finally reached the very walls of Paris.

Finally the time had come for me to stir myself into action...

The battle for Paris was a disgusting affair. The idea of fighting foreign troops in the streets of the capital is offensive to all Frenchmen. It was, however, necessary.

Napoleon was far away from the city at the time, and the defence was in the very capable hands of Marshal Marmont. The Emperor, still refusing to entertain the possibility of defeat, was engaged in preparing one of his extraordinary master stokes. His customary consummate optimism, and certainty that he could outwit and outmanoeuvre his enemies, still held the spellbound loyalty and trust of the army. And certainly his inspired plan to march his soldiers away from Paris – ultimately to entrap the occupying Prussians therein, by cutting their communications, and meanwhile dividing and thus weakening the other two armies – was indeed characteristic of his genius.

But time was not on his side.

The civil authorities were in a panic. Napoleon's brother Joseph was wringing his hands in despair, not knowing what he should do as the sound of gunfire and the stench of smoke pervaded the Paris streets, while its confused citizens cowered in fear.

The Empress and the King of Rome left Paris, soon to be followed by the entire Imperial Court. It must have been an odd sight to see the dilapidated state of the once grand coaches laden with the hastily salvaged remnants of Imperial grandeur. Such disarray was undignified, to say the least. The streams of evacuating Parisiens must have found it a confusing moment to see the lumbering exit of those whom they had once believed to be something exceptional amongst humanity.

I was determined that I would not be joining them. After all,

Governments had come and gone before, and I saw no reason why I should participate. Thus, as Marshal Marmont signed the capitulation of Paris on March the thirtieth, and the Bonaparte brothers, Joseph and Jerome, rode out to follow their departed sister-in-law, I set about my business.

I have always remained faithful to anyone as long as they remained faithful to themselves, according to the rule of common sense. If you will judge me according to this great rule you will be forced to recognise that I had always been extraordinarily consistent.

Misguided though it may appear, I could never be what I consider to be a creature vile enough, or sufficiently unworthy, to submit my intelligence or to sacrifice my country unconditionally to an individual, whoever he may be – however well born, or however gifted.

I had liked Napoleon. Even loved him. But the duty of good Frenchmen was to consider the fate of an invaded France. How much she had against her, poor France. It was, therefore, now necessary to decide what form of government would enable her to meet this catastrophic situation.

I had resolved that I would remain in Paris to safeguard the interests of the French people. And as the foreign troops swarmed into the city, setting up their bivouacs in the Paris boulevards, and grazing their horses by the banks of the Seine, I strengthened that resolve – and prepared my own plans.

At Fontainebleau, meanwhile, I was aware that the Emperor Napoleon had returned to concentrate his troops, and consolidate his own doubtless magnificent plans, which I knew would still retain the formidable support of the army.

I therefore paid Marshal Marmont a little visit on that night of the thirtieth as he surrendered Paris. We conversed long and constructively, and I returned home at a late hour to gather some rest before the important events of the morrow.

The Tsar and the Allied commanders would enter the gates of Paris in the morning, and I would have to make sure that they respected the integrity of France by being met by a Frenchman. Furthermore, it would be necessary to convene a meeting of the

Senate, so that we could take the obligatory procedures to officially depose the Emperor Napoleon, and form a provisional government until such times as the succession was agreed upon.

Yes, the coming days would be busy. Very busy indeed.

* * *

'I am deeply honoured to welcome your Imperial Majesty to reside beneath my humble roof during your stay in Paris.'

I bowed to the tall lithe figure as he approached, on foot, the steps to my home. From the Place de la Concorde where once, not so very long ago, Madame la Guillotine had wreaked her bloody revenge upon another tyranny. This time it would be more civilised, I hoped.

I was aware that the staring attention of the pressing crowds was closely observing every word and action of both myself and the tall white figure who now bounded towards me, a smile of genuine delight and calm assurance emanating with sparkling radiance from his handsome golden features.

The people of Paris were still. Silent. What an extraordinary morning it had been for them. First, the entry of the Allies. Then, the massive review of those variously clad uniformed troops in the centre of their city, the strangest of which were those barbaric looking Cossacks, whose foreignness was the source of an uninhibited fascination for the civilised Parisians.

Rumours were rife in Paris. No one knew exactly what was going on. All they knew was that the fighting had ceased, the Imperial court had disappeared, and they were suddenly swamped with foreign troops. Thus I had spent the morning in drafting a proclamation for the confused People that would explain the situation, and allay their fears of further bloodshed.

'My dear Prince! I am delighted to renew our acquaintance…'

The smile was dazzling as he displayed his magnetic charm most effectively for the onlookers.

'I have determined to stay in your house that I may avail myself of your assistance. You have the complete confidence of myself, and of the allies. We do not wish to settle anything until we have heard from you. You know France – her needs and desires. Say what you believe we ought to do, and we shall do it.'

With these words the Tsar of Russia entered my house under the silent gaze of the people of Paris. But I noticed that as the affable Alexander genially ascended my steps by my side, graciously waving with friendly and unaffected charm at the hushed Parisians, here and there isolated shouts of 'peacemaker' rose from the huddled masses. It was my hope that this sentiment would soon spread through the city in that strange manner that remains a mystery to human beings, but is nonetheless the work of some force of enthusiasm's momentum.

Shortly after the ceremonial arrival of the Tsar, the King of Prussia and Prince Schwarzenburg, commander-in-chief of the allied forces, arrived. Dalberg was with me, of course. Also Count Nesselrode and the Prince of Liechenstein, and the Tsar's Corsican assistant, Pozzo di Borgo, who loathed his fellow countryman who had become an Emperor. Thus the little gathering in my salon was complete. No time was wasted, as we met to decide the fate of France.

Alexander, with his characteristic sense of mission, dramatically announced that there were four choices with which we were now faced: to re-open negotiations with Napoleon; to establish some form of Regency; to recall the Bourbons; or to place Bernadotte upon the throne of France. And as he enunciated the propositions that were to be conjectured, it was immediately obvious towards whom his personal choice inclined. He was clearly disposed to appoint Jean-Baptiste Bernadotte, the Crown Prince of Sweden

How do the circled patterns of time repeat themselves? My mind fleetingly recalled another meeting in this fair city, at another time, long ago. Then too had the name 'Bernadotte' been proposed. I smiled to myself. How strange is life…

But my own mind was made up. I knew the choice that France must make. And, when I had quietly listened to the others debate their preferences, I firmly explained and asserted my view.

* * *

'Brandy sire?'

The Tsar and I were alone in my favourite room. The long meeting had been concluded, and my proposals had been accepted. Yet still the Tsar appeared to hold a measure of reserve regarding the decision. Perhaps he required a deeper explanation of my view? Perhaps he hoped to change my mind. Perhaps he simply required a moment to assure himself that France was being served of its best interest, for he did not personally approve my choice.

Whatever his reason, he seemed to want to converse alone before the official evening functions. Thus we found ourselves together, before the blazing flames of my fire in the library. It was a pleasant moment, in a relaxed atmosphere. He was an earnest young man, the Tsar, and I knew his concern for the people of France was deeply genuine. He too was a man of destiny, and honestly regarded himself as an instrument of the Almighty. Never had that been more evident than now.

'Prince...' He was staring into the rich brown liquid in his glass as the lights from the chandelier glinted their reflection from its glowing depths. His handsome brow was creased in a deep frown, and he paused as I awkwardly seated myself opposite him, stretching my throbbing leg towards the heat of the leaping flames.

'I have prayed hard, Prince, that God will guide me towards the decision that is right for the nation of France. A decision that will be both best for her people, as well as according the peaceful interests of the other great Nations of Europe.' He paused, looking up into my face. 'It is a difficult decision, and that is why I have sought your advice, my friend...'

Again he hesitated, his eyes now moving to stare thoughtfully into the fire. 'I accept your thinking, sir, but I myself have a deep respect and admiration for the Prince Royal of Sweden. He is a strong man, with a balanced sense of priority. Furthermore, he appears to understand the needs of France – and of Europe. His militaristic talents would make him a strong ally...' His voice rose in a growing, earnest urgency. '...Were he to become King of France, I cannot help but feel that...'

'Sire, the people of France are tired.' My firm interruption halted his rising passion, and returned his troubled gaze to meet mine. 'They are tired of Revolution. Tired of War. Tired of fighting. They have sacrificed millions of lives, for twenty years. And for what? They are hungry. Hungry for Peace.'

I stopped, choosing my next words carefully, for I understood the Tsar's thoughts. 'Sire, I agree with you regarding the Crown Prince of Sweden. Sweden is indeed fortunate to have found such a man to lead them and re-build their country. I am certain that he will restore to them their lost greatness, and furthermore stabilize that whole important area of northern Europe. I assure you, sire, I could not think more highly of this brilliant man. I have long held a deep respect for both him and his remarkable talents. Indeed, I confess to contributing my modest influence towards his accession to the Swedish throne!'

I twinkled a returning smile as I saw the Tsar's face momentarily smile in amusement. Becoming serious once more, I continued, leaning forward slightly to emphasise my own sense of urgency.

'And yet, sire, as I too have deeply pondered the possibility of this extraordinary man becoming King of France, I have nonetheless arrived at the profoundly certain conclusion that it is impossible. France would never accept another military leader at the moment. If she did want a soldier then she would keep the one she has. He's the first in the world, as I said at our meeting earlier.

'But sire, the pain of the recent wars is still too fresh in their memories. Moreover, there are Bonapartist supporters remaining, and where they are active, as inevitably they will be, they could become even more potentially destructive by dividing the army into Bonaparte/Bernadotte factions. The former would consider Bernadotte a traitor, the latter, a hero. No sire, it is asking for trouble. The army must remain united and loyal to the constitutional Head of State.'

I stopped, fortifying myself with a draft from my brandy glass.

I was aware that the Tsar was listening attentively, taking in everything I said with an intelligent understanding.

As I slowly lowered my glass, I looked with an expression of fixed certainty into the light blue eyes of the Russian Emperor. Quietly I finished, steadfastly maintaining my resolve.

'Sire, France is a country wracked by pain and disillusionment. We must provide for her a new order, an order based, as I said at the meeting earlier, upon a principle. And that principle must be Legitimacy. With this principle we are strong, we meet no resistance. Sire, our legitimacy in Europe lies in the return of the Bourbons. There is no other choice that is appropriate for the interests of France.'

As I finished, the Tsar continued to stare thoughtfully into my eyes during the silence that fell between us. His face remained expressionless, yet I knew that he had been moved by my purposeful pronouncements of what I believed to be the best interests of France.

Eventually he responded, his voice low and resigned. 'I myself have no predilection for the Bourbons. They are my cousins! Yet my own preference is for Bernadotte. A regency is out of the question – and so is the recall of Bonaparte…' His voice trailed off slightly. Perhaps he was remembering how once he had admired so much that now deposed Emperor.

'All the same, Prince Talleyrand, you are a man with great political insight and vision. There is none other that I would trust more deeply than you to give an objective political decision that is in the best interests of France. I am after all a Russian, and the others…' He broke off, a suddenly rueful expression spreading across his face as he reluctantly accepted that he must now totally concede to my choice. 'Very well, Prince – it shall be the Bourbons.'

He rose abruptly, draining his glass. Looking at his timepiece, he reminded me, as I too struggled to my feet, that we were now delayed for our attendance of the evening entertainments.

As I awkwardly found my balance, I felt an odd hollowness in my chest. Pausing for a moment, I leaned on my stick, pensively looking into the hissing depths of the fire.

'He was a great man.' I was as startled as the Tsar to hear the words issue so unexpectedly from my lips in a low murmur. 'Sword of France...'

'What did you say, my friend?'

The genial face of the Tsar was smiling into mine as he now briskly prepared to depart.

I looked unseeingly at the golden haloed head before me. Into my thoughts suddenly flooded the sweet memories of bygone days, when the challenge of radical change had offered such heady promises – and the vision of that thin, long-haired young man with the strange grey eyes of genius had seemed to be the answer for Liberty.

Huskily I answered the enquiring blue gaze of the affable Russian, aware that my voice was barely audible. 'He was a great man, Napoleon. Once...'

I felt an unaccustomed lump in my throat, and now I saw the Tsar too swallow as, bowing his head slightly, he acknowledged my emotion. Taking my arm he now gently urged me to accompany him.

'Come Prince, we must attend the opera. We shall be late if we do not make haste.'

My emotions were contained, though my thoughts still observed their sadness as later, at the Opera House, the crowds stood to cheer both the Tsar's presence – and my own.

'Peacemaker!' they shouted to the tall golden figure. The sentiment had spread, I thought. How fickle are the loyalties of men to other men. But who was I to make judgments of them?

Chapter XXIV

The vast rooms of the Palace of Fontainebleau were enveloped in darkness. Throughout, the thick shapes of furniture, clad in their protective coverings of coarse cloth, stood like solid sentinels, thrusting their bulky forms into the clinging shadows. Waiting...

Outside, the formal gardens were still and silent. Even the creatures of night were subdued, somehow affected by the sombre atmosphere that had invaded this stately residence of Kings and Emperors. Nearby, in the surrounding vicinity, the murmured conversations of thousands of soldiers muttered ceaselessly into the night.

And back in the Palace the listening silence thickened. Slowly – ineluctably – it stiffened its merciless grip.

Unblinkingly stared the burning eyes of Napoleon Bonaparte at the square colourless shape of the covered painting, hanging eerily above the fireplace. How strange. He didn't seem to be able to blink. His red, aching eyes were transfixed by the ugly form, unable to tear their fixed gaze from its sightless presence. It was horrible – *horrible*. Yet even as he recoiled from the sight of something that appalled him so much, Napoleon was still unable to wrench his gaze away from it. It's like the blind eye of destiny, he thought. The eyelid of God finally shuts...

He shuddered. Suddenly he was cold, even though he could feel beads of sweat breaking out on his forehead. His mind felt hollow. He was incapable of thinking anymore. He felt entirely numb.

'Sire, are you alright…?'

The familiar sound of Caulaincourt's voice floated into his hearing. How odd that it didn't seem any louder than the cracklings and hissings of the fire, or the creaks of the windows, or the groans of the ceiling… It was just there amongst that strange, deafening yet silent cacophony. And he – he, Napoleon – was not part of it. He was watching it, somehow floating – like Caulaincourt's voice.

Why? Why had they covered that painting…? Who had had the audacity to do it without his permission? He liked that painting. What did they mean by it? Had they known…?

The momentary rush of indignant, coherent thought left him, fading his pattern of thought once more into that odd oblivion of nothingness…

'Sire, please…are you alright?'

The urgency in Caulaincourt's voice was now accompanied by what seemed to Napoleon to be a pressure on his arm. Now the Emperor was at last able to pull his gaze from the covered picture. Dropping his eyes, he looked at Caulaincourt's hand resting in concern upon his arm. Expressionless, he stared at it. Then, moving his eyes, he looked at the small bottle, which he clutched in his own hand.

As he felt the affectionate touch of the man who was looking down at him from his standing position, Napoleon raised his head, his haggard features forcing themselves into a smile. Caulaincourt… He patted the hand that still rested on his arm. He was always there. On that dreadful journey back from Moscow. And now too… He closed his eyes as he thought of the past few days. Caulaincourt, unconvincingly reassured by the wordless nod of his master, reluctantly withdrew.

Napoleon, slumped more deeply into his chair, slowly opened his stinging eyelids. The dancing lights in the fireplace before him seemed to be unnatural, glaring and moving in strange jagged patterns. Unreal. At last he blinked. Looking at the bottle in his hand again, his thoughts gradually acquired a vague coherence.

Glancing around the dim shadows of the empty room, he

smiled grimly to himself. Alone! Yes, he was alone. But what they didn't know was that he'd always felt alone. This strange feeling of numb detachment was not alien to him. He had often felt it before. Often...

'To be alone is not necessarily to be lonely.' Suddenly he remembered saying those words not long ago. He had had a presentiment that day; he remembered it clearly. Involuntarily he looked up at the blank square on the wall. The blind eye of destiny... Shivering, he leaned forward to poke the fire. He must avert his gaze from that ugly monstrosity. It was like a deformity.

Eugènie! It was to Eugènie he had said those words. He could remember it distinctly. For a moment, as he looked into the fire, he could see the burning logs in her fireplace. He felt he could almost see her seated – as he was now – before the flames, staring steadily into their depths, in her own sad solitude. She was waiting too – for that husband of hers. He who waited near Paris to hear if he was, after all, to become the next King of France.

He snarled bitterly to himself. Again his thoughts seemed to go momentarily numb. He couldn't think of that man. Mark Anthony! Indeed. Yet somehow he could feel no hatred for him...

Eugènie, what were her thoughts now? he wondered. She, to whom he had surrendered his sword. How clever 'they' were to send poor Eugènie. He would have resisted anyone else...What pain she must have endured...

...And Josephine, dear, beloved Josephine. Was she too alone, by another fireplace at Malmaison...? He had heard that the Tsar was going to call on her. He smiled to himself. She would plead for her children. Perhaps even for him. Good, gentle Josephine. Lovingly he thought back to the years of the Consulate, and before. How happy they had been then. But she had been right: she *was* his lucky charm. It had all gone so terribly wrong after the divorce...

He winced. The thought seemed to induce a pain in his stomach. How strange it was, he thought suddenly, that he was thinking of these two. Not of his wife Marie Louise, whose only thought was to claim the protection of her father. Fickle creature. Nor indeed did he think of his brothers and sisters. They would survive. He had assured their financial situations. That was all they cared about anyway.

But his son? What of his son? That was different. He closed his eyes. For the first time he felt the prick of tears. Would he ever see his child again? He, who meant everything to him...

Now, suddenly, an anger seemed to surge up from the depths of his being, consuming him in its raw eruption. Damn them – damn them all! Bitterly he thought of his Marshals. They too had only wanted money and titles. Vain bastards. How they had flattered him when it had suited them. At least Bernadotte had been more straightforward about where he had stood all these years. But, those others... He flushed as he remembered the scene earlier that day.

'Abdicate! Abdicate!'

Had they not been aware of how contemptible their bilious howlings were? They had behaved like a pack of frightened schoolchildren. And Marmont...?

Marmont... Napoleon felt a bursting of pressure inside his head as he thought of the man. He, who had gone over to the Austrians, taking his soldiers with him and destroying the solid support of the army. Weak bastard. A wave of disgust swept over him. Such people were beneath contempt. But then he knew why Caulaincourt, who had been going back and forth to Paris on his behalf, had informed him of the meeting that Marmont had had with Talleyrand. His lip curled as he thought of it. Stupid man – what had he been told by that slippery reptile...?

He closed his eyes, banishing the cripplingly painful thought from his mind. Talleyrand. He couldn't think of him. And what made it worse was that he had once been so fond of that unspeakable traitor. Talleyrand...

Napoleon leaned his head against the back of the chair. He felt tired. Terribly, dreadfully tired. He had done as they asked: abdicated. Well, let them have their damned Bourbons. Ungrateful bastards. They'd soon learn the error of their ways.

His eyes were irresistibly drawn to the blank square on the

wall. He was mesmerised by it once more. But now it seemed to be no longer empty. He blinked, but still he saw that dread image smiling down at him. Was it the candles…? The light from the fireplace…? Why was the bloody face of the Duc d'Enghien staring down at him from that yowling monstrosity on the wall? Again and again he blinked. Still the image remained – grinning relentlessly at him.

Suddenly he knew that the face of that young man had always been with him. He had never been able to rid himself of that guilt, even when he had been able to bury it beneath the glitter of his success. And yet, now he knew, it had always been there, the ghost of that young Bourbon prince. Even though he was sure that what he had done at that time had been right, the feeling of guilt had nonetheless rooted itself deeply in his conscience. He had killed a Bourbon. 'Murdered,' they said…

Well, now they had wreaked their revenge. Even at this moment Louis XVIII was being proclaimed the legitimate King of France. The Bourbons had won, after all. Napoleon dropped his head. Suddenly he was overcome by a consuming sensation of despair. What had it all been about? Destiny? Why…?

The numbness returned to grip his mind. The fire was swimming before him. The sound of silence deafened his thoughts. Lifting the small bottle closer to his un-focusing eyes, he tried to stare at it. How many years had this been carried around his neck in battle, just in case…? Now, when he knew he could no longer bear this life any more, it was still with him…

'The Emperor of Elba!' The title sizzled in his brain. How dare they? How *dare* they humiliate him…! Quickly he unscrewed the small top from the bottle. Throwing back his head, he drank from it, draining every drop of its contents before, lowering his arm in exhaustion, he dropped it onto the floor.

Limp with despair, he watched it roll away from him. An idea is greater than a man, he thought, as the creeping darkness of oblivion swept over him…

* * *

But time would not spare him so easily. He too was to suffer the humiliation that he had inflicted upon others, and like Prometheus he would be bound to a rock, there to endure the taunts of his memory that would remind him of his once supreme greatness.

Caulaincourt found his master convulsed in the paroxysms of the poison's pain. But the small bottle had for too long been carried around Napoleon's neck without replacement of its contents, and the once deadly potion had lost its strength.

* * *

Paris had now grown used to the romantic Tsar, and a mounting feeling of gaiety had engulfed the capital as he stayed on to ensure the smooth transition of government, of which I had become the provisional Head until the arrival of Louis XVIII. But at the Grand Procession of the victorious Sovereigns through the cheering crowds of Paris, there was one unsmiling face. And though he rode tall and nobly at the right hand of the Tsar, Bernadotte's impassive expression betrayed in its paleness a deep unhappiness. As I looked at him, I wondered if it was disappointment at his unrealised hopes of not ascending the throne of France. Or was it the uneasy quiet of subdued expressions as he passed by his once fellow Frenchmen…?

Yet somehow, I felt I knew the real source of his unhappiness. His thoughts were with another man who, like him, had that same Nobility of Spirit; though there would be those who would forever dispute that characteristic – of both of them. Nonetheless, these two rivals had shared something between them for many long and eventful years, and a mutual admiration had been their bond.

I knew that as he rode through the thronging masses, the Prince Royal of Sweden's thoughts were far away from the ringing chimes of freedom here in Paris. They were with the small man, in his black hat and shabby General's uniform, who even now was bound for the southern coast of France, and his new home of Elba. Alone. In a small black carriage.

* * *

Napoleon would not, of course, stay on that Mediterranean island. And, after his unsuccessful efforts in 1815 to recover his former throne, he would end his days as the prisoner of his most hated enemy, the English, on that godforsaken rock in the South Atlantic, St Helena.

Josephine, his lucky charm, was to die within a month of the Emperor's departure from Fontainebleau. She had caught a cold while walking with the Tsar in the Park at Malmaison, and, already weakened by her years of hopeless despair, succumbed to the relief of death.

Bernadotte left Paris as quickly as he could, politely declining the Tsar's invitations to share longer the honours of celebration. His wife Désirée remained in Paris, and she would not rejoin her husband for nine more years, by which time her son would be married to Josephine's grand-daughter – and Napoleon Bonaparte, her first love, would be dead.

I? Well, I would continue to serve France according to how I believed I could best appropriate my talents for her interests.

The Bourbons? Perhaps it was, after all, a mistake to return them to power, even though it had been much diminished. The French people never entirely trusted them again. Perhaps I had underestimated the festering resentments from the time of the Revolution. But I believe that I represented for France that which was best for her at the time. I am certain there was no alternative in 1814.

I have told the story of this strange period in History as I have seen it. Others, doubtless, see it from a different viewpoint, with varying emphases. But human beings are limited, and we can only relate things as and how we see them ourselves. Thereby, somehow, we justify our own actions, even when others condemn them.

Napoleon Bonaparte was a genius. At no time before or since

has there been a human being quite like him. We who were privileged to participate in the events of that time feel as amazed as the onlooker at the enormity of the changes that took place. And no one can ever deny that it was the magnitude of his unique vision that wrenched Europe out of her eighteenth century inertia, and into the challenges of modern thought.

* * *

Who knows the nature of genius? I suspect the truth is that we never shall. All we do know is that when such a comet travels through time we are transported higher into the realms of happiness that are created. His ideas and dreams of glory exceeded those of any ordinary Human Being. Yet are we also plunged into greater depths of gloom when the brilliant light extinguishes?

But all who knew Napoleon of the Consulate loved him. For his nobility of spirit, and his singularity of purpose. And, like the comets in the Heavens, his light will last in the memories and imaginations of men – because he loved them, though he failed to make them understand his vision.